THE SHIP WHO WON

ANNE McCAFFREY
JODY LYNN NYE

BAEN

THE SHIP WHO WON

This is a work of fiction. All the characters and events portrayed in this book are fictional, and any resemblance to real people or incidents is purely coincidental.

A Baen Books Original

Baen Publishing Enterprises
P.O. Box 1403
Riverdale, N.Y. 10471

ISBN: 0-671-87657-0

Cover art by Stephen Hickman

First paperback printing, May 1995

Distributed by Simon & Schuster
1230 Avenue of the Americas
New York, N.Y. 10020

Library of Congress Catalog Number: 93-43510

Typeset by Windhaven Press, Auburn, N.H.
Printed in the United States of America

FIRST CONTACT

"Lightning?" Keff asked Alteis softly. "What causes the lightning, sir?"

The oldster with white-shot black fur studied his lips carefully as he spoke, but then his gaze wandered off over Keff's head. When it returned to Keff, there was a blankness in his eyes that showed he hadn't understood, or had forgotten the question.

"He doesn't know," Keff said with a sigh. "Aren't you curious? Didn't you ever try to find out?" Keff asked Brannel.

"Not!" Brannel exclaimed. The bold young villager seemed nervous for the first time since Keff's arrival. "One curious, all—" He brought his hands together in a thunderclap. "All . . . all . . ."

"All punished for one person's curiosity? But why?" Keff demanded. "By whom?"

For answer Brannel aimed his three-fingered hand at the mountains. Keff peered up at the distant heights.

"Huh?" Carialle broadcast to Keff. "Did I miss something?"

"Punishment from the mountains?" Keff asked. "By his body language Brannel holds whatever comes from there in healthy respect, but he doesn't like it."

"Typical of religions," Carialle sniffed. She focused her cameras on the mountain peak in the direction Keff faced and zoomed in. "Say, there *are* structures up there, Keff. What are they? Temples? Shrines? Who built them?"

Keff pointed and turned to Brannel. "What are . . . ?" he began. His question was abruptly interrupted when a beam of hot light shot from the peak of the tallest mountain to strike directly at Keff's feet. Hot light engulfed him. The air turned fiery in his throat. The image of Brannel's face, agape, swam before his eyes, faded to a black shadow on his retinas, then flew upward into a cloudless sky blacker than space.

BOOKS IN THIS SERIES

✦ CHAPTER ONE

The ironbound door at the end of the narrow passage-way creaked open. An ancient man peered out and focused wrinkle-lapped eyes on Keff. Keff knew what the old one saw: a mature man, not overly tall, whose wavy brown hair, only just beginning to be shot with gray, was arrayed above a mild yet bull-like brow and deep-set blue eyes. A nose whose craggy shape suggested it may or may not have been broken at some time in the past, and a mouth framed by humor lines added to the impression of one who was tough yet instinctively gentle. He was dressed in a simple tunic but carried a sword at his side with the easy air of someone who knew how to use it. The oldster wore the shapeless garments of one who has ceased to care for any attribute but warmth and convenience. They stud-ied each other for a moment. Keff dipped his head slightly in greeting.

"Is your master at home?"

"I have no master. Get ye gone to whence ye came," the ancient spat, eyes blazing. Keff knew at once that this was no serving man; he'd just insulted the High Wizard Zarelb himself! He straightened his shoulders, going on guard but seeking to look friendly and non-threatening.

"Nay, sir," Keff said. "I must speak to you." Rats crept out of the doorway only inches from his feet and skittered away through the gutters along the walls. A disgusting place, but Keff had his mission to think of.

"Get ye gone," the old man repeated. "I've nothing for you." He tried to close the heavy, planked door. Keff pushed his gauntleted forearm into the narrowing crack and held it open. The old man backed away a pace, his eyes showing fear.

"I know you have the Scroll of Almon," Keff said, keeping his voice gentle. "I need it, good sir, to save the people of Harimm. Please give it to me, sir. I will harm you not."

"Very well, young man," the wizard said. "Since you threaten me, I will cede the scroll."

Keff relaxed slightly, with an inward grin. Then he caught a gleam in the old man's eye, which focused over Keff's shoulder. Spinning on his heel, Keff whipped his narrow sword out of its scabbard. Its lighted point picked out glints in the eyes and off the sword-blades of the three ruffians who had stepped into the street behind him. He was trapped.

One of the ruffians showed blackened stumps of teeth in a broad grin. "Going somewhere, sonny?" he asked.

"I go where duty takes me," Keff said.

"Take him, boys!"

His sword on high, the ruffian charged. Keff immediately blocked the man's chop, and riposted, flinging the man's heavy sword away with a clever twist of his slender blade that left the man's chest unguarded and vulnerable. He lunged, seeking his enemy's heart with his blade. Stumbling away with more haste than grace, the man spat, gathered himself, and charged again, this time followed by the other two. Keff turned into a whirlwind, parrying, thrusting, and striking, holding the three men at bay. A near strike by one of his opponents streaked along the wall by his cheek. He jumped away and parried just before an enemy skewered him.

"Yoicks!" he cried, dancing in again. "Have at you!"

He lunged, and the hot point of his epee struck the middle of the chief thug's chest. The body sank to the ground, and vanished.

"There!" Keff shouted, flicking the sword back and forth, leaving a Z etched in white light on the air. "You are not invincible. Surrender or die!"

Keff's renewed energy seemed to confuse the two remaining ruffians, who fought disjointedly, sometimes getting in each other's way while Keff's blade found its mark again and again, sinking its light into arms, shoulders, chests. In a lightning-fast sequence, first one, then the other foe left his guard open a moment too long. With groans, the villains sank to the ground, whereupon they too vanished. Putting the epee back into his belt, Keff turned to confront the ancient wizard, who stood watching the proceedings with a neutral eye.

"In the name of the people of Harimm, I claim the Scroll," Keff said grandly, extending a hand. "Unless you have other surprises for me?"

"Nay, nay." The old man fumbled in the battered leather scrip at his side. From it he took a roll of parchment, yellowed and crackling with age. Keff stared at it with awe. He bowed to the wizard, who gave him a grudging look of respect.

The scroll lifted out of the wizard's hand and floated toward Keff. Hovering in the air, it unrolled slowly. Keff squinted at what was revealed within: spidery tracings in fading brown ink, depicting mountains, roads, and rivers. "A map!" he breathed.

"Hold it," the wizard said, his voice unaccountably

changing from a cracked baritone to a pleasant female alto. "We're in range of the comsats." Door, rats, and aged figure vanished, leaving blank walls.

"Oh, spacedust," Keff said, unstrapping his belt and laser epee and throwing himself into the crash seat at the control console. "I was enjoying that. Whew! Good workout!" He pulled his sweaty tunic off over his head, and mopped his face with the tails. The dark curls of hair on his broad chest may have been shot through here and there with white ones, but he was grinning like a boy.

"You nearly got yourself spitted back there," said the disembodied voice of Carialle, simultaneously sending and acknowledging ID signals to the SSS-900. "Watch your back better next time."

"What'd I get for that?" Keff asked.

"No points for unfinished tasks. Maps are always unknowns. You'll have to follow it and see," Carialle said coyly. The image of a gorgeous lady dressed in floating sky blue chiffon and gauze and a pointed hennin appeared briefly on a screen next to her titanium column. The lovely rose-and-cream complected visage smiled down on Keff. "Nice footwork, good sir knight," the Lady Fair said, and vanished. "SSS-900, this is the CK-963 requesting permission to approach and dock—Hello, Simeon!"

"Carialle!" The voice of the station controller came through the box. "Welcome back! Permission granted, babe. And that's SSS-900-C, now, C for Channa. A lot's happened in the year since you've been away. Keff, are you there?"

Keff leaned in toward the pickup. "Right here, Simeon. We're within half a billion klicks. Should be with you soon."

"It'll be good to have you on board," Simeon said. "We're a little disarrayed right now, to put it mildly, but you didn't come to see me for my housekeeping."

"No, cookie, but you give such good decontam a girl can hardly stay away," Carialle quipped with a naughty chuckle.

"Dragon's teeth, Simeon!" Keff suddenly exclaimed, staring at his scopes. "What happened around here?"
"Well, if you really want to know . . ."

The scout ship threaded its way through an increasingly cluttered maze of junk and debris as they neared the rotating dumbbell shape of Station SSS-900. After viewing Keff's cause for alarm, Carialle put her repulsors on full to avoid the very real possibility of intersecting with one of the floating chunks of metal debris that shared a Trojan point with the station. Skiffs and tugs moved amidst the shattered parts of ships and satellites, scavenging. A pair of battered tugs with scoops on the front, looking ridiculously like gigantic vacuum cleaners, described regular rows as they sieved up microfine spacedust that could hole hulls and vanes of passing ships without ever being detected by the crews inside. The cleanup tugs sent hails as Carialle passed them in a smooth arc, synchronizing herself to the spin of the space station. The north docking ring was being repaired, so with a flick of her controls, Carialle increased thrust and caught up with the south end. Lights began to chase around the lip of one of the docking bays on the ring, and she made for it.

" . . . so that was the last we saw of the pirate Belazir and his bully boys," Simeon finished, sounding weary. "For good, I hope. My shell has been put in a more damage resistant casing and resealed in its pillar. We've spent the last six months healing and picking up the pieces. Still waiting for replacement parts. The insurance company is being sticky and querying every fardling item on the list, but no one's surprised about that. Fleet ships are remaining in the area. We've put in for a permanent patrol, maybe a small garrison."

"You have had a hell of a time," Carialle said, sympathetically.

"Now let's hear the good news," Simeon said, with a sudden surge of energy in his voice. "Where've you been all this time?"

Carialle simulated a trumpet playing a fanfare.

"We're pleased to announce that star GZA-906-M has two planets with oxygen-breathing life," Keff said.

"Congratulations, you two!" Simeon said, sending an audio burst that sounded like thousands of people cheering. He paused, very briefly. "I'm sending a simultaneous message to Xeno and Explorations. They're standing by for a full report with samples and graphs, but me first! I want to hear it all."

Carialle accessed her library files and tight-beamed the star chart and xeno file to Simeon's personal receiving frequency. "This is a precis of what we'll give to Xeno and the benchmarkers," she said. "We'll spare you the boring stuff."

"If there's any bad news," Keff began, "it's that there's no sentient life on planet four, and planet three's is too far down the tech scale to join Central Worlds as a trading partner. But they were glad to see us."

"He thinks," Carialle interrupted, with a snort. "I really never knew what the Beasts Blatisant thought." Keff shot an exasperated glance at her pillar, which she ignored. She clicked through the directory on the file and brought up the profile on the natives of Iricon III.

"Why do you call them the Beasts Blatisant?" Simeon asked, scanning the video of the skinny, hairy hexapedal beings, whose faces resembled those of intelligent grasshoppers.

"Listen to the audio," Carialle said, laughing. "They use

a complex form of communication which we have a socio-logical aversion to understanding. Keff thought I was blowing smoke, so to speak."

"That's not true, Cari," Keff protested. "My initial con-clusion," he stressed to Simeon, "was that they had no need for a complex spoken language. They live right in the swamps," Keff said, narrating the video that played off the datahedron. "As you can see, they travel either on all sixes or upright on four with two manipulative limbs. There are numerous predators that eat Beasts, among other things, and the simple spoken language is sufficient to relay infor-mation about them. Maintaining life is simple. You can see that fruit and edible vegetables grow in abundance right there in the swamp. The overlay shows which plants are dangerous."

"Not too many," Simeon said, noting the international symbols for poisonous and toxic compounds: a skull and crossbones and a small round face with its tongue out.

"Of course the first berry tried by my knight errant, and I especially stress the errant," Carialle said, "was those raspberry red ones on the left, marked with Mr. Yucky Face."

"Well, the natives were eating them, and their biology isn't that unlike Terran reptiles." Keff grimaced as he admitted, "but the berries gave me fierce stomach cramps. I was rolling all over the place clutching my belly. The Beasts thought it was funny." The video duly showed the hexapods, hooting, standing over a prone and writhing Keff.

"It was, a little," Carialle added, "once I got over being worried that he hadn't eaten something lethal. I told him to wait for the full analysis—"

"That would have taken *hours*," Keff interjected. "Our social interaction was happening in *realtime*."

"Well, you certainly made an impression."

"Did you understand the Beasts Blatisant? How'd the IT program go?" asked Simeon, changing the subject.

IT stood for Intentional Translator, the universal simultaneous language translation program that Keff had started before he graduated from school. IT was in a constant state of being perfected, adding referents and standards from each new alien language recorded by Central Worlds exploration teams. The brawn had more faith in his invention than his brain partner, who never relied on IT more than necessary. Carialle teased Keff mightily over the mistakes the IT made, but all the chaffing was affectionately meant. Brain and brawn had been together fourteen years out of a twenty-five-year mission, and were close and caring friends. For all the badinage she tossed his way, Carialle never let anyone else take the mickey out of her partner within her hearing.

Now she sniffed. "Still flawed, since IT uses only the symbology of alien life-forms already discovered. Even with the addition of the Blaize Modification for sign language, I think that it still fails to *anticipate*. I mean, who the hell knows what referents and standards new alien races will use?"

"Sustained use of a symbol in context suggests that it has meaning," Keff argued. "That's the basis of the program."

"How do you tell the difference between a repeated movement with meaning and one without?" Carialle asked, reviving the old argument. "Supposing a jellyfish's wiggle is sometimes for propulsion and sometimes for dissemination of information? Listen, Simeon, you be the judge."

"All right," the station manager said, amused.

"What if members of a new race have mouths and talk, but impart any information of real importance in some other way? Say, with a couple of sharp poots out the sphincter?"

"It was the berries," Keff said. "Their diet caused the repeating, er, repeats."

"Maybe that . . . habit . . . had some relevance in the beginning of their civilization," Carialle said with acerbity. "However, Simeon, once Keff got the translator working on their verbal language, we found that at first they just parroted back to him anything he said, like a primitive AI pattern, gradually forming sentences, using words of their own and anything they heard him say. It seemed useful at first. We thought they'd learn Standard at light-speed, long before Keff could pick up on the intricacies of their language, but that wasn't what happened."

"They parroted the language right, but they didn't really understand what I was saying," Keff said, alternating his narrative automatically with Carialle's. "No true comprehension."

"In the meantime, the flatulence was bothering him, not only because it seemed to be ubiquitous, but because it seemed to be controllable."

"I didn't know if it was supposed to annoy me, or if it meant something. Then we started studying them more closely."

The video cut from one scene to another of the skinny, hairy aliens diving for ichthyoids and eels, which they captured with their middle pair of limbs. More footage showed them eating voraciously; teaching their young to hunt; questing for smaller food animals and hiding from larger and more dangerous beasties. Not much of the land was dry, and what vegetation grew there was sought after by all the hungry species.

Early tapes showed that, at first, the Beasts seemed to be afraid of Keff, behaving as if they thought he was going to attack them. Over the course of a few days, as he seemed to be neither aggressive nor helpless, they investigated him further. When they dined, he ate a meal from his own supplies beside them.

"Then, keeping my distance, I started asking them questions, putting a clear rising interrogative into my tone of voice that I had heard their young use when asking for instruction. That seemed to please them, even though they were puzzled why an obviously mature being needed what seemed to be survival information. Interspecies communication and cooperation was unknown to them." Keff watched as Carialle skipped through the data to another event. "This was the potlatch. Before it really got started, the Beasts ate kilos of those bean-berries."

"Keff had decided then that they couldn't be too intelligent, doing something like that to themselves. Eating foods that caused them obvious distress for pure ceremony's sake seemed downright dumb."

"I was disappointed. Then the IT started kicking back patterns to me on the Beasts' noises. Then I felt downright dumb." Keff had the good grace to grin at himself.

"And what happened, ah, in the end?" Simeon asked.

Keff grinned sheepishly. "Oh, Carialle was right, of course. The red berries were the key to their formal communication. I had to give points for repetition of, er, body language. So, I programmed the IT to pick up what the Blatisants meant, not just what they said, taking in all movement or sounds to analyze for meaning. It didn't always work right . . ."

"Hah!" Carialle interrupted, in triumph. "He admits it!"

" . . . but soon, I was getting the sense of what they were really communicating. The verbal was little more than protective coloration. The Blatisants do have a natural gift for mimicry. The IT worked fine—well, mostly. The system's just going to require more testing, that's all."

"It always requires more testing," Carialle remarked in a

long-suffering voice. "One day we're going to miss something we really need."

Keff was unperturbed. "Maybe IT needs an AI element to test each set of physical movements or gestures for meaning on the spot and relay it to the running glossary. I'm going to use IT on humans next, see if I can refine the quirks that way when I already know what a being is communicating."

"If it works," Simeon said, with rising interest, "and you can read body language, it'll put you far beyond any means of translation that's ever been done. They'll call you a mind-reader. Softshells so seldom say what they mean—but they do express it through their attitudes and gestures. I can think of a thousand practical uses for IT right here in Central Worlds."

"As for the Blatisants, there's no reason not to recommend further investigation to award them ISS status, since it's clear they are sentient and have an ongoing civilization, however primitive," Keff said. "And that's what I'm going to tell the Central Committee in my report. Iricon III's got to go on the list."

"I wish I could be a mouse in the wall," Simeon said, chuckling with mischievous glee, "when an evaluation team has to talk with your Beasts. The whole party's going to sound like a raft of untuned engines. I know CenCom's going to be happy to hear about another race of sentients."

"I know," Keff said, a little sadly, "but it's not *the* race, you know." To Keff and Carialle, the designation meant that most elusive of holy grails, an alien race culturally and technologically advanced enough to meet humanity on its own terms, having independently achieved computer science and space travel.

"If anyone's going to find *the* race, it's likely to be you two," Simeon said with open sincerity.

Carialle closed the last kilometers to the docking bay and

shut off her engines as the magnetic grapples pulled her close, and the vacuum seal snugged around the airlock.

"Home again," she sighed.

The lights on the board started flashing as Simeon sent a burst requesting decontamination for the CK-963. Keff pushed back from the monitor panels and went back to his cabin to make certain everything personal was locked down before the decontam crew came on board.

"We're empty on everything, Simeon," Carialle said. "Protein vats are at the low ebb, my nutrients are redlining, fuel cells down. Fill 'er up."

"We're a bit short on some supplies at the moment," Simeon said, "but I'll give you what I can." There was a brief pause, and his voice returned. "I've checked for mail. Keff has two parcels. The manifests are for circuits, and for a 'Rotoflex.' What's that?"

"Hah!" said Keff, pleased. "Exercise equipment. A Rotoflex helps build chest and back muscles without strain on the intercostals." He flattened his hands over his ribs and breathed deeply to demonstrate.

"All we need is more clang-and-bump deadware on *my deck*," Carialle said with the noise that served her for a sigh.

"Where's your shipment, Carialle?" Keff asked innocently. "I thought you were sending for a body from Moto-Prosthetics."

"Well, you thought wrong," Carialle said, exasperated that he was bringing up their old argument. "I'm happy in my skin, thank you."

"You'd love being mobile, lady fair," Keff said. "All the things you miss staying in one place! You can't imagine. Tell her, Simeon."

"She travels more than I do, Sir Galahad. Forget it."

"Anyone else have messages for us?" Carialle asked.

"Not that I have on record, but I'll put out a query to show you're in dock."

Keff picked his sodden tunic off the console and stood up.

"I'd better go and let the medicals have their poke at me," he said. "Will you take care of the rest of the computer debriefing, my lady Cari, or do you want me to stay and make sure they don't poke in anywhere you don't want them?"

"Nay, good sir knight," Carialle responded, still playing the game. "You have coursed long and far, and deserve reward."

"The only rewards I want," Keff said wistfully, "are a beer that hasn't been frozen for a year, and a little companionship—not that you aren't the perfect companion, lady fair"—he kissed his hand to the titanium column—"but as the prophet said, let there be spaces in your togetherness. If you'll excuse me?"

"Well, don't space yourself too far," Carialle said. Keff grinned. Carialle followed him on her internal cameras to his cabin, where, in deference to those spaces he mentioned, she stopped. She heard the sonic-shower turn on and off, and the hiss of his closet door. He came out of the cabin pulling on a new, dry tunic, his curly hair tousled.

"Ta-ta," Keff said. "I go to confess all and slay a beer or two."

Before the airlock sealed, Carialle had opened up her public memory banks to Simeon, transferring full copies of their datafiles on the Iricon mission. Xeno were on line in seconds, asking her for in-depth, eyewitness commentary on their exploration. Keff, in Medical, was probably answering some of the same questions. Xeno liked subjective accounts as well as mechanical recordings.

At the same time Carialle carried on her conversation with Simeon, she oversaw the decontam crew and loading staff, and relaxed a little herself after what had been an arduous journey. A few days here, and she'd feel ready to go out and knit the galactic spiral into a sweater.

Keff's medical examination, under the capable stethoscope of Dr. Chaundra, took less than fifteen minutes, but the interview with Xeno went on for hours. By the time he had recited from memory everything he thought or observed about the Beasts Blatisant he was wrung out and dry.

"You know, Keff," Darvi, the xenologist, said, shutting down his clipboard terminal on the Beast Blatisant file, "if I didn't know you personally, I'd have to think you were a little nuts, giving alien races silly names like that. Beasts Blatisant. Sea Nymphs. Losels—that was the last one I remember."

"Don't you ever play Myths and Legends, Darvi?" Keff asked, eyes innocent.

"Not in years. It's a kid game, isn't it?"

"No! Nothing wrong with my mind, *nyuk-nyuk*," Keff said, rubbing knuckles on his own pate and pulling a face. The xenologist looked worried for a moment, then relaxed as he realized Keff was teasing him. "Seriously, it's self-defense against boredom. After fourteen years of this job, one gets fardling tired of referring to a species as 'the indigenous race' or 'the inhabitants of Zoocon I.' I'm not an AI drone, and neither is Carialle."

"Well, the names are still silly."

"Humankind is a silly race," Keff said lightly. "I'm just indulging in innocent fun."

He didn't want to get into what he and Carialle considered the serious aspects of the game, the points of honor, the satisfaction of laying successes at the feet of his lady fair. It wasn't as if he and Carialle couldn't tell the difference between play and reality. The game had permeated their life and given it shape and texture, becoming more than a game, *meaning* more. He'd never tell this space-dry plodder about the time five years back that he actually stood vigil throughout a long, lonely night lit by a single candle to earn his knighthood. *I guess you just had to be there,* he thought. "If that's all?" he asked, standing up quickly.

Darvi waved a stylus at him, already engrossed in the files. Keff escaped before the man thought of something else to ask and hurried down the curving hall to the nearest lift.

Keff had learned about Myths and Legends in primary school. A gang of his friends used to get together once a week (more often when they dared and homework permitted) to play after class. Keff liked being able to live out some of his heroic fantasies and, briefly, *be* a knight battling evil and bringing good to all the world. As he grew up and learned that the galaxy was a billion times larger than his one small colony planet, the compulsion to do good grew, as did his private determination that he could make a difference, no matter how minute. He managed not to divulge this compulsion during his psychiatric interviews on his admission to Brawn Training and kept his altruism private. Nonetheless, as a knight of old, Keff performed his assigned tasks with energy and devotion, vowing that no ill or evil would ever be done by him. In a quiet way, he applied the rules of the game to his own life.

As it happened, Carialle also loved M&L, but more for the strategy and research that went into formulating the quests than the adventuring. After they were paired, they had simply fallen into playing the game to while away the long days and months between stars. He could put no finger on a particular moment when they began to make it a lifestyle: Keff the eternal knight errant and Carialle his lady fair. To Keff this was the natural extension of an adolescent interest that had matured along with him.

As soon as he'd heard that the CX-963 was in need of a brawn, his romantic nature required him to apply for the position as Carialle's brawn. He'd heard—who hadn't?— about the devastating space storm and collision that had cost Fanine Takajima-Morrow's life and almost took Carialle's sanity.

She'd had to undergo a long recovery period when the Mutant Minorities (MM) and Society for the Preservation of the Rights of Intelligent Minorities (SPRIM) boffins wondered if she'd ever be willing to go into space again. They rejoiced when she announced that not only was she ready to fly, but ready to interview brawns as well. Keff had wanted that assignment badly. Reading her file had given him an intense *need* to protect Carialle. A ridiculous notion, when he ruefully considered that she had the resources of a brainship at her synapse ends, but her vulnerability had been demonstrated during that storm. The protective aspect of his nature vibrated at the challenge to keep her from any further harm.

Though she seldom talked about it, he suspected she still had nightmares about her ordeal—in those random hours when a brain might drop into dreamtime. She also proved to be the best of partners and companions. He liked her, her interests, her hobbies, didn't mind her faults or her tendency to be right more often than he was. She taught him patience. He taught her to swear in ninety languages as a creative means of dispelling tension. They bolstered one another. The trust between them was as deep as space and felt as ancient and as new at the same time. The fourteen years of their partnership had flown by, literally and figuratively. Within Keff's system of values, to be paired with a brainship was the greatest honor a mere human could be accorded, and he knew it.

The lift slowed to a creaky halt and the doors opened. Keff had been on SSS-900 often enough to turn to port as he hit the corridor, in the direction of the spacer bar he liked to patronize while on station.

Word had gotten around that he was back, probably the helpful Simeon's doing. A dark brown stout already separating from its creamy crown was waiting for him on the polished steel bar. It was the first thing on which he focused.

"Ah!" he cried, moving toward the beer with both hands out. "Come to Keff."

A hand reached into his field of vision and smartly slapped his wrist before he could touch the mug handle. Keff tilted a reproachful eye upward.

"How's your credit?" the bartender asked, then tipped him a wicked wink. She was a woman of his own age with nut-brown hair cut close to her head and the milk-fair skin of the lifelong spacer of European descent. "Just kidding. Drink up, Keff. This one's on the house. It's good to see you."

"Blessings on you and on this establishment, Mariad, and on your brewers, wherever they are," Keff said, and put his nose into the foam and slowly tipped his head back and the glass up. The mug was empty when he set it down. "Ahhhh. Same again, please."

Cheers and applause erupted from the tables and Keff waved in acknowledgment that his feat had been witnessed. A couple of people gave him thumbs up before returning to their conversations and dart games.

"You can always tell a light-year spacer by the way he refuels in port," said one man, coming forward to clasp Keff's hand. His thin, melancholy face was contorted into an odd smile.

Keff stood up and slapped him on the back. "Baran Larrimer! I didn't know you and Shelby were within a million light years of here."

An old friend, Larrimer was half of a brain/brawn team

assigned to the Central Worlds defense fleet. Keff suddenly remembered Simeon's briefing about naval support. Larrimer must have known exactly what Keff had been told. The older brawn gave him a tired grimace and nodded at the questioning expression on his face.

"Got to keep our eyes open," he said simply.

"And you are not keeping yours open," said a voice. A tiny arm slipped around Keff's waist and squeezed. He glanced down into a small, heart-shaped face. "Good to see you, Keff."

"Susa Gren!" Keff lifted the young woman clean off the ground in a sweeping hug and set her down for a huge kiss, which she returned with interest. "So you and Marliban are here, too?"

"Courier duty for a trading contingent," Susa said in a low voice, her dark eyes crinkling wryly at the corners. She tilted her head toward a group of hooded aliens sitting isolated around a table in the corner. "Hoping to sell Simeon a load of protector/detectors. They plain forgot that Marl's a brain and could hear every word. The things they said in front of him! Which he quite rightly passed straight on to Simeon, so, dear me, didn't they have a hard time bargaining their wares. I'd half a mind to tell CenCom that those idiots can find their own way home if they won't show a brainship more respect. But," she sighed, "it's paying work."

Marl had only been in service for two—no, it was three years now—and was still too far down in debt to Central Worlds for his shell and education to refuse assignments, especially ones that paid as well as first-class courier work. Susa owed megacredits, too. She had made herself responsible for the debts of her parents, who had borrowed heavily to make an independent go of it on a mining world, and had failed. Fortunately not fatally, but the disaster had left them with only a subsistence allowance. Keff liked the spunky young woman, admired her drive and wit, her springy step and dainty, attractive figure. The two of them had always had an affinity which Carialle had duly noted, commenting a trifle bluntly that the ideal playmate for a brawn was another brawn. Few others could understand the dedication a brawn had for his brainship nor match the lifelong relationship.

"Susa," he said suddenly. "Do you have some time? Can you sit and talk for a while?"

Her eyes twinkled as if she had read his mind. "I've nothing to do and nowhere to go. Marl and I have liberty until those drones want to go home. Buy me a drink?"

Larrimer stood up, tactfully ignoring the increasing aura of intimacy between the other two brawns. He slapped his credit chit down on the bar and beckoned to Mariad.

"Come by if you have a moment, Keff," he said. "Shelby would be glad to see you."

"I will," Keff said, absently swatting a palm toward Larrimer's hand, which caught his in a firm clasp. "Safe going."

He and Susa sat down together in a booth. Mariad delivered a pair of Guinnesses and, with a motherly cluck, sashayed away.

"You're looking well," Susa said, scanning his face with a more than friendly concern. "You have a tan!"

"I got it on our last planetfall," Keff said. "Hasn't had time to fade yet."

"Well, I think you look good with a little color in your face," she declared. Her mouth crooked into a one-sided grin. "How far down does it go?"

Keff waggled his eyebrows at her. "Maybe in a while I'll let you see."

"Any of those deep scratches dangerous?" Carialle asked, swiveling an optical pickup out on a stalk to oversee the techs checking her outsides. The ship lay horizontally to the "dry dock" pier, giving the technicians the maximum expanse of hull to examine.

"Most of 'em are no problem. I'm putting setpatch in the one nearest your fuel lines," the coveralled man said, spreading a gray goo over the place. It hardened slowly, acquiring a silver sheen that blended with the rest of the hull plates. "Don't think it'll split in temperature extremes, ma'am, but it's thinner there, of course. This'll protect you more."

"Many thanks," Carialle said. When the patching compound dried, she tested her new skin for resonance and found its density matched well. In no time she'd forget she had a wrinkle under the dressing. Her audit program also found that the fee for materials was comfortingly low, compared to having the plate removed and hammered, or replaced entirely.

Overhead, a spider-armed crane swung its burden over her bow, dropping snakelike hoses toward her open cargo hull. The crates of xeno material had already been taken away in a specially sealed container. A suited and hooded worker had already cleaned the nooks and niches, making sure no stray native spores had hooked a ride to the Central Worlds. The crane's operator directed the various flexible tubes to the appropriate valves. Fuel was first, and Carialle flipped open her fuel toggle as the stout hose reached it. The narrow tube which fed her protein vats had a numbered filter at its spigot end. Carialle recorded that number in her files in case there were any impurities in the final product. Thankfully, the conduit that fed the carbo-protein sludge to Keff's food synthesizer was opaque. The peristaltic pulse of the thick stuff always made Cari think of quicksand, of sand-colored octopi creeping along an ocean floor, of week-old oatmeal. Her attention diverted momentarily to the dock, where a front-end loader was rolling toward her with a couple of containers, one large and one small, with bar-code tags addressed to Keff. She signaled her okay to the driver to load them in her cargo bay.

Another tech, a short, stout woman wearing thick-soled magnetic boots, approached her airlock and held up a small item. "This is for you from the station-master, Carialle. Permission to come aboard?"

Carialle focused on the datahedron in her fingers and felt a twitch of curiosity.

"Permission granted," she said. The tech clanked her way into the airlock and turned sideways to match the up/down orientation of Carialle's decks, then marched carefully toward the main cabin. "Did he say what it was?"

"No, ma'am. It's a surprise."

"Oh, Simeon!" Carialle exclaimed over the station-master's private channel. "Cats! Thank you!" She scanned the contents of the hedron back and forth. "Almost a real-time week of video footage. Wherever did you get it?"

"From a biologist who breeds domestic felines. He was out here two months ago. The hedron contains compressed videos of his cats and kittens, and he threw in some videos of wild felines he took on a couple of the colony worlds. Thought you'd like it."

"Simeon, it's wonderful. What can I swap you for it?"

The station-master's voice was sheepish. "You don't *need* to swap, Cari, but if you happened to have a spare painting? And I'm quite willing to sweeten the swap."

"Oh, no. I'd be cheating *you*. It isn't as if they're music. They're nothing."

"That isn't true, and you know it. You're a brain's artist."

With little reluctance, Carialle let Simeon tap into her video systems and directed him to the corner of the main cabin where her painting gear was stowed.

To any planetbound home-owner the cabin looked spotless, but to another spacer, it was a magpie's nest. Keff's exercise equipment occupied much of one end of the cabin. At the other, Carialle's specially adapted rack of painting equipment took up a largish section of floor space, not to mention wall space where her finished work hung— the ones she didn't give away or *throw* away. Those few permitted to see Cari's paintings were apt to call them "masterpieces," but she disclaimed that.

Not having a softshell body with hands to manage the mechanics of the art, she had had customized gear built to achieve the desired effect. The canvases she used were very thin, porous blocks of cells that she could flood individually with paint, like pixels on a computer screen, until it oozed together. The results almost resembled brush strokes. With the advance of technological subtleties, partly thanks to Moto-Prosthetics, Carialle had designed arms that could hold actual fiber brushes and airbrushes, to apply paints to the surface of the canvases over the base work.

What had started as therapy after her narrow escape from death had become a successful and rewarding hobby. An occasional sale of a picture helped to fill the larder or the fuel tank when bonuses were scarce, and the odd gift of an unlooked-for screen-canvas did much to placate occasionally fratchety bureaucrats. The sophisticated servo arms pulled one microfiber canvas after another out of the enameled, cabinet-mounted rack to show Simeon, who appreciated all and made sensible comments about several.

"That one's available," Carialle said, mechanical hands turning over a night-black spacescape, a full-color sketch of a small nocturnal animal, and a study of a crystalline mineral deposit embedded in a meteor. "This one I gave Keff. This one I'm keeping. This one's not finished. Hmm. These two are available. So's this one."

Much of what Carialle rendered wouldn't be visible to the unenhanced eyes of a softshell artist, but the sensory apparatus available to a shellperson gave color and light to scenes that would otherwise seem to the naked eye to be only black with white pinpoints of stars.

"That's good." Simeon directed her camera to a spacescape of a battered scout ship traveling against the distant cloudlike mist of an ion storm that partially overlaid the corona of a star like a veil. The canvas itself wasn't rectangular in shape, but had a gentle irregular outline that complimented the subject.

"Um," Carialle said. Her eye, on tight microscopic adjustment, picked up flaws in some individual cells of paint. They were red instead of carmine, and the shading wasn't subtle enough. "It's not finished yet."

"You mean you're not through fiddling with it. Give over, girl. I like it."

"It's yours, then," Carialle said with an audible sigh of resignation. The servo picked it out of the rack and headed for the airlock on its small track-treads. Carialle activated a camera on the outside of her hull to spot a technician in the landing bay. "Barkley, would you mind taking something for the station-master?" she said, putting her voice on speaker.

"Sure wouldn't, Carialle," the mech-tech said, with a brilliant smile at the visible camera. The servo met her edge of the dock, and handed the painting to her.

"You've got talent, gal," Simeon said, still sharing her video system as she watched the tech leave the bay. "Thank you. I'll treasure it."

"It's nothing," Carialle said modestly. "Just a hobby."

"Fardles. Say, I've got a good idea. Why don't you do a gallery showing next time you're in port? We have plenty of traders and bigwigs coming through who would pay good credit for original art. Not to mention the added cachet that it's painted by a brainship."

"We-ell . . . " Carialle said, considering.

"I'll give you free space near the concessions for the first week, so you're not losing anything on the cost of location. If you feel shy about showing off, you can do it by invitation only, but I warn you, word will spread."

"You've persuaded me," Carialle said.

"My intentions are purely honorable," Simeon replied gallantly. "Frag it!" he exclaimed. The speed of transmission on his frequency increased to a microsquirt. "You're as loaded and ready as you're going to get, Carialle. Put it together and scram off this station. The Inspector General wants a meeting with you in fifteen minutes. He just told me to route a message through to you. I'm delaying it as long as I dare."

"Oh, no!" Carialle said at the same speed. "I have no intention of letting Dr. Sennet 'I am a psychologist' Maxwell-Corey pick through my brains every single fardling time I make stationfall. I'm cured, damn it! I don't need constant monitoring."

"You'd better scoot now, Cari. My walls-with-ears have heard rumors that he thinks your 'obsession' with things like Myths and Legends makes your sanity highly suspect. When he hears the latest report—your Beasts Blatisant— you're going to be in for another long psychological profile session, and Keff along with you. Even Maxwell-Corey has to justify his job to someone."

"Damn him! We haven't finished loading my supplies! I only have half a vat of nutrients, and most of the stuff Keff ordered is still in your stores."

"Sorry, honey. It'll still be here when you come back. I can send you a 'squirt after he's gone."

Carialle considered swiftly whether it was worth calling in a complaint to SPRIM over the Inspector General and his obsessive desire to prove her unfit for service. He was witch-hunting, of that she was sure, and she wasn't going to be the witch involved. Wasn't it bad enough that he insisted on making her relive a sixteen-year-old tragedy every time they met? One day there was going to be a big battle, but she didn't feel like taking him on yet.

Simeon was right. The CK-963 was through with decontamination and repairs. Only half a second had passed during their conversation. Simeon could hold up the IG's missive only a few minutes before the delay would cause the obstreperous Maxwell-Corey to demand an inquiry.

"Open up for me, Simeon. I've got to find Keff."

"No problem," the station-master said. "I know where he went."

"Keff," said the wall over his head. "Emergency transmission from Carialle."

Keff tilted his head up lazily. "I'm busy, Simeon. Privacy." Susa's hand reached up, tangled in his hair, and pulled it down again. He breathed in the young woman's scent, moved his hands in delightful counterpoint under her body, one down from the curve of her shoulder, pushing the thin cloth of her ship-suit down; one upward, caressing her buttocks and delicate waist. She locked her legs with his, started her free hand toward his waistband, feeling for the fastening.

"Emergency *priority* transmission from Carialle," Simeon repeated.

Reluctantly, Keff unlocked his lips from Susa's. Her eyes filled with concern, she nodded. Without moving his head, he said, "All right, Simeon. Put it through."

"Keff," Carialle's voice rang with agitation. "Get down here immediately. We've got to lift ship ASAP."

"Why?" Keff asked irritably. "You couldn't have finished loading already."

"Haven't. Can't wait. Got to go. Get here, stat!"

Sighing, Keff rolled off Susa and petulantly addressed

the ceiling. "What about my shore leave? Ladylove, while I like nothing better in the galaxy than being with you ninety-nine percent of the time, there *is* that one percent when we poor shell-less ones need—"

Carialle cut him off. "Keff, the Inspector General's on station."

"What?" Keff sat up.

"He's demanding another meeting, and you know what that means. We've got to get as far away from here as we can, right away."

Keff was already struggling back into his ship-suit. "Are we refueled? How much supplies are on board?"

Simeon's voice issued from the concealed speaker. "About a third full," he said. "But it's all I can give you right now. I told you supplies were short. Your food's about the same."

"We can't go far on that. About one long run, or two short ones." Keff stood, jamming feet into boots. Susa sat up and began pulling the top of her coverall over her bare shoulders. She shot Keff a look of regret mingled with understanding.

"We'll get missing supplies elsewhere," Carialle promised. "What's the safest vector out of here, Simeon?"

"I'll leave," Susa said, rising from the edge of the bed. She put a delicate hand on his arm. Keff stooped down and kissed her. "The less I hear, the less I have to confess if someone asks me under oath. Safe going, you two." She gave Keff a longing glance under her dark lashes. "Next time."

Just like that, she was gone, no complaints, no recriminations. Keff admired her for that. As usual, Carialle was correct: a brawn's ideal playmate was another brawn. It didn't stop him feeling frustrated over his thwarted sexual encounter, but it was better to spend that energy in a useful manner. Hopping into his right boot, he hurried out into the corridor. Ahead of him, Susa headed for a lift. Keff deliberately turned around, seeking a different route to his ship.

"Keep me out of Maxwell-Corey's way, Simeon." He ran around the curve of the station until he came to another lift. He punched the button, pacing anxiously until the doors opened.

"You're okay on that path," the station-master said, his voice following Keff. The brawn stepped into the empty car, and the doors slid shut behind him. "All right, this just became an express. Brace yourself."

"What about G sector?" Carialle was asking as Keff came aboard the CK-963. All the screens in the main cabin were full of star charts. Keff nodded Carialle's position in the main column and threw himself into his crash couch as he started going down the pre-launch list.

"Okay if you don't head toward Saffron. That's where the Fleet ships last traced Belazir's people. You *don't* want to meet them."

"Fragging well right we don't."

"What about M sector?" Keff said, peering at the chart directly in front of him. "We had good luck there last time."

"Last time you had your clock cleaned by the Losels," Carialle reminded him, not in too much of a hurry to tease. "You call that good luck?"

"There're still a few systems in that area we wanted to check. They fitted the profile for supporting complex life-forms," Keff said, unperturbed. "We would have tried MBA-487-J, except you ran short of fuel hotdogging it and we had to limp back here. Remember, Cari?"

"It could happen any time we run into bad luck," Carialle replied, not eager to discuss her own mistakes. "We're running out of time."

"What about vectoring up over the Central Worlds cluster? Toward galactic 'up'?"

"Maxwell-Corey's going toward DND-922-Z when he leaves here," Simeon said.

Carialle tsk-tsked. "We can't risk having him following our scent."

Keff stared at the overview on the tank. "How about we head out in a completely new direction? See what's out there thataway?"

"What's your advice, Simeon?" Carialle asked, locking down any loose items and sliding her airlock shut with a sharp hiss. Her gauges zoomed as she engaged her own power. Nutrients, fuel, power cells all showed less than half full. She hated lifting off under these circumstances, but she had no choice. The alternative was weeks of interrogation, and possibly being grounded—unfairly!—at the end of it.

"I've got an interesting anomaly you might investigate," Simeon said, downloading a file to Carialle's memory. "Here's a report I received from a freighter captain who made a jump through R sector to get here. His spectroscopes picked up unusual power emanations in the vicinity of RNJ-599-B. We've no records of habitation anywhere around there. Could be interesting."

"G-type stars," Keff noted approvingly. "Yes, I see what he meant. Spectroanalysis, Cari?"

"All the signs are there that RNJ could have generated planets," the brain replied. "What does Exploration say?"

"No one's done any investigation in that part of R sector yet," Simeon said blandly, carefully emotionless.

"No one?" Carialle asked, scrolling through the files. "Hmmm! Oh, yes!"

"So we'll be the first?" Keff said, catching the excitement in Carialle's voice. The burning desire to go somewhere and see something *first*, before any other

Central Worlder, overrode the fears of being caught by the Inspector General.

"I can't locate any reference to so much as a robot drone," Carialle said, displaying star maps empty of neon-colored benchmarks or route vectors. Keff beamed.

"And to seek out new worlds, to boldly go . . ."

"Oh, shush," Carialle said severely. "You just want to be the first to leave your footprints in the sand."

"You've got twelve seconds to company," Simeon said. "Don't tell me where you're going. What I don't know I can't lie about. Go with my blessings, and come back safely. Soon."

"Will do," Keff said, strapping in. "Thanks for everything, Simeon. Cari, ready to—"

The words were hardly out of his mouth before the CK-963 unlatched the docking ring and lit portside thrusters.

✪ CHAPTER TWO

The Inspector General's angry voice pounded out of the audio pickup on Simeon's private frequency.

"CK-963, respond!"

"Discovered!" Keff cried, slapping the arm of his couch. The next burst of harsh sound made him yelp with mock alarm. "Catch us if you can, you cockatrice!"

"Hush!" Carialle answered the hail in an innocent voice, purposely made audible for her brawn's sake. "S . . . S-nine . . . dred. H . . . ving trou—" Keff was helpless with laughter. "Pl . . . s repeat mes . . . g?"

"I said get back here! You have an appointment with me as of ten hundred hours prime meridian time, and it is now ten fifteen." Carialle could almost picture his plump, mustachioed face turning red with apoplexy. "How dare you blast out of here without my permission? I want to see you!"

"Sorr . . . " Carialle said, "br . . . king up. Will send back mission reports, General."

"That was clear as a bell, Carialle!" the angry voice hammered at the speaker diaphragm. "There is no static interference on your transmission. You make a one-eighty and get back here. I expect to see you in ninety minutes. Maxwell-Corey out."

"Oops," said Keff, cheerfully. He tilted his head out of his impact couch toward her pillar and winked. His deep-set blue eyes twinkled. "M-C won't believe that last phrase was a fluke of clear space, will he?"

"He'll have to," Carialle said firmly. "I'm not going back to have my cerebellum cased, not a chance. Bureaucratic time-waster! I know I'm fine. You know you're fine. Why do we always have to go bend over and cough every time we make planetfall and explore a new world? I landed, got steam-cleaned and decontaminated, made our report with words and pictures to Xeno and Exploration. I refuse to have another mental going-over just because of my past experiences."

"Good of Simeon to tip us off," Keff said, running down the ship status report on his personal screen. "I hope he won't catch too much flak for it. But look at this! Thirty percent food and fuel?"

"I know," Carialle said contritely, "but what else could I do?"

"Not a blessed, or unblessed thing," Keff agreed. "Frankly, I prefer the odds as opposed to what we'd have to go through to wait for Simeon's next shipments. Full tanks and complete commissary do not, in my book, equate with peace of mind if M-C's about. Eventually we will have to go back, you know."

"Yes, if only to make certain Simeon's coped with the man. Before we do though, I'll just send Simeon a microsquirt to be sure Maxwell-Corey's left for D sector. . . ."

"Or someplace else equally distant from us. It isn't as if we can't hang out in space for a while on iron rations until Sime sends you an all-clear burst," Keff offered bravely, although Carialle could see he didn't look forward to the notion.

"If the IG is sneaky enough . . ."

" . . . And he is if anyone deserves that adjective. . . ."

" . . . to scan message files he'll know when Simeon knows where we are, and he could put a tag on us so no station will supply the 963."

"We shall not come to that sorry pass, my lady fair," Keff said, lapsing into his Sir Galahad pose. "In the meantime, let us fly on toward R sector and whatever may await us there." He made an enthusiastic and elaborate flourish and ended up pointing toward the bow.

Carialle had to laugh.

"Oh, yes," she said. "Now, where were we?" The Wizard was back on the wall, and he spoke in the creaking tenor of an old, old man. "Good sir knight, thou hast fairly won this scroll. Hast anything thou wish to ask me?"

Grinning, Keff buckled on his epee and went to face him.

While Keff chased men-at-arms all over her main cabin, Carialle devoted most of her attention to eluding the Inspector General's attempts to follow her vector.

As soon as she cut off Maxwell-Corey's angry message, she detected the launch of a message drone from the SSS-900, undoubtedly containing an official summons. As plenty of traffic was always flying into the station's space, it took no great skill to divert the heat-seeking flyer onto the trail of another outgoing vessel. Nothing, and certainly not an unbrained droid, could outmaneuver a brainship. By the time the mistake was discovered, she'd be out of this sector entirely, and on her way to an unknown quadrant of the galaxy.

Later, when she felt less threatened by him, she'd compose a message complaining of what was really becoming harassing behavior to SPRIM. She'd had that old nuisance on her tail long enough. Running free, in full control of her engines and her faculties, was one of the most important things in her life. Every time that right was threatened, Carialle reacted in a way that probably justified the IG's claim of dangerous excitability.

In the distance, she picked up indications of two small ships following her initial vector. All right, score one up for the IG: he'd known she'd resist his orders and had ordered a couple of scouts to chase her down. That could also mean that he might have even put out an alarm that she was a danger to herself and her brawn, and must be brought back willingly or unwillingly. Would the small scouts have picked up her power emissions? She ought to have been one jump ahead of old Sennet and expected this sort of antic. She ought to have lain quiescent. Oh well. She really couldn't contest the fact that proximity to the IG did put her in a state of confusion. She adjusted her adrenals. Calm down, girl. Calm down. Think!

Quick perusal of her starchart showed the migration of an ion storm only a couple of thousand klicks away. Carialle made for it. She skimmed the storm's margin. Then, letting her computers plot the greatest possible radiation her shields could take without buckling, she slid nimbly over the surface, a surfer riding dangerous waters. The sensation was glorious! Ordinary pilots, unable to feel the pressures on their ships' skins as she did, would hesitate to follow. Nor could their scopes detect her in the wash of ion static. Shortly, Carialle was certain she had shaken off her tails. She turned a sharp perpendicular from the ion storm, and watched its opalescent halos recede behind her as she kicked her engines up to full speed.

Returning to the game, she found Keff studying the floating map holograph over a cold one at the "village pub." He glanced up at her pillar when she hailed him.

"I take it we're free of unwanted company?"

"With a sprinkling of luck and the invincibility of our radiation proof panels," Carialle said, "we've evaded the minions of the evil wizard. Now it's time for a brew." She tested herself for adrenaline fatigue, and allowed herself a brief feed of protein and vitamin B-complex.

Keff tipped his glass up to her. Quick analysis told her that though the golden beverage looked like beer, it was the non-alcoholic electrolyte-replenisher Keff used after workouts. "Here's to your swift feet and clever ways, my lovely, and confusion to our enemies. Er, did my coffee come aboard?"

"Yes, sir," she replied, flashing the image of a saluting marine on the wall. "The storesmaster just had time to break out a little of the good stuff when Simeon passed the word down. I even got you a small quantity of chocolate. Best Demubian." Keff beamed.

"Ah, Cari, now I know the ways you love me. Did you have time to load any of my *special* orders?" he asked, with a quirk of his head.

"Now that you mention it, there were two boxes in the cargo hold with your name on them," Carialle said.

Clang. BUMP! *Clang.* BUMP!

The shining contraption of steel that was the Rotoflex had taken little time to put together, still less to watch the instructional video on how to use it. Keff sat on the leatherette-covered, modified saddle with a stirrup-shaped, metal pulley in each outstretched hand. His broad face red from the effort, Keff slowly brought one fist around until it touched his collarbone, then let it out again. The heavy cables sang as they strained against the resistance coils, and relaxed with a heavy thump when Keff reached full extension. Squeezing his eyes shut, he dragged in the other fist. The tendons on his neck stood out cordlike under his sweat-glistening skin.

"Two hundred and three," he grunted. "Uhhh! Two hundred and four. Two . . ."

"Look at me," Carialle said, dropping into the bass octave and adopting the spiel technique of so many tri-vid commercials. "Before I started the muscle-up exercise program I was a forty-four-kilogram weakling. *Now* look at me. You, too, can . . ."

"All right," Keff said, letting go of the hand-weights. They swung in noisy counterpoint until the metal cables retracted into their arms. He arose from the exerciser seat and toweled off with the cloth slung over the end of his weight bench. "I can acknowledge a hint when it's delivered with a sledgehammer. I just wanted to see how much this machine can take."

"Don't you mean how much *you* can take? One day you're going to rupture something," Carialle warned. She noted Keff's respiration at over two hundred pulses per minute, but it was dropping rapidly.

"Most accidents happen in the home," Keff said, with a grin.

"I really was sorry I had to interrupt your tryst with Susa," Carialle said for the twentieth time that shift.

"No problem," Keff said, and Carialle could tell that this time he meant it. "It would have been a more pleasant way to get my heart rate up, but this did nicely, thank you." He yawned and rolled his shoulders to ease them, shooting one arm forward, then the other. "I'm for a shower and bed, lady dear."

"Sleep well, knight in shining muscles."

Shortly, the interior was quiet but for the muted sounds of machinery humming and gurgling. The SSS-900 technicians had done their work well, for all they'd been rushed by circumstances to finish. Carialle ran over the systems one at a time, logging in repair or replacement against the appropriate component. That sort of accounting took up little time. Carialle found herself longing for company. A perverse notion since she knew it would be hours now before Keff woke up.

Carialle was not yet so far away from some of the miners' routes that she couldn't have exchanged gossip with other ships in the sector, but she didn't dare open up channels for fear of tipping off Maxwell-Corey to their whereabouts. The enforced isolation of silent running left her plenty of time for her thoughts.

Keff groaned softly in his sleep. Carialle activated the camera just inside his closed door for a brief look, then dimmed the lights and left him alone. The brawn was faceup on his bunk with one arm across his forehead and right eye. The thin thermal cover had been pushed down and was draped modestly across his groin and one leg, which twitched now and again. One of his precious collection of real-books lay open facedown on the nightstand. The tableau was worthy of a painting by the Old Masters of Earth—Hercules resting from his labors. Frustrated from missing his close encounter of the female kind, Keff had exercised himself into a stiff mass of sinews. His muscles were paying him back for the abuse by making his rest uneasy. He'd rise for his next shift aching in every joint, until he worked the stiffness out again. As the years went by it took longer for Keff to limber up, but he kept at it, taking pride in his excellent physical condition.

Softshells were, in Carialle's opinion, funny people. They'd go to such lengths to build up their bodies which then had to be maintained with a significant effort, disproportionate to the long-term effect. They were so unprotected. Even the stress of exercise, which they considered healthy, was damaging to some of them. They strove to accomplish goals which would have perished in a few generations, leaving no trace of their passing. Yet they cheerfully continued to "do" their mite, hoping something would survive to be admired by another generation or species.

Carialle was very fond of Keff. She didn't want him anguished or disabled. He had been instrumental in restoring her to a useful existence and while he wasn't Fanine—who could be?—he had many endearing qualities. He had brought her back to wanting to live, and then he had neatly caught her up in his own special goal—to find a species Humanity could freely interact with, make cultural and scientific exchanges, open sociological vistas. She was concerned that his short life span, and the even shorter term of their contract with Central Worlds Exploration, would be insufficient to accomplish the goal they had set for themselves. She would have to continue it on her own one day. What if the beings they sought did not, after all, exist?

Shellpeople had good memories but not infallible ones, she reminded herself. In three hundred, four hundred years, would she even be able to remember Keff? Would she want to, lest the memory be as painful as the anticipation of such loss was now? *If I find them after you're . . . well, I'll make sure they're named after you,* she vowed silently, listening to his quiet breathing. That immortality at least she could offer him.

So far, in light of that lofty goal, the aliens that the CK team had encountered were disappointing. Though interesting to the animal behaviorist and xenobiologist, Losels, Wyverns, Hydrae, and the Rodents of Unusual Size, et cetera ad nauseam, were all non-sentient.

To date, the CK's one reasonable hope of finding an equal or superior species came five years and four months before, when they had intercepted a radio transmission from a race of beings who sounded marvelously civilized and intelligent. As Keff had scrambled to make IT understand them, he and Carialle became excited, thinking that they had found *the* species with whom they could exchange culture and technology. They soon discovered that the inhabitants of Jove II existed in an atmosphere and pressure that made it utterly impractical to establish a physical presence. Pen pals only. Central Worlds would have to limit any interaction to radio contact with these Acid Breathers. Not a total loss, but not the real thing. Not *contact*.

Maybe this time on *this* mission into R sector, there would be something worthwhile, the real gold that didn't turn to sand when rapped on the anvil. That hope lured them farther into unexplored space, away from the *known* galaxy, and communication with friends and other B&B ship partnerships. Carialle chose not to admit to Keff that she was as hooked on First Contact as he was. Not only was there the intellectual and emotional thrill of being the first human team to see something totally new, but also the bogies had less chance of crowding in on her . . . if she looked further and further ahead.

For a shellperson, with advanced data-retrieval capabilities and superfast recall, every memory existed as if it had happened only moments before. Forgetting required a specific effort: the decision to wipe an event out of one's databanks. In some cases, that fine a memory was a curse, forcing Carialle to reexamine over and over again the events leading up to the accident. Again and again she was tormented as the merciless and inexorable sequence pushed its way, still crystal clear, to the surface—as it did once more during this silent running.

Sixteen years ago, on behalf of the Courier Service, she and her first brawn, Fanine, paid a covert call to a small space-repair facility on the edge of Central Worlds space. Spacers who stopped there had complained to CenCom of being fleeced. Huge, sometimes ruinously expensive purchases with seemingly faultless electronic documentation were charged against travelers' personal numbers, often months after they had left SSS-267. Fanine discreetly gathered evidence of a complex system of graft, payoffs and kickbacks, confirming CenCom's suspicions. She had sent out a message to say they had corroborative details and were returning with it.

They never expected sabotage, but they should have—Carialle corrected herself: *she* should have—been paying closer attention to what the dock hands were doing in the final check-over they gave her before the CF-963 departed. Carialle could still remember how the fuel felt as it glugged into her tank: cold, strangely cold, as if it had been chilled in vacuum. She could have refused that load of fuel, should have.

As the ship flew back toward the Central Worlds, the particulate matter diluted in the tanks was kept quiescent by the real fuel. Gradually, her engines sipped away that buffer, finally reaching the compound in the bottom of her tanks. When there was more aggregate than fuel, the charge reached critical mass, and ignited.

Her sensors shut down at the moment of explosion but that moment—10:54:02.351—was etched in her memory. That was the moment when Fanine's life ended and Carialle was cast out to float in darkness.

She became aware first of the bitter cold. Her internal temperature should have been a constant 37° Celsius, and cabin temperature holding at approximately twenty-one. Carialle sent an impulse to adjust the heat but could not find it. Motor functions were at a remove, just out of her reach. She felt as if all her limbs—for a brainship, all the motor synapses—and most horribly, her vision, had been removed. She was blind and helpless. Almost all of her external systems were gone except for a very few sound and skin sensors. She called out soundlessly for Fanine: for an answer that would never come.

Shock numbed the terror at first. She was oddly detached, as if this could not be happening to her. Impassively she reviewed what she *knew*. There had been an explosion. Hull integrity had been breached. She could not communicate with Fanine. Probably Fanine was dead. Carialle had no visual sensing equipment, or no control of it, if it still remained intact. Not being able to see was the worst part. If she could see, she could assess the situation and make an objective judgment. She had sustenance and air recirculation, so the emergency power supply had survived when ship systems were cut, and she retained her store of chemical compounds and enzymes.

First priority was to signal for help. Feeling her way through the damaged net of synapses, she detected the connection for the rescue beacon. Without knowing whether it worked or not, Carialle activated it, then settled in to keep from going mad.

She started by keeping track of the hours by counting seconds. Without a clock, she had no way of knowing how accurate her timekeeping was, but it occupied part of her mind with numbing lines of numbers. She went too quickly through her supply of endorphins and serotonin. Within a few hours she was forced to fall back on stress-management techniques taught to an unwilling Carialle when she was much younger and thought she was immortal by patient instructors who knew better. She sang every song and instrumental musical composition she knew, recited poems from the Middle Ages of Earth forward, translated works of literature from one language into another, cast them in verse, set them to music, meditated, and shouted inside her own skull.

That was because most of her wanted to curl up in a ball in the darkest corner of her mind and whimper. She knew all the stories of brains who suffered sensory deprivation. Tales of hysteria and insanity were the horror stories young shellchildren told one another at night in primary education crèches. Like the progression of a fatal disease, they recounted the symptoms. First came fear, then disbelief, then despair. Hallucinations would begin as the brain synapses, desperate for stimulation, fired off random neural patterns that the conscious mind would struggle to translate as rational, and finally, the brain would fall into irrevocable madness. Carialle shuddered as she remembered how the children whispered to each other in supersonic voices that only the computer monitors could pick up that after a while, you'd begin to hear things, and imagine things, and feel things that weren't there.

To her horror, she realized that it was happening to her. Deprived of sight, other than the unchanging starscape, sound, and tactile sensation, memory drive systems failing, freezing in the darkness, she was beginning to feel hammering at her shell, to hear vibrations through her very body. Something was touching her.

Suddenly she knew that it wasn't her imagination. Somebody had responded to her beacon after who-knew-how-long, and was coming to get her. Galvanized, Carialle sent out the command along her comlinks on every frequency, cried out on local audio pickups, hoping she was being heard and understood.

"I am here! I am alive!" she shouted, on every frequency. "Help me!"

But the beings on her shell paid no attention. Their movements didn't pause at all. The busy scratching continued.

Her mind, previously drifting perilously toward madness, focused on this single fact, tried to think of ways to alert the beings on the other side of the barrier to her presence. She felt pieces being torn away from her skin, sensor links severed, leaving nerve endings shrieking agony as they died. At first she thought that her "rescuers" were cutting through a burned, blasted hull to get to her, but the tapping and scraping went on too long. The strangers were performing salvage on her shell, with her still alive within it! This was the ultimate violation; the equivalent of mutilation for transplants. She screamed and twitched and tried to call their attention to *her*, but they didn't listen, didn't hear, didn't stop.

Who were they? Any spacefarer from Central Worlds knew the emblem of a brainship. Even land dwellers had at least seen tri-dee images of the protective titanium pillar in which a shellperson was encased. Not to know, to be attempting to open her shell without care for the person inside meant that they must not be from the Central Worlds or any system connected to it. Aliens? Could her attackers be from an extra-central system?

When she was convinced that the salvagers were just about to sever her connections to her food and air recycling system, the scratching stopped. As suddenly as the intrusion had begun, Carialle was alone again. Realizing that she was now on the thin edge of sanity, she forced herself to count, thinking of the shape of each number, tasting it, pretending to feel it and push it onward as she thought, tasted, and pretended to feel the next number, and the next, and the next. She hadn't realized how different numbers *were*, individuals in their own right, varying in many ways each from the other, one after the other.

Three million, six hundred twenty-four thousand, five hundred and eighty three seconds later, an alert military transport pilot recognized the beacon signal. He took her shell into the hold of his craft. He did what he could in the matter of first aid to a shellperson—restored her vision. When he brought her to the nearest space station and technicians were rushed to her aid, she was awash in her own wastes and she couldn't convince anyone that what she was sure had happened —the salvage of her damaged hull by aliens—was a true version of her experiences. There was no evidence that anything had touched her ship after the accident. None of the damage could even be reasonably attributable to anything but the explosion and the impacts made by hurtling space junk. They showed her the twisted shard of metal that was all that had been left of her life-support system. What had saved her was that the open end had been seared shut in the heat of the explosion. Otherwise she would have been exposed directly to vacuum. But the end was smooth, and showed no signs of interference. Because of the accretion of waste they thought that her strange experience must be hallucinatory. Carialle alone knew she hadn't imagined it. There had been someone out there. There had!

The children's tales, thankfully, had not turned out to be true. She had made it to the other side of her ordeal with her mind intact, though a price had to be extracted from her before she was whole again. For a long time, Carialle was terrified of the dark, and she begged not to be left alone. Dr. Dray Perez-Como, her primary care physician, assigned a roster of volunteers to stay with her at all times, and made sure she could see light from whichever of her optical pickups she turned on. She had nightmares all the time about the salvage operation, listening to the sounds of her body being torn apart while she screamed helplessly in the dark. She fought depression with every means of her powerful mind and will, but without a diversion, something that would absorb her waking mind, she seemed to have "dreams" of some sort whenever her concentration was not focused.

One of her therapists suggested to Carialle that she could recreate the "sights" that tormented her by painting the images that tried to take control of her mind. Learning to manipulate brushes, mixing paints—at first she gravitated toward the darkest colors and slathered them on canvas so that not a single centimeter remained "light." Then, gradually, with healing and careful, loving therapy, details emerged: sketchily at first; a swath of dark umber, or a wisp of yellow. In the painstaking, meticulous fashion of any shellperson, her work became more graphic, then she began to experiment with color, character, and dimension. Carialle herself became fascinated with the effect of color, concentrated on delicately shading tones, one into another, sometimes using no more than one fine hair on the brush. In her absorption with the mechanics of the profession, she discovered that she genuinely enjoyed painting. The avocation couldn't change the facts of the tragedy she had suffered, but it gave her a splendid outlet for her fears.

By the time she could deal with those, she became aware of the absence of details; details of her schooling, her early years in Central's main training facility, the training itself as well as the expertise she had once had. She had to rebuild her memory from scratch. Much had been lost. She'd lost vocabulary in the languages she'd once been fluent in, scientific data including formulae and equations, navigation. Ironically, she could recall the details of the accident itself, too vividly for peace of mind. Despite meticulously relearning all the missing details concerning her first brawn, Fanine—all the relevant facts, where their assignments had taken them—these were just facts. No memory of shared experiences, fears, worries, fun, quarrels remained. The absence was shattering.

Ships did mourn the loss of their brawns: even if the brawn lived to retire at a ripe old age for a dirtside refuge. Carialle was *expected* to mourn: encouraged to do so. She was aware only of a vague remorse for surviving a situation that had ended the life of someone else. But she could not remember quite enough about Fanine or their relationship to experience genuine grief. Had they even liked one another? Carialle listened to hedrons of their mission reports and communiques. All of these could be taken one way or the other. The nine years they had spent together had been reduced to strict reportage with no personal involvement that Cari could recall.

As occupational therapy, Carialle took a job routing communication signals coming in to CenCom, a sort of glorified directory-assistance. It was busywork, taking little effort or intellect to do well. The advantage lay in the fact that voices and faces surrounded her.

She was ready for a new ship within two years of her rescue, and thank God for required insurance. As soon as the last synapse connection was hooked up and she was conscious again, Carialle felt an incredible elation: she was whole again, and strong. This was the way she was meant to be: capable of sailing through space, available and eager for important missions. Her destiny was not to answer communication systems or scuttle on a grav-carrier through corridors filled with softshells.

The expenses of the rescue operation and her medical care had been assumed by CenCom since that last mission had been hazardous, but the new CX-963 got quite a shock at the escalation of price in ship hulls. Her insurance had been based on *purchase*, not replacement price. She'd done a preliminary assessment of the cost but erroneously based her figures on those of her original ship-self. Her savings vanished in the margin between the two as unseen as a carbon meteor in atmosphere. She'd have no options on missions: she'd have to take any and many, and at once, to begin paying her enlarged debt.

Concurrently her doctors and CenCom urged her to choose a new brawn. After losing her last so spectacularly,

Carialle was reluctant to start the procedure; another choice might end in another death. She agreed to see one man who came particularly well recommended, but she couldn't relate at all to him and he left in the shortest possible courteous time. She didn't *have* to have a brawn, did she? Brainships could go on solo missions or on temporary assignments. She might accept one on those terms. Her doctors and CenCom said they'd check into that possibility and left her alone again.

Though there were rarely so many, nine B&B ships were currently on the Regulus CenCom base, either between missions or refitting. She did have the chance to speak with other shellpeople. She was made to feel welcome to join their conference conversations. She knew that they knew her recent history but no one would have brought the subject up unless she did. And she didn't. But she could listen to the amiable, often hilarious, and sometimes brutally frank, conversations of her peers. The refits were five 800s and two 700s with such brilliant careers that Carialle felt unequal to addressing them at all: the eighth was preparing for a long mission, and there was herself. On an open channel, the brainships did have a tendency to brag about their current partner, how he or she did this and that, and was so good at sports/music/gaming/dancing, or how silly he or she could be about such and such—but hadn't they discovered Planet B or Moon C together, or managed to get germdogs to Colony X and save ninety percent of the afflicted from horrible deaths? The 800s were fond of reciting the silly misunderstandings that could occur between brain and brawn. Within Carialle, a wistfulness began to grow: the sense of what she, partnerless, was lacking.

When the FC-840 related having to mortgage her hull again to bail her brawn out of the clutches of a local gambling casino, Carialle realized with a sense of relief that she'd never have had that kind of trouble with Fanine. That was the first of the feelings, if not specific memories, that resurfaced, the fact that she had respected Fanine's good sense. More memories emerged, slowly at first, but all reassuring ones, all emphasizing the fact that she and Fanine had been *friends* as well as co-workers. Inevitably, during this process, Carialle became aware that she was lonely.

With that awareness, she announced to CenCom that she would now be willing to meet with brawns for the purpose of initiating a new partnership. At once she was inundated with applications, as if everyone had been poised to respond to that willingness. She wondered just how much the conversations of the other brainships had been calculated to stir her to that decision. They had all been keeping an eye on her.

The first day of interviews with prospective partners was hectic, exciting, a whirl of courtship. Deliberately Carialle avoided meeting any who were physically similar to Fanine, who had been a tall, rather plain brunet with large hands and feet, or anyone from Fanine's home planet. Fortunately there were few with either disqualification. None of the first lot, male or female, quite suited, although each did give Carialle a characteristic to add to her wish-list of the perfect brawn.

Keff was her first visitor on the morning of the second day. His broad, cheerful face and plummy voice appealed to her at once. He never seemed to stop moving. She followed him with amusement as he explored the cabin, pointing out every admirable detail. They talked about hobbies. When he insisted that he would want to bring his personal gym along with him, they got into a silly quarrel over the softshell obsession with physical fitness. Instead of being angry at his obduracy in not recognizing her sovereignty over her own decks, Carialle found herself laughing.

Even when he was driving a point home, Keff's manner was engaging, and he was willing to listen to her. She informed CenCom that she was willing to enter a brain/brawn contract. Keff moved aboard at once, and his progressive-resistance gear came with him.

Just how carefully CenCom had orchestrated the affair, Carialle didn't care. CenCom, after all, had been matching brains with brawns for a very long time; they must have the hang of it now. Keff and Carialle complemented one another in so many ways. They shared drive, hope, and intelligence. Even during the interview Keff had managed to reawaken in Carialle the sense of humor which she had thought unlikely to be resuscitated.

In a very few days, as they awaited their first assignment, it was as if she'd never been paired with anyone else but Keff. What he said about spending almost all their time together went double for her. Each of them did pursue his or her private thoughts and interests, but they did their best work together. Keff was like the other half of her soul.

Despite her recent trauma, Carialle was a well-adjusted shellperson as indeed her recovery had proved. She was proud of having the superior capabilities that made it possible to multiplex several tasks at once. She felt sorry for nonshell humans. The enhanced functions available to any shellperson, most especially a brainship, were so far beyond the scope of "normal" humans. She felt lucky to have been born under the circumstances that led to her being enshelled.

Several hundred years before, scientists had tried to find a way to rehabilitate children who were of normal intelligence but whose bodies were useless. By connecting brain synapses to special nodes, the intelligent child could manipulate a shell with extendable pseudopods that would allow it to move, manipulate tools or keyboards. An extension of that principle resulted in the first spaceships totally controlled by encapsulated human beings. Other "shellpeople," trained for multiplexing, ran complicated industrial plants, or space stations, and cities. From the moment a baby was accepted for the life of a shellperson, he or she was conditioned to consider that life preferable to "softshells" who were so limited in abilities and lifespans.

One of the more famous brainships, the HN-832, or the Helva-Niall, had been nicknamed "the ship who sang," having developed a multivoice capability as her hobby. Though she docked in CenCom environs but rarely, Helva's adventures inspired all young shellpeople. Although Carialle was deeply disappointed to discover she had only an average talent for music, she was encouraged to find some other recreational outlet. It had taken a disaster for Carialle to find that painting suited her.

Encapsulated at three months and taught mostly by artificial intelligence programs and other shellpeople, Carialle had no self-image as an ordinary human. While she had pictures of her family and thought they looked like pleasant folks, she felt distinct from them.

Once Carialle had gone beyond the "black" period of her painting, her therapists had asked her to paint a self-portrait. It was a clumsy effort since she knew they wanted a "human" look while Carialle saw herself as a ship so that was what she produced: the conical prow of the graceful and accurately detailed spaceship framed an oval blob with markings that could just barely be considered "features" and blond locks that overlaid certain ordinary ship sensors. Her female sibling had had long blond hair.

After a good deal of conferencing, Dr. Dray and his staff decided that perhaps this was a valid self-image and not a bad one: in fact a meld of fact (the ship) and fiction (her actual facial contours). There were enough shellpeople now,

Dr. Dray remarked, so that it was almost expectable that they saw themselves as a separate and distinct species. In fact, Carialle showed a very healthy shellperson attitude in not representing herself with a perfect human body, since it was something she never had and never could have.

Simeon's gift to Carialle was particularly appropriate. Carialle was very fond of cats, with their furry faces and expressive tails, and watched tapes of their sinuous play in odd moments of relaxation. She saw softshells as two distinct and interesting species, some members of which were more attractive than others.

As human beings went, Carialle considered Keff very handsome. In less hurried situations, his boyish curls and the twinkle in his deep-set blue eyes had earned him many a conquest. Carialle knew intellectually that he was good-looking and desirable, but she was not at all consumed with any sensuality toward him, or any other human being. She found humans, male and female, rather badly designed as opposed to some aliens she had met. If Man was the highest achievement of Nature's grand design, then Nature had a sense of humor.

Whereas prosthetics had been the way damaged adults replaced lost limbs or senses, the new Moto-Prosthetics line went further than that by presenting the handicapped with such refined functions that no "physical" handicap remained. For the shellperson, it meant they could "inhabit" functional alter-bodies and experience the full range of human experiences firsthand. That knocked a lot of notions of limitations or restrictions into an archaic cocked hat. Since Keff had first heard about Moto-Prosthetic bodies for brains, he had nagged Carialle to order one. She evaded a direct "no" because she valued Keff, respected his notion that she should have the chance to experience life outside the shell, join him in his projects with an immediacy that she could not enjoy encapsulated.

The idea was shudderingly repulsive to her. Maybe if Moto-Prosthetics had been available before her accident, she might have been more receptive to his idea. But to leave the safety of her shell—well, not really leave it, but to seem to leave it—to be vulnerable—though he insisted she review diagrams and manuals that conclusively demonstrated how sturdy and flexible the M-P body was—was anathema. Why Keff felt she should be like other humans, often clumsy, rather delicate, and definitely vulnerable, she couldn't quite decide.

She started Simeon's gift tape to end that unproductive, and somewhat disturbing line of thought. Although Carialle had a library that included tapes of every sort of creature or avian that had been discovered, she most enjoyed the grace of cats, the smooth sinuousness of their musculature. This datahedron started with a huge spotted feline creeping forward, one fluid movement at a time, head and back remaining low and out of sight as if it progressed along under a solid plank. It was invisible to the prong-horned sheep on the other side of the undergrowth. Carialle watched with admiration as the cat twitched, gathered itself, sprang, and immediately stretched out in a full gallop after its prey. She froze the frame, then scrolled it backward slightly to the moment when the beautiful creature leapt forward, appreciating the graceful arc of its back, the stretch of its forelimbs, the elongated power of the hindquarters. She began to consider the composition of the painting she would make: the fleeing sheep was frozen with its silly face wild-eyed and splay-legged ahead of the gorgeous, silken threat behind it.

As she planned out her picture, she ran gravitational analyses, probable radiation effects of a yellow-gold sun, position of blip possibly indicating planet, and a computer model, and made a few idle bets with herself on whether they'd find an alien species, and what it'd look like.

❑ CHAPTER THREE

Keff ignored the sharp twigs digging into the belly of his environment suit as he wriggled forward for a better look. Beyond the thin shield of thorny-leafed shrubbery was a marvel, and he couldn't believe what he was seeing. Closing with his target would not, could not, alter what he was viewing at a distance, not unless someone was having fun with optical illusions—but he painfully inched forward anyway. Not a hundred meters away, hewing the hard fields and hauling up root crops, was a work force of bipedal, bilaterally symmetrical beings, heterogeneous with regard to sex, apparently mammalian in character, with superior cranial development. In fact, except for the light pelt of fur covering all but lips, palms, soles, small rings around the eyes, and perhaps the places Keff couldn't see underneath their simple garments, they were remarkably like human beings. Fuzzy humans.

"Perfect!" he breathed into his oral pickup, not for the first time since he'd started relaying information to Carialle. "They are absolutely perfect in every way."

"Human-chauvinist," Carialle's voice said softly through

the mastoid-bone implant behind his ear. "Just because they're shaped like Homo sapiens doesn't make them any more perfect than any other sentient humanoid or human-like race we've ever encountered."

"Yes, but think of it," Keff said, watching a female, breasts heavy with milk, carrying her small offspring in a sling on her back while she worked. "So *incredibly* similar to us."

"Speak for yourself," Carialle said, with a sniff.

"Well, they are almost exactly like humans."

"Except for the fur, yes, and the hound-dog faces, exactly."

"Their faces aren't really that much like dogs'," Keff protested, but as usual, Carialle's artistic eye had pinned down and identified the similarity. It was the manelike ruff of hair around the faces of the mature males that had thrown off his guess. "A suggestion of dog, perhaps, but no more than that last group looked like pigs. I think we've found the grail, Cari."

A gust of cold wind blew through the brush, fluttering the folds of loose cloth at the back of Keff's suit. His ears, nose, and fingers were chilly and growing stiff, but he ignored the discomfort in his delight with the objects of his study. On RNJ-599-B-V they had struck *gold*. Though it would be a long time before the people he was watching would ever meet them on their own terms in space.

Coming in toward the planet, Carialle had unleashed the usual exploratory devices to give them some idea of geography and terrain.

The main continent was in the northern hemisphere of the planet. Except for the polar ice cap, it was divided roughly into four regions by a high, vast mountain range not unlike the European Alps of old Earth. Like the four smaller mountain ranges in each of the quadrants, it had been volcanic at one time, but none of the cones showed any signs of activity.

The team had been on planet for several days already, viewing this and other groups of the natives from different vantage points. Carialle was parked in a gully in the eastern quadrant, four kilometers from Keff's current location, invisible to anyone on foot. It was a reasonable hiding place, she had said, because they hadn't seen any evidence during their approach of technology such as radar or tracking devices. Occasional power fluctuations pinged the needles on Carialle's gauges, but since they seemed to occur at random, they *might* just be natural surges in the planet's magnetic field. But Carialle was skeptical, since the surges were more powerful than one should expect from a magnetic field, and were diffuse and of brief duration, which made it difficult for her to pin the phenomenon down to a location smaller than five degrees of planetary arc. Her professional curiosity was determined to find a logical answer.

Keff was more involved with what he could see with his own eyes—his wonderful aliens. He studied the tool with which the nearest male was chipping at the ground. The heavy metal head, made of a slagged iron/copper alloy, was laboriously holed through in two places, where dowels or nails secured it to the flat meter-and-a-half long handle. Sinew or twine wound around and around making doubly sure that the worker wouldn't lose the hoe face on the back swing. By squeezing his eyelids, Keff activated the telephoto function in his contact lenses and took a closer look. The tools were crude in manufacture but shrewdly designed for most effective use. And yet no technology must exist for repair: the perimeter of the field was littered with pieces of discarded, broken implements. These people might have discovered smelting, but welding was still beyond them. Still, they'd moved from hunter/gatherer to farming and animal husbandry. Small but well-tended small flower and herb gardens bordered the field and the front of a man-high cave mouth.

"They seem to be at the late Bronze or early Iron Age stage of development," Keff murmured. "Speaking anthropologically, this would be the perfect species for a long-term surveillance to see if this society will parallel human development." He parted the undergrowth, keeping well back from the opening in the leaves. "Except for having only three fingers and a thumb on each hand, they've got the right kind of manipulative limbs to attain a high technological level."

"Close enough for government work," Carialle said, reasonably. "I can't see that the lack of one digit would interfere with their ability to make more complex tools, since clearly they're using some already."

"No," Keff said. "I'd be more disappointed if they didn't have thumbs. A new species of humanoid! I can write a paper about them." Keff's breath quickened with his enthusiasm. "Parallel development to Homo sapiens terraneum? Evolution accomplished separately from Earth-born humanity?"

"It's far more likely that they were seeded here thousands of years ago," Carialle suggested, knowing that she'd better dampen his enthusiasm before it got out of hand. "Maybe a forgotten colony?"

"But the physical differences would take eons to evolve," Keff said. The odds against parallel development were staggering, but the notion that they might have found an unknown cousin of their own race strongly appealed to him. "Of course, scientifically speaking, we'd have to consider that possibility, especially in the light of the number of colonial ventures that never sent back a 'safe down' message."

"Yes, we should seriously consider that aspect," Carialle said, but without sarcasm.

By thrusting out the angle of his jawbone, Keff increased the gain on his long-distance microphone to listen in on the natives as they called out to one another. All the inhabitants of this locale were harvesting root produce. If any kind of formal schooling existed for the young, it must be suspended until the crops were brought in. Typical of farm cultures, all life revolved around the cycle of the crops. Humanoids of every age and size were in or around the broad fields, digging up the roots. They seemed to be divided into groups of eight to ten, under the supervision of a crew boss, either male or female, who worked alongside them. No overseer was visible, so everyone apparently knew his or her job and got on with it. Slackers were persuaded by glares and peer pressure to persevere. Keff wondered if workers were chosen for their jobs by skill, or if one inherited certain tasks or crop rows by familial clan.

Well out of the way of the crews, small children minding babies huddled as near as they could to a low cavern entrance from which Carialle had picked up heat source traces, suggesting that entrance led to their habitation. It made sense for the aborigines to live underground, where the constant temperature was approximately 14° C, making it warmer than it was on the surface. Such an accommodation would be simple to heat, with the earth itself as insulation. Only hunger could have driven Keff out to farm or hunt in this cold, day after day.

Keff could not have designed a world more likely to be dependent upon subsistence culture. The days were long, but the temperature did not vary between sunup and sundown. Only the hardiest of people would survive to breed: and the hardiest of plants. It couldn't be easy to raise crops in this stony ground, either. Keff rubbed a pinch of it between his finger and thumb.

"High concentration of silicate clay in that soil," Carialle said, noticing his action. "Makes it tough going, both for the farmer and the crop."

"Needs more sand and more fertilizer," Keff said. "And more water. When we get to know one another, we can advise them of irrigation and soil enrichment methods. See that flat panlike depression at the head of the field? That's where they pour water brought uphill by hand." A line of crude barrels nestled against the hillside bore out his theory.

Dirt-encrusted roots of various lengths, shapes, and colors piled up in respectable quantity beside the diggers, whose fur quickly assumed the dull dun of the soil.

"It's incredible that they're getting as much of a yield as they are," Keff remarked. "They must have the science of farming knocked into them."

"Survival," Carialle said. "Think what they could do with fertilized soil and steady rainfall. The atmosphere here has less than eight percent humidity. Strange, when you consider they're in the way of prevailing continental winds, between the ocean and that mountain range. There should be plenty of rain, and no need for such toil as *that*."

Under the direction of a middle-aged male with a light-brown pelt, youngsters working with the digging crews threw piles of the roots onto groundsheets, which were pulled behind shaggy six-legged pack beasts up and down the rows. When each sheet was full, the beast was led away and another took its place.

"So what's the next step in this production line?" Keff asked, shifting slightly to see.

The female led the beast to a square marked out by hand-sized rocks, making sure nothing fell off as she guided the animal over the rock boundary. Once inside, she detached the groundsheet. Turning the beast, she led it back to the field where more folded groundsheets were piled.

"But if they live in the cave, over there," Keff said, in surprise, "why are they leaving the food over here?"

"Maybe the roots need to dry out a little before they can be stored, so they won't rot," Carialle said. "Or maybe they stink. You find out for yourself when we make contact. Here, visitor, eat roots. Good!"

"No, thanks," Keff said.

The six-legged draft animal waited placidly while the young female attached a new sheet to its harness. The beast bore a passing resemblance to a Terran shire horse, except for the six legs and a double dip of its spine over the extra set of shoulder-hips. Under layers of brown dust, its coat was thick and plushy: good protection against the cold wind. Some of the garments and tool pouches worn by the aborigines were undoubtedly manufactured out of such hide. Keff gazed curiously at the creature's feet. Not at all hooflike: each had three stubby toes with blunt claws and a thick sole that looked as tough as stone. The pack beast walked with the same patient gait whether the travois behind it was fully loaded or not.

"Strong," Keff said. "I bet one of those six-legged packs—hmm, six-packs!—could haul you uphill."

Carialle snorted. "I'd like to see it try."

Team leaders called out orders with hand signals, directing workers to new rows. The workers chattered among themselves, shouting cheerfully while they stripped roots and banged them on the ground to loosen some of the clinging soil. Carialle could almost hear Xeno gibbering with joy when they saw the hedrons she was recording for them.

"Funny," Keff said, after a while. "I feel as if I should understand what they're saying. The pace of their conversation is similar to Standard. There's cadence, but measured, not too fast, and it's not inflected like, say, Old Terran Asian."

A thickly furred mother called to her child, playing in a depression of the dusty earth with a handful of other naked tykes. It ignored her and went on with its game, a serious matter of the placement of pebbles. The mother called again, her voice on a rising note of annoyance. When the child turned to look, she repeated her command, punctuating her words with a spiraling gesture of her right hand. The child, eyes wide with alarm, stood up at once and ran over. After getting a smack on the bottom for disobedience, the child listened to instructions, then ran away, past the cave entrance and around the rise of the hill.

"Verrrry interesting," Keff said. "She didn't *say* anything different, but that child certainly paid attention when she made that hand gesture. Somewhere along the line they've evolved a somatic element in their language."

"Or the other way around," Carialle suggested, focusing on the gesture and replaying it in extreme close-up. "How do you know the hand signals didn't come first?"

"I'd have to make a study on it," Keff said seriously, "but I'd speculate because common, everyday symbols are handled with verbal phrases, the hand signals probably came later. I wonder why it evolved that way?"

"Could a percentage of them be partially hearing-impaired or deaf?"

"Not when they have such marked cadence and rhythm in their speech," Keff replied. "I doubt this level of agriculturalist would evolve lipreading. Hmm. I could compare it to the Saxon/Norman juxtaposition on Old Earth. Maybe they've been conquered by another tribe who primarily use sign language for communication. Or it might be the signs come from their religious life, and mama was telling baby that God would be unhappy if he didn't snap to it."

"Ugh. Invisible blackmail."

Keff patted the remote IT unit propped almost underneath his chin. "I want to talk to some of these people and see how long it takes my unit to translate. I'm dying to see what similarities there are between their language structure and Standard's." He started to gather himself up to stand.

"Not so fast," Carialle said, her voice ringing in his mastoid-bone implant. He winced. "When something seems too good to be true, it probably is. I think we need to do more observation."

"Cari, we've watched half a dozen of these groups already. They're all alike, even to the size of the flower gardens. When am I going to get to talk to one of them?"

The brain's voice hinted of uneasiness. "There's something, well, odd and seedy about this place. Have you noticed how old all these artifacts are?"

Keff shrugged. "Usable tools passed down from generation to generation. Not uncommon in a developing civilization."

"I think it's just the opposite. Look at that!"

Coming toward the work party in the field were two furry humanoid males. Between them on a makeshift woven net of rough cords, they carefully bore a hemispherical, shieldlike object full of sloshing liquid. They were led by the excited child who had been sent off by his mother. He shouted triumphantly to the teams of workers who set down their tools and rubbed the dust out of their fur as they came over for a drink. Patiently, each waited his or her turn to use the crude wooden dippers, then went immediately back to the fields.

"Water break," Keff observed, propping his chin on his palm. "Interesting bucket."

"It looks more like a microwave raydome to me, Keff," Carialle said. "Whaddayou know! They're using the remains of a piece of advanced technical equipment to haul water."

"By Saint George and Saint Vidicon, you're right! It

does look like a raydome. So the civilization's not evolving, but in the last stages of decline," Keff said, thoughtfully, tapping his cheek with his fingertips. "I wonder if they had a war, eons ago, and the opposing forces blew themselves out of civilization. It's so horribly cold and dry here that we could very well be seeing the survivors of a comet strike."

Carialle ran through her photo maps of the planet taken from space. "No ruins of cities above ground. No signatures of decaying radiation that I saw, except for those sourceless power surges—and by the way, I just felt another one. Could they be from the planet's magnetic disturbance? There are heavy electromagnetic bursts throughout the fabric of the planet, and they don't seem to be coming from anywhere. I suppose they *could* be natural but — it's certainly puzzling. Possibly there was a Pyrrhic victory and both sides declined past survival point so that they ended up back in the Stone Age. Dawn of Furry Mankind, second day."

"Now that you mention it, I do recognize some of the pieces they made their tools out of," Keff said. He watched an adolescent female guiding two six-packs in a tandem yoke pulling a plow over part of the field that had been harvested. "Yours is probably the best explanation, unless they're a hard-line back-to-nature sect doing this on purpose, and I doubt that very much. But that plowshare looks more to me like part of a shuttlecraft fin. Especially if their bucket has a ninety-seven-point resemblance to a raydome. Sad. A viable culture reduced to noble primitives with only vestiges of their civilization."

"That's what we'll call them, then," Carialle said, promptly. "Noble Primitives."

"Seconded. The motion is carried."

Another young female and her docile six-pack dragged a full load of roots toward the stone square. Keff shifted to watch her.

"Hey, the last load of roots is gone! I didn't see anyone move it."

"We weren't paying attention," Carialle said. "The ground's uneven. There might be a root cellar near that square, with another crew of workers. If you walk over the ground nearby I could do a sounding and find it. If it's unheated that would explain why it's not as easy to pick out as their living quarters."

Keff heard a whirring noise behind him and shifted as silently as he could. "Am I well enough camouflaged?"

"Don't worry, Keff," Carialle said in his ear. "It's just another globe-frog."

"Damn. I hope they don't see me."

Beside the six-packs, one of the few examples of animal life on RNJ were small green amphibioids that meandered over the rocky plains, probably from scarce water source to water source, in clear globular cases full of water. Outside their shells they'd be about a foot long, with delicate limbs and big, flat paws that drove the spheres across dry land. Keff had dubbed them "globe-frogs." The leader was followed by two more. Globe-frogs were curious as cats, and all of them seemed fascinated by Keff.

"Poor things, like living tumbleweeds," Carialle said, sympathetically.

"The intelligent life isn't much better off," Keff said. "It's dry as dust around here."

"Terrible when sentient beings are reduced to mere survival," Carialle agreed.

"Oops," Keff said, in resignation. "They see me. Here they come. Damn it, woman, stop laughing."

"It's your animal magnetism," Carialle said, amused.

The frogs rolled nearer, spreading out into a line; perhaps to get a look at all sides of him, or perhaps as a safety precaution. If he suddenly sprang and attacked, he could only get one. The rumble of their cases on the ground sounded like thunder to him.

"Shoo," Keff said, trying to wave them off before the field workers came over to investigate. He glanced at the workers. Luckily, none were paying attention to the frogs. "Cari, where's the nearest water supply?"

"Back where the raydomeful came from. About two kilometers north northeast."

"Go that way," Keff said, pointing, with his hand bent up close to his body. "Water. You don't want me. Vamoose. Scram." He flicked his fingers. "Go! *Please.*"

The frogs fixed him with their bulbous black eyes and halted their globes about a meter away from him. One of them opened its small mouth to reveal short, sharp teeth and a pale, blue-green tongue. With frantic gestures, Keff beseeched them to move off. The frogs exchanged glances and rolled away, amazingly in the direction he had indicated. A small child playing in a nearby shallow ditch shrieked with delight when it saw the frogs passing and ran after them. The frogs paddled faster, but the tot caught up, and fetched one of the globes a kick that propelled it over the crest of the hill. The others hastily followed, avoiding their gleeful pursuer. The light rumbling died away.

"Whew!" Keff said. "Those frogs nearly blew my cover. I'd better reveal myself now before someone discovers me by accident."

"Not yet! We don't have enough data to prove the Noble Primitives are nonhostile."

"That's a chance we always take, lady fair. Or why else are we here?"

"Look, we know the villagers we've observed do not leave their sites. I haven't been able to tell an inhabitant of one village from the inhabitant of any other. And you sure don't look like any Noble Primitive. I really don't like risking your being attacked. I'm four kilometers away from you so I can't pull your softshell behind out of trouble, you know. My servos would take hours to get to your position."

Keff flexed his muscles and wished he could take a good stretch first. "If I approach them peacefully, they should at least give me a hearing."

"And when you explain that you're from off-planet? Are they ready for an advanced civilization like ours?"

"They have a right to our advantages, to our help in getting themselves back on their feet. Look how wretchedly they live. Think of the raydome, and the other stuff we've seen. They once had a high-tech civilization. Central Worlds can help them. It's our duty to give them a chance to improve their miserable lot, bring them back to this century. They *were* once our equals. They deserve a chance to be so again, Carialle."

"Thou hast a heart as well as a brain, sir knight. Okay."

Before they had settled how to make the approach, shouting broke out on the work site. Keff glanced up. Two big males were standing nose to nose exchanging insults. One male whipped a knife made of a shard of blued metal out of his tool bag; another relic that had been worn to a mere streak from sharpening. The male he was facing retreated and picked up a digging tool with a ground-down end. Yelling, the knife-wielder lunged in at him, knife over his head. The children scattered in every direction, screaming. Before the pikeman could bring up his weapon, the first male had drawn blood. Two crew leaders rushed up to try to pull them apart. The wounded male, red blood turning dark brown as it mixed with the dust in his body-fur, snarled over the peacemaker's head at his foe. With a roar, he shook himself loose.

"I think you missed your chance for a peaceful approach, Keff."

"Um," Keff said. "He who spies and runs away lives to chat another day."

While the combatants circled each other, ringed by a watching crowd, Keff backed away on his hands and knees through the bush. Cursing the pins and needles in his legs, Keff managed to get to his feet and started downhill toward the gully where Carialle was concealed.

Carialle launched gracefully out of the gully and turned into the face of planetary rotation toward another spot on the day-side which her monitors said showed signs of life.

"May as well ring the front doorbell this time," Keff said. "No sense letting them get distracted over something else. If only I'd moved sooner!"

"No sense having a post mortem over it," Carialle said firmly. "You can amaze *these* natives with how much you already know about them."

Reversing to a tail-first position just at the top of atmosphere, Carialle lowered herself gently through the thin clouds and cleaved through a clear sky onto a rocky field in plain sight of the workers. Switching on all her exterior cameras, she laughed, and put the results on monitor for Keff.

"I could paint a gorgeous picture," she said. "Portrait of blinding astonishment."

"Another regional mutation," Keff said, studying the screen. "They're still beautiful, still the same root stock, but their faces look a little like sheep."

"Perfectly suited for open-mouthed goggling," Carialle said promptly. "I wonder what causes such diversity amidst the groups. Radiation? Evolution based on function and lifestyle?"

"Why would they *need* to look like sheep?" Keff said, shrugging out of the crash straps.

"Maybe they were behind the door when ape faces like yours were handed out," Carialle said teasingly, then turned to business. "I'm reading signs of more underground heat sources. One habitation, three entrances. Ambient air temperature, fourteen degrees. This place is *cold*."

"I'll wear a sweater, Mom. Here goes!"

As Keff waited impatiently in the airlock, checking his equipment carriers and biting on the implanted mouth contact to make sure it was functioning properly, Carialle lowered the ramp. Slowly, she opened the airlock. A hundred yards beyond it, Keff saw a crowd of the sheep-faced Noble Primitives gathered at the edge of the crop field, still gaping at the tall silver cylinder.

Taking a deep breath, Keff stepped out onto the ramp, hand raised, palm outward, weaponless. The IT was slung on a strap around his neck so he let his other hand hang loosely at his side.

"Hail, friends!" he called to the aliens huddled on the edge of the dusty field. "I come in peace."

He walked toward the crowd. The Primitives stared at him, the adults' faces expressionless underneath the fur masks, the children openly awestruck. Cautiously, Keff raised his other hand away from his body so they could see it, and smiled.

"They're not afraid of you, Keff," Carialle said, monitoring the Noble Primitives' vital signs. "In fact, they're not even surprised. Now that's odd!"

"Why does one of the mages come to us?" Alteis said, worriedly, as the stranger approached them, showing his teeth. "What have we done wrong? We have kept up with the harvest. All proceeds on schedule. The roots are nearly all harvested. They are of good quality."

Brannel snorted, a sharp breath ruffling the fur on his upper lip, and turned an uncaring shoulder toward the oldster. Old Alteis was so afraid of the mages that he would do himself an injury one day if the overlords were *really* displeased. He stared at the approaching mage. The male was shorter than he, but possessed of a mighty build and an assured, cocky walk. Unusual for a mage, his hands showed that they were not unacquainted with hard work. The outthrust of the cleft chin showed that he knew his high place, and yet his dark, peaty blue eyes were full of good humor. Brannel searched his memory, but was certain he had never encountered this overlord before.

"He is one we do not know," Brannel said quickly in an undertone out of the side of his mouth. "Perhaps he is here to tell us he is our new master."

"Klemay is our master," Alteis said, his ruff and mustache indignantly erect on his leathery face.

"But Klemay has not been seen for a month," Brannel said. "I saw the fire in the mountains, I told you. Since then, no power has erupted from Klemay's peak."

"Perhaps this one serves Klemay," Mrana, mate of Alteis, suggested placatingly. Surreptitiously, she brushed the worst of the dust off the face of one of her children. None of them looked their best at harvest time when little effort could be wasted on mere appearance. The overlord must understand that.

"Servers serve," Brannel snorted. "No overlord serves another but those of the Five Points. Klemay was not a high mage."

"Do not speak of things you do not understand," Alteis said, as alarmed as that foolish male ever became. "The mages will hear you."

"The mages are not listening," Brannel said.

Alteis was about to discipline him further, but the overlord was within hearing range now. The stranger came closer and stopped a couple of paces away. All the workers bowed their heads, shooting occasional brief glances at the visitor. Alteis stepped forward to meet him and bowed low.

"What is your will, lord?" he asked.

Instead of answering him directly, the mage picked up the box that hung around his neck and pushed it nearly underneath Alteis's chin. He spoke to the leader at some length. Though Brannel listened carefully, the words meant nothing. Alteis waited, then repeated his words clearly in case the overlord had not understood him. The mage smiled, head tilted to one side, uncomprehending.

"What may I and my fellow workers do to serve you, exalted one?" Brannel asked, coming forward to stand beside Alteis. He, too, bowed low to show respect, although the germ of an idea was beginning to take shape in his mind. He tilted his chin down only the barest respectable fraction so he could study the visitor.

The male fiddled with the small box on his breast, which emitted sounds. He spoke over it, possibly reciting an incantation. That was not unusual; all the overlords Brannel had ever seen talked to themselves sometimes. Many objects of power were ranged about this one's strongly built form. Yet he did not appear to understand the language of the people, nor did he speak it. He hadn't even acknowledged Brannel's use of mage-talk, which had been cleverly inserted into his query.

Puzzled, Brannel wrinkled his forehead. His fellow servers stayed at a respectful distance, showing proper fear and respect to one of the great overlords. They were not puzzled: they had no thoughts of their own to puzzle them or so Brannel opined. So he took as close a look at this puzzling overlord as possible.

The male appeared to be of the pure blood of the Magi, showing all three signs: clear skin, whole hand, and bright eyes. His clothing did not resemble that which overlords wore. Then Brannel arrived at a strange conclusion: this male was *not* an overlord. He could not speak either language, he did not wear garments like an overlord, he did not act like an overlord, and he had clearly not come from the high places of the East. The worker male's curiosity welled up until he could no longer contain the question.

"Who are you?" he asked.

Alteis grabbed him by the ruff and yanked him back into the midst of the crowd of shocked workers.

"How dare you speak to an overlord like that, you young puppy?" he said, almost growling. "Keep your eyes down and your mouth shut!"

"He is not an overlord, Alteis," Brannel said, growing more certain of this every passing moment.

"Nonsense," Fralim said, closing his hand painfully on Brannel's upper arm. Alteis's son was bigger and stronger than he was, but Fralim couldn't see the fur on his own skin. He loomed over Brannel, showing his teeth, but Brannel knew half the ferocity was from fear. "He's got all his fingers, hasn't he? The finger of authority has not been amputated. He can use the objects of power. I ask forgiveness, honored lord," Fralim said, speaking in an abject tone to the stranger.

"He does not speak our language, Fralim," Brannel said clearly. "Nor does he understand the speech of the Magi. All the Magi speak the linga esoterka, which I understand. I will prove it. Master," he said, addressing Keff in mage-talk, "what is thy will?"

The stranger smiled in a friendly fashion and spoke again, holding the box out to him.

The experiment didn't impress Brannel's fellow workers. They continued to glance up at the newcomer with awe and mindless adoration in their eyes, like the herd beasts they so resembled.

"Keff," the stranger said, nodding several times and pointing to himself. He shifted his hand toward Brannel. "An dew?"

The others ducked. When the finger of authority was pointed at one of them, it sometimes meant that divine discipline was forthcoming. Brannel tried to hide that he, too, had flinched, but the gesture seemed merely a request for information.

"Brannel," he said, hand over pounding heart. The reply delighted the stranger, who picked up a rock.

"An dwattis zis?" he asked.

"Rock," Brannel said. He approached until he was merely a pace from the overlord. "What is this?" he asked, very daringly, reaching out to touch the mage's tunic sleeve.

"Brannel, no!" Alteis wailed. "You'll die for laying hands on one of them!"

Anything was better than living out his life among morons, Brannel thought in disgust. No bolt of punishment came. Instead, Keff said, "Sliv."

"Sliv," Brannel repeated, considering. It sounded almost like the real word. Ozran was great! he thought in gratitude. Perhaps Keff *was* a mage, but from a distant part of the world.

They began to exchange the words for objects. Keff led Brannel to different parts of the holding, pointing and making his query. Brannel, becoming more interested by the minute, gave him the words and listened carefully to the stranger-words with which Keff identified the same things. Keff was freely offering Brannel a chance to exchange information, to know his words in trade for his own. Language was power, Brannel knew, and power held the key to self-determination.

Behind them, the villagers followed in a huddled group, never daring to come close, but unable to stay away as Brannel claimed the entire, and apparently friendly, attention of a mage. Fralim was muttering to himself. It might have meant trouble, since Fralim saw himself as the heir to village leadership after Alteis, but he was too much in awe of the seeming-mage and had already forgotten some of what had happened. If Brannel managed to distract him long enough afterward, Fralim would forget forever the details of his grudge. It would disappear into the grayness of memory that troubled nearly every server on Ozran. Brannel decided to take advantage of the situation, and named every single worker to the mage. Fralim whitened under his fur, but he smiled back, teeth gritted, when Keff repeated his name.

The stranger-mage asked about every type of root, every kind of flower and herb in the sheltered garden by the cavern mouth. Twice, he tried to enter the home-cavern, but stopped when he saw Brannel pause nervously on the threshold. The worker was more convinced than he was of anything else in his life that this mage was not as other mages: he didn't know entry to the home site between dawn and dusk was forbidden under pain of reprisal.

Toward evening, the prepared food for the villagers appeared in the stone square, as it did several times every day. Brannel would have to pretend to eat and just hope that he could control his rumbling guts until he had a chance to assuage his hunger from his secret cache. He'd worked a long, hard day before he'd had to stimulate his wits to meet the demands of this unexpected event.

Muttering began among the crowd at their heels. The children were hungry, too, and had neither the manners nor the wit to keep their voices down. Not wishing to incur the wrath of the visiting mage, Alteis and Mrana were discussing whether or not they dared offer such poor fare to the great one. Should they, or shouldn't they, interrupt the great one's visit at all by letting mere workers eat? What to do?

Brannel took care of the problem. Keeping a respectful

distance, he led Keff to the stone square and picked up the lid of one of the huge covered dishes. With one hand, he made as if to eat from the steaming tureen of legume stew.

Keff's eyes widened in understanding and he smiled. Though he waved away offers of food, he encouraged the villagers with friendly gestures to come forward and eat. Knowing that Alteis was watching, Brannel was forced to join them. He consumed a few tiny mouthfuls as slowly as he dared.

Fortunately, he had plenty of interruptions which concealed his reluctance to eat. Keff questioned him on the names of the foodstuffs, and what each was made of, pointing to raw vegetables and making an interrogative noise.

"Stewed orange root," Brannel said, pointing out the appropriate field to the mage. "Grain bread." Some of the grain the plough animals ate served to demonstrate what kind. "Legume stew. Sliced tuber fried in bean oil." Beans were unavailable, having been harvested and gathered in by the mages the month before, so he used small stones approximately the right size, and pretended to squeeze them. Keff understood. Brannel knew he did. He was as excited as the mage when the box began to make some of the right sounds, as if finding them on its tongue: frot, brot, brat, bret, bread.

"Bread! That's right," Brannel said, enthusiastically, as Keff repeated what the box said. "That's right, Mage-lord: bread!"

Keff slapped Brannel hard on the back. The worker jumped and caught his breath, but it was a gesture of friendliness, not disapproval—as if Keff was just another worker, a neighbor . . . a—a friend. He tried to smile. The others fell to their knees and covered their heads with their arms, fearing the thunderbolt about to descend.

"Bread," Keff repeated happily. "I think I've got it."

"Do you?" Carialle asked in his ear. "And does the rain in Spain fall mainly in the plain?"

"Ozran, I think," Keff said, subvocalizing as the villagers picked themselves off the ground and came around cautiously to inspect Brannel who was smiling. Keff himself was wild with glee, but restraining himself for fear of scaring the natives further. "I can hardly believe it. I'm making progress faster than I even dared to hope. There's some Ancient Terran forms in their speech, Carialle, embedded in the alien forms, of course. I believe the Ozrans had contact with humankind, maybe millenia ago, significant contact that altered or added to the functionalism of their language. Are there any records in the archives for first contact in this sector?"

"I'll put a trace through," Carialle said, initiating the search sequence and letting it go through an automatic AI program. A couple of circuits "clicked," and the library program began to hum quietly to itself.

By means of Keff's contact button, Carialle focused on the antics of the natives. A few of the females were picking up the spilled dishes with a cautious eye on Keff, never venturing too close to him. The large, black-furred male and the elderly salt-and-pepper male examined a protesting Brannel. The slender male tried without success to wave them off.

"What is wrong with these people?"

"Mm-mm? I don't know. They're looking Brannel over for damages or marks or something. What did they expect to happen when I patted him on the back?"

"I don't know. Bodily contact shouldn't be dangerous. I wish you could get close enough to them so I could read their vital signs and do a chemspec analysis of their skin."

Keff stood at a distance from the villagers, nodding and smiling at any who would meet his eyes, but the moment he took a step toward one, that one moved a step back. "They won't let me, that's obvious. Why are most of them so downright scared of me, but not surprised to see me?"

"Maybe they have legends about deities that look like you," Carialle said with wry humor. "You may be fulfilling some long-awaited prophecy. 'The bare-faced one will come out of the sky and set us free.'"

"No," Keff said, thoughtfully. "I think the reaction is more immediate, more present day. Whatever it is, they're most courteous and absolutely cooperative: an ethnologist's dream. I'm making real progress in communications. I think I've found the 'to be' verb, but I'm not sure I'm parsing it correctly yet. Brannel keeps grinning at me when I ask what something 'is.'"

"Keep going," Carialle said encouragingly. "Faint heart never won fair lady. You're all getting along so well there."

With every evidence of annoyance, Brannel fought free of the hands of his comrades. He smoothed his ruffled fur and glared at the others, his aspect one of long suffering. He returned to Keff, his expression saying, "Let's resume the language lesson, and pay no more attention to *those* people."

"I'd love to know what's going on," Keff said out loud in Standard, with a polite smile, "but I'm going to have to learn a lot more before I can ask the right questions about your social situation here."

One of the other Noble Primitives muttered under his breath. Brannel turned on him and hissed out a sharp phrase that needed no translation: even the sound of it was insulting. Keff moved between them to defuse a potential argument, and that made the other Primitive back off sharply. Keff got Brannel's attention and pointed to the raydome water carrier. Listening to prompts from the IT program through his implant, he attempted to put together a whole sentence of pidgin Ozran.

"What are that?" Keff asked. "Eh? Did I get that right?"

From Brannel's merry expression, he hadn't. He grinned, giving the local man his most winsome smile. "Well, *teach* me then, can you?"

Emboldened by Keff's friendly manner, the Noble Primitive laughed, a harsh sound; more of a cackle than a guffaw.

"So," Keff asked, trying again in Ozran, "what are yes?" He whispered an aside to Carialle. "I don't know even how to ask 'what's right?' yet. I must sound like the most amazing idiot."

"What *is* that. What *are* those," Brannel said, with emphasis, picking up one stone in one hand, a handful of stones in the other, and displaying first one and then the other. He had correctly assumed Keff was trying to ask about singular and plural forms and had demonstrated the difference. The others were still staring dumbly, unable to understand what was going on. Keff was elated by his success.

"Incredible. You may have found the only intelligent man on the planet," Carialle said, monitoring as the IT program recorded the correct uses of the verb, and postulated forms and suffixes for other verbs in its file, shuffling the onomatopoeic transliterations down like cards. "Certainly the only one of this bunch who understands abstract questions."

"He's a find," Keff agreed. "A natural linguist. It could have taken me days to elicit what he's offering freely and, I might add, intelligently. It's going to take me more time to figure out that sign language, but if anyone can put me on the right track, it's Brannel."

Having penetrated the mystery of verbal declension, Keff and Brannel sat down together beside the fire and began a basic conversation.

"Do you see how he's trying to use my words, too?" Keff subvocalized to Carialle.

Using informal signs and the growing lexicon in the IT program, Keff asked Brannel about the below ground habitation.

" . . . Heat from . . . earth," Brannel said, patting the ground by his thigh. IT left audio gaps where it lacked sufficient glossary and grammar, but for Keff it was enough to tell him what he wanted to know.

"A geothermal heating system. It's so cold out; why can't you enter now?" Keff said, making a cave by arching his finger and thumb on the ground and walking his other hand on two fingers toward it.

"Not," Brannel said firmly, with a deliberate sign of his left hand. The IT struggled to translate. "Not cave day. We are . . . work . . . day."

"Oh," Carialle said. "A cultural ban to keep the slackers out on the field during working hours. Ask him if he knows what causes the power surges I'm picking up."

Keff relayed the question. The others who were paying attention shot sulky glances toward Brannel. The dun-colored male started to speak, then stopped when an older female let out a whimper of fear. "Not," he said shortly.

"I guess he doesn't know," Keff said to Carialle. "You, sir," he said, going over to address the eldest male, Alteis, who immediately cowered. "Where comes strong heat from sky?" He pantomimed arcs overhead. "What makes strong heat?"

With a yell, one of the small boys—Keff thought it might be the same one who had defied his mother's orders—traced a jagged line in the sky. The he dove into his mother's lap for safety. An adolescent female, Nona, Keff thought her name was, glanced up at him in terror, and quickly averted her eyes to the ground. The others murmured among themselves, but no one looked or spoke.

"Lightning?" Keff asked Alteis softly. "What causes the lightning, sir?"

The oldster with white-shot black fur studied his lips carefully as he spoke, then turned for help to Brannel, who remained stoically silent. Keff repeated his question. The old male nodded solemnly, as if considering an answer, but then his gaze wandered off over Keff's head. When it returned to Keff, there was a blankness in his eyes that showed he hadn't understood a thing, or had already forgotten the question.

"He doesn't know," Keff said with a sigh. "Well, we're back to basics. Where does the food go for storage?" he asked. He gestured at the stone square and held up one of the roots Brannel had used as an example. "Where roots go?"

Brannel shrugged and muttered something. "Not know," IT amplified and relayed. "Roots go, food comes."

"A culture in which food preparation is a sacred mystery?" Carialle said, with increasing interest. "Now, that's bizarre. If we take that back to Xeno, we'll deserve a bonus."

"Aren't you curious? Didn't you ever try to find out?" Keff asked Brannel.

"Not!" Brannel exclaimed. The bold villager seemed nervous for almost the first time since Keff had arrived. "One curious, all—" He brought his hands together in a thunderclap. "All . . . all," he said, getting up and drawing a circle in the air around an adult male, an adult female, and three children. He pantomimed beating the male, and shoved the food bowls away from the female and children with his foot. Most of the fur-faced humanoids shuddered and one of the children burst into tears.

"All punished for one person's curiosity? But why?" Keff demanded. "By whom?"

For answer Brannel aimed his three-fingered hand at the mountains, with a scornful expression that plainly said that Keff should already know that. Keff peered up at the distant heights.

"Huh?" Carialle said. "Did I miss something?"

"Punishment from the mountains? Is it a sacred tradition associated with the mountains?" Keff asked. "By his body language Brannel holds whatever comes from there in healthy respect, but he doesn't like it."

"Typical of religions," Carialle sniffed. She focused her cameras on the mountain peak in the direction Keff faced and zoomed in for a closer look. "Say, there are structures up there, Keff. They're blended in so well I didn't detect them on initial sweep. What are they? Temples? Shrines? Who built them?"

Keff pointed, and turned to Brannel.

"What are . . . ?" he began. His question was abruptly interrupted when a beam of hot light shot from the peak of the tallest mountain in the range to strike directly at Keff's feet. Hot light engulfed him. "Wha—?" he mouthed. His hand dropped to his side, slamming into his leg with the force of a wrecking ball. The air turned fiery in his throat, drying his mouth and turning his tongue to leather. Humming filled his ears. The image of Brannel's face, agape, swam before his eyes, faded to a black shadow on his retinas, then flew upward into a cloudless sky blacker than space.

The bright bolt of light overpowered the aperture of the tiny contact-button camera, but Carialle's external cameras recorded the whole thing. Keff stood rigid for a moment after the beam struck, then slowly, slowly keeled over and slumped to the ground in a heap. His vital-sign monitor shrieked as all activity flatlined. To all appearances he was dead.

"Keff!" Carialle screamed. Her system demanded adrenaline. She fought it, forcing serotonin and endorphins into her bloodstream for calm. It took only milliseconds until she was in control of herself again. She had to be, for Keff's sake.

In the next few milliseconds, her circuits raced through a diagnostic, checking the implants to be sure there was no system failure. All showed green.

"Keff," she said, raising the volume in his implant. "Can you hear me?" He gave no answer.

Carialle sent her circuits through a diagnostic, checking the implants to be sure there was no system failure. All showed green except the video of the contact camera, which gradually cleared. Before Carialle could panic further, the contacts began sending again. Keff's vitals returned, thready but true. He was alive! Carialle was overjoyed. But Keff was in danger. Whatever caused that burst of power to strike at his feet like a well-aimed thunderbolt might recur. She had to get him out of there. A bolt like that couldn't be natural, but further analysis must wait. Keff was hurt and needed attention. That was her primary concern. How could she get him back?

The small servos in her ship might be able to pick him up, but were intended for transit over relatively level floors. Fully loaded they wouldn't be able to transport Keff's weight across the rough terrain. For the first time, she wished she had gotten a Moto-Prosthetic body as Keff had been nagging her to do. She longed for two legs and two strong arms.

Hold it! A body was available to her: that of the only intelligent man on the planet. When the bolt had struck, Brannel, with admirably quick reflexes, had flung himself out of the way, rolling over the stony ground to a sheltered place beneath the rise. The other villagers had run hell-for-leather back toward their cavern, but Brannel was still only a few meters away from Keff's body. Carialle read his infrared signal and heartbeat: he was ten meters from Keff's body. She opened a voice-link through IT and routed it via the contact button.

"Brannel," she called, amplifying the small speaker as much as she could without distortion. "Brannel, pick up Keff. Bring Keff home." The IT blanked on the word home. She spun through the vocabulary database looking for an equivalent. "Bring Keff to Keff's cave, Brannel!" Her voice rose toward hysteria. She flattened her tones and increased endorphins and proteins to her nutrients to counter the effects of her agitation.

"Mage Keff?" Brannel asked. He raised his head cautiously from the shelter of his hiding place, fearing another bolt from the mountains. "Keff speaks?"

Keff lay in a heap on the ground, mouth agape, eyes half open with the whites showing. Brannel, knowing that sometimes bolts continued to burn and crackle after the initial lightning, kept a respectful distance.

"Bring Keff to Keff's cave," a disembodied voice pleaded. A female's voice it was, coming from underneath the mage's chin. Some kind of familiar spirit? Brannel rocked back and forth, struggling with ambivalent desires. Keff had been kind to him. He wanted to do the mage's wishes. He also wasn't going to put himself in danger for the sake of one of Them whom the mage-bolts had struck down. Was Keff Klemay's successor and that was why he had come to visit their farm holding? Only his right to succeed Klemay had just been challenged by the bolt.

Across the field, the silver cylinder dropped its ramp, clearly awaiting the arrival of its master. Brannel looked from the prone body at his feet to the mysterious mobile stronghold. Stooping, he stared into Keff's eyes. A pulse twitched faintly there. The mage was still alive, if unconscious.

"Bring Keff to Keff's cave," the voice said again, in a crisp but persuasive tone. "Come, Brannel. Bring Keff."

"All right," Brannel said at last, his curiosity about the silver cylinder overpowering his sense of caution. This would be the first time he had been invited into a mage's stronghold. Who knew what wonders would open up to him within Keff's tower?

Drawing one of the limp arms over his shoulder, Brannel hefted Keff and stood up. After years of hard work, carrying the body of a man smaller than himself wasn't much of an effort. It was also the first time he'd laid hands on a mage. With a guilty thrill, he bore Keff's dead weight toward the silver tower.

At the foot of the ramp, Brannel paused to watch the smooth door withdraw upward with a quiet hiss. He stared up at it, wondering what kind of door opened without hands to push it.

"Come, Brannel," the silky persuasive voice said from the weight on his back.

Brannel obeyed. Under his rough, bare feet, the ramp boomed hollowly. The air smelled different inside. As he set foot over the threshold into the dim, narrow anteroom, lights went on. The walls were smooth, like the surface of unruffled water, meeting the ceiling and walls in perfect corners. Such ideal workmanship aroused Brannel's admiration. But what else would one expect from a mage? he chided himself.

In front of him was a corridor. Narrow bands of bluish light like the sun through clouds illuminated themselves. Along the walls at Brannel's eye level, orange-red bands flickered into life, moving onward until they reached the walls' end. The colored lights returned to the beginning and waited.

"I follow thee. Is that right?" Brannel asked in mage-speak, cautiously stepping into the corridor.

"Come," the disembodied voice said in common Ozran and the sound echoed all around him. Mage Keff was certainly a powerful wizard to have a house that talked.

Carialle was relieved that Brannel hadn't been frightened by a disembodied voice or the sight of an interplanetary ship. He was cautious, but she gave him credit for that. She had the lights guide him to the wall where Keff's weight bench was stored. It slid noiselessly out at knee level before the Noble Primitive who didn't need to be told that that was where he was to lay Keff's body.

"The only intelligent man on the planet," Carialle said quietly to herself.

Brannel straightened up and took a good, long look at the cabin, beginning to turn on his callused heels. As he caught sight of the monitors showing various angles of the crop field outside, and the close-up of his fellow Noble Primitives crouched in a huddle at the cave mouth, he let out a sound close to a derisive laugh.

Carialle turned her internal monitors to concentrate on Keff's vital signs. Respiration had begun again and his eyes twitched under their long-lashed lids.

Brannel started to walk the perimeter of the cabin. He was careful to touch nothing, though occasionally he leaned close and sniffed at a piece of equipment. At Keff's exercise machines, he took a deeper breath and straightened up with a snort and a puzzled look on his face.

"Thank you for your help, Brannel," Carialle said, using the IT through her own speakers. "You can go now. Keff will also thank you later."

Brannel showed no signs of being ready to depart. In fact, he didn't seem to have heard her at all. He was wandering around the main cabin with the light of wonder in his eyes beginning to alter. Carialle didn't like the speculative look on his face. She was grateful enough to the furry male for rescuing Keff to let him have a brief tour of the facilities, but no more than that.

"Thank you, Brannel. Good-bye, Brannel," Carialle said, her tone becoming more pointed. "You can go. Please. Now. Go. Leave!"

Brannel heard the staccato words spoken by the mage's familiar in a much less friendly tone than it had used to coax him inside Keff's stronghold. He didn't want to leave such a fascinating place. Many objects lured him to examine them, many small enough to be concealed in the hand. Some of them might even be objects of power. Surely the great mage would not miss a small one.

He focused on a flattened ovoid of shiny white the size of his hand lying on a narrow shelf below a rack of large stiff squares that looked to be made of wood. Even the quickest glance at the white thing told him that it had the five depressions of an item of power in its surface. His breathing quickened as he reached out to pick it up.

"No!" said the voice. "That's my palette." Out of the wall shot a hand made of black metal and slapped his wrist. Surprised, he dropped the white thing. Before it hit the floor, another black hand jumped away from the wall and caught it. Brannel backed away as the lower hand passed the white object to the upper hand, which replaced it on the shelf.

Thwarted, Brannel looked around for another easily portable item. Showing his long teeth in an ingratiating smile and wondering where the unseen watcher was concealed, he sidled purposefully toward another small device on top of a table studded with sparkling lights. His hand lifted, almost of its own volition, toward his objective.

"Oh, no, you don't," Carialle said firmly, startling him into dropping Keff's pedometer back onto the monitor board. She watched as he swiveled his head around, trying to discover where she was. "Didn't anyone ever tell you shoplifting is rude?"

He backed away, with his hands held ostentatiously behind him.

"You're not going to leave on your own, are you?" Carialle said. "Perhaps a little push is in order."

Starting at the far side of the main cabin, Carialle generated complex and sour sonic tones guaranteed to be painful to humanoid ears. The male fell to his knees with his hands over his ears, his sheep's face twisted into a rictus. Carialle turned up the volume and purposefully began to sweep the noise along her array of speakers toward the airlock. Protesting, Brannel was driven, stumbling and crawling, out onto the ramp. As soon as she turned off the noise, he did an abrupt about-face and tried to rush back in. She let loose with a loud burst like a thousand hives of bees and slid the door shut in his face before he could cross the threshold.

"Some people just do not know when to leave," Carialle grumbled, as she ordered out a couple of servos to begin first aid on Keff.

Driven out into the open air by the sharp sounds, Brannel hurried away from the flying castle and over the hill. On the other side of the field, the others were crouched in a noisy conference, arms waving, probably discussing the strange mage. No one paid any attention to him, which was good. He had much to think about, and he was hungry. He'd been forced to consume some of the woozy food. He hoped he hadn't had enough to dull what he had learned this day.

During his youth, when he had fallen ill with fever, vomiting and headache, he had been unable to eat any of the food provided by the overlords. His parents had an argument that night about whether or not to beg Klemay for medical help. Brannel's mother thought such a request would be approved since Brannel was a sturdy lad and would grow to be a strong worker. His father did not want to ask, fearing punishment for approaching one of the high ones. Brannel overheard the discussion, wondering if he was going to die.

In the morning, the floating eye came from Klemay to oversee the day's work. Brannel's mother did not go running out to abase herself before it. Though he was no better, she seemed to have forgotten all about the urgency of summoning help for him. She settled Brannel, swathed in hides, at the edge of the field, and patted his leg affectionately before beginning her duties. She *had* forgotten her concern of the previous night. So had his father. Brannel was not resentful. This was the way it had always been with the people. The curious thing was that *he* remembered. Yesterday had not disappeared into an undifferentiated grayness of mist and memory. Everything that he'd heard or seen was as clear to him as if it was still happening. The only thing that was different between yesterday and the day before was that he had not eaten.

Thereafter, he had avoided eating the people's food whenever possible. He experimented with edible native plants that grew down by the river, but lived mostly by stealing raw vegetables and grain from standing crops or from the plough-beasts' mangers. As a result, he grew bigger and stronger than any of his fellows. If his mother remarked upon it at all, when the vague fuzz of memory lifted, she was grateful that she had produced a fine strong big son to work for the overlord. His wits sharpened, and anything he heard he remembered forever. He didn't want to lose the gift by poisoning himself with the people's food. So far, the mages had had no cause to suspect him of being different from the rest of his village. And he was careful *not* to be disobedient or bring himself to their attention.

The worst fate he could imagine was losing his clarity of mind.

That clear mind now puzzled over Keff: was he or was he not a mage? He possessed objects of power, but he spoke no mage-talk. His house familiar knew none of their language either, but it used the same means that Mage Klemay did to drive him out, as the workers of his cave were driven by hideous noises outside to work every day of their lives. Keff seemed to have power yet he was struck down all unaware by the mage-bolt. Could Keff not have sensed it coming?

Once on the far side of the field, Brannel squeezed between bushes to the slope that led to his hiding place near the river. Observed only by a few green-balls, he ate some raw roots from the supply that he had concealed there in straw two nightfalls before. All the harvests had been good this year. No one had noticed how many basket loads he had removed, or if they had, they didn't remember. Their forgetfulness was to his advantage.

His hunger now satisfied, Brannel made his way back to the cavern, to listen to the remarkable happenings of the day, the new mage, and how the mage had been struck down. No one thought to ask what had happened to this mage and Brannel did not enlighten them. They'd have forgotten in the morning anyway. When night's darkness fell, they all swarmed back into the warm cave. As they found their night places, Alteis looked at his son, his face screwed as he tried to remember something he had intended to ask Brannel, but gave up the effort after a long moment.

¤ CHAPTER FOUR

At a casual glance, the council room of the High Mage of the South appeared to be occupied by only one man, Nokias himself, in the thronelike hover-chair in the center, picked out by the slanting rays of the afternoon sun. Plennafrey realized, as she directed her floating spy-eye to gaze around the palatial chamber, that more presence and power was represented there and then than almost anywhere else on Ozran. She was proud to be included in that number allied to Nokias, proud but awed.

Closest to the rear of the hover-chair hung the simple silver globes of his trusted chief servants, ready to serve the High Mage, but also guarding him. They were the eyes in the back of his head, not actual fleshly eyes as Plennafrey had imagined when she was a child. Ranged in random display about the great chamber were the more ornate globe eyes of the mages and magesses. In the darkest corner hovered the sphere belonging to gloomy Howet. Mage-height above all the others flew the spy-eye of Asedow, glaring scornfully down on everyone else. Iranika's red ball drifted near the huge open window that looked out upon the mountain range, seemingly inattentive to the High Mage's discourse. Immediately before Nokias at eye level floated the gleaming metallic pink and gold eye of Potria, an ambitious and dangerous enchantress. As if sensing her regard, Potria's spy-eye turned toward hers, and Plennafrey turned hers just in time to be gazing at High Mage Nokias before the mystical aperture focused.

At home in her fortress sanctuary many klicks distant, Plenna felt her cheeks redden. It would not do to attract attention, nor would her inexperience excuse an open act of discourtesy. That was how mages died. For security, she tightened her fingers and thumb in the five depressions on her belt buckle, her personal object of power, and began to draw from it the weblike framework of a spell that would both protect her and injure or kill anyone who tried to cross its boundaries as well as generate an atmosphere of self-deprecation and effacement. Her magical defenses were as great as any mage's: lack of experience was her weakness. Plennafrey was the most junior of all the mages, the sole survivor of her family. She had taken her father's place only two years ago. Thankfully, Potria appeared not to have taken offense, and the pink-gold spy-eye spun in air to stare at each of its fellows in turn. Plenna directed her blue-green spy eye to efface itself so as not to arouse further notice, and let the spell stand down, inactive but ready.

"We should move now to take over Klemay's stronghold," Potria's mental voice announced. Musical as a horn call, it had a strong, deep flavor that rumbled with mystic force. On the walls, the mystic art of the ancients quivered slightly, setting the patterns in motion within their deeply carved frames.

"Counsel first, Lady Potria," Nokias said, mildly. He was a lean, ruddy-faced man, not so tall as Plennafrey's late father, but with larger hands and feet out of proportion to his small stature. His light brown eyes, wide and innocent, belied the quick mind behind them. He snapped his long fingers and a servant bearing a tray appeared before him. The fur-face knelt at Nokias's feet and filled the exquisite goblet with sparkling green wine. The High Mage of the South appeared to study the liquid, as if seeking advice within its emerald lights. "My good brother to the east, Ferngal, also has a claim on Klemay's estate. After all, it was his argument with our late brother that led to his property becoming . . . available."

Silence fell in the room as the mages considered that position.

"Klemay's realm lies on the border between East and South," said Asedow's voice from the electric blue sphere. "It belongs not to Ferngal nor to us until one puts a claim on it. Let us make sure the successful claim is ours!"

"Do you hope for such a swift promotion, taking right of leadership like that?" Nokias asked mildly, setting down the half-empty goblet and tapping the base with one great hand. A mental murmur passed between some of the other mages. Plenna knew, as all of them did, how ambitious Asedow was. The man was not yet bold enough nor strong enough to challenge Nokias for the seat of Mage of the South. He had a tendency to charge into situations, not watching his back as carefully as he might. Plennafrey had overheard others saying that it probably wouldn't be long before carrion birds were squabbling over *Asedow's* property.

"Klemay carried a staff of power that drew most strongly from the Core of Ozran," Asedow stated. "Long as your forearm, with a knob on the end that looked like a great red jewel. He could control the lightning with it. I move to take possession of it."

"What you can take, you can keep," Nokias said. The words were spoken quietly, yet they held as much threat as a rumbling volcano. Even then, Asedow did not concede. Unless he *was* baiting Nokias into a challenge, Plenna thought, with a thrill of terror. Not now, when they were facing a challenge from a rival faction! Cautiously, she made her spy-eye dip toward the floor, where it would be out of the way of flying strikes of power. She'd heard of one mage crisped to ash and cinders by a blast sent through his spy-eye.

Nokias was the only one who noticed her cautious deployment and turned a kindly, amused glance in her drone's direction. She felt he could see her through its contracting pupil as she really was: a lass of barely twenty years, with a pixie's pointed chin and large, dark eyes wide with alarm. Ashamed of showing weakness, Plenna bravely levitated her eye to a level just slightly below the level held by the others. Nokias began to study a corner of the ceiling as if meditating on its relevance to the subject at hand.

"There is something stirring in the East," Iranika said in her gravelly mental voice, rose-colored spy-eye bobbing with her efforts to keep it steady. She was an elderly magess who lived at the extreme end of the southern mountain range. Plennafrey had never met her in person, nor was she likely to. The old woman stayed discreetly in her well-guarded fortress lest her aging reflexes fail to stop an assassination attempt. "Twice now I have felt unusual emanations in the ley lines. I suspect connivance, perhaps an upcoming effort by the eastern powers to take over some southern territory."

"I, too, have my suspicions," Nokias said, nodding.

Iranika snorted. "The Mage of the East wants his realm to spread out like sunrise and cover the whole of Ozran. Action is required lest he thinks you weak. Some of you fly on magic-back at once to Klemay's mountain. The power must be seized now! Strange portents are abroad."

"'Some of you' fly to the mountain? You will not be of our number, sister?" Howet rumbled from his corner.

"Nay. I have no need of additional power, as some feel they do," Iranika said, an unsubtle thrust at Asedow, who ignored it since she sided with him to attack. "I have enough. But I don't want Klemay's trove falling into the hands of the East by default."

"One might say the same about yours," Potria said offensively. "Why, I should claim yours now before your chair falls vacant, lest someone move upon it from the West."

"You are welcome to try, girl," Iranika said, turning her eye fully upon Potria's.

"Shall I show you how I'll do it?" Potria asked, her voice ringing in the huge chamber. The pink-gold sphere loomed toward the red. Both levitated toward the ceiling as they threw threats back and forth.

Plenna's eye's-eye view wobbled as she prepared for what looked like another contretemps between the two women. As Asedow yearned for the seat of Mage of the South, Potria craved Iranika's hoard of magical devices. Though Nokias was the senior mage in this quarter, Plennafrey had heard he held the seat only because Iranika didn't want it. She wished she was as secure in her position as the old woman. Plennafrey would have given a great deal to know if old Iranika kept her place by right or by bluff. If one was seen as weakening, one became an almost certain victim of assassination, and one's items of power would be gone even before the carrion birds arrived to circle around the corpse.

To achieve promotion in the hierarchy, a mage or magess must challenge and win against senior enchanters. Such battles were not always fatal, nor were they always magical. Sometimes, such matters were accomplished by suborning a mage's servants to steal artifacts that weakened power to the point where the mage could be overcome by devious means. Kills gave one more status. Plennafrey knew that, but she was reluctant to take lives. Even *thoughts* of theft and murder did not come easily to her, though she was learning them as a plain matter of survival. Another way to get promotion was to acquire magical paraphernalia from a secret cache left by the Ancient Ones or the Old Ones—such things were not unknown—or to take them from a mage no longer using them. Plenna wouldn't get much of Klemay's hoard unless she was bold. She was determined to claim *something* no matter what it cost her.

The items of power that descended from the Ancient Ones to the Old Ones and thence to the mages varied in design, but all had the same property, the ability to draw power from the Core of Ozran, the mystic source. There seemed to be no particular pattern the Ancient Ones followed in creating objects that channeled power: amulets, rings, wands, maces, staves, and objects of mysterious shape that had to be mounted in belts or bracelets to be carried. Plennafrey had even heard of a gauntlet the shape of an animal's head. Nokias bore upon his wrist the Great Ring of Ozran and also possessed amulets of varying and strange shapes. His followers had fewer, but all these artifacts had one feature in common: the five depressions into which one fit one's fingertips when issuing the mental or verbal Words of Command.

"Enough bickering," Nokias said wearily. "Are we agreed then? To take what we can of Klemay's power? What we find shall be shared between us according to seniority." Nokias settled back, the look in his eyes indicating he did not expect a challenge. "And strength."

"Agreed," the voice issued forth from Potria's spy-eye.

"Yes," boomed Howet.

"All right," Asedow agreed sourly.

"Yes." Plenna added her soft murmur, which was almost unheard among the other equally low voices around the great room.

Iranika alone remained silent, having had her say.

"Then the eyes have it," Nokias said, jovially, slapping his huge hands together.

Plennafrey joined in the chorus of groans that echoed through the chamber. That joke was old when the Ancient Ones walked Ozran.

"How shall we do this thing, High Mage?" Potria asked. "Open attack or stealth?"

"Stealth implies we have something to hide," Asedow said at once. "Ancient treasures belong to anyone who can claim and hold them. I say we go in force and challenge Ferngal openly."

"Ah!" Potria cried suddenly. "Ferngal and the Easterlings are on the move at this very moment! I sense a disruption in the lines of power in the debated lands! *Unusual* emanations of power."

"Ferngal would not dare!" Asedow declared.

"Wait," Nokias said, his brows drawn over thoughtful eyes. His gaze grew unfocused. "I sense what you do, Potria. Dyrene"—he raised a hand to one of his minions hovering just behind her master's chair. "You have a spy-eye in the vicinity. Investigate."

"I obey, High Mage," Dyrene's voice said. The young woman was monitoring several eyes at once for Nokias, to keep the High Mage from having to occupy his attention with simple reconnaissance. "Hmm—hmmm! It is not Ferngal, magical ones. There is a silver cylinder in the crop fields among the workers. It is huge, High Mage, as large as a tower. I do not know how it got there! There is a man nearby and . . . I do not know this person."

Iranika cackled to herself. The other spy-eyes spun on hers, pupils dilated to show the fury of their operators.

"You knew about it all the time, old woman," Potria said, accusingly.

"I detected it many hours ago," Iranika said, maddeningly coy. "I told you there had been strange movement in the ley lines, but did you listen? Did you think to check for yourselves? I have been watching. The great silver cylinder fell through the sky with fire at its base. A veritable flying fortress. It is a power object of incredible force. The man who came from within has been consorting with Klemay's peasants."

"He is not tied to the Core of Ozran," Nokias declared after a moment's concentration, "and so he is not a mage. That will make him easy to capture. We will find out who he is and whence he comes. Lend me your eyes, Dyrene. Open to me."

"I obey, lord," the tinny voice said.

Concentrating on his target, the Mage of the South laid his left hand across his right wrist to activate the Great Ring, and raised both hands toward the window. A bolt of crackling, scarlet fire lanced from his fingertips into the sky.

"He falls, High Mage," Dyrene reported.

"I must see this stranger for myself," Iranika said. Without asking for leave, her spy-eye rose toward the great window.

"Wait, high ones!" Dyrene called. "A peasant moves the stranger's body. He carries it toward the silver tower." After a moment, when all the spy-eyes hovered around Dyrene's sphere, "It is sealed inside."

Iranika groaned.

"I want this silver cylinder," Asedow said in great excitement. "What forces it would command! High Mage, I claim it!"

"I challenge you, Asedow," Potria shrilled at once. "I claim both the tower and the being."

Other voices raised in the argument: some supporting Potria, some Asedow, while there were even a few clamoring for *their* right to take possession of the new artifacts. Nokias ignored these. Potria and Asedow would be permitted to make the initial attempt. Subsequent challengers would take on the winner, if Nokias himself did not claim liege right to the prizes.

"The challenge is heard and witnessed," Nokias declared, shouting over the din. He raised the hand holding the Great Ring. With a squawk, Plenna sent her spy-eye to take refuge underneath Nokias's floating chair and warded the windows of her mountain home. Humming, scarlet power beams lanced in through Nokias's open window, one from each of the two mages in their mountain strongholds. They struck together in a crashing explosion sealed by the Great Ring. "And the contest begins."

All the eyes flew out of the arching stone casement behind the challengers to have a look at the objects of contention.

"It is bigger than huge," Plennafrey observed, spiraling her eye around and around the silver tower. "How beautiful it is!"

"There are runes inscribed here," Iranika's old voice said. Plennafrey felt the faint pull of the old woman trying to attract attention, and followed the impulse to the red spy-eye floating near the broad base. "Come here and see. I have not seen anything in all my archives which resemble these."

"I spy, with my little eye, an enigma of huge and significant proportions," Nokias said, his golden sphere hovering behind them as they tried to puzzle out the runes.

"It is a marvelous illusion," Howet said, streaking back a distance to take in the whole object. "How do I know this isn't a great trick by Ferngal? Metal and fire—that's no miracle, High Mage. I can build something like this myself."

"It is most original in design," Nokias said.

"Ferngal hasn't the imagination," Potria protested.

"It's lovely," Plenna said, admiring the smooth lines.

Iranika sputtered. "Lovely but useless!"

"How do you know?" Potria snapped.

While her servos were taking care of Keff, Carialle kept vigil on the mountain range to the south. No rain was falling, so where had that lightning, if it *was* lightning, come from? An electrical discharge of that much force had to have a source. She didn't read anything appropriate in that direction, not even a concentration of conductive ore in the mountains that could act as a natural capacitor. The fact that the bolt had fallen so neatly at Keff's feet suggested deliberate action.

The air around her felt ionized, empty, almost brittle. After the bolt had struck, the atmosphere slowly began to return to normal, as if the elements were flowing like water filling in where a stone had hit the surface of a pond.

Her sensors picked up faint rumbling, and the air around her drained again. This time she felt a wind blowing hard toward the mountain range. Suddenly the scarlet bolts struck again, two jagged spears converging on one distant peak. Then, like smithereens scattering from under a blacksmith's hammer, minute particles flew outward from the point of impact toward her.

She focused quickly on the incoming missiles. They were too regular in shape to be shards of rock, and also appeared to be flying under their own power, even increasing in speed. The analysis arrived only seconds before the artifacts did, showing perfect spheres, smooth and vividly colored, with one sector sliced off the front of each to show a lenslike aperture. Strangely, she scanned no mechanisms inside. They appeared to be hollow.

The spheres spiraled around and over her, as if some fantastic juggler was keeping all those balls in the air at once. Carialle became aware of faint, low-frequency transmissions. The spheres were sending data back to some source. She plugged the IT into her external array.

Her first assumption—that the data was meant only for whatever had sent each—changed as she observed the alternating pattern of transmission and the faint responses to the broadcasts from the nontransmitting spheres. They were *talking* to each other. By pinning down the frequency, she was able to hear voices.

Using what vocabulary and grammar Keff had recorded from Brannel and the others, she tried to get a sense of the conversation.

The IT left long, untranslatable gaps in the transcript. The Ozran language was as complex as Standard. Keff had only barely begun to analyze its syntax and amass vocabulary. Carialle recorded everything, whether she understood it or not.

"Darn you, Keff, wake up," she said. This was *his* specialty. He knew how to tweak the IT, to adjust the arcane device to the variables and parameters of language. The snatches of words she did understand tantalized her.

"Come here," one of the colored balls said to the others in a high-pitched voice. " . . . (something) not . . . like (untranslatable)."

" . . . (untranslatable) . . . how do . . . know . . ." Carialle heard a deep masculine voice say, followed by a word Brannel had been using to refer to Keff, then another unintelligible sentence.

" . . . (untranslatable)."

"How do you know?"

An entire sentence came through in clear translation. Carialle perked up her audio sensors, straining to hear more. She ordered the servo beside the weight bench to nudge Keff's shoulder.

"Keff. Keff, wake up! I need you. You have to hear this. Aargh!" She growled in frustration, the bass notes of her voice vibrating the tannoy diaphragms. "We get a group of uninhibited, fluent native speakers, situated who knows where, and you're taking a nap!"

The strange power arcs that she had sensed when they first landed were stronger now. Did that power support the hollow spheres and make them function? Whoever was running the system was using up massive power like air: free, limitless, and easy. She found it hard to believe it could be the indigenous Noble Primitives. They didn't have anything more technologically advanced than beast harness. Carialle should now look for a separate sect, the "overlords" of this culture.

She scanned her planetary maps for a power source and was thwarted once again by the lack of focus. The lines of force seemed to be everywhere and anywhere, defying analysis. If there had been less electromagnetic activity in the atmosphere, it would have been easier. Its very abundance prevented her from tracing it. Carialle was fascinated but nervous. With Keff hurt, she'd rather study the situation from a safer distance until she could figure out who was controlling things, and what with.

No time to make a pretty takeoff. On command, Carialle's servo robots threw their padded arms across Keff's forehead, neck, chest, hips, and legs, securing him to the weight bench. Carialle started launch procedures. None of the Noble Primitives were outside, so she wouldn't scare them or fry them when she took off. The flying eye-balls would have to shift for themselves. She kicked the engines to launch.

Everything was go and on green. Only she wasn't moving.

Increasing power almost to the red line, she felt the heat of her thrusters as they started to slag the mineral-heavy clay under her landing gear, but she hadn't risen a centimeter.

"What kind of fardling place is this?" Carialle demanded. "What's holding me?" She shut down thrust, then gunned it again, hoping to break free of the invisible bonds. Shut down, thrust! Shut down, thrust! No go. She was trapped. She felt a rising panic and sharply put it down. Reality check: this could not be happening to a ship of her capabilities.

Carialle ran through a complete diagnostic and found every system normal. She found it hard to believe what her systems told her. She could detect no power plant on this planet, certainly not one strong enough to hold her with thrusters on full blast. She should at least have felt a *twitch* as such power cut in. Some incredible alien *force* of unknown potency was holding her surface-bound.

"No," she whispered. "Not again."

Objectively, the concept of such huge, wild power controlled with such ease fascinated the unemotional, calculating part of Carialle's mind. Subjectively, she was frightened. She cut her engines and let them cool.

Rescue from this situation seemed unlikely. Not even Simeon had known their exact destination. Sector R was large and unexplored. Nevertheless, she told herself staunchly, Central Worlds had to be warned about the power anomaly so no one else would make the mistake of setting down on this planet. She readied an emergency drone and prepared it to launch, filling its small memory with all the data she and Keff had already gathered about Ozran. She opened the small drone hatch and launched it. Its jets did not ignite. The invisible force held it as firmly as it did her.

Frequency analysis showed that an uncapsuled mayday

was unlikely to penetrate the ambient electromagnetic noise. Even if she could have gotten one in orbit, who was likely to hear it in the next hundred years? She and Keff were on their own.

"Ooooh." A heartfelt groan from the exercise equipment announced Keff's return to consciousness.

"How do you feel?" she asked, switching voice location to the speaker nearest him.

"Horrible." Keff started to sit up but immediately regretted any upward movement. A sharp, seemingly pointed pain like a saw was attempting to remove the rear of his skull. He put a hand to the back of his head, clamped his eyes shut, then opened them as wide as he could, hoping to dispel his fuzzy vision. His eyelids felt thick and gritty. He took a few deep breaths and began to shiver. "Why is it cold in here, Cari? I'm chilled to the bone."

"Ambient temperature of this planet *is* uncomfortably low for humans," Carialle said, brisk with relief at his recovery.

"Brrr! You're telling me!" Keff slid his legs around and put his feet on the ground. His sight cleared and he realized that he was sitting on his weight bench. Carialle's servos waited respectfully a few paces away. "How did I get in here? The last thing I remember was talking to Brannel out in the field. What's happened?"

"Brannel brought you in, my poor wounded knight. Are you sure you're well enough to comprehend all?" Carialle's voice sounded light and casual, but Keff wasn't fooled. She was very upset.

The first thing to do was to dissolve the headache and restore his energy. Pulling an exercise towel over his shoulders like a cape and moving slowly so as not to jar his head more than necessary, Keff got to the food synthesizer.

"Hangover cure number five, and a high-carb warm-up," he ordered. The synthesizer whirred obediently. He drank what appeared in the hatch and shuddered as it oozed down to his stomach. He burped. "I needed that. And I need some food, too. Warm, high protein.

"While I replenish myself, tell all, fair lady," Keff said. "I can take it." With far more confidence than he felt, he smiled at her central pillar and waited.

"Now, let's see, where were we?" she began in a tone that was firm enough, but his long association with Carialle told him that she was considerably agitated. "You got hit by scarlet lightning. Not, I think, a natural phenomenon, since none of the necessary meteorological conditions existed. There's also the problem with its accuracy, landing right at your feet and knocking you, and you only, unconscious. I *refuse* to entertain coincidence. Someone shot that lightning right at you! I persuaded Brannel to bring you inside."

"You did?" Keff was admiring, knowing how little of the language she would have had to do any persuading.

"After he scooted, and not without persuasion, I add for accuracy's sake, we had a plague of what I would normally class as reconnaissance drones, except they have no perceptible internal mechanisms whatsoever, not even flight or anti-grav gear." Carialle's screens shifted to views of the outside, telephoto and close-angle. Small, colored spheres hovered at some distance, flat apertures all facing the brainship.

"Someone has very pretty eyes," Keff said with interest. "No visible means of support, as you say. Curious." The buzzer sounded on the food hatch, and he retrieved the large, steaming bowl. "Ahhh!"

On the screen, a waveguide graph showing frequency modulation had been added beside the image of each drone. The various sound levels rose and fell in patterns.

"Here's what I picked up on the supersonics."

"Such low frequencies," Keff said, reading the graphs. "They can't be transmitting very sophisticated data."

"They're broadcasting voice signals to one another," Carialle said. "I ran the tapes through IT, and here's what I got." She played the datafile at slightly higher than normal speed to get through it all. Keff's eyebrows went up at the full sentence in clear Standard. He went to the console where Carialle had allowed him to install IT's mainframe and fiddled with the controls.

"Hmm! More vocabulary, verbs, and I dare to suggest we've got a few colloquialisms or ejaculations, though I've no referents to translate them fully. This is a pretty how-de-do, isn't it? Whoever's running these artifacts is undoubtedly responsible for the unexpected power emissions the freighter captain reported to Simeon." He straightened up and cocked his head wryly at Carialle's pillar. "Well, my lady, I don't fancy sneak attacks with high-powered weapons. I'd rather not sit and analyze language in the middle of a war zone. Since we're not armed for this party, why don't we take off, and file a partial report on Ozran to be completed by somebody with better shields?"

Carialle made an exasperated noise. "I would take off in a Jovian second, but we are being held in place by a tractor beam of some kind. I can read neither the source nor the direction the power is coming from. It's completely impossible, but I can't move a centimeter. I've been burning fuel trying to take off over and over—and you know we don't have reserves to spare."

Keff finished his meal and put the crockery into the synthesizer's hatch. With food in his belly, he felt himself again. His head had ceased to revolve, and the cold had receded from his bones and muscles.

"That's why I'm your brawn," he said, lightly. "I go and find out these things."

"Sacrificing yourself again, Keff? To pairs of roving eyes?" Carialle tried to sound flip, but Keff wasn't fooled.

He smiled winningly at her central pillar. All his protective instincts were awake and functioning.

"You are my lady," he said, with a gallant gesture. "I seek the object of my quest to lay at your feet. In this case, information. Perhaps an Ozran's metabolism only gets a minor shock when touched with this mystical power beam. We don't know that the folk on the other end are hostile."

"*Anything* that ties my tail down is hostile."

"You shall not be held in durance vile while I, your champion, live." Keff picked up the portable IT unit, checked it for damage, and slung it around his chest. "At least I can find Brannel and ask him what hit me."

"Don't be hasty," Carialle urged. On the main screen she displayed her recording of the attack on Keff. "The equation has changed. We've gone suddenly from dealing with indigenous peasantry at no level of technology to an unknown life-form with a higher technology than *we* have. This is what you're up against."

Keff sat back down and concentrated on the screen, running the frames back and forth one at a time, then at speed.

"Good! Now I know what I need to ask about," he said, pointing. "Do you see that? Brannel knew what the lightning was, he knew it was coming, *and* he got out of its way. Look at those reflexes! Hmmm. The bolt came from the mountains to the south. Southwest. I wonder what the terms are for compass directions in Ozran? I can draw him a compass rose in the dust, with planetary sunrise for east . . ."

Carialle interrupted him by filling the main cabin with a siren wail.

"Keff, you're not listening. It might be too dangerous. To unknown powers who can tie up a full-size spaceship, one human male isn't a threat. And they've downed you once already."

"It's not that easy to kill Von Scoyk-Larsens," Keff said, smiling. "They may be surprised I'm still moving around. Or as I said, perhaps they didn't think the red bolt would affect me the way it did. In any case, can you think of a way to get us out of here unless I do?"

Carialle sighed. "Okay, okay, gird your manly loins and join the fray, Sir Galahad! But if you fall down and break both your legs don't come running to me."

"Nay, my lady," Keff said with a grin and a salute to her titanium pillar. "With my shield or upon it. Back soon."

¤ CHAPTER FIVE

Keff walked into the airlock. He twitched down his tunic, checked his equipment, and concentrated on loosening his muscles one at a time until he stood poised and ready on the balls of his feet. With one final deep breath for confidence, he nodded to Carialle's camera and stepped forward.

Regretting more every second that she had been talked into his proposed course of action, Carialle slid open her airlock and dropped the ramp slowly to the ground. As she suspected, the flying eyes drifted closer to see what was going on. She fretted, wondering if they were capable of shooting at Keff. He had no shields, but he was right: if he didn't find the solution, they'd never be able to leave this place.

Keff walked out to the top of the ramp and held out both hands, palms up, to the levitating spheres. "I come in peace," he said.

The spheres surged forward in one great mass, then *flit!*, they disappeared in the direction of the distant mountains.

"That's rung the bell," Keff said, with satisfaction. "Spies of the evil wizard, my lady, cannot stand where good walks."

A whining alarm sounded. Carialle read her monitors.

"Do you feel it? The mean humidity of the immediate atmosphere has dropped. Those arching lines of stray power I felt crisscrossing overhead are strengthening directly above us. Power surge building, building . . ."

"I feel it," Keff said, licking dry lips. "My nape hair is standing up. Look!" he shouted, his voice ringing. "Here come our visitors!"

Nothing existed beyond three hundred meters away, but from that distance at point south-southwest, two objects came hurtling out of nonexistence one after the other, gaining dimensionality as they neared Carialle, until she could see them clearly. It took Keff a few long milliseconds more, but he gasped when his eyes caught sight of the new arrivals.

"Not the drones again," Keff said. "It's our wizard!"

"Not *a* wizard," Carialle corrected him. "Two."

Keff nodded as the second one exploded into sight after the first. "They're not Noble Primitives. They're another species entirely." He gawked. "Look at them, Cari! Actual humanoids, just like us!"

Carialle zoomed her lenses in for a good look. For once Keff's wishful thinking had come true. The visitor closest to Carialle's video pickup could have been any middle-aged man on any of the Central Worlds. Unlike the cave-dwelling farmers, the visitor had smooth facial skin with neither pelt, nor beard, nor mustache; and the hands were equipped with four fingers and an opposable thumb.

"Extraordinary. Vital signs, pulse elevated at eighty-five beats per minute, to judge by human standards from the flushed complexion and his expression. He's panting and cursing about something. Respiration between forty and sixty," Carialle reported through Keff's mastoid implant.

"Just like humans in stress!" Keff repeated, beatifically.

"So were Brannel and his people," Carialle replied, overlaying charts on her screen for comparison. "Except for superficial differences in appearance, this male and our Noble Primitives are alike. That's interesting. Did this new species evolve from the first group? If so, why didn't the Noble Primitive line dead-end? They should have ceased to exist when a superior mutation arose. And if the bald-faced ones evolved from the hairy ones, why are there so many different configurations of Noble Primitives like sheep, dogs, cats, and camels?"

"That's something I can ask them," Keff said, now sub-vocalizing as the first airborne rider neared him. He started to signal to the newcomer.

The barefaced male exhibited the haughty mien of one who expected to be treated as a superior being. He had beautiful, long-fingered hands folded over a slight belly indicative of a sedentary lifestyle and good food. Upright and dignified, he rode in an ornate contraption which resembled a chair with a toboggan runner for a base. In profile, it was an uncial "h" with an extended and flared bottom serif, a chariot without horses. Like the metal globes that had heralded the visitors' arrival, the dark green chair hovered meters above the ground with no visible means of propulsion.

"What is holding that up?" Keff asked. "Skyhooks?"

"Sheer, bloody, pure power," Carialle said. "Though, by the shell that preserves me, I can't see how he's manipulating it. He hasn't moved an extra muscle, but he's maneuvering like a space jockey."

"Psi," Keff said. "They've exhibited teleportation, and now telekinesis. *Super* psi. All the mentat races humankind has encountered in the galaxy rolled *together* aren't as strong as these people. And they're *so* like humans. Hey, friend!" Keff waved an arm.

Paying no attention to Keff, the sledlike throne veered close to Carialle's skin and then spun on its axis to face the pink-gold chariot that followed, making the occupant of that one pull up sharply to avoid a midair collision. She sat up tall in her seat, eyes blazing with blue-green fire, waves of crisp bronze hair almost crackling with fury about her set face. Her slim figure attired in floating robes of ochre and gold chiffon, she seemed an ethereal being, except for her expression of extreme annoyance. She waved her long, thin hands in complex gestures and the man responded sneeringly in kind. Keff's mouth had dropped open.

"More sign language," Carialle said, watching the woman's gestures with a critical eye. "New symbols. IT didn't have them in the glossary before."

"I'm in love," Keff said, dreamily. "Or at least in lust. Who is she?"

"I don't know, but she and that male are angry at each other. They're fighting over something."

"I hope she wins." Keff sighed, making mooncalf eyes at the new arrival. "She sure is beautiful. That's some figure she's got. And that hair! Just the same color as her skin. Wonderful." The female sailed overhead and Keff's eyes lit up as he detected a lingering scent. "And she's wearing the most delicious perfume."

Carialle noted the rise in his circulation and respiration and cleared her throat impatiently.

"Keff! She's an indigenous inhabitant of a planet we happen to be studying. Please disengage fifteen-year-old hormones and re-enable forty-five-year-old brain. We need to figure out who they are so we can free my tail and get off this planet."

"I can't compartmentalize as easily as you can," Keff grumbled. "Can I help it if I appreciate an attractive lady?"

"I'm no more immune to beauty than you are," Carialle reminded him. "But if she's responsible for our troubles, I want to know why. I particularly want to know *how!*"

Across the field, some of the Noble Primitives had emerged from their burrow. Stooping in postures indicative of respect and healthy fear, they scurried toward the floating chairs, halting some distance away. Keff noticed Brannel among them, standing more erect than any of the others. Still defying authority, Keff thought, with wry admiration.

"Do you want to ask him what's going on?" Carialle said through the implant.

"Remember what he said about being punished for curiosity," Keff reminded her. "These are the people he's afraid of. If I single him out, he's in for it. I'll catch him later for a private talk."

The elder, Alteis, approached and bowed low to the two chair-holders. They ignored him, continuing to circle at ten meters, calling out at one another.

"I knew I could not trust you to wait for Nokias to lead us here, Asedow," Potria shouted angrily. "One day, your eagerness to thrust out your hand for power will result in having it cut off at the shoulder."

"You taunt me for breaking the rules when you also didn't wait," Asedow retorted. "Where's Nokias, then?"

"I couldn't let you claim by default," Potria said, "so your action forced me to follow at once. Now that I am here, I restate that I should possess the silver cylinder and the being inside. I will use it with greater responsibility than you."

"The Ancient Ones would laugh at your disingenuousness, Potria," Asedow said, scornfully. "You want them just to keep them from me. I declare," he shouted to the skies, "that I am the legitimate keeper of these artifacts sent down through the ages to me, and by my hope of promotion, I will use them wisely and well."

Potria circled Asedow, trying to get nearer to the great cylinder, but he cut her off again and again. She directed her chair to fly up and over him. He veered upward in a flash, cackling maddeningly. She hated him, hated him for thwarting her. At one time they had been friends, even toyed with the idea of becoming lovers. She had hoped that they could have been allies, taking power from Nokias and that bitch Iranika and ruling the South between them despite the fact that the first laws of the First Mages said only one might lead. She and Asedow could never agree on who that would be. As now, he wouldn't support *her* claim, and she wouldn't support his. So they were forced to follow archaic laws whose reasoning was laid down thousands of years ago and might never be changed. The two of them were set against one another like mad vermin in a too-small cage. She or Asedow must conquer, must be the clear winner in the final contest. Potria had determined in her deepest heart that *she* would be the victor.

The rustle in her mystic hearing told her that Asedow was gathering power from the ley lines for an attack. He had but to chase her away or knock her unconscious, and the contest was his. Killing was unnecessary and would only serve to make High Mage Nokias angry by depriving him of a strong subject and ally. Potria began to wind in the threads of power between her fingers, gathering and gathering until she had a web large enough to throw over him. It would contain the force of Asedow's spell and knock him out.

"That one is unworthy," she heard Asedow call out. "Let me win, not her!"

Stretching the smothering web on her thumbs, she spread out her arms wide in the prayer sign, hands upright and palms properly turned in toward her to contain the blessing.

"In the name of Ureth, the Mother World of Paradise, I call all powers to serve me in this battle," she chanted.

Asedow flashed past her in his chariot, throwing his spell. Raising herself, Potria dropped her spread counter-spell on top of him and laughed as his own blast of power caught him. His chair wobbled unsteadily to a halt a hundred meters distant. His cursing was audible and he was very angry. He switched his chair about on its axis. She saw his face, dark with blood as a thundercloud. He panted heavily.

"Thought you would have an easy win, did you?" Potria called, tauntingly. She began to ready an attack of her own. Something not fatal but *appropriate*.

She felt disturbances in the ether. More mages were coming, probably attracted by the buildup of power in this barren, uninteresting place. Potria changed the character of the cantrip she was molding. If she was to have an audience, she would give a good show and make a proper fool of Asedow.

By now, her opponent hovered invisible in a spell-cloud of dark green smoke that roiled and rumbled. Potria fancied she even saw miniature lightnings flash within its depths. He, too, had observed the arrival of more of their magical brethren, and it made him impatient. He struck while his spell was still insufficiently prepared. Potria laughed and raised a single, slim hand, fingers spread. The force bounced off the globe of protection she had wrought about herself, rushed outward, and exploded on contact with the nearest solid object, a tree, setting it ablaze. Some of it rebounded upon Asedow, shaking his chariot so hard that he nearly lost control of it.

Having warded off Asedow's pathetic attack, Potria stole

a swift look at the newly arrived mages. They were all minor lights from the East, probably upset that she and Asedow had crossed the border into their putative realm. By convention, they were bound to stay out of the middle of a fairly joined battle, and so they hovered on the sidelines, swearing about the invasion by southern mages. So long as they kept out of her way until she won, she didn't care what they thought of her.

Keff saw the five new arrivals blink into existence, well beyond the battleground. The first two came to such a screeching halt that he wondered if they had hurried to the scene at a dead run and were having trouble braking. The others proceeded with more caution toward the circling combatants.

"The first arrivals remind me of something," Keff said, "but I can't put my finger on what. Great effect, that sudden stop!"

"It looked like Singularity Drive," Carialle said, critically. "Interesting that they've duplicated the effect unprotected and in atmosphere."

"That's big magic," Keff said.

The new five were no sooner at the edge of the field than the magiman and magiwoman let off their latest volley at each other.

Smoke exploded in a plume from the green storm cloud. It was shot along its expanse with lightning and booms of thunder. Enwrapping the magiwoman in its snakelike coils, it closed into a murky sphere with the golden female at its center. Lights flashed inside and Keff heard a scream. Whether it was fury, fear, or pain he couldn't determine.

Suddenly, the sphere broke apart. The smoke dissipated on the evening sky, leaving the female free. Her hair had escaped from its elegant coif and stood out in crackling tendrils. The shoulder of her robe was burned away, showing the tawny flesh beneath. Eyes sparking, she levitated upward, arms gathering and gathering armfuls of nothing to her breast. Her hands chopped forward, and lightning, liquid electricity, flew at her opponent.

The male crossed his forearms before himself in a gesture intended to ward away the attack, but only managed to deflect some of it. Tiny fingers of white heat peppered his legs and the runner of his chair, burning holes in his robe and scorching the vehicle's ornamentation. In order to escape, he had to move away from Carialle toward the open fields, where the lightning ceased to pursue him. Triumphantly, the female sailed in and spiraled around the brainship in a kind of victory lap. In front of the ship, a translucent brick wall built itself up row by row, until it was as tall as Carialle herself.

Keff stared.

"Are they fighting over us?" he asked in disbelief.

Carialle took umbrage at the suggestion. "How dare they?" she said. "This is my ship, not the competition trophy!"

The male did not intend to give up easily. As soon as the cloud of lightning was gone, he headed back toward the ship. Between his hands a blue-white globe was forming. He threw it directly at the brick wall and the enchantress behind it.

The female was insufficiently prepared and the ball caught her in the belly. It knocked her chair back hundreds of meters, past the hovering strangers who hastily shifted out of her way. The illusory wall vanished. With a cry, the female flew in, arching her fingers like a cat's claws. Scarlet fire shot from each one, focusing on the male. His chair bounced up in the air and turned a full loop. Miraculously, he kept his seat. He tried to regain his original position near Carialle.

"They *are* fighting over me. The unmitigated gall of the creatures!"

At the first sign of mystic lightning, the workers had judiciously fled to a safe distance from which they avidly watched the battle. Ignoring Alteis's hissed commands to keep his head down, Brannel watched the overlords hungrily, as his eyes had earlier fed on Keff. Maybe this time a miracle would occur and one of them would drop an object of power. In the confusion of battle, it would go unnoticed until he, Brannel, dove for it and made it his own. Mere possession of an object of power might not make one a mage, but he wanted to find out. All his life he had cherished dreams of learning to fly or control lightning.

The odds against his success were immense. The mages were the mages, and the workers were the workers, to live, die, or serve at the whim of their overlords, never permitted to look above their lowly station. Until today, when Mage Keff arrived out of the sky, Brannel had never thought there was a third way of life. The stranger was not a mage by Ozran standards, since the overlords were fighting over him as if he wasn't there; but he was certainly not a worker. He must be something in between, a stepping stone from peasant to power. Brannel knew Keff could' help him rise above his lowborn status and gain a place among mages, but how to win his favor and his aid? He had already been of service to Mage Keff. Perhaps he could render other services, provided that Keff survived the contest going on above his head.

Brannel had recognized Magess Potria and Mage Asedow by their colors while his peers were too afraid to lift their heads out of the dust. He'd give his heart and the rest of his fingers to be able to spin spells as they did. In spite of the damage that the combatants were doing to one another, not a tendril of smoke nor a tongue of flame had even come close to Keff, who was watching the battle rage calmly and without fear. Brannel admired the stranger's courage. Keff would be a powerful mentor. Together they would fight the current order, letting worthy ones from the lowest caste ascend to rule as their intelligence merited. That is, if Keff survived the war in which he was one of the prizes.

"A world of wizards, my lady!" Keff chortled gleefully to Carialle. "They're doing magic! No wonder you can't find a power source. There isn't one. This is pure evocation of power from the astral plane of the galaxy."

The beautiful woman zipped past him in her floating chair, hands busy between making signs and spells. He adjusted IT to register all motions and divide them between language and ritual by repeat usage and context. He was also picking up on a second spoken language or dialect. IT had informed him that Brannel had used some of the terms, and Keff wondered at the linguistic shift from one species to the other.

"Magical evocation is hardly scientific, Keff," Carialle reminded him. "They're getting power from somewhere, that's for sure. I can even follow some of the buildup a short way out, but then I lose it in the random emanations."

"It comes from the ether," Keff said, rapt. "It's magic."

"Stop calling it that. We're not playing the game now," Carialle said sharply. "We're witnessing sophisticated manipulation of power, not abracadabra-something-out-of-nothing."

"Look at it logically," Keff said, watching the male lob a hand-sized ball of flame over his head at his opponent. "How else would you explain being able to fly without engines or to appear in midair?"

"Telekinesis."

"And how about knitting lightning between your hands? Or causing smoke and fireballs without fuel? This is the stuff of legends. Magic."

"It's sophisticated legerdemain, I'll grant that much, but there's a logical explanation, too."

Keff laughed. "There *is* a logical explanation. We've discovered a planet where the laws of magic *are* the laws of science."

"Well, there's physics, anyhow," Carialle said. "Our magimen up there are beginning to fatigue. Their energy levels aren't infinite."

Ripostes and return attacks were slowing down. The magiwoman maintained an expression of grim amusement throughout the conflict, while the magiman couldn't disguise his annoyance.

As if attracted by the conflict, a bunch of globe-frogs appeared out of the brushy undergrowth at the edge of the crop fields. They rolled into the midst of the Noble Primitives, who were huddled into the gap, watching the aerial battle. The indigenes avoided contact with the small creatures by kicking out at them so that the globes turned away. The little group trundled their conveyances laboriously out into the open and paused underneath the sky-borne battle. Keff watched their bright black eyes focus on the combatants. They seemed fascinated.

"Look, Carialle," Keff said, directing his contact-button camera toward them. "Are they attracted by motion, or light? You'd think they'd be afraid of violent beings much larger than themselves."

"Perhaps they are attracted to power, like moths to a candle flame," Carialle said, "although, mind you, I've never seen moths or candles in person. I'm not an expert in animal behaviorism, but I don't think the attraction is unusual. Incautious, to the point of self-destructive, perhaps. Either of our psi-users up there could wipe them out with less power than it would take to hold up those chairs."

The two mages, sailing past, parrying one another's magic bolts and making their own thrusts, ignored the cluster which trailed them around the field. At last the little creatures gave up their hopeless pursuit, and rolled in a group toward Keff and Carialle.

"Your animal magnetism operating again," Carialle noted. The globe-frogs, paddling hard on the inner wall of their spherelike conveyances with their oversize paws, steered over the rocky ground and up the ramp, making for the inside of the ship. "Ooops, wait a minute! You can't come in here. Out!" she said, in full voice on her hatchway speakers. "Scat!"

The frogs ignored her. She tracked them with her internal cameras and directed her servos into the airlock to herd them out the door again. The frogs made a few determined tries to get past the low-built robots. Thwarted, they reversed position inside their globes and paddled the other way.

"Pests," Carialle said. "Is everyone on this planet intent on a free tour of my interior?"

The globe-frogs rolled noisily down the ramp and off the rise toward the underbrush at the opposite end of the clearing. Keff watched them disappear.

"I wonder if they're just attracted to any vibrations or emissions," he said.

"Could be— Heads up!" Carialle trumpeted suddenly. She put her servos into full reverse to get them out of Keff's way. Without waiting to ask why or what, Keff dove sideways into Carialle's hatch and hit the floor. A split second later, he felt a flamethrowerlike blast of heat almost singe his cheek. If he'd remained standing where he was, he'd have gotten a faceful of fire.

"They're out of control! Get in here!" Carialle cried.

Keff complied. The battle had become more serious, and the magic-users had given up caring where their bolts hit. Another spell flared out of the tips of the woman's fingers at the male, only a dozen meters from Keff.

The brawn tucked and rolled through the inner door. Carialle slid the airlock door shut almost on his heels. Keff heard a whine of stressed metal as something else hit the side of the ship.

"Yow!" Carialle protested. "That blast was cold! *How* are they doing that?"

Keff ran to the central cabin viewscreens and dropped into his crash seat.

"Full view, please, Cari!"

The brain obliged, filling the three surrounding walls with a 270° panorama.

Keff spun his pilot's couch to follow the green contrail across the sky, as the male magician retreated to the far end of the combat zone. He looked frustrated. The last, unsuccessful blast that hit Carialle's flank must have been his. The female, beautiful, powerful, sitting up high in her chair, prepared another attack with busy hands. Her green eyes were dulling, as if she didn't care where her strike might land. The five magimen on the sidelines looked bored and angry, just barely restraining themselves from interfering. The battle would end soon, one way or another.

Even inside the ship, Keff felt the sudden change in the atmosphere. His hair, including his eyebrows and eyelashes and the hair on his arms, crackled with static. Something momentous was imminent. He leaned in toward the central screen.

Out of nothingness, three new arrivals in hover-chairs blinked into the heart of the battle zone. Inadvertently Keff recoiled against the back of his chair.

"Yow! They mean business," Carialle said. "No hundred meters of clearance space. Just smack, right into the middle."

The spells the combatants were building dissipated like colored smoke on the wind. Carialle's gauges showed a distinct drop in the electromagnetic fields. The mage and magess dropped their hands stiffly onto their chair arms and glared at the obstacles now hovering between them. If looks could have ignited rocket fuel, the thwarted combatants would have set Carialle's tanks ablaze. Whatever was powering them had been cut off by the three in the center.

"Uh-oh. The Big Mountain Men are here," Keff said, flippantly, his face guarded.

The newcomers' chairs were bigger and gaudier than any Keff and Carialle had yet seen. A host of smaller seats, containing lesser magicians, popped in to hover at a respectful distance outside the circle. Their presence was ignored by the three males who were obviously about to discipline the combatants.

"Introductions," Keff said, monitoring IT. "High and mighty. The lad in the gold is Nokias, the one in black is Ferngal, and the silver one in the middle who looks so nervous is Chaumel. He's a diplomat."

Carialle observed the placatory gestures of the mage in the silver chair. "I don't think that Ferngal and Nokias like each other much."

But Chaumel, nodding and smiling, floated suavely back and forth between the gold and black in his silver chair and managed to persuade them to nod at one another with civility if not friendliness. The lesser magicians promptly polarized into two groups, reflecting their loyalties.

"Compliments to the Big Mountain Men from my pretty lady and her friend," Keff continued. "She's Potria, and he's Asedow. One of the sideliners says they were

something—bold? cocky?—to come here. Aha, that's what
that word Brannel used meant: forbidden! That gives me
some roots for some of the other things they're saying. I'll
have to backtrack the datahedrons—I think a territorial
dispute is going on."

Nokias and Ferngal each spoke at some length. Keff
was able to translate a few of the compliments the magimen paid to each other.

"Something about high mountains," he said, running IT
over contextual data. "Yes, I think that repeated word must
be 'power,' so Ferngal is referring to Nokias as having
power as high, I mean, strong as the high mountains and
deep as its roots." He laughed. "It's the same pun we have
in Standard, Cari. He used the same word Brannel used
for the food 'roots.' The farmers and the magicians do use
two different dialects, but they're related. It's the cognitive
differences I find fascinating. Completely alien to any language in my databanks."

"All this intellectual analysis is very amusing," Carialle
said, "but what are they saying? And more to the point,
how does it affect *us*?"

She shifted cameras to pick up Potria and Asedow on
separate screens. After the speeches by the two principals,
the original combatants were allowed their say, which they
had with many interruptions from the other and much
pointing towards Carialle.

"Those are definitively possessive gestures," Keff said
uneasily.

"No one puts a claim on *my ship*," Carialle said firmly.
"Which one of them has a tractor beam on me? I want it
off."

Keff listened to the translator and shook his head. "Neither one did it, I think. It may be a natural phenomenon."

"Then why isn't it grounding any of those chairs?"

"Cari, we don't know that's what is happening."

"I have a pretty well-developed sense of survival, and that's exactly what it's telling me."

"Well, then, we'll tell them you own your ship, and they can't have it," Keff said, reasonably. "Wait, the diplomat's talking."

The silver-robed magician had his hands raised for attention and spoke to the assemblage at some length, only glancing over his shoulder occasionally. Asedow and Potria stopped shouting at each other, and the other two Big Mountain Men looked thoughtful. Keff tilted his head in amusement.

"Look at that: Chaumel's got them all calmed down. Say, he's coming this way."

The silver chariot left the others and floated toward Carialle, settling delicately a dozen feet from the end of the ramp. The two camps of magicians hovered expectantly over the middle of the field, with expressions that ranged from nervous curiosity to open avarice. The magician rose and walked off the end of the chair's finial to stand beside it. Hands folded over his belly, he bowed to the ship.

"So they can stand," Carialle said. "I gather from the shock on the faces of our Noble Primitives over there that that's unusual. I guess these magicians don't go around on foot very often."

"No, indeed. When you have mystic powers from the astral plane, I suppose auto-ambulatory locomotion is relegated to the peasants."

"He's waiting for something. Does he expect us to signal him? Invite him in for tea?"

Keff peered closely at Chaumel's image. "I think we'd better wait and let him make the first move. Ah! He's coming to pay us a visit. A state visit, my lady."

Chaumel got over his internal debate and, with solemn dignity, made his way to the end of the ramp, every step slow and ponderous. He reached the tip and paused, bowing deeply once again.

"I feel honored," Carialle said. "If I'd'a known he was coming I'd'a baked a cake."

◘ CHAPTER SIX

"The initiative is ours now," Keff said. He kept watch on the small screen of his Intentional Translator as it processed all the hedrons Carialle had recorded while he was unconscious and combined it with the dialogue he had garnered from Brannel and the magicians' discussions. The last hedron popped out of the slot, and Keff slapped it into his portable IT unit on the control panel. "That's it. We have a working vocabulary of Ozran. I can talk with him."

"Enough to ask intelligent questions?" Carialle asked. "Enough to negotiate diplomatically for our release, and inform them, 'by the way, folks, we're from another planet'?"

"Nope," Keff said, matter-of-factly. "Enough to ask stupid questions and gather more information. IT will pick up on the answers I get and, I *hope*, translate them from context."

"That IT has never been worth the electrons to blow it up," Carialle said in a flat voice.

"Easy, easy, lady," Keff said, smiling at her pillar.

"Sorry," she said. "I'm letting the situation get to me. I don't like being out of control of my own functions."

"I understand perfectly," Keff said. "That's why the sooner I go out and face this fellow the better, whether or not I have a perfect working knowledge of his language."

"If you say something insulting by accident, I don't think you'll survive a second blast of that lightning."

"If they're at all as similar to humans as they look, their curiosity will prevent them killing me until they learn all about me. By then, we'll be friends."

"Good sir knight, you assume them to be equal in courtesy to your good self," Carialle said.

"I must face the enchanter's knight, if only for the sake of chivalry."

"Sir Keff, I don't like you leaving the Castle Strong when there's a dozen enchanters out there capable of flinging bolts of solid power down your gullet, and there's not a thing I can do to protect you."

"The quest *must* continue, Carialle."

"Well . . ." she said, then snorted. "I'm being too protective, aren't I? It isn't exactly first contact if you stay inside and let them pelt away at us. And we'll never get out of here. We have to establish communications. Xeno will die of mortification if we don't, and there go our bonuses."

"That's the spirit," Keff said, buckling on his equipment harness.

Carialle tested her exterior links to IT. "Anything we say will come out in pidgin Ozran. Right?"

Keff paused, looked up at her pillar. "Should you speak at all? Are they ready for the concept of a talking ship?"

"Were we ready for flying chairs?" Carialle countered. "We're at least as strange to them as they are to us."

"I'd rather not have them know you can talk," Keff said thoughtfully.

"But they already know I can speak independently. I

talked to Brannel while you were unconscious. Unless he thought you were having an out-of-body experience."

"Supposing Brannel had the nerve to approach our magicians, he wouldn't be able to explain the voice he heard. He was gutsy with me, but you'll notice on the screen that he's staying well out of the way of the chair-riders. They're in charge and he's a mere peon."

"He is scared of them," Carialle agreed. "Remember how he explained punishment came from the mountains when one of his people is too curious. It's no problem for them to dispense punishment. They're endlessly creative when it comes to going on the offensive."

"Contrariwise, I take leave to doubt that any of the magicians would give him a hearing if he did come forward with the information. There's a big crowd of Brannel's folk out there on the perimeter and the wizards haven't so much as glanced their way. No one pays the least attention to the peasants. Your secret is still safe. That's why I want you to keep quiet unless need arises."

"All right," Carialle said at last. "I'll keep mumchance. But, if you're in danger . . . I don't know what I'll do."

"Agreed." And Keff shot her column an approving grin.

"Let's test the system," Carialle said. The small screen to the right of the main computer lit up with a line diagram of Keff's body. He rose and stood before it, holding his arms away from his sides to duplicate the posture.

"Testing," he said. "Mah, may, mee, mo, mu. The quick brown fox jumped over the lazy dog. Maxwell-Corey is a fardling, fossicking, meddling moron." He repeated the phrases in a subvocal whisper. Small green lights in the image's cheeks lit up.

"Got you," Carialle's voice said in his ear. Lights for the mastoid implants clicked on, followed by the fiber optic pickups implanted in the skin at the outer corners of his eyes. "I'm not trusting the contact buttons alone. The lightning earlier knocked them out for a while." Heart, respiration, skin tension monitors in his chest cavity and the muscles of his thighs lighted green. The lights flicked out and came on again as Carialle did double backup tests. "You're wired for sound and ready to go. I can see, hear, and just about feel anything that happens to you."

"Good," Keff said, relaxing into parade rest. "Our guest is waiting."

"Here comes the stranger."

Keff's implant translated Asedow's comment as he stepped outside. He assumed the same air of dignity that Chaumel displayed and walked to the bottom of the ramp. He paused, wondering if he should stay there, which gave him a psychological advantage over his visitor who had to look up at him. Or join the fellow on the ground as a mark of courtesy. With a smile, he sidestepped. Chaumel backed up slightly to make room for him. Face-to-face with the silver magician, Keff raised his hand, palm out.

"Greetings," he said. "I am Keff."

The eyewitness report had been correct, Chaumel realized with a start. The stranger was one of them. The oddest thing was that he did not recognize him. There were only a few hundred of the caste on all of Ozran. A family of mages could not conceal a son like this one, grown to mature manhood and in possession of such an incredible power-focus as the silver cylinder.

"Greetings, high one," Chaumel said politely, with the merest dip of a nod. "I am Chaumel. You honor us with your presence."

The man cocked his head, as if listening to something far away, before he responded. Chaumel sensed the faintest hint of power during the pause, and yet, as Nokias had informed him, it did not come from the Core of Ozran. When at last he spoke, the stranger's words were arranged in uneducated sentences, mixed with the odd word of gibberish.

"Welcome," he said. "It is . . . my *honor* meet you."

Chaumel drew back half a pace. The truth was that the stranger did not understand the language. What could possibly explain such an anomaly as a mage who used power that did not come from the core of all and a man of Ozran who did not know the tongue?

The stranger seemed to guess what he was thinking and continued although not ten words in twenty made sense. And the intelligible was unbelievable.

"I come from the stars," Keff said, pointing upward. He gestured behind him at the brainship, flattened his hand out horizontally, then made it tip up and sink heel first toward the ground. "I flew here in the, er, silver house. I come from another world."

" . . . Not . . . here," Chaumel said. IT missed some of the vocabulary but not the sense. He beckoned to Keff, turned his back on the rest of his people.

"You don't want me to talk about it here?" Keff said in a much lower voice.

"No," Chaumel said, with a cautious glance over his shoulder at the other two Big Mountain Men. "Come . . . mountain . . . me." IT rewound the phrase and restated the translation using full context. "Come back to my mountain with me. We'll talk there."

"No, thanks," Keff said, with a shake of his head. "Let's talk here. It's all right. Why don't you ask the others—uh!"

"Keff!" Carialle's voice thudded against his brain. He knew then why all the Noble Primitives were so submissive and eager to avoid trouble. Chaumel had taken a gadget like a skinny flashlight from a sling on his belt and jabbed it into Keff's side. Fire raced from his rib cage up his neck and through his backbone, burning away any control he had over his own muscles. For the second time in as many hours, he collapsed bonelessly to the ground. The difference this time was that he remained conscious of everything going on around him. Directly in front of his eyes, he saw that, under the hem of his ankle-length robe, Chaumel wore black and silver boots. They had very thick soles. Even though the ground under his cheek was dry, dust seemed not to adhere to the black material, which appeared to be some kind of animal hide, maybe skin from a six-pack. He became aware that Carialle was speaking.

" . . . Fardle it, Keff! Why didn't you stay clear of him? I know you're conscious. Can you move at all?"

Chaumel's feet clumped backward and to one side, out from Keff's limited field of vision. Suddenly, the ground shot away. Unable to order his muscles to move, Keff felt his head sag limply to one side. He saw, almost disinterestedly, that he was floating on air. It felt as if he were being carried on a short mattress.

Unceremoniously, Keff was dumped off the invisible mattress onto the footrest of Chaumel's chariot, his head tilted at an uncomfortable upward angle. The magician stepped inside the U formed by Keff's body and sat down on the ornamented throne. The whole contraption rose suddenly into the air.

"Telekinesis," Keff muttered into the dental implant. He found he was slowly regaining control of his body. A finger twitched. A muscle in his right calf contracted. It tingled. Then he was aware that the chair was rising above the fields, saw the upper curve of the underground cavern in which Brannel's people lived, the mountains beyond, very high, higher than he thought.

"Good!" Carialle's relief was audible. "You're still connected. I thought I might lose the links again when he hit you with that device."

"Wand," Keff said. He could move his eyes now, and he fixed them on the silver magician's belt. "Wand."

"It looked like a wand. Acted more like a cattle prod." There was a momentary pause. "No electrical damage. It seems to have affected synaptic response. That is one sophisticated psi device."

"Magic," Keff hissed quietly.

"We'll argue about that later. Can you get free?"

"No," Keff said. "Motor responses slowed."

"Blast and damn it, Galahad! I can't come and get you. You're a hundred meters in the air already. All right, I can track you wherever you're going."

Carialle was upset. Keff didn't want her to be upset, but he was all but motionless. He managed to move his head to a slightly more comfortable position, panting with the strain of such a minor accommodation. Empathic and psionic beings in the galaxy had been encountered before, but these people's talents were so much stronger than any other. Keff was awed by a telekinetic power strong enough to carry the chair, Chaumel, and him with no apparent effort. Such strength was beyond known scientific reality.

"Magic," he murmured.

"I do not believe in magic," Carialle said firmly. "Not with all this stray electromagnetic current about."

"Even magic must have physics," Keff argued.

"Bah." Carialle began to run through possibilities, some of which bordered a trifle on the magic she denied, but *something* which would bring Keff back where he belonged—inside her hull—and both of them off this planet as soon as her paralysis, like Keff's, showed any signs of wearing off.

Brannel hid alone in the bushes at the far end of the field, waiting to see if Mage Keff came out again. After offering respect to the magelords, the rest of his folk had taken advantage of the great ones' disinterest in them and rushed home to where it was warm.

The worker male was curious. Perhaps now that the battle was over, the magelords would go away so he could approach Keff on his own. To his dismay, the high ones showed no signs of departing. They awaited the same event he did: the emergence of Magelord Keff. He was awestruck as he watched Chaumel the Silver approach the great tower on foot. The mage waited, eyes on the tight-fitting door, face full of the same anticipation Brannel felt.

Keff did not come. Perhaps Keff was making them all play into his hands. Perhaps he was wiser than the magelords. That would be most satisfyingly ironic.

Instead, when Keff emerged and exchanged words with the mage, he suddenly collapsed. Then he was bundled onto the chariot of Chaumel the Silver and carried away. All Brannel's dreams of freedom and glory died in that instant. All the treasures in the silver tower were now out of his reach and would be forever.

He muttered to himself all the way back to the cave. Fralim caught him, asked him what he was on about.

"We ought to follow and save Magelord Keff."

"Save a mage? You must be mad," Fralim said. "It is night. Come inside and go to sleep. There will be more work in the morning."

Depressed, Brannel turned and followed the chief's son into the warmth.

¤ CHAPTER SEVEN

"Why . . . make things more . . . harderest . . . than need?" Chaumel muttered as he steered the chair away from the plain. IT found the root for the missing words and relayed the question to Keff through his ear-link. "Why must you make things more difficult than they need to be? I want to talk . . . in early . . ."

"My apologies, honored one," Keff said haltingly.

He had sufficiently recovered from the bolt to sit up on the end of Chaumel's chair. The magician leaned forward to clasp Keff's shoulder and pulled him back a few inches. Once he looked down, the brawn was grateful for the reassuring contact. From the hundred meters Carialle had last reported, they had ascended to at least two hundred and were still rising. He still had no idea how it was done, but he was beginning to enjoy this unusual ride.

The view was marvelous. The seven-meter square where Brannel and his people laid their gathered crops and the mound under which the home cavern lay had each shrunk to an area smaller than Keff's fingernail. On the flattened hilltop, the brainship was a shining figure like a literary statuette. Nearby, the miniature chairs, each containing a colorfully dressed doll, were rising to disperse.

Keff noticed suddenly that their progress was not unattended. Gold and black eye spheres flanked the silver chair as it rose higher still and began to fly in the direction of the darkening sky. More spheres, in different colors, hung behind like wary sparrows trailing a crow, never getting too close. This had to be the hierarchy again, Keff thought. He doubted this constituted an honor guard since he had gathered that Nokias and Ferngal outranked Chaumel. More on the order of keeping watch on both the Silver Mage and the stranger. Keff grinned and waved at them.

"Hi, Mum," he said.

"It'll take you hours at that rate to reach one of those mountain ranges," Carialle said through the implant. "I'd like to know how long he can fly that thing before he has to refuel or rest, or whatever."

Keff turned to Chaumel.

"Where are we . . ."

Even before the question was completely out of his mouth, the view changed.

" . . . going?"

Keff gaped. They were no longer hanging above Brannel's fields. Between one meter and another the silver chariot had transferred effortlessly to a point above snow-capped mountain peaks. The drop in temperature was so sudden Keff suffered a violent, involuntary shudder before he knew he was cold.

"—Ramjamming fardling flatulating dagnabbing planet!" Carialle's voice, missing from his consciousness for just moments, reasserted itself at full volume. "There you are! You are one hundred and seventy four kilometers northeast from your previous position."

"Lady dear, what language!" Keff gasped out between chatters. "Not at all suitable for *my* lady fair."

"But appropriate! You've been missing a long time. Confound it, I was worried!"

"It only felt like a second to me," Keff said, apologetically.

"Fifty-three hundredths of a second," Carialle said crisply. "Which felt like eons to my processing gear. I had to trace your vital signs through I don't know how many power areas before I found you. Luckily your evil wizard told us you were going to a *mountain*. That did cut down by about fifty percent the terrain I had to sweep."

"We teleported," Keff said, wonderingly. "*I* . . . teleported! I didn't feel as if I was. It's effortless!"

"I hate it," Carialle replied. "You were off the air while you were in transit. I didn't know where you had gone, or if you were still alive. Confound these people with their unelectronic toys and nonmechanical machines!"

"My . . . mountain home," Chaumel announced, interrupting Keff's subvocal argument. The silver magician pointed downward toward a gabled structure built onto the very crest of the highest peak in the range.

"How lovely," Keff said, hoping one of the expressions he had gleaned from Carialle's tapes of the broadcasting drones was appropriate. By Chaumel's pleased expression, it was.

At first all he could see was the balcony, cantilevered out over a bottomless chasm, smoky purple and black in the light of the setting sun. Set into the mountaintop were tall, arched glass windows, shining with the last highlights of day. They were distinguishable from the blue-white ice cap only because they were flat and smooth. What little could be seen of the rest of the mountain was jagged outthrusts and steep ravines.

"Mighty . . . not . . . from the ground," Chaumel said, pantomiming something trying to come up from underneath and being met above by a fist. IT rewound the comment and translated it in Keff's ear as "This is a mighty stronghold. Nothing can reach us from the ground."

"No, to be sure." Well, that stood to reason. No mage would want to live in a bastion that could be climbed to. Much less accessible if it could be reached only by an aerial route.

The balcony, as they got nearer, was as large as a commercial heliport, with designated landing pads marked out in different colored flush-set paving stones. One square, nearest the tall glass doors, was silver-gray, obviously reserved for the lord of the manor.

The chariot swung in a smooth curve over the pad and set down on it as daintily as a feather. As soon as it landed, the flock of spy-eyes turned and flew away. Chaumel gestured for Keff to get down.

The brawn stepped off the finial onto the dull stone tiles, and found himself dancing to try and keep his balance. The floor was smooth and slick, frictionless as a track-ball surface. Losing his footing, Keff sprawled backward, catching himself with his hands flat behind him, and struggled to an upright position. The feel of the floor disconcerted him. It was heavy with power. He didn't hear it or feel it, but he sensed it. The sensation was extremely unnerving. He rubbed his palms together.

"What's the matter?" Carialle asked. "The view keeps changing. Ah, that's better. Hmm. No, it isn't. What's that dreadful vibration? It feels mechanical."

"Don't know," Keff said subvocally, testing the floor with a cautious hand. Though dry to look at, it felt tacky, almost clammy. "Slippery," he added, with a smile up at his host.

Dark brows drawn into an impatient V, Chaumel gestured for Keff to get up. Very carefully, using his hands, Keff got to his knees, and tentatively, to his feet. Chaumel nodded, turned, and strode through the tall double doors. Walking ding-toed like a waterfowl, Keff followed as quickly as he could, if only to get off the surface.

Each time he put a foot down, the disturbing vibration rattled up his leg into his spine. Keff forced himself to ignore it as he tried to catch up with Chaumel.

The silver magiman nattered on, half to Keff, half to himself. Keff boosted the gain on IT to pick up every word, to play back later.

The glass doors opened out from a grand chamber like a ballroom or a throne room. Ceilings were unusually high, with fantastic ornamentation. Keff stared straight up at a painted and gilded trompe l'oeil fresco of soaring native avians in a cloud-dotted sky. Windows of glass, rock crystal, and colored minerals were set at every level on the wall. There was one skylight cut pielike into the ceiling. Considering that his host and his people flew almost everywhere, Keff wasn't surprised at the attention paid to the upper reaches of the rooms. The magifolk seemed to like light, and living inside a mountain was likely to cause claustrophobia. The walls were hewn out of the natural granite, but the floor everywhere was that disconcerting track-ball surface.

"This (thing) . . . mine . . . old," Chaumel said, gesturing casually at a couple of framed pieces of art displayed on the wall. Keff glanced at the first one to figure out what it represented, and then wished he hadn't. The moire abstract seemed to move by itself in nauseous patterns. Keff hastily glanced away, dashing tears from his eyes and controlling the roil of his stomach.

"Most original," he said, gasping. Chaumel paused briefly in his chattering to beam at Keff's evident perspicacity and pointed out another stomach-twister. Keff carefully kept his gaze aimed below the level of the frames, offering compliments without looking. Staring at the silver magician's heels and the hem of his robe, Keff padded faster to catch up.

They passed over a threshold into an anteroom where several servants were sweeping and dusting. Except when raising their eyes to acknowledge the presence of their master, they also made a point of watching the ground in front of them. It was no consolation to Keff to realize that others had the same reaction to the "artwork."

Chaumel was the only bare-skin Keff saw. The staff appeared to consist solely of fur-skinned Noble Primitives, like Brannel, but instead of having just four fingers on each hand, some had all five.

"The missing links?" Keff asked Carialle. These beings looked like a combination between Chaumel's people and Brannel's. Though their faces were hairy, they did not bear the animal cast to their features that the various villagers had. They looked more humanly diversified. "Do you suppose that the farther you go away from the overlords, the more changes you find in facial structure?" He stopped to study the face of a furry-faced maiden, who reddened under her pelt and dropped her eyes shyly. She twisted her duster between her hands.

"Ahem! A geographical cause isn't logical," Carialle said, "although you might postulate inbreeding between the two races. That would mean that the races are genetically close. Very interesting."

Chaumel, noticing he'd lost his audience, detoured back, directed Keff away from the serving maid and toward a stone archway.

"Will you look at the workmanship in that?" Keff said, admiringly. "Very fine, Chaumel."

"I'm glad you . . ." the magiman said, moving on through the doorway into a wide corridor. "Now, this . . . my father . . ."

"This" proved to be a tapestry woven, Carialle informed

Keff after a microscopic peek, of dyed vegetable fibers blended with embroidered colorful figures in six-pack hair.

"Old," she said. "At least four hundred years. And expert craftwork, I might add."

"Lovely," Keff said, making sure the contact button scanned it in full for his xenology records. "Er, high worker-ship, Chaumel."

His host was delighted, and took him by the arm to show him every item displayed in the long hall.

Chaumel was evidently an enthusiastic collector of objets d'art and, except for the nauseating pictures, had a well-developed appreciation of beauty. Keff had no trouble admiring handsomely made chairs, incidental tables, and pedestals of wood and stone; more tapestries; pieces of scientific equipment that had fallen into disuse and been adapted for other purposes. A primitive chariot, evidently the precursor of the elegant chairs Chaumel and his people used, was enshrined underneath the picture of a bearded man in a silver robe. Chaumel also owned some paintings and representational art executed with great skill that were not only not uncomfortable but a pleasure to behold. Keff exclaimed over everything, recording it, hoping that he was also gathering clues to help free Carialle so they could leave Ozran as soon as possible.

A few of Chaumel's treasures absolutely defied description. Keff would have judged them to be sculpture or statuary, but some of the vertical and horizontal surfaces showed wear, the polished appearance of long use. They were furniture, but for what kind of being?

"What is this, Chaumel?" Keff asked, drawing the magi-man's attention to a small grouping arranged in an alcove. He pointed to one item. It looked like a low-set painter's easel from which a pair of hardwood tines rose in a V. "This is very old."

"Ah!" the magiman said, eagerly. " . . . from old, old day-day." IT promptly interpreted into "from ancient days," and recorded the usage.

"I'm getting a reading of between one thousand six hundred and one thousand nine hundred years," Carialle said, confirming Chaumel's statement. The magiman gave Keff a curious look.

"Surely your people didn't use these things," Keff said. "Can't sit on them, see?" He made as if to sit down on the narrow horizontal ledge at just above knee level.

Chaumel grinned and shook his head. "Old Ones used . . . sit-lie," he said.

"They weren't humanoid?" Keff asked, and then clarified as the magiman looked confused. "Not like you, or me, or your servants?"

"Not, not. Before New Ones, we."

"Then the humanoids were not the native race on this planet," Carialle said excitedly into Keff's implant. "They *are* travelers. They settled here alongside the indigenous beings and shared their culture."

"That would explain the linguistic anomalies," Keff said. "And that awful artwork in the grand hall." Then speaking aloud, he added, "Are there any of the Old Ones left, Chaumel?"

"Not, not. Many days gone. Worked, move from empty land to mountain. Gave us, gave them." Chaumel struggled with a pantomime. "All . . . gone."

"I think I understand. You helped them move out of the valleys, and they gave you . . . what? Then they all died? What caused that? A plague?"

Chaumel suddenly grew wary. He muttered and moved on to the next grouping of artifacts. He paused dramatically before one item displayed on a wooden pedestal. The gray stone object, about fifty centimeters high, resembled an oddly twisted urn with an off-center opening.

"Old-*Old*-Ones," he said with awe, placing his hands possessively on the urn.

"Old Ones—Ancient Ones?" Keff asked, gesturing one step farther back with his hand.

"Yes," Chaumel said. He caressed the stone. Keff moved closer so Carialle could take a reading through the contact button.

"It's even older than the Old Ones' chair, if that's what that was. Much older. Ask if this is a religious artifact. Are the Ancient Ones their gods?" Carialle asked.

"Did you, your father-father, bring Ancient Ones with you to Ozran?" Keff asked.

"Not *our* ancestors," Chaumel said, laying three imaginary objects in a row. "Ozran: Ancient Ones; Old Ones; New Ones, we. Ancient," he added, holding out the wand in his belt.

"Carialle, I think he means that artifact is a leftover from the original culture. It *is* ancient, but there has been some modification on it, dating a couple thousand years back." Then aloud, he said to Chaumel. "So they passed usable items down. Did the Ancient Ones look like the Old Ones? Were they their ancestors?"

Chaumel shrugged.

"It looks like an entirely different culture, Keff," Carialle said, processing the image and running a schematic overlay of all the pieces in the hall. "There're very few Ancient One artifacts here to judge by, but my reconstruction program suggests different body types for the Ancients and the Old Ones. Similar, though. Both species were upright and had rearward-bending, jointed lower limbs—can't tell how many, but the Old One furniture is built for larger creatures. Not quite as big as humanoids, though."

"It sounds as if one species succeeded after another," Keff said. "The Old Ones moved in to live with the Ancient Ones, and many generations later after the Ancients died off, the New Ones arrived and cohabited with the Old Ones. They are the third in a series of races to live on this planet: the aborigines, the Old Ones, and the New Ones, or magic-using humanoids."

Carialle snorted. "Doesn't say much for Ozran as a host for life-forms, if two intelligent races in a row died off within a few millenia."

"And the humanoids are reduced to a nontechnological existence," Keff said, only half listening to Chaumel, who was lecturing him with an intent expression on his broad-cheeked face. "Could it have something to do with the force-field holding you down? They got stuck here?"

"Whatever trapped me did it selectively, Keff!" Carialle said. "I'd landed and taken off six times on Ozran already. It was deliberate, and I want to know who and why."

"Another mystery to investigate. But I also want to know why the Old Ones moved up here, away from their source of food," Keff said. "Since they seem to be dependant on what's grown here, that's a sociological anomaly."

"Ah," Carialle said, reading newly translated old data from IT. "The Old Ones didn't move up here with the New Ones' help, Keff. They were up here when the humanoids came. They found Ancient artifacts in the valleys."

"So these New Ones had some predilection for talent when they came here, but their contact with the Old Ones increased it to what we see in them now. Two space-going races, Carialle!" Keff said, greatly excited. "I want to know if we can find out more about the pure alien culture. Later on, let's see if we can trace them back to their original systems. Pity there's so little left: after several hundred years of humanoid rule, it's all mixed up together."

"Isn't the synthesis as rare?" Carialle asked, pointedly.

"In our culture, yes. Makes it obvious where the sign

language comes from, too," Keff said. "It's a relic from one of the previous races—useful symbology that helps make the magic work. The Old Ones may never have shared the humanoid language, being the host race, but somehow they made themselves understood to the new-comers. Worth at least a paper to *Galactic Geographic*. Clearly, Chaumel here doesn't know what the Ancients were like."

The magiman, watching Keff talking to himself, heard his name and Keff's question. He shook his head regret-fully. "I do not. Much before days of me."

"Where do your people come from?" Keff asked. "What star, where out there?" He gestured up at the sky.

"I do not know that also. Where from do yours come?" Chaumel asked, a keen eye holding Keff's.

The brawn tried to think of a way to explain the Central Worlds with the limited vocabulary at his disposal and raised his hands helplessly.

"Vain hope." Carialle sighed. "I'm still trying to find any records of settlements in this sector. Big zero. If I could get a message out, I could have Central Worlds do a full-scan search of the old records."

"So where do the Noble Primitives fit in, Chaumel?" Keff asked, throwing a friendly arm over the man's shoul-der before he could start a lecture on the next objet d'art. He pointed at a male servant wearing a long, white robe, who hurried away, wide-eyed, when he noticed the bare-skinned ones looking at him. "I notice that the servants here have lighter pelts than the people in the farm village." He gestured behind him, hoping that Chaumel would understand he meant where they had just come from. He tweaked a lock of his own hair, rubbing his fingers together to indicate "thin," then ran his fingers down his own face and held out his hand.

"They're handsomer. And some of them have five

fingers, like mine." Keff waggled his forefinger. "Why do the ones in the valley have only four?" He bent the finger under his palm.

"Oh," Chaumel said, laughing. He stated something in a friendly, offhanded way that the IT couldn't translate, scissors-chopping his own forefinger with his other hand to demonstrate what he meant. " . . . when of few days—babies. Low mind. . . . no curiosity . . . worker." He made the scissors motion again.

"What?" Carialle shrieked in Keff's ear. "It's not a mutation. It's *mutilation*. There aren't two brands of humanoids, just one, with most of the poor things exploited by a lucky few."

Keff was shocked into silence. Fortunately, Chaumel seemed to expect no reply. Carialle continued to speak in a low voice while Keff nodded and smiled at the magiman.

"Moreover, he's been referring to the Noble Primitives as property. When he mentioned his possessions, IT went back and translated his term for the villagers as 'chattel.' I do not like these people. Evil wizards, indeed!"

"Er, very nice," Keff said in Ozran, for lack of any good reply. Chaumel beamed.

"We care for them, we who commune with the Core of Ozran. We lead our weaker brothers. We guard as they working hard in the valleys to raise food for us all."

"Enslave them, you mean," Carialle sniffed. "And they live up here in comfort while Brannel's people freeze. He looks so warm and friendly—for a slave trader. Look at his eyes. Dead as microchips."

"Weaker? Do you mean feeble-minded? The people down in the valleys have strong bodies but, er, they don't seem very bright," Keff said. "These, your servants, are much more intelligent than any of the ones we met." He didn't mention Brannel.

"Ah," Chaumel said, guardedly casual, "the workers eat stupid, not question . . . who know better, overlords."

"You mean you put something in the food to keep them stupid and docile so they won't question their servitude? That's monstrous," Keff said, but he kept smiling.

Chaumel didn't understand the last word. He bowed deeply. "Thank you. Use talent, over many years gone, we give them," he pantomimed over his own wrist and arm, showed it growing thicker, "more skin, hair, grow dense flesh . . ."

IT riffled through a list of synonyms. Keff seized upon one. "Muscles?" he asked. IT repeated Chaumel's last word, evidently satisfied with Keff's definition.

"Yes," Chaumel said. "Good for living . . . cold valleys. Hard work!"

"You mean you can skimp on the central heat if you give them greater endurance," Carialle said, contemptuously. "You bloodsucker."

Chaumel frowned, almost as if he had heard Carialle's tone.

"Hush! Er, I don't know if this is a taboo question, Chaumel," Keff began, rubbing his chin with thumb and forefinger, "but you interbreed with the servant class, too, don't you? Bare-skins with fur-skins, make babies?"

"Not I," the silver magiman explained hastily. "But yes. Some lower . . . mages and magesses have faces with hair. Never make their places as mages of . . . but not everyone is . . . sent for mightiness."

"Destined for greatness," Keff corrected IT. IT repeated the word. "So why are you not great? I mean," he rephrased his statement for tact, "not one of the mages of—IT, put in that phrase he used?"

"Oh, I am good—satisfied to be what I am," Chaumel said, complacently folding his fingers over his well-padded rib cage.

"If they're already being drugged, why amputate their fingers?" Carialle wanted to know.

"What do fingers have to do with the magic?" Keff asked, making a hey-presto gesture.

"Ah," Chaumel said. Taking Keff's arm firmly under his own, he escorted him down the hall to a low door set deeply into the stone walls. Servants passing by showed Keff the whites of their eyes as Chaumel slipped the silver wand out of his belt and pointed at the lock. Some of the fur-skins hurried faster as the red fire lanced laserlike into the keyhole. One or two, wearing the same keen expression as Brannel, peered in as the door opened. Shooting a cold glance to speed the nosy ones on their way, Chaumel urged Keff inside.

The darkness lifted as soon as they stepped over the threshold, a milky glow coming directly from the substance of the walls.

"Cari, is that radioactive?" Keff asked. His whisper was amplified in a ghostly rush of sound by the rough stone.

"No. In fact, I'm getting no readings on the light at all. Strange."

"Magic!"

"Cut that out," Carialle said sulkily. "I say it's a form of energy with which I am unacquainted."

In contrast to all the other chambers Keff had seen in Chaumel's eyrie, this room had a low, unadorned ceiling of rough granite less than an arm's length above their heads. Keff felt as though he needed to stoop to avoid hitting the roof.

Chaumel moved across the floor like a man in a chapel. The furnishings of the narrow room carried out that impression. At the end opposite the door was a molded, silver table not unlike an altar, upon which rested five objects arranged in a circle on an embroidered cloth. Keff tiptoed forward behind Chaumel.

The items themselves were not particularly impressive: a metal bangle about twelve centimeters across, a silver tube, a flattened disk pierced with half-moon shapes all around the edge, a wedge of clear crystal with a piece of dull metal fused to the blunt end, and a hollow cylinder like an empty jelly jar.

"What are they?" Keff asked.

"Objects of power," Chaumel replied. One by one he lifted them and displayed them for Keff. Returning to the bangle, Chaumel turned it over so Keff could see its inner arc. Five depressions about two centimeters apart were molded into its otherwise smooth curve. In turn, he showed the markings on each one. With the last, he inserted the tips of his fingers into the depressions and wielded it away from Keff.

"Ah," Keff said, enlightened. "You need five digits to use these."

"So the amputation is to keep the servers from organizing a palace revolt," Carialle said. "Any uppity server just wouldn't have the physical dexterity to use them."

"Mmm," Keff said. "How old are they?" He moved closer to the altar and bent over the cloth.

"Old, old," Chaumel said, patting the jelly jar.

"Old Ones," Carialle verified, running a scan through Keff's ocular implants. "So is the bangle. The other three are Ancient, with some subsequent modifications by the Old Ones. All of them have five pressure plates incorporated into the design. That's why Brannel tried to take my palette. It has five depressions, just like these items. He probably thought it was a power piece, like these."

"There's coincidence for you: both the alien races here were pentadactyl, like humans. I wonder if that's a recurring trait throughout the galaxy for technologically capable races," Keff said. "Five-fingered hands."

Chaumel certainly seemed proud of his. Setting down

the jelly jar, he rubbed his hands together, then flicked invisible dust motes off his nails, taking time to admire both fronts and backs.

"Well, they are shapely hands," Carialle said. "They wouldn't be out of place in Michelangelo's Sistine Chapel frescoes except for the bizarre proportions."

Keff took a good look at Chaumel's hands. For the first time he noticed that the thumbs, which he had noted as being rather long, bore lifelike prostheses, complete with nails and tiny wisps of hair, that made the tips fan out to the same distance as the forefingers. The little fingers were of equal length to the ring fingers, jarring the eye, making the fingers look like a thick fringe cut straight across. Absently conscious of Keff's stare, Chaumel pulled at his little fingers.

"Is he trying to make them longer by doing that?" Carialle asked. "It's physically impossible, but I suppose telling him that won't make him stop. Superstitions are superstitions."

"That's er, grotesque, Chaumel," Keff said, smiling with what he hoped was an expression of admiration.

"Thank you, Keff." The silver magiman bowed.

"Show me how the objects of power work," Keff said, pointing at the table. "I'd welcome a chance to watch without being the target."

Chaumel was all too happy to oblige.

"Now you see how these are," he said graciously. He chose the ring and the tube, putting his favorite, the wand, back in its belt holster. "This way."

On the way out of the narrow room, Chaumel resumed his monologue. This time it seemed to involve the provenance and ownership of the items.

"We are proud of our toys," Carialle said deprecatingly. "Nothing up my sleeve, alakazam!"

"Whoops!" Keff said, as Chaumel held out his hand and

a huge crockery vase appeared on the palm. "Alakazam, indeed!"

With a small smile, Chaumel blew on the crock, sending it flying down the hall as if skidding on ice. He raised the tube, aimed it, and squeezed lightly. The crock froze in place, then, in delayed reaction, it burst apart into a shower of jet-propelled sand, peppering the walls and the two men.

"Marvelous!" Keff said, applauding. He spat out sand. "Bravo! Do it again!"

Obligingly, Chaumel created a wide ceramic platter. "My mother this belonged to. I do not *ever* like this," he said. With a twist of his wrist, it followed the crock. Instead of the tube, the silver magiman operated the ring. With a crack, the platter exploded into fragments. A glass goblet, then a pitcher appeared out of the air. Chaumel set them dancing around one another, then fused them into one piece with a dash of scarlet lightning from his wand. They dropped to the ground, spraying fragments of glass everywhere.

"And what do you do for an encore?" Keff asked, surveying the hall, now littered with debris.

"Hmmph!" Chaumel said. He waved the wand, and three apron-clad domestics appeared, followed by brooms and pails. Leaving the magical items floating on the air, he clapped his hands together. The servers set hastily to work cleaning up. Chaumel folded his arms together with satisfaction and turned a smug face to Keff.

"I see. You get all the fun, and they do all the nasty bits," Keff said, nodding. "Bravo anyway."

"I was following the energy buildup during that little Wild West show," Carialle said in Keff's ear. "There is no connection between what Chaumel does with his toys, that hum in the floors, and any energy source except a slight response from that random mess in the sky. Geothermal is silent. And before you ask, he hasn't got a generator. Ask him where they get their power from."

"Where do your magical talents come from?" Keff asked the silver magiman. He imitated Potria's spell-casting technique, gathering in armfuls of air and thrusting his hands forward. Chaumel ducked to one side. His face paled, and he stared balefully at Keff.

"I guess it isn't just sign language," Keff said sheepishly. "Genuine functionalism of symbols. Sorry for the breach in etiquette, old fellow. But could the New Ones do that," he started to make the gesture but pointedly held back from finishing it, "when they came to Ozran?"

"Some. Most learned from Old Ones," Chaumel said, not really caring. He flipped the wand into the air. It twirled end over end, then vanished and reappeared in his side-slung holster.

"Flying?" Keff said, imitating the way the silver magiman's chair swooped and turned. "Learned from Old Ones?"

"Yes. Gave learning to us for giving to them."

"Incredible," Keff said, with a whistle. "What I wouldn't give for magic lessons. But where does the power come from?"

Chaumel looked beatific. "From the Core of Ozran," he said, hands raised in a mystical gesture.

"What is that? Is it a physical thing, or a philosophical center?"

"It is the Core," Chaumel said, impatiently, shaking his head at Keff's denseness. The brawn shrugged.

"The Core is the Core," he said. "Of course. Non-sequitur. Chaumel, my ship can't move from where it landed. Does the Core of Ozran have something to do with that?"

"Perhaps, perhaps."

Keff pressed him. "I'd really like an answer to that,

Chaumel. It's sort of important to me, in a strange sort of way," he said, shrugging diffidently.

Chaumel irritably shook his head and waved his hands.

"I'll tackle him again later, Cari," Keff said under his breath.

"Now is better . . . What's that sound?" Carialle said, interrupting herself.

Keff looked around. "I didn't hear anything."

But Chaumel had. Like a hunting dog hearing a horn, he turned his head. Keff felt a rise of static, raising the hair on the back of his neck.

"There it is again," Carialle said. "Approximately fifty thousand cycles. Now I'm showing serious power fluctuations where you are. What Chaumel was doing in the hallway was a spit in the ocean compared with this."

Chaumel grabbed Keff's arm and made a spiraling gesture upward with one finger.

"This way, in haste!" Chaumel said, pushing him through the hallway toward the great room and the landing pad beyond. His hand flew above his head, repeating the spiral over and over. "Haste, haste!"

¤ CHAPTER EIGHT

Night had fallen over the mountains. The new arrivals seemed to glow with their own ghostlight as they flew through the purple-dark sky toward Chaumel's balcony. Keff, concealed with Chaumel behind a curtain in the tall glass door, recognized Ferngal, Nokias, Potria, and some of the lesser magimen and magiwomen from that afternoon. There were plenty of new faces, including some in chairs as fancy as Chaumel's own.

"The big chaps and their circle of intimates, no doubt. Wish I had a chance to put on my best bib and tucker," Keff murmured to Carialle. To his host, he said, "Shouldn't we go out and greet them, Chaumel?"

"Hutt!" Chaumel said, hurriedly putting a hand to his lips, and raising the wand at his belt in threat to back up his command. Silently, he pantomimed putting one object after another in a row. " . . . (untranslatable) . . ."

"I think I understand you," Keff said, interrupting IT's attempt to locate roots for the phrase. "Order of precedence. Protocol. You're waiting for everyone to land."

Pursing his lips, Chaumel nodded curtly and returned

to studying the scene. One at a time, like a flock of enormous migratory birds, the chariots queued up beyond the lip of the landing zone. Some jockeyed for better position, then resumed their places as a sharp word came from one of the occupants of the more elaborate chairs. Keff sensed that adherence to protocol was strictly enforced among the magifolk. Behave or get blasted, he thought.

As soon as the last one was in place, Chaumel threw open the great doors and stood to one side, bowing. Hastily, Keff followed suit. Five of the chairs flew forward and set down all at once in the nearest squares. Their occupants rose and stepped majestically toward them.

"Zolaika, High Magess of the North," Chaumel said, bowing deeply. "I greet you."

"Chaumel," the tiny, old woman of the leaf-green chariot said, with a slight inclination of her head. She sailed regally into the center of the grand hall and stood there, five feet above the ground as if fixed in glass.

"Ilnir, High Mage of the Isles." Chaumel bowed to a lean man in purple with a hooked nose and a domed, bald head. Nokias started forward, but Chaumel held up an apologetic finger. "Ferngal, High Mage of the East, I greet you."

Nokias's face crimsoned in the reflected light from the ballroom. He stepped forward after Ferngal strode past with a smug half-grin on his face. "I had forgotten, brother Chaumel. Forgive my discourtesy."

"Forgive mine, high one," Chaumel said, suavely, holding his hands high and apart. "Ureth help me, but you could never be less than courteous. Be greeted, Nokias, High Mage of the South."

Gravely, the golden magiman entered and took his place at the south point of the center ring. He was followed by Omri of the West, a flamboyantly handsome man dressed fittingly in peacock blue. Chaumel gave him an elaborate salute.

With less ceremony and markedly less deference, Chaumel greeted the rest of the visiting magi.

"He outranks these people," Carialle said in Keff's implant. "He's making it clear they're lucky to get the time of day out of him. I'm not sure where he stands in the society. He's probably not quite of the rank of the first five, but he's got a lot of power."

"And me where he wants us," Keff said in a sour tone.

As Nokias had, a few of the lesser ones were compelled to take an unexpected backseat to some of their fellows. Chaumel was firm as he indicated demotions and ignored those who conceded with bad grace. Keff wondered if the order of precedence was liquid and altered frequently. He saw a few exchanges of hot glares and curt gestures, but no one spoke or swung a wand.

Potria and Asedow had had time to change clothes and freshen up after their battle. Potria undulated off her pink-gold chariot swathed in an opaque gown of a cloth so fine it pulsed at wrists and throat with her heartbeat. Her perfume should have been illegal. Asedow, still in dark green, wore several chains and wristlets of hammered and pierced metal that clanked together as he walked. The two elbowed one another as they approached Chaumel, striving to be admitted first. Chaumel broke the deadlock by bowing over Potria's hand, but waving Asedow through behind her back. Potria smirked for receiving extra attention from the host, but Asedow had preceded her into the hall, dark green robes aswirl. As Carialle and Keff had observed before, Chaumel was a diplomat.

"How does one get promoted?" he asked Chaumel, who bowed the last of the magifolk, a slender girl in a primrose robe, into the ballroom. "What criteria do you use to tell who's on first?"

"I will explain in time," the silver mage said. "Come."

Taking Keff firmly by the upper arm, he went forth to make small talk with his many visitors. He brought Keff to bow to Zolaika who began an incomprehensible conversation with Chaumel literally over Keff's head because the host rose several feet to float on the same level as the lady. Keff stood, staring up at the verbal Ping-Pong match, wishing the IT was faster at simultaneous translation. He heard his name several times, but caught little of the context. Most of it was in the alternate, alien-flavored dialect, peppered with a few hand gestures. Keff only recognized the signs for "help" and "honor."

"I hope you're taking all this down so I can work on it later," he said in a subvocal mutter to Carialle. Hands behind his back, he twisted to survey the rest of the hall.

"With my tongue out," Carialle said. "My, you certainly brought out the numbers. Everyone wants a peep at you. What would you be willing to bet that everyone who could reasonably expect admittance is here. I wonder how many are sitting home, trying to think up a good excuse to call?"

"No bet," Keff said cheerfully. "Oh, look, the decorator's been in."

The big room, which had been empty until the guests arrived, was beginning to fill in with appropriate pieces of furniture. Two rows of sconces bearing burning torches appeared at intervals along the walls. Three magifolk chatting near the double doors discovered a couch behind them and sat down. Spider-legged chairs chased mages through the room, only to place themselves in a correct and timely manner, for the mages never once looked behind to see if there was something there to be sat on: a seat was assumed. Fat, ferny plants in huge crockery pots grew up around two magimen who huddled against one wall, talking in furtive undertones.

A wing chair nudged the back of Zolaika's knees while

an ottoman insinuated itself lovingly under the old woman's feet. She made herself comfortable as several of the junior magifolk came to pay their respects. A small table with a round, rimmed top appeared in their midst. Several set down their magical items, initiating an apparent truce for the duration.

After kissing Zolaika's hand, Chaumel detached himself from the group and steered Keff toward the next of the high magimen in the room. Engrossed in a conversation, Ilnir barely glanced at Keff, but accorded Chaumel a courteous nod as he made an important point using his wrist-thick magic mace for emphasis. A carved pedestal appeared under Ilnir's elbow and he leaned upon it.

Each of the higher magimen had a number of sycophants, male and female, as escort. Potria, gorgeous in her floating, low-cut peach gown, was among the number surrounding Nokias. Asedow was right beside her. They glared at Chaumel, evidently taking personally the slight done to their chief. As Chaumel and Keff passed by, they raised their voices with the complaint that they had been wrongly prevented from finishing their contest.

Ferngal and Nokias were standing together near the crystal windows beyond their individual circles. The two were exchanging pleasantries with one another, but not really communicating. Keff, boosting the gain of his audio pickup with a pressure of his jaw muscles, actually heard one of them pass a remark about the weather.

Chaumel stopped equidistant between the two high mages. His hand concealed in a fold of his silver robe, he used sharp pokes to direct Keff to bow first to Ferngal, then Nokias. Keff offered a few polite words to each. IT was working overtime processing the small talk it was picking up, but it gave him the necessary polite phrases slowly enough to recite accurately without resorting to IT's speaker.

"I feel like a trained monkey," Keff subvocalized.

As he straightened up, Carialle got a look at his audience. "That's what they think you are, too. They seem surprised that you can actually speak."

Chaumel turned him away from his two important guests and tilted his head conspiratorially close.

"You see, my young friend, I would have preferred to have you all to myself, but I can't refuse access to the preeminent magis when they decide to call at my humble home for an evening. One climbs higher by power . . . (power-plays, IT suggested) managed, as ordered by the instructions left us by our ancestors. Such power-plays determine one's height (rank, IT whispered). Also, deaths. They are most facile at these."

"Deaths?" Keff asked. "You mean, you all move up one when someone dies?"

"Yes, but also when one *makes* a death," Chaumel said, with an uneasy backward glance at the high mages. Keff goggled.

"You mean you move up when you kill someone?"

"Sounds like the promotion lists in the space service to me," Carialle remarked to Keff.

"Ah, but not only that, but through getting more secrets and magical possessions from those, and more. But Ferngal of the East has just, er, discarded . . ."

"Disposed of," Carialle supplied.

" . . . Mage Klemay in a duel, so he has raised/ascended over Mage Nokias of the South. I must incorporate the change of status smoothly, though"—his face took on an exaggerated mask of tragedy—"it pains me to see the embarrassment it causes my friend, Nokias. We attempt to make all in harmony."

Keff thought privately that Chaumel didn't look that uncomfortable. He looked like he was enjoying the discomfiture of the Mage of the South.

"This is a nasty brood. They make a point of scoring off one another," Carialle observed. "The only thing that harmonizes around here is the color-coordinated outfits and chariots. Did you notice? Everyone has a totem color. I wonder if they inherit it, earn it, or just choose it." She giggled in Keff's ear. "And what happens when someone else has the one you want?"

"Another assassination, I'm sure," Keff said, bowing and smiling to one side as Ferngal made for Ilnir's group.

As the black-clad magiman's circle drifted off, Nokias's minions spread out a little, as if grateful for the breathing room. Keff turned to Potria and gave her his most winning smile, but she looked down her nose at him.

"How nice to see you again, my lady," he said in slow but clear Ozran. The lovely bronze woman turned pointedly and looked off in another direction. The puff of gold hair over her right ear obscured her face from him completely. Keff sighed.

"No sale," Carialle said. "You might as well have been talking to her chair. Tsk-tsk, tsk-tsk. Your hormones don't have much sense."

"Thank you for that cold shower, my lady," Keff said, half to Potria, half to Carialle. "You're a heartless woman, you are." The brain chuckled in his ear.

"She's not that different from anyone else here. I've never seen such a bundle of tough babies in my life. Stay on your guard. Don't reveal more about us than you have to. We're vulnerable enough as it is. I don't like people who mutilate and enslave thousands, not to mention capturing helpless ships."

"Your mind is like unto my mind, lady dear," Keff said lightly. "*That* one doesn't look so tough."

Near the wall, almost hiding in the curtains behind a rose-robed crone was the last magiwoman Chaumel had bowed into the room. IT·reminded him her name was

Plennafrey. Self-effacing in her simple primrose gown and metallic blue-green shoulder-to-floor sash, her big, dark eyes, pointed chin, and broad cheekbones gave her a gamin look. She glanced toward Keff and immediately turned away. Keff admired her hair, ink-black with rusty highlights, woven into a simple four-strand plait that fell most of the way down her back.

"I feel sorry for her," Keff said. "She looks as though she's out of her depth. She's not mean enough."

Carialle gave him the raspberry. "You always do fall for the naive look," she said. "That's why it's always so easy to lure you into trouble in Myths and Legends."

"Oho, you've admitted it, lady. Now I'll be on guard against you."

"Just you watch it with these people and worry about me later. They're not fish-eating swamp dwellers like the Beasts Blatisant."

Keff had time to nod politely to the tall girl before Chaumel yanked him away to meet the last of the five high magimen. "I know how she feels, Cari. I'm not used to dealing with advanced societies that are more complicated and devious than the one I come from. Give me the half-naked swamp dwellers every time."

"Look at that," Potria said, sourly. "My claim, and Chaumel is parading it around as if he discovered it."

"Mine," Asedow said. "We have not yet settled the question of ownership."

"He has a kind face," Plennafrey offered in a tiny voice. Potria spun in a storm of pink-gold and glared at her.

"You are mad. It is not fully Ozran, so it is no better than a beast, like the peasants."

Remembering her resolution to be bolder no matter how terrified she felt, Plennafrey cleared her throat.

"I am sure he is not a mere thing, Potria. He looks a true

man." In fact, she found his looks appealing. His twinkling eyes reminded her of happy days, something she hadn't known since long before her father died. If only she could have such a man in her life, it would no longer be lonely.

Potria turned away, disgusted. "I have been deprived of my rights."

"*You* have? *I* spoke first." Asedow's eyes glittered.

"I was winning," Potria said, lips curled back from gritted white teeth. She flashed a hand signal under Asedow's nose. He backed off, making a sign of protection. Plenna watched, wild-eyed. Although she knew they wouldn't dare to rejoin their magical battle in here, neither of them was above a knife in the ribs.

Suddenly, she felt a wall of force intrude between the combatants. The thought of a possible incident must also have occurred to Nokias. Asedow and Potria retreated another hand-span apart, continuing to harangue one another. Plenna glanced over at the other groups of mages. They were beginning to stare. Nokias, having been disgraced once already this evening, would be furious if his underlings embarrassed him in front of the whole assemblage.

Asedow was getting louder, his hands flying in the old signs, emphasizing his point. "It is to my honor, and the tower and the beast will come to me!"

Potria's hands waved just as excitedly. "You have no honor. Your mother was a fur-skin with a dray-beast jaw, and your father was drunk when he took her!"

At the murderous look in Asedow's eye, Plenna warded herself and planted her hand firmly over her belt buckle beneath the concealing sash. At least she could help prevent the argument from spreading. With an act of will, she cushioned the air around them so no sound escaped past their small circle. That deadened the shouting, but it didn't prevent others from seeing the pantomime the two were throwing at one another.

"How dare you!" Zolaika's chair swooped in on the pair, knocking them apart with a blast of force which dispelled Plenna's cloud of silence. "You profane the sacred signs in a petty brawl!"

"She seeks to take what is rightfully mine," Asedow bellowed. Freed, his voice threatened to shake down the ceiling.

"High one, I appeal to you," Potria said, turning to the senior magess. "I challenged for the divine objects and I claim them as my property." She pointed at Keff.

Keff was taken aback.

"Now just a minute here," he said, starting forward as he recognized the words. "I'm no one's chattel."

"Hutt!" Zolaika ordered, pointing an irregular, hand-sized form at him. Keff ducked, fearing another bolt of scarlet lightning. Chaumel pulled him back and, keeping a hand firmly on his shoulder, offered a placatory word to Potria.

"She's not the enchantress I thought she was," Keff said sadly to Carialle.

"A regular La Belle Dame Sans Merci," Carialle said. "Treat with courtesy, at a respectable distance."

"Speaking of stating one's rights," Ferngal said as he and the other high magimen moved forward. He folded his long fingers in the air before him and studied them. "May I mention that the objects were found in Klemay's territory, which is now my domain, so I have the prior claim. The tower and the male are mine." He crushed his palms together deliberately.

"But before that, they were in my venue," the old woman in red cried out from her place by the window. Her chair lifted high into the air. "I had seen the silver object and the being near my village when first it fell on Ozran. I claim precedence over you for the find, Ferngal!"

"I am no one's find!" Keff said, breaking away from Chaumel. "I'm a free man. My ship is *my* magical object, no one else's."

"I'm *mine*," Carialle crisply reminded him.

"I'd better keep you a piece of magical esoterica, lady, or they'll kill me without hesitation over a talking ship with its own brain."

La Belle Dame Sans Merci raised a shrill outcry. Chaumel, eager to keep the peace in his own home, flew to the center of the room and raised his hands.

"Mages and magesses and honored guest, the hour is come! Let us *dine*. We will discuss this situation much more reasonably when we all have had a bite and a sup. Please!" He clapped his hands, and a handful of servants appeared, bearing steaming trays. At a wave of their master's hand they fanned out among the guests, offering tasty-smelling hors d'oeuvres. Keff sniffed appreciatively.

"Don't touch," Carialle cautioned him. "You don't know what's in them."

"I know," Keff said, "but I'm starved. It's been hours since I had that hot meal." He felt his stomach threatening to rumble and compressed his diaphragm to prevent it being heard. He concentrated on looking politely disinterested.

Chaumel clapped his hands, and fur-faced musicians strumming oddly shaped instruments suddenly appeared here and there about the room. They passed among the guests, smiling politely. Chaumel nodded with satisfaction, and signaled again.

More Noble Primitives appeared out of the air, this time with goblets and pitchers of sparkling liquids in jewel colors. A chair hobbled up to Keff and edged its seat sideways toward his legs, as if offering him a chance to sit down.

"No thanks," he said, stepping away a pace. The chair, unperturbed, tottered on toward the next person standing next to him. "Look around, Cari! It's like Merlin's household in *The Sword in the Stone*. I feel a little drunk on glory, Cari. We've discovered a race of magicians. This is the pinnacle of our careers. We could retire tomorrow and they'd talk about us until the end of time."

"Once we get off this rock and go home! I keep telling you, Keff, what they're doing isn't magic. It can't be. Real magic shouldn't require *power*, least of all the kind of power they're sucking out of the surrounding area. Mental power possibly, but not battery-generator type power, which is what is coming along those electromagnetic lines in the air."

"Well, there's invocation of power as well as evocation, drawing it into you for use," Keff said, trying to remember the phrases out of the Myths and Legends rule book.

Carialle seemed to read his mind. "Don't talk about a game! This is real life. This isn't magic. Ah! There it is: proof."

Keff glanced up. Chaumel was bowing to something hovering before him at eye level. It was a box of some kind. It drifted slightly so that the flat side that had been directed at Chaumel was pointing at him. Looking out from behind a glass panel was a man's face, dark-skinned and ancient beyond age. The puckered eyelids compressed as the man peered intently at Keff.

"See? It's a monitor," Carialle said. "A com unit. It's a device, *not* magic, *not* evoked from the person of the user. He's transmitting his image through it, probably because he's too weak to be here in person."

"Maybe the box is just a relic from the old days," Keff said, but his grand theory did have a few holes in it. "Look, there's nothing feeding it."

"You don't need cable to transmit power, Keff. You know that. Even Chaumel isn't magicking the food up himself. He's calling it from somewhere. Probably in the depths of the dungeon, there's a host of fuzzy-faced cooks working their heads off, and furry sommeliers decanting wine. I think he's acting like the teleportative equivalent of a maitre d'."

"All right, I concede that they *might* be technicians. What I want to know is just what they want with us so badly that they have to trap us in place."

"What we appear to be, or at least I appear to be, is a superior technical gizmo. Your girlfriend and her green sidekick at least don't want something this big to get away. The greed, by the way, is not limited to those two. At least eighty percent of the people here experience increased respiration and heartbeat when they look at you and the IT box, and by proxy, me. It's absolutely indecent."

Chaumel went around the room like a zephyr, defusing arguments and urging people to sit down to prepare for the meal. Keff admired his knack of having every detail at his fingertips. Couches with attached tables appeared out of the ether. The guests disported themselves languidly on the velvet covers while the tables adjusted themselves to be in easy range. The canape servers vanished in midstep and the remains of the hors d'oeuvres with them. Napery, silver, and a translucent dinner service appeared on every table followed by one, two, three sparkling crystal goblets, all of different design. White, embroidered napkins opened out and spread themselves on each lap.

Something caught Keff squarely in the belly and behind the knees, making him fold up. A padded seat caught him, lifted him up and forward several feet into the heart of the circle of magifolk, and the tray across his middle clamped firmly down on the other arm of the chair. Under his heels, a broad bar braced itself to give him support. A napkin puffed up, settled like swansdown on his thighs.

"Oh, I'm not hungry," he said to the air. The invisible maitre d' paid no attention to his protest. He was favored with china and crystal, and a small finger bowl on a doily. He picked up a goblet to examine it. Though the glass was wafer-thin, it had been incised delicately with arabesques and intricate interlocking diamonds.

"How beautiful."

"Now that is contemporary. Not bad," Carialle said, with grudging approval. Keff turned the goblet and let it catch the torchlight. He pinged it with a fingernail and listened to the sweet song.

A hairy-faced server bearing an earthen pitcher appeared next to Keff to fill his glass with dark golden wine. Keff smiled at him and sniffed the liquid. It was fragrant, like honey and herbs.

"Don't drink that," Carialle said, after a slight hesitation to assess the readouts from Keff's olfactory implant. "Full of sulfites, and just in case you think the Borgias were a fun family, enough strychnine in it to kill you six times over."

Shocked, Keff pushed the glass away. It vanished and was replaced by an empty one. Another server hovered and poured a cedar-red potation into its bowl. He smiled at the furry-faced female who tipped up the corners of her mouth tentatively before hurrying away to the next person.

"Who put poison in my wine?" Keff whispered, staring around him.

Chaumel glanced over at him with a concerned expression. Keff nodded and smiled to show that everything was all right. The silver magiman nodded back and went on his way from one guest to another.

"I don't know," Carialle said. "It wasn't and *isn't* in the pitcher, but I wasn't quick enough to follow the burst of energy back to its originator. Seems it isn't an unknown incident, though."

All around the room, a Noble Primitive was appearing beside each mage. Full of curiosity, Keff eyed them. Each bore a different cast of features, some more animal than others, so they were undoubtedly from the magimen's home provinces. Asedow's servant did look like a six-pack. The pretty girl's servant was hardly mutated at all, except for something about the eyes that suggested felines. Potria didn't look at her pig-person, but stiff-armed her goblet toward him. Cautiously, the Noble Primitive took a sip. Nothing happened to him, but two other servants nearby fell over on the floor in fits of internal anguish. They vanished and were replaced by others. Whites showing all around the irises of his eyes, the pig-man handed the goblet back to his mistress, and waited, hands clenched, for her nod of approval. Other mages, their first drink satisfactory, held their glasses aloft, calling loudly to the wine servers for refills.

"Food-tasters! There's more in heaven and on earth than is dreamed of in your philosophy, Horatio," Keff said.

"Hmph!" Carialle said. "That's an understatement. I wish you could see what I do. Those langorous poses are just that: poses. I'm recording everything for your benefit, and it's taking approximately eighteen percent of my total memory capacity to absorb it. I'm not merely monitoring three language forms. There is a lot more going on sub rosa. Every one of our magifolk is tensed up so much I don't know how they can swallow. The air is full of power transmissions, odd miniature gravity wells, low-frequency signals, microwaves, you name it."

"Can you trace any of it back? What is it all for?"

"The low-frequency stuff is easy to read. It's chatter. They're sending private messages to one another, forming conspiracies and so on against, as nearly as I can tell, everyone else in the room. The power signals correspond to dirty tricks like the poison in your wine. As for the microwaves, I can't tell what they're for. The transmission is slightly askew to anything I've dealt with before, and I can't intercept it anyway because I'm not on the receiving end."

"Tight point-to-point beam?"

"I wish *I* could transmit something with as little spill-over," Carialle admitted. "Somebody is very good at what they're doing."

IT continued to translate, but most of what it reported was small talk, mostly on the taste of the wine and the current berry harvests. With their chairs bobbing up and down to add emphasis to their discourse, two magiwomen were conversing about architecture. A couple of the magifolk here and there leaned their heads toward one another as if sharing a confidence, but their lips weren't moving. Keff suspected the same kind of transference that the magifolk used to control their eye spheres. He looked up, wondering where all the spy-eyes had gone. That afternoon on the field the air had been thick with them.

Keff contrasted the soup that appeared in huge silver tureens with the swill that Brannel's people had to eat. And he and Cari were still not free to leave the planet. Still, in spite of the shortcomings, he had a feeling of satisfaction.

"This is the race everyone in Exploration has always dreamed of finding," he said, surveying the magifolk. "Our technical equals, Cari. And against all odds, a humanoid race that evolved parallel to our own. They're incredible."

"Incredible when they amputate fingers from babies?" asked Carialle. "And keep a whole segment of the race under their long thumbs with drugged food and drink? If they're our equals, thank you, I'll stay unequal. Besides, they don't appear to be makers, they're users. Chaumel's mighty proud of those techno-toys left to him by the Old Ones and the Ancient Ones, but he doesn't know how to fix 'em. And neither does anyone else. Over there, in the corner."

Keff glanced over as Carialle directed. On the floor lay Chaumel's jelly jar. He gasped.

"Does he know he lost it?"

"He didn't lose it. I saw him drop it there. It doesn't work anymore, so he discarded it. Everybody else has looked at it with burning greed in their eyes and, as soon as they realized it doesn't work anymore, ignored it. They're operators, not engineers."

"They're still tool-using beings with an advanced civilization who have technical advantages, if you must call it that, superior in many ways to ours. If we can bring them into the Central Worlds, I'm sure they'll be able to teach us plenty."

"We already know all about corruption, thank you," Carialle said.

A servant stepped forward, bowed, and presented the tureen to him. Keff sniffed. The soup smelled wonderful. He gave them a tight smile. Another popped into being beside him bearing a large spoon, and ladled some into the bowl on his tray. The rich golden broth was thick with chunks of red and green vegetables and tiny, doughnut-shaped pasta. Keff poked through it with his silver spoon.

"Cari, I'm starved. Is any of this safe to eat? They didn't assign me a food-taster, even if I'd trust one."

"Hold up a bite, and I'll tell you if anyone's spiked it." Keff obliged, pretending he was cooling the soup with his breath. "Nope. Go ahead."

"Ahhhh." Keff raised it all the way to his lips.

His chair jerked sideways in midair. The stream of soup went flying off into the air past his cheek and vanished before it splashed onto his shoulder. He found himself facing Omri.

"Tell me, strange one," said the peacock-clad mage, lounging back on his floating couch, one hand idly spooning up soup and letting it dribble back into his bowl. "Where do you come from?"

"Watch it," Carialle barked.

"From far away, honored sir," Keff said. "A world that circles a sun a long way from here."

"That's impossible."

Keff found himself spun halfway around until he was nose to nose with a woman in brown with night-black eyes.

"There are no other suns. Only ours."

Keff opened his mouth to reply, but before he could get the words out, his chair whirled again.

"Pay no attention to Lacia. She's a revisionist," said Ferngal. His voice was friendly, but his eyes were two dead circles of dark blue slate. "Tell me more about this star. What is its name?"

"Calonia," Keff said.

"That leaves them none the wiser," Carialle said.

"That leaves us none the wiser," Chaumel echoed, turning Keff's seat in a flat counterclockwise spin three-quarters around. "How far is it from here, and how long did it take you to get here?" Keff opened his mouth to address Chaumel, but the silver magiman became a blur.

"What power do your people have?" Asedow asked. Whoosh!

"How many are they?" demanded Zolaika. Hard jerk, reverse spin.

"Why did you come here?" asked a plump man in bright yellow. Blur.

"What do you want on Ozran?" Nokias asked. Keff tried to force out an answer.

"Not—" Short jerk sideways.

"How did you obtain possession of the silver tower?" Potria asked.

"It's my sh—" Two half-arcs in violently different directions, until he ended up facing an image of Ferngal that swayed and bobbed.

"Will more of your folk be coming here?" Keff heard. His stomach was beginning to head for his esophagus.

"I . . ." he began, but his chair shifted again, this time to twin images of Ilnir, who gabbled something at him in a hoarse voice that was indistinguishable from the roar in his ears.

"Hey!" Keff protested weakly.

"The Siege Perilous, Galahad," Carialle quipped. "Be strong, be resolute, be brave."

"I'm starting to get motion sick," Keff said. "Even flyer training wasn't like this! I feel like a nardling lazy Susan." The chair twisted until it was facing away from Ilnir. A blurred figure of primrose yellow and teal at the corner of his eye sat up slightly.

Beside Keff's hand, a small glass appeared. It was filled with a sparkling liquid of very pale green. Keff's vision abruptly cleared. Was he being offered another shot of poison? The silver blob that was Chaumel shot a suspicious look at the tall girl, then nodded to Keff. The brawn started to take the ornate cup, when two more tasters abruptly keeled over and let their glasses crash to the ground. Two more servants appeared, always four-fingered fur-faces. Keff regarded the cup suspiciously.

"What about it, Cari? Is it safe to drink?"

"It's a motion sickness drug," Carialle said, after a quick spectroanalysis. Hastily, before he was moved again, Keff gulped down the green liquid. It tasted pleasantly of mint and gently heated his stomach. In no time, Keff felt much better, able to endure this ordeal. He winked at the pretty girl the next time he was whirled past her. She returned him a tentative grin.

The Siege Perilous halted for a moment and Keff realized his soup plate had vanished. In its place was a crescent-shaped basket of fruit and a plate of salad. His fellow diners were also being favored with the next course. Some of them, with bored expressions, waved it away and were instantly served tall, narrow crockery bowls with salt-encrusted rims. Before he spun away again, he watched Zolaika pull something from it and yank apart a nasty-looking crustacean.

"Ugh," Keff said. "No fish course for me."

Thanks to the young woman's potion he felt well enough to eat. While trying to field questions from the magifolk, he picked up one small piece of fruit after another. Carialle tested them for suspicious additives.

"No," Carialle said. "No, no, no, yes—oops, not anymore. No, no, yes!"

Before it could be tainted by long-distance assassins, Keff popped the chunk of fruit in his mouth without looking at it. It burst in a delightful gush of soft flesh and slightly tart juice. His next half-answer was garbled, impeded by berry pulp, but it didn't matter, since he was never allowed to finish a sentence anyway before the next mage greedily snatched him away from his current inquisitor. He swallowed and sought for another wholesome bite.

The basket disappeared out from under his hand and was replaced by the nauseating crock. His fingers splashed into the watery gray sauce. It sent up an overwhelming odor of rotting oil. Keff's stomach, tantalized by the morsel of fruit, almost whimpered. He held his breath until his invisible waiter got the hint and took the crock away. In its place was a succulent-smelling vol au vent covered with a cream gravy.

"No!" said Carialle as he reached for his fork.

"Oh, Cari." His chair revolved, pinning him to the back, and the meat pastry evaporated in a cloud of steam. "Oh, damn."

"Why have you come to Ozran?" Ilnir asked. "You have not answered me."

"I haven't been allowed," Keff said, bracing himself, expecting any moment to be turned to face another magiman. When the chair didn't move, he sat up straighter.

"We come to explore. This planet looked interesting, so we landed."

"We?" Ilnir asked. "Are there more of you in your silver tower?"

"Oops," Carialle said.

"Me and my ship," Keff explained hastily. "When you travel alone as I do, you start talking out loud."

"And do you hear answers?" Asedow asked to the general laughter of his fellows. Keff smiled.

"Wouldn't that be something?" Keff answered sweetly. Asedow smirked.

"That man's been zinged and he doesn't even know it," Carialle said.

"Look, I'm no danger to you," Keff said earnestly. "I'd appreciate it if you would release my ship and let me go on my way."

"Oh, not yet," Chaumel said, with a slight smile Keff didn't like at all. "You have only just arrived. Please allow us to show you our hospitality."

"You are too kind," Keff said firmly. "But I must continue on my way."

The spin took him by surprise.

"Why are you in such a hurry to leave?" Zolaika asked, narrowing her eyes at him. The face with the monitor, hovering beside her, looked him up and down and said something in the secondary, more formal dialect. Keff batted the IT unit slung around his chest, which burped out a halting query.

"What tellest thou from us?"

"What will I say about you?" Keff repeated, and thought fast. "Well, that you are an advanced and erudite people with a strong culture that would be interesting to study."

He was slammed sideways by the force of the reverse spin.

"You would send others here?" Ferngal asked.

"Not if you didn't want me to," Keff said. "If you prefer to remain undisturbed, I assure you, you will be." He suffered a fast spin toward Omri.

"We'll remain more undisturbed if you don't go back to make a report at all," the peacock magiman said. A halfwhirl this time, and he ended up before Potria.

"Oh, come, friends," she said, with a winning smile. "Why assume ill where none exists? Stranger, you shall enjoy your time here with us, I promise you. To our new friendship." She flicked her fingers. A cup of opal glass materialized in front of her and skimmed across the air to Keff's tray. Keff, surprised and gratified, picked it up and tilted it to her in salute.

"What's in it, Cari?" he subvocalized.

"Yum. It's a nice mugful of mind-wipe," she said. "Stabilized sodium pentothal and a few other goodies guaranteed to make her the apple of your eye." Keff gave the enchantress a smile full of charm and a polite nod, raised the goblet to her once again, and put it down untasted. "Sorry, ma'am. I don't drink."

The bronze woman swept her hand angrily to one side, and the goblet vanished.

"Nice try, peachie," Cari said, triumphantly.

Keff seized a miniature dumpling from the next plate that landed on his tray.

"Yes," Carialle whispered. Keff popped it into his mouth and swallowed. His greed amused the magifolk of the south, whose chairs bobbed up and down in time to their laughter. He smiled kindly at them and decided to turn the tables.

"I am very interested in your society. How are you governed? Who is in charge of decision-making that affects you all?"

That simple question started a philosophical discussion that fast deteriorated into a shouted argument, resulting in the death or discomfort of six more fur-skinned foodtasters. Keff smiled and nodded and tried to follow it all while he swallowed a few bites.

Following Carialle's instructions, he waved away the next two dishes, took a morsel from the third, ignored the next three when Carialle found native trace elements that would upset his digestive tract, and ate several delightful mouthfuls from the last, crisp, hot pastries stuffed with fresh vegetables. Each dish was more succulent and appealing than the one before it.

"I can't get over the variety of magic going on in here," Keff whispered, toying with a soufflé that all but defied gravity.

"If it was really magic, they could magic up what you wanted to eat and not just what they want you to have. As for the rest, you know what I think."

"Well, the food is perfect," Keff said stubbornly. "No burnt spots, no failed sauces, no gristle. That sounds like magic."

"Oh, maybe it's food-synths instead," Carialle countered. "If I was working for Chaumel, I'd be terrified of making mistakes and ruining the food. Wouldn't you?"

Keff sighed. "At least I still have my aliens."

"Enough of this tittle-tattle," Chaumel called out, rising. He clapped his hands. The assemblage craned their necks to look at him. "A little entertainment, my friends?" He brought his hands together again.

Between Nokias and Ferngal, a fur-skinned tumbler appeared halfway through a back flip and bounded into the center of the room. Keff's chair automatically backed up until it was between two others, leaving the middle of the circle open. A narrow cable suspended from the ceiling came into being. On it, a male and a female hung ankle to ankle ten meters above the ground. Starting slowly, they revolved faster until they were spinning flat out, parallel to the floor. There was a patter of insincere applause. The rope and acrobats vanished, and the tumbler leaped into the air, turned a double somersault, and landed on one hand. A small animal with an ornamented collar appeared standing on his upturned feet. It did flips on its perch, as the male boosted it into the air with thrusts of his powerful legs. Omri yawned. The male and his pet disappeared to make room for a whole troupe of juvenile tumblers.

Keff heard a gush of wind from the open windows. The night air blew a cloud of dust over the luminescent parapet, but it never reached the open door. Chaumel flashed his wand across in a warding gesture. The dust beat itself against a bellying, invisible barrier and fell to the floor.

"Was that part of the entertainment?" Keff said subvocally.

"Another one of those power drains," Carialle said. "Somehow, what they do sucks all the energy, all the cohesive force out of the surrounding ecology. The air outside of Chaumel's little mountain nest is dead, clear to where I am."

"Magic doesn't have to come from somewhere," Keff said.

"Keff, physics! Power is leaching toward your location. Therefore logic suggests it is being drawn in that direction by need."

"Magic doesn't depend on physics. But I concede your point."

"It's true whether or not you believe in it. The concentrated force-fields are weakening everywhere but there."

"Any chance it weakened enough to let you go?"

There was a slight pause. "No."

A prestidigitator and his slender, golden-furred assistant suddenly appeared in midair, floating down toward the floor while performing difficult sleight-of-hand involving fire and silk cloths. They held up hoops, and acrobats bounded out of the walls to fly through them. More acrobats materialized to catch the flyers, then disappeared as soon as they were safely down. Keff watched in fascination, admiring the dramatic timing. Apparently, the spectacle failed to maintain the interest of the other guests. His chair jerked roughly forward toward Lacia, nearly ramming him through the back. The acrobats had to leap swiftly to one side to avoid being run over.

"You are a spy for a faction on the other side of Ozran, aren't you?" she demanded.

"There aren't any other factions on Ozran, madam," Keff said. "I scanned from space. All habitations are limited to this continent in the northern hemisphere and the archipelago to the southwest."

"You must have come from one of them, then," she said. "Whose spy are you?"

Just like that, the interrogation began all over again. Instead of letting him have time to answer their demands, they seemed to be vying with one another to escalate their accusations of what they suspected him of doing on Ozran. Potria, still angry, didn't bother to speak to him, but occasionally snatched him away from another magifolk just for the pleasure of seeing his gasping discomfort. Asedow joined in the game, tugging Keff away from his rival. Chaumel, too, decided to assert his authority as curator of the curiosity, pulling him away from other magifolk to prevent him answering their questions. In the turmoil, Keff spun around faster and faster, growing more irked by the moment at the magi using him as a pawn. He kept his hands clamped to his chair arms, his teeth gritted tightly as he strove to keep from being sick. Their voices chattered and shrilled like a flock of birds.

"Who are you . . . ?"

"I demand to know . . . !"

"What are you . . . ?"

"Tell me. . . ."

"How do . . . ?"

"Why . . . ?"

"What . . . ?"

Fed up at last, Keff shouted at the featureless mass of color. "Enough of this boorish interrogation. I'm not playing anymore!"

Heedless of the speed at which he was spinning, he pushed away his tray, stepped out from the footrest, and went down, down, down. . . .

✿ CHAPTER NINE

Keff fell down and down toward a dark abyss. Frigid winds screamed upward, freezing his face and his hands, which were thrust above his head by his descent. The horizontal blur that was the faces and costumes of the magifolk was replaced by a vertical blur of gray and black and tan. He was falling through a narrow tunnel of rough stone occasionally lit by streaks of garishly colored light. His hands grasped out at nothing; his feet sought for support and found none.

Gargoyle faces leered at him, gibbering. Flying creatures with dozens of clawed feet swooped down to worry his hair and shoulders. Momentum snapped his head back so he was staring up at a point of light far, far above him that swayed with every one of his heartbeats. The movement made him giddy. His stomach squeezed hard against his rib cage. He was in danger of losing what little he had been able to eat. The wind bit at his ears, and his teeth chattered. He forced his mouth closed, sought for control.

"Carialle, help! I'm falling! Where am I?"

The brain's tone was puzzled.

"You haven't moved at all, Keff. You're still in the middle of Chaumel's dining room. Everyone is watching you, and having a good time, I might add. Er, you're staring at the ceiling."

Keff tried to justify her observation with the terrifying sensation of falling, the close stone walls, and the gargoyles, and suddenly all fear fled. He was furious. The abyss was an illusion! It was all an illusion cast to punish him. Damn their manipulation!

"That is enough of this nonsense!" he bellowed.

Abruptly, all sensation stopped. The buzzing he suddenly felt through his feet bothered him, so he moved, and found himself lurching about on the slick floor, struggling for balance. With a yelp, he tripped forward, painfully bruising his palms and knees. He blinked energetically, and the points of light around him became ensconced torches, and the pale oval Plennafrey's face. She looked concerned. Keff guessed that she was the one who had broken the spell holding his mind enthralled.

"Thank you," he said. His voice sounded hollow in his own ears. He sat back on his haunches and gathered himself to stand up.

He became aware that the other magifolk were glaring at the young woman. Chaumel was angry, Nokias shocked, Potria mute with outrage. Plenna lifted her small chin and stared back unflinchingly at her superiors. Keff wondered how he had ever thought her to be weak. She was magnificent.

"Her heartbeat's up. Respiration, too. She's in trouble with them," Carialle said. "She's the junior member here— I'd say the youngest, too, by a decade—and she spoiled her seniors' fun. Naughty. Oops, more power spikes."

Keff felt insubstantial tendrils of thought trying to insinuate themselves into his mind. They were rudely slapped away by a new touch, one that felt/scented lightly of wildflowers. Plennafrey was defending him. Another sally by other minds managed to get an image of bloody, half-eaten corpses burning in a wasteland into his consciousness before they were washed out by fresh, cool air.

"Keff, what's wrong?" Carialle asked. "Adrenaline just kicked up."

"Psychic attacks," he said, through gritted teeth. "Trying to control my mind."

He fought to think of anything but the pictures hammering at his consciousness. He pictured a cold beer, until it dissolved inexorably into a river of green, steaming poison. He switched to the image of dancing in an anti-grav disco with a dozen girls. They became vulpine-winged harpies picking at his flesh as he swung on a gibbet. Keff thought deliberately of exercise, mentally pulling the Rotoflex handles to his chest one at a time, concentrating on the burn of his chest and neck muscles. Such a small focus seemed to bewilder his tormentors as they sought to corrupt that one thought and regain control.

Sooner or later the magifolk would break through, and he would never know the difference between his own consciousness and what they planted in his thoughts. He felt a twinge of despair. Nothing in his long travels had prepared him to defend himself against this kind of power. How much more could he withstand? If they continued, he'd soon be blurting out the story of his life—and his life with Carialle.

Not that—he wouldn't! Angrily, he steeled his will. If he couldn't protect himself, he couldn't guard Carialle. Even at the cost of his own life he must prevent them from finding out about her. Her danger would be worse than his, and worse than what had happened to her that time before they became partners.

The Rotoflex handles of his imagination became knives

that he plunged agonizingly again and again into his own breast. He forced his mental self to drop them. They burst into flames that rose up to burn his arms. He could feel the hair crackling on his forearms. Then a soft rain began to fall. The fire died with hisses of disappointment. Keff almost smiled. Plennafrey again.

He was grateful for the young magiwoman's intercession. How long could she hold out against the combined force of her elders? He could almost feel the mental sparks flying between Plennafrey and the others. She was actually holding her own, which was causing consternation and outrage among them. The outwardly calm standoff threatened to turn into worse.

"Small power spikes," Carialle announced. "A jab to the right. Ooh, a counter to the left. A roundhouse punch—what was that?"

Keff felt himself gripped by an invisible force. Slowly, like the rope-dancers, he began to revolve in midair, this time without his chair. He turned faster and faster and faster. What little remained of his original delight at having discovered a race of magicians was fast disappearing in the waves of nausea roiling his long-suffering stomach. He tried to touch the floor, or one of the other mages, but nothing was within reach. Faster, faster, faster he turned, until the room was divided into strata of light and color. Images began to invade his consciousness, accompanied by shrieks tinged with fear and anger, shriveling his nerves. He could feel nothing but pain, and the roaring in his head overwhelmed his other senses.

Keff felt a touch on the arm, and suddenly he was staggering weak-kneed across the slick floor behind Plennafrey. She had abandoned the battle in favor of saving him. Holding his hand firmly, she made for the open doors.

Chaumel's transparent wall proved no barrier. Plennafrey

plunged her hand under her sash to her belt, and a hole
opened in the wall just before they reached it, letting a cloud
of dust whip past them into the room. Coughing, she and
Keff dashed out onto the landing pad. Keff remembered
what Carialle had said about color coordination and ran after
the girl toward the blue-green chair at the extreme edge of
the balcony. His feet were unsteady on the humming floor,
but he forced himself to cover the distance almost on the
young woman's heels.

She threw herself into her chariot, hoisted him in, too.
Without ceremony, the chair swept off into the night.
Behind him, Keff saw other magifolk running for their
chairs. He saw Chaumel shake a fist up at them, and suddenly, the image blanked out.

They emerged into a vast, torchlit, stony cavern that
extended off into the distance to both left and right.
Plenna paused a split second and turned the chair to the
right. Her big, dark eyes were wide open, her head turning
to see first one side, then the other as they passed. Keff
hung on as the chair skipped up to miss a stalagmite and
ducked a low cave mouth. He gasped. The air tasted moist
and mineral heavy.

"Where are you?" Carialle's voice exploded in his ear.
"Damnation, I hate that!"

"Watch the volume, Cari!"

Sound level much abated, Carialle continued. "You are
approximately nine hundred meters directly below your
previous location, heading south along a huge system of
connected underground caverns. Hmm!"

"What?" he demanded, then bit his tongue as Plennafrey's chair dodged through a narrow pipe and out into a
cavern the bottom of which dropped away like the illusion-
ary abyss.

"I'm reading some of those electromagnetic lines down

there, not far from you, but not intersecting the tunnel you are currently traveling."

"Where are we going?" he asked the girl.

"Where we will be safe," she said curtly. Her forehead was wrinkled and she was hunched forward as if straining to push something with her shoulders.

"Is there something wrong?"

"It's the lee lines," she said. "Where we are is weak. I'm drawing on ones very far away. We must reach the strong ones to escape, but Chaumel stops me."

"Lee lines?" Keff said, asking for further explanation. Then a memory struck him and he sent IT running through similar-sounding names in Standard language. It came up with "ley," which it defined as "adjective, archaic, related to mystical power." Very similar, Keff noted, and turned his head to mention it.

The chair bounced, hitting a small outcropping of rock, and Keff felt his rump leave the platform. He gripped the edges until his knuckles whitened. The air whistled in his ears.

"What if you can't reach the strong ley lines?" he shouted.

"We can get most of the way to my stronghold through down here," the girl said, not looking down at him. "It will take longer, but the mountains are hollow below. Oh!"

Ahead of them, the air thickened, and a dozen chariots took shape. These swooped in at Keff and the girl, who took a hairpin curve in midair and looped back toward the narrow passage. Keff caught a glimpse of Chaumel in the lead, glittering like a star. The silver mage grinned ferociously at them.

Asedow spurred his green chariot faster to beat Chaumel to Plenna's vehicle. He succeeded only in creating a minor traffic jam blocking the neck of stone as

Plennafrey disappeared into it. By the time they straightened themselves out, their prey had a head start.

Plennafrey retraced their path through the forest of onyx pillars. Keff leaned back against her knees as she cut a particularly sharp turn to avoid the same outcropping as on the way out. Keff glanced up at her face and found it calm, intense, alert, pale and lovely as a lily. He shook his head, wondering how he had possibly missed noticing her before. He risked a quick glance back.

Far behind them, the magimen in pursuit were coming to grief amidst the stalactite clusters. Keff heard shouts of anger, then warning, and not long after, a crash. Their pursuers were down to eleven.

"The passage widens out beyond the junction where you first appeared," Carialle said, narrating from her soundings of the underground system. "Life-forms ahead."

They swooped under a low overhang that marked the boundary of the next limestone bubble cavern. Keff smelled food and squinted ahead in the torchlight. The smell of hot food blended with the cold, wet, limestone scent of the caves. Before them lay the subterranean kitchens whose existence Carialle had postulated. Compared to the frosty ambient temperature above, this place was positively tropical. Keff felt his cheeks reddening from the heat that washed them. Plennafrey turned slightly pink. Scores of fur-faced cooks and assistants hurried around like ants, carrying pots and pans to the huge, multi-burner stoves lined up against the walls or hauling full platters of cooked food to vast tables that ran down the center of the chamber.

"Natural gas, geothermal heat," Carialle said. "The catering service for the nine circles of Hell."

In one corner, discarded like toy dishes in a doll's tea set, were hundreds of bowls, plates, and platters, sent back untouched from upstairs by fussy diners.

"What a waste," Keff said as they passed over the trash heap. The reeking fumes of deteriorating food made his eyes water. He gasped.

Avoiding a low point in the ceiling, the chariot bore down on the cooks, who dropped their pans and dishes and dove for cover. The bottom of the runner struck something soft, but kept going. Keff glanced behind them and saw the ruins of a tall cake and the pastry chef's stricken face.

"Sorry!" Keff called.

Behind them, the magimen on their chariots swooped into the cavern, shouting for Plennafrey to surrender her prize. Bolts of red fire struck past them, impacting the stone walls with explosive reports. Chunks of stone rained down on the screaming cooks. Plennafrey jerked the chariot downward, and a lightning stroke passed over them, shattering a stalactite into bits just before they reached it. Keff threw his hands up before his face just a split second too late, and ended up spitting out limestone sand.

"Don't damage anything!" Chaumel yelled. "My kitchen!" Keff saw him frantically making warding symbols with his hands, sending spells to protect his property.

Plennafrey stole a look over her shoulder and poured on the speed. She pulled Keff's body back against her legs. He looked up at her for explanation.

She said, "I need my hands," and immediately began weaving her own enchantments in a series of complex passes. Keff braced himself between the end of the chariot back and the chair legs to keep Plennafrey from bouncing out of her seat.

The cavern narrowed sharply at its far end, forcing them farther and farther toward the floor. Fur-faced Noble Primitives who had been throwing themselves down to get out of their way went entirely flat or slammed into the wall as Plennafrey's chariot flashed by. Females shrieked and males let out hoarse-voiced cries of alarm.

Scarlet fire ricocheted from wall to wall, missing the blue-green chariot by hand-spans. The young magiwoman launched off fist-sized globes of smoky nothingness, flinging them behind her back. Keff, intent on the wall above the cave mouth zooming toward them, heard cries and protests, followed by a series of explosive puffs.

Plennafrey resumed control of her chair just in time to direct them sharply down and into the stone tunnel. This must have been the central corridor of Chaumel's underground complex. Hundreds of Noble Primitives dropped their burdens and dove for cover as he and Plennafrey zoomed through. Skillfully zigzagging, dipping, and rising, she avoided each living being and stone pillar in the long tube.

"She's good on this thing," Keff confided to Carialle. "What a rocket-cycle jockey she'd make."

To right and left, several smaller tunnels offered themselves. Plennafrey glanced at each one as they passed. With the inadequate light of torches, Keff could see no details more than a dozen feet up each one. The magiwoman bit her lip, then banked a turn into the ninth right.

"Keff, not that one!" Carialle said urgently.

"Aha!"

Keff heard Chaumel's crow of victory, and view-halloo cries from the other pursuers. He wondered why they sounded so pleased.

Plenna dodged against the left wall to avoid colliding with a grossly-wheeled wagon pulled by six-packs and piled high with garbage. There was barely enough space for both of them, but somehow the magiwoman made it by. After a short interval, Keff heard a few loud scrapes, and a couple of hard splats, followed by furious and derisive yells. Two more magimen would be abandoning the race as they went home to clean refuse out of their gorgeous robes. Another scrape ended in a sickening-sounding crunch. Keff guessed the magiman on that chariot had misjudged the space between the cart and the wall. That left eight in pursuit. Keff risked a glance. The silver glimmer at the front was Chaumel, and behind him the dark green of Asedow, the pink-gold of Potria, Nokias's gold, and the shadow that was Ferngal were grouped in his wake. More ranged behind them, but he couldn't identify them.

Plennafrey wound her way through the irregular, narrowing corridor, tossing spells over her shoulder to slow her pursuers.

"I would turn around and weave a web to snare them," she said, "but I dare not take my eyes off our path."

"I agree with you wholeheartedly, lady," Keff said. "Keep your eyes on the road. Look, it's lighter up ahead."

A lessening of the gloom before them suggested a larger chamber, with more room to maneuver. Plenna crested the high threshold and let out a moan of dismay. The room widened out into a big cavern, but it was as smooth and featureless as a bubble. Racks and racks of bottles lined the lower half of the walls. No spaces between them suggested any way out.

"A dead end," Keff said, in a flat tone. "We're in Chaumel's wine cellar. No wonder he was gloating."

"I was trying to tell you," Carialle spoke up in a contrite voice. "You weren't listening."

"I'm sorry, Cari. It was a wild ride," Keff said.

Plennafrey turned in a loop that brought Keff's heart up into his throat and made for the narrow entrance, but it was suddenly filled by Chaumel and the rest of the posse. Plennafrey reversed her chair until she was hovering in the center of the room. Eight chairs surrounded her, looking like a hanging jury.

" . . . And it looks like it's over."

"There you are, my friends. You left us too soon," Chaumel said. "Magess Plennafrey, you overreached yourself. You misunderstand how reluctant we are to allow such prizes as this stranger and his tower to be won by the least of our number."

Keff felt Plenna's knees tighten against his back.

"Perhaps he does not want to be anyone's property," she said. "I will leave him his freedom."

"You do not have the right to make that choice, Magess," Nokias said. He stretched out his arms and planted one big hand across the ring that encircled his other wrist. Keff braced himself as red bolts shot out of the bracelet, enveloping him and the floating chair.

An invisible rod collected the bolts, diverting them harmlessly down into nothingness. The astonished look on Nokias's face said that he neither expected Plennafrey to defy him nor to be able to counteract his attack.

"That's what hit you on the plain," Carialle whispered in Keff's ear. "Same frequency. It must have been Nokias. My, he looks surprised."

The other magimen lifted their objects of power, preparing an all-out assault on their errant member.

"Please, friends," Chaumel said, moving between them toward the wary pair in the center. His eyes were glowing with a mad, inner light. "Allow me."

He took the wand from the sleeve on his belt and raised it. Keff glanced up at Plennafrey. The magiwoman, glaring defiance, began to wind up air in her arms.

"I see what she's doing," Carialle said, her voice alarmed. "Keff, tell her not to teleport again. I won't—"

The cavern exploded in a brilliant white flash.

Except for the absence of eight angry magimen, Keff and Plennafrey might not have moved. They were in the center of a globe hewn from the bare rock. Then Keff noticed that the walls were rougher and the ceiling not so high. Plennafrey hastily brought the chair to earth. She sighed a deep breath of relief. Keff seconded it.

He sprang up and offered her his hand. With a small smile, she reached out and took it, allowing him to assist her from the chair.

"My lady, I want to thank you very sincerely for saving my life," Keff said, bowing over their joined hands. When he looked up, Plenna was pink, but whether with pleasure or embarrassment Keff wasn't sure.

"I could not let them treat you like chattel," she said. "I feel you are a true man for all you are not one of us."

"A true man offers homage to a true lady," Keff said, bowing again. Plennafrey freed herself and turned away, clutching her hand against herself shyly. Keff smiled.

"What pretty manners you have," Carialle's voice said. It sounded thin and very far away. "You're forty-five degrees of planetary arc away from your previous location. I just had time to trace you before your power burst dissipated. You're in a small bubble pocket along another one of those long cavern complexes. What is this place?"

"I was just about to ask that." Keff looked around him. "Lady, where are we?"

Unlike Chaumel's wine cellar, this place didn't smell overpoweringly of wet limestone and yeast. The slight mineral scent of the air mixed with a fragrant, powdery perfume. Though large, the room had the sensation of intimacy. A comfortable-looking, overstuffed chair sprawled in the midst of little tables, fat floor pillows, and toy animals. Against one wall, a small bed lay securely tucked up beneath a thick but worn counterpane beside a table of trinkets. Above it, a hanging lamp with a cobalt-blue shade, small and bright like a jewel, glowed comfortingly. Keff knew it to be the private bower of a young lady who had taken her place as an adult but was not quite ready to give up precious childhood treasures.

"It is my . . . place," Plennafrey said. IT missed the adjective, but Keff suspected the missing word was "secret" or "private." Seeing the young woman's shy pride, he felt sure no other eyes but his had ever seen this sanctuary. "We are safe here."

"I'm honored," Keff said sincerely, returning his gaze to Plennafrey. She smiled at him, watchful. He glanced down at the bedside shelf, chose a circular frame from which the images of several people projected slightly. He picked it up, brought it close to his eyes for Carialle to analyze.

"Holography," Carialle said at once. "Well, not exactly. Similar effect, but different technique."

Keff turned the frame in his hands. The man standing at the rear was tall and thin, with black hair and serious eyebrows. He had his hands on the shoulders of two boys who resembled him closely. The small girl in the center of the grouping had to be a younger version of Plennafrey. "Your family?"

"Yes."

"Handsome folks. Where do they live?"

She looked away. "They're all dead," she said.

"I am sorry," Keff said.

Plennafrey turned her face back toward him, and her eyes were red, the lashes fringed with tears. She fumbled with the long, metallic sash, lifted it up over her head, and flung it as far across the room as she could. It jangled against the wall and slithered to the floor.

"I hate what that means. I hate being a magess. I would have been so happy if not for . . ." IT tried to translate her speech, and fell back to suggesting roots for the words she used. None of it made much sense to Keff, but Carialle interrupted him.

"I think she killed them, Keff," she said, alarmed. "Didn't Chaumel say that the only way to advance in the ranks was by stealing artifacts and committing murder? You're shut up in a cave with a madwoman. Don't make her angry. Get out of there."

"I don't believe that," Keff said firmly. "They all died, you said? Do you want to tell me about it?" He took both the girl's hands in his. She flinched, trying to pull away, but Keff, with a kind, patient expression, kept a steady, gentle pressure on her wrists. He led her to the overstuffed footrest and made her sit down. "Tell me. Your family died, and you inherited the power objects they had, is that right? You don't mean you were actually instrumental in their deaths."

"I do," Plenna said, her nose red. "I did it. My father was a very powerful mage. He . . . ed Nokias himself."

"Rival," IT rapped out crisply. Keff nodded.

"They both wished the position of Mage of the South, but Nokias took it. Losing the office troubled him. Over days and days—time, he went—" Helplessly, she fluttered fingers in the vicinity of her temple, not daring to say the word out loud.

"He went mad," Keff said. Plenna dropped her eyes.

"Yes. He swore he would rival the Ancient Ones. Then he decided having children had diminished his power. He wanted to destroy us to get it back."

"Horrible," Keff said. "He *was* mad. No one in his right mind would ever think of killing his children."

"Don't say that!" Plennafrey begged him. "I loved my father. He had to keep his position. You don't know what it's like on Ozran. Any sign of weakness, and someone else will . . . step in."

"Go on," Keff said gravely. Aided occasionally by IT, Plennafrey continued.

"There is not much to tell. Father tried many rituals to

build up his connection with the Core of Ozran and thereby increase his power, but they were always unsuccessful. One day, two years ago, I was studying ley lines, and I felt hostile power stronging up. . . ."

"Building up," interjected IT.

"As I had been taught to do, I defended myself, making power walls. . . ."

"Warding?" Keff asked, listening to IT's dissection of the roots of her phrase.

"Yes, and feeding power back along the lines from which they came. There was more than I had ever felt." The girl's pupils dilated, making her eyes black as she relived the scene. "I was out on our balcony. Then I was surrounded by hot fire. I built up and threw the power away from me as hard as I could. It took all the strength I had. The power rushed back upon its sender. It went past me into our stronghold. I felt an explosion inside our home. That was when I knew what I had done. I ran." Her face was pale and haunted. "The door of my father's sanctum was blown outward. My brothers lay in the hall beyond. All dead. All dead. And all my fault." Tears started running down her cheeks. She dabbed at them with the edge of a yellow sleeve. "Nokias and the others came to the stronghold. They said I had made my first coup. I had achieved the office of magess. I didn't want it. I had force-killed my family."

"But you didn't do it on purpose," Keff said, feeling in his tunic pocket for a handkerchief and extending it to her. "It was an accident."

"I could have let my father succeed. Then he and my brothers might be alive," Plennafrey said. "I should have known." A tear snaked down her cheek. Angrily, she wiped her eye and sat with the cloth crumpled in her fists.

"You fought for your life. That's normal. You shouldn't have to sacrifice yourself for anyone's power grab."

"But he was my father! I respected his will. Is it not like that where you live?" the girl asked.

"No," Keff said with more emphasis than he intended. "No father would do what he did. To us, life is sacred."

Plenna stared at her hands. She gave a little sigh. "I wish I lived there, too."

"I hate this world more than ever," said Carialle, for whom special intervention to save her life had begun before she was born. "Corruption is rewarded, child murder not even blinked at; power is the most important thing, over family, life, sanity. Let's have them put an interdict on this place when we get out of here. They haven't got space travel, so we don't have to worry about them showing up in the Central Worlds for millenia more to come."

"We have to get out of here first," Keff reminded her. "Perhaps we can help them to straighten things out before we go."

Carialle sighed. "Of course you're right, knight in shining armor. Whatever we can do, we should. I simply cannot countenance what this poor girl went through."

Keff turned to Plennafrey. She stared down toward the floor, not seeing it, but thinking of her past.

"Please, Plennafrey," Keff said, imbuing the Ozran phrases with as much persuasive charm in his voice as possible, "I'm new to your world. I want to learn about you and your people. You interest me very much. What is this?" he asked, picking up the nearest unidentifiable gewgaw.

Distracted, she looked up. Keff held the little cylinder up to her, and she smiled.

"It is a music," she said. At her direction, he shook the box back and forth, then set it down. The sides popped open, and a sweet, tinny melody poured out. "I have had that since, oh, since a child."

"Is it old?"

"Oh, a few generations. My father's father's father," she giggled, counting on her fingers, "made it for his wife."

"It's beautiful. And what's this?" Keff got up and reached for a short coiled string and the pendant bauble at the end of it. The opaline substance glittered blue, green, and red in the lamplight.

"It's a plaything," Plennafrey said, with a hint of her natural vitality returning to her face. "It takes some skill to use. No magic. I am very good with it. My brothers were never as skilled."

"Show me," Keff said. She stood up beside him and wound the string around the central core of the pendant. Inserting her forefinger through the loop at the string's end, she cradled the toy, then threw it. It spooled out and smacked back into her palm. She flicked it again, but this time moved her hand so the pendant ricocheted past her head, dove between their knees, then shot back into her hand.

"A yo-yo!" Keff said, delighted.

"You have such things?" Plennafrey asked. She smiled up into his face.

Keff grinned. "Oh, yes. This is far nicer than the ones I used to play with. In fact, it's a work of art. Can I try?"

"All right." Plenna peeled the string off her finger and extended the toy to him. He accepted it, his hands cradling hers for just a moment. He did a few straight passes with the yo-yo, then made it fly around the world, then swung it in a trapeze.

"You are very good, too," Plenna said, happily. "Will you show me how you did the last thing?"

"It would be my pleasure," Keff told her. He returned the toy to her hands. As his palms touched hers, he felt an almost electric shock. He became aware they were standing very close, their thighs brushing slightly so that he could feel the heat of her body. Her breath caught, then came more quickly. His respiration sped up to match hers. To his delight and astonishment he knew that she was as attracted to him as he was to her. The yo-yo slipped unnoticed to the hassock as he clasped her hands tightly. She smiled at him, her eyes full of trust and wonder. Before she said a word, his arms slid along hers, encompassing her narrow waist, hands flat against her back. She didn't protest, but pressed her slim body to his. He felt her quiver slightly, then she nestled urgently against him, settling her head on his shoulder. Her skin was warm through the thin stuff of her dress, and her flowery, spicy scent tantalized him.

She felt so natural in his arms he had to remind himself that she was an alien being, then he discarded inhibition. If things didn't work out physically, well, they were sharing the intense closeness of people who had been in danger together, a kind of comfort in itself. Yet he let himself believe that all would be as he desired it. There were too many other outward similarities to humanity in Plennafrey's people. With luck, they made love the same way.

Plennafrey had none of the seductive art of the gauze-draped Potria, but he found her genuine responsiveness much more desirable. While her elders were tormenting Keff, it had probably not occurred to her to think of him as anything but an abused "toy."

She was merely being kind to an outsider, or less charitably, to a dumb animal that couldn't defend itself. Now that they were together, intriguing chemistry bubbled up between them. He watched the long fringe of her lashes lift to reveal her large, dark eyes. He admired the long throat and the way her pulse jumped in the small shadow at the hollow inside her collarbone. The corners of her mouth lifted while she, too, stopped to study him.

"What are you thinking?" he asked, looking up at her.

"I am thinking that you are handsome," she said.

"Well, you are very beautiful, lady magess," he whispered, bending down to kiss the curve of her shoulder.

"I hate being a magess," Plennafrey said in a voice that was nearly a sob.

"But I am glad you are a magess," Keff said. "If you hadn't been, I would never have met you, and you are the nicest thing I have seen since I came to Ozran."

He put his hand under her chin, stroked her soft throat with a gentle finger like petting a cat. Almost felinely, Plenna closed her eyes to long slits and let her head drift back, looking like she wanted to purr. She raised her face to his, and her hand crept up the back of his neck to pull his head down to her level. Keff tasted cherries and cinnamon on her lips, delighted to lose himself in her perfume. He deepened the kiss, and Plenna responded with ardor. He bent down to kiss the curve of her shoulder, felt her brush her cheek against his ear.

Suddenly she let go of him and stepped back, looking up at him half-expectantly, half-afraid. Keff gathered up her hands and kissed them, pulled Plenna close, and brushed her lips with soft, feather-light caresses until they opened. She sighed.

"Sight and sound off, please, Cari," Keff whispered. Plennafrey nestled her head into the curve of his shoulder, and he kissed her.

Carialle considered for a moment before shutting off the sensory monitors. While in a potentially hostile environment, especially with hostiles in pursuit, it was against Courier Service rules to break off all communications.

The Ozran female let out a wordless cry, and Keff matched it with a heartfelt moan. Carialle weighed the requirement with Keff's right to privacy and decided a limited signal wasn't unreasonable. Such a request was permissible as long as the brain maintained some kind of contact with her brawn partner.

"As you wish, my knight errant," she said, hastily turning off the eye and mouth implants. She monitored transmission of his cardial and pulmonary receivers instead. They were getting a strenuous workout.

With her brawn otherwise occupied, Carialle turned her attention to the outside of Ozran. Most of the power and radio signals were still clustered on and inside Chaumel's peak. Each magiman and magiwoman proved to have a slightly different radio frequency which she or he used for communication, so Carialle could distinguish them. The eight remaining hunters who had pursued Keff and his girlfriend down the subterranean passages fanned out again and again across the planetary surface, and regrouped. The search was proving futile. Carialle mentally sent them a raspberry.

"Bad luck, you brutes," she said, merrily.

On the plain, the eye-globes came out of nowhere and circled around and around her. Carialle peered at each one closely, and recorded its burblings to the others through IT. Keff was building up a pretty good Ozran vocabulary and grammar, so she could understand the messages of frustration and fury that they broadcast to one another.

Some time later, Keff's heartbeat slowed down to its resting rate. His brain waves showed he had drifted off to sleep. Carialle occupied herself in the hours before dawn by doing maintenance on her computer systems and keeping an eye on the hunters who had to be wearing themselves out by now.

Carialle gave Keff a decent interval to wipe out sleep toxins, and then switched on again. Her video monitors beside his eyes offered her a most romantic tableau.

On the small bed against the bower wall, the young

magiwoman was cuddled up against Keff's body. They were both naked, and his dark-haired, muscular arm was thrown protectively over her narrow, pale waist. Their ankles overlapped and then he started running a toe up and down her calf. Carialle took the opportunity to scan Keff's companion and found her readings of great interest.

Keff snorted softly, the sound he always made when he was on the edge of wakefulness.

"Ahem!" Carialle said, just loudly enough to alert, but not loud enough to startle Keff. "Are you certain this is what Central Worlds means by first contact?"

Keff gave a deep and throaty chuckle. "Ah, but it *was* first contact, my lady," he said, allowing her to infer the double or triple entendre.

"A gentleman never kisses and tells, you muscled ape," Carialle chided him. He laughed softly. The girl stirred slightly in her sleep, and her hand settled upon the hair on his chest. She smiled gently, dreaming. "Keff, I have something I need to tell you about Plennafrey, in fact about all the Ozrans: they're human."

"Very similar, but they're humanity's cousins," Keff corrected her. "And wait until I show the tapes to Xeno. Not of this, of course. They'll go wild."

"She *is* human, Keff. She must be the descendant of some lost colony or military ship that landed here eons ago. Her reactions, both emotional and bodily, let alone blood pressure, structure, systems—she was close enough to your contact implants for me to make sure. And I *am* sure. We have met the Ozrans, and they is us."

"Genetic scan?" Keff was disappointed. Carialle could tell he was still hoping, but he was a good enough exobiologist to realize he knew it himself.

"Bring me a lock of her hair, and I'll prove it."

"Oh, well," he said, gathering Plennafrey closer and tucking her head into his shoulder. "I can still rejoice in having found a mutation of humanity that has such powerful TK abilities."

Carialle sighed. Bless his stubbornness, she thought.

"It's not TK. It's sophisticated tool-using. Take away her toys and see if she can do any of her magic tricks."

Keff reached over the edge of the small bed and picked up the heavy belt by its buckle. He weighed it in his hand, then let it slip on his palm so his fingers were pointing toward the five depressions. "Does that mean I can use these things, too?"

"I should say so."

The links of the belt clanked softly together. The slight noise was enough to wake the young magiwoman in alarm. She sat up, her large eyes scanning the chamber.

"Who is here?" she asked. Keff held out her belt to her and she snatched it protectively.

"Only me," Keff said. "I'm sorry. I wanted to see how it worked. I didn't mean to wake you up."

Plenna looked apologetic for having overreacted to simple curiosity, and offered the belt to him with both hands and a warning. "We mustn't use it here. It is the reason that my bower is secure. We are just on the very edge of the ley lines, so my belt buckle and sash resonate too slightly to be noticed by any other mage." She swept a hand around. "Everything in this room was brought here by hand. Or fashioned by hand from new materials, using no power."

"That's in the best magical tradition," Keff noted approvingly. "That means there's no 'vibes' left over from previous users. In this case, tracers or finding spells."

"Or circuits," Carialle said. "How does their magic work?"

Her question went unanswered. Before Keff could relay it to Plenna, he found himself gawking up toward the ceiling. As neatly as a conjurer pulling handkerchiefs out of his sleeve, the air disgorged Chaumel's flying chair, followed by Potria's, then Asedow's. Chaumel swooped low over the bed. The silver mage glared at them through bloodshot eyes.

"What a pretty place," he said, showing all his teeth in a mirthless grin. "I'll want to investigate it later on." He eyed Plennafrey's slender nakedness with an arrogant possessiveness. "Possibly with your . . . close assistance, my lady. You've been having a nice time while we've looked everywhere for you!"

Keff and Plennafrey scrambled for their clothes. One by one, the other hunters appeared, crowding the low bubble of stone.

"Ah, the chase becomes interesting again," Potria said. She didn't look her best. The chiffon of her gown drooped limply like peach-colored lettuce, and her eye makeup had smeared from lines to bruises. "I was getting so *bored* running after shadows."

"Yes, the prey emerges once again," Chaumel said. "But this time the predators are ready."

Plenna glared at Chaumel as she threw her primrose dress over her head.

"We should never have traveled in here by chair," she snarled. Keff stepped into his trousers and yanked on his right boot.

"That is correct," Chaumel said, easily, sitting back with his abnormally long fingers tented on his belly. "It took us some time to find the vein by which the heart of Ozran fed your power, but we have you at last. We will pass judgment on you later, young magess, but at this moment, we wish our prize returned to us."

The two stood transfixed as Nokias, Ferngal, and Omri slid their chairs into line beside their companion.

"Your disobedience will have to be paid for," Nokias said sternly to Plenna.

The young woman bowed her head, clasping her belt

and sash in her hands. "I apologize for my disrespect, High Mage," she said, contritely. Keff was shocked by her sudden descent into submissiveness.

Nokias smiled, making Keff want to ram the mage's teeth down his skinny throat. "My child, you were rash. I can forgive."

The golden chair angled slightly, making to set down in the clear space between Plenna's small bed and her table. With lightning reflexes, Plennafrey grabbed Keff's hand, jumped over the lower limb of the chair, and dashed for her own chair. Clutching his armload of clothes and one boot, Keff had a split second to brace himself as Plenna launched the blue-green chariot into the gap left by Nokias and zoomed out into one of the tunnels that led out of the bubble.

Keff threw his legs around the edges of Plennafrey's chariot to brace himself while he shrugged into his tunic. The strap of the IT box was clamped tightly in his teeth. He disengaged it, dragged it out from under his shirt, and put it around his neck where it belonged. His boot would have to wait.

"Well done, my lady," he shouted. His voice echoed off the walls of the small passage that wound, widened, and narrowed about them.

"How *dare* they invade my sanctum!" Plennafrey fumed. Instead of being frightened by the appearance of the other mages, she was furious. "It goes beyond discourtesy. It is—like invading my mind! How *dare* they? Oh, I feel so stupid for teleporting in. I should never have done that."

"I'm responsible again, Plenna," Keff said contritely. He hung on as she negotiated a sharp turn. He pulled his legs up just in time. The edge of the chair almost nipped a stone outcropping. Plennafrey's hand settled softly on his shoulder, and he reached up to squeeze it. "You were saving my life."

"Oh, I do not blame you, Keff," she said. "If only I had been thinking clearly. It is all my fault. You couldn't know what I should have kept in mind, what I have been trained in all my life!" Her hand tightened in his, and he let it go. "It is just that now I don't know where we can go."

The posse was once again in pursuit. Keff heard shouting and bone-chilling scrapes as the hunters organized themselves a single-file line and attempted to follow. This tunnel was narrower than the ones underneath Chaumel's castle. A fallen stalactite aimed a toothlike pike at them, which Plenna dodged with difficulty. She scraped a few shards of wood off the side of her vehicle on the opposite wall. Keff curled his legs up under his chin away from the edge and prayed he wouldn't bounce off.

"Usually I enter on foot," Plenna said apologetically. "A chair was never meant to pass this way."

Keff was sure that Chaumel and the others were figuring that out now. The swearing and crashing sounds were getting louder and more emphatic. If Plenna wasn't such a good pilot, they'd be coming to grief on the rocks, too.

"Can't we teleport out of here?" Keff asked.

"We can't teleport out of a place," Plenna said, staring ahead of them. "Only in. Almost there. Hold on."

Keff, gripping the legs of her chair, got brief impressions of a series of vast caverns and corkscrewing passages as they looped and flitted through a passage that wound in an ever-widening spiral without the walls ever spreading farther apart. To Keff's relief, they emerged into the open air. They were over a steep-sided, narrow, dry riverbed bounded by dun-colored brush and scrub trees. He had a mere glimpse of the partly-concealed stone niche where Plenna almost certainly landed her chair when here by herself, then they were out over the ravine heading into the sunrise. Keff's stomach turned over when he realized how high up they were. He chided himself for a practical coward; he wasn't afraid of heights in vacuum, but where gravity ruled, he was acrophobic.

He turned at the sound of a shout. Through a lucky fluke, Chaumel and Asedow were almost immediately behind them. The others were probably still trying to get out of Plenna's labyrinth, or had crashed into the stone walls. As soon as he was clear, Asedow raised his mace. Red fire lanced out at them. Plenna, apparently intuiting where Asedow would strike, dodged up and down, slewing sideways to let the beams pass. The dry brush of the deep river vale smoldered and caught fire.

Chaumel was more subtle. Keff felt something creep into his mind and take hold. He suddenly thought he was being carried in the jaws of a dragon. Fiery breath crept along his back and into his hair, growing hotter. The fierce, white teeth were about to bite down on him, severing his legs. He groaned, clenching his jaws, as he fought the illusion's hold on his mind. The image vanished in the sweet breeze Keff had come to associate with Plenna, but it was followed immediately by another horrible illusion. She batted it away at once without losing her concentration on the battle. Chaumel was ready with the next sally.

"Don't want them taking my mind!" Keff ground out, battling images of clutching octopi with needle-sharp teeth set in a ring.

"Concentrate, Keff," Carialle said. "Those devious bastards can't find a crack if you keep your focus small. Think of an equation. Six to the eighth power is . . . ?"

"Times six is thirty six, times six is two hundred sixteen, times six is . . ." Keff recited.

Plennafrey started forming small balls of gray nothingness between her hands. Her chair wheeled on its own axis, bringing her face-to-face with her pursuers. They peeled off to the sides like expert dog-fighters, but not before she had flung her spells at them. Explosions echoed down the valley. Ferngal's chair tipped over backward, sending him plummeting into the ravine. Keff heard his cry before the magiman vanished in midair. The black chair vanished, too. Nokias zoomed in toward them, his hand laid across his spell-casting ring. Plenna threw up a wall of protection just in time to shield them from the scarlet lightning.

"Divided by fourteen is . . . ? Come on!" Carialle said. "To the nearest integer."

One by one, the last three mages appeared out of the cave mouth and joined in the aerial battle. Keff couldn't watch Plenna weaving spells anymore because the webs made him think of giant spiders, which the illusion-casters made creep toward him, threatening to eat him. He drove them away with numbers.

"How long is a ninety-five kilohertz radio wave?" Carialle pressed him. "Keff, late-breaking headline: a couple hundred chariots just left Chaumel's residence. They're *all* coming for you. Teleporting . . . now!"

"We're too vulnerable," Keff shouted hoarsely. "If they get through to my mind the way they did in the banquet hall, I'll end up their plaything. If they don't shoot us first!"

All six of the remaining mages positioned themselves around Plenna like the sides of a cube, converging on her, throwing their diverse spells and illusions. Hands flying, Plennafrey warded herself and Keff in a translucent globe of energy. Carialle's voice became suffused with static.

Suddenly, the chair under him dropped. Spells and lightning bolts, along with the shield-globe, vanished. The sides of the ravine shot upward like the stone walls in his nightmare.

"What happened?" he shouted. All the other mages were falling, too, their faces frozen with fear. Before his question was completely out of his mouth, the terrifying fall ceased. Keff felt his hair crackle with static electricity, and bright sparks seemed to fly around all the mages' chariots. Unhesitatingly, Plenna angled her chair upward, flying out of the canyon. She crested the ridge and ran flat out toward the east. "What was that?"

"Didn't you pay the power bill?" Carialle asked, in his ear. "That was a full blackout, a tremendous drop along the electromagnetic lines. I think you overloaded the circuits of whatever's powering them, but they're back on line. Fortunately, it got everybody at once, not just you."

"Are you all right?" Keff asked.

The yearning and frustration in the brain's voice was unmistakable. "For that one moment I was free, but *un*fortunately I was too slow to take off! All the power on the planet is draining toward you—even the plants seem to be losing their color. Everyone is out in full force after you. Keff, get her to bring you here!"

Like a hive of angry hornets, swarms of chariots poured over the ridge in pursuit. Scarlet bolts whipped past Keff's ear. He grabbed Plennafrey's knee, and turned his face up to her.

"Plenna, if you can't teleport out, we have to teleport *into* somewhere—my ship!" She nodded curtly.

Over his head, the girl's arms wove and wove. Keff watched the mass of chairs fill the air behind them. He prayed they wouldn't suffer another magical blackout.

"Great Mother Planet of Paradise, aid me!" Plenna threw up her arms, and the whole scene, angry magicians and all, vanished.

¤ CHAPTER TEN

Plonk! The chariot was abruptly surrounded by the walls of Carialle's main cabin.

"That was a tight fit," Carialle remarked on her main speaker. "You're nearly close enough to the bulkhead to meld with the paint."

"But we made it," Keff said, scrambling out. Gratefully, he stretched his legs and reached high over his head with joined hands until his back cracked in seven places. "Ahhh . . ."

Plenna rose and stared around her in wonder. "Yes, we made it. So this is what the tower looks like inside. It is like a home, but so many strange things!"

"I think she likes it," Carialle said, approvingly.

"Well, what's not to like?" Keff said. "Are the magimen still coming?"

"They don't know where you've gone. They'll figure it out soon enough, but I'm generating white noise to mask my interior. It's making the spy-eyes crazy, but that's all right with me, the nasty little metal mosquitoes."

"It is *not* you talking," Plennafrey said, watching his lips as Carialle made her latest statement. "There *is* a second voice, a female's. Your tower can speak?"

Keff, realizing the habits of fourteen years were stronger than discretion, glanced at Carialle's pillar and pulled an apologetic face.

"Oops," Carialle said.

"Er, it's not a tower, Plenna. It's a ship," Keff explained.

"And it's not his. It's mine." Carialle manifested her Myths and Legends image of the Lady Fair on the main screen. With tremendous and admirable self-control, Plennafrey just caught her mouth before it could drop open. She eyed the gorgeous silhouette, evidently contrasting her own disheveled costume unfavorably with the rose-colored gauze and satin of the Lady.

"You're . . . only a picture," Plenna said at last.

"You want me three-dimensional?" Cari said, making her image "step" off the wall and assume a moving holographic image. She held out her hands, making her long sleeves flutter with a whisper of silk. "As you wish. But I am real. I exist inside the walls of this ship. I am the other half of Keff's team. My name is Carialle."

The fierce expression Plenna wore told Carialle that Plenna was jealous of all things pertaining to Keff. That needed to be handled when the crisis had passed. To the magiwoman's credit, she understood that, too.

"I greet you, Carialle," Plenna said politely.

"She's a winner, Keff," Cari said, pitching her statement for Keff's mastoid implant only. "Pretty, too. And just a little taller than you are. That must have made things interesting."

Keff colored satisfactorily. "Now that we're all acquainted, we have to talk seriously before Chaumel and his Wild Hunt catch up with us. What in the name of Daylight Savings Time just happened out there?"

"I have never seen the High Mages so . . . so insane,"

Plennafrey offered, shaking her head. "They have gone beyond reason."

"That's not what I mean," Keff said. "The magic stopped all at once when we were hanging over that riverbed."

"It has happened before," Plenna said, nodding gravely. "But not when I was in the sky. That was terrible."

"The huge drain on power obviously caused some kind of imbalance in the system," Carialle said. She plotted a chair for her image to sit down on and gestured for the other two to seat themselves. "The drop came after the whole grid of what the lady called 'ley lines' bottomed out all over the planet. There was, for an instant, no more power to call. It came back after you all suffered a kind of blackout. Look."

In their midst, Carialle projected a two-meter, three-dimensional image of Ozran, showing the ley lines etched in purple over the dun, green, and blue globe. Geographical features, including individual peaks and valleys on the continents, took shape.

"Oh," Plenna breathed, recognizing some of the terrain. "Is this what Ozran looks like?"

"That's right," Keff said.

"How wonderful," she said, beaming at Carialle for the first time. "To be able to make beautiful pictures like that."

Carialle ducked her head politely, acknowledging the compliment.

"Thank you, miss. Now, this is the normal flow of those mysterious electromagnetic waves. Here's what happened when you got that blast of dust in Chaumel's stronghold."

The translucent globe turned until the large continent in the northern hemisphere was facing Keff and Plennafrey. The dark lines thickened toward a peak on a mountain spine in the southeast region, thinning everywhere else. What remained were small "peaks" on the lines here and there. "I think these are the mages who didn't come to dinner. Now here"—the configurations changed slightly, the bulges shifting southward— "is what happened when you escaped from the dinner party. And this next matches the moment when you teleported to Magess Plennafrey's sanctum sanctorum."

The purple lines performed complicated dances. First, a slight bulge opened out in lines near a river valley in the southernmost mountain range of the continent, corresponding to a slight drop in the forces in the southeast. Chaumel's peak was nearly invisible amidst the power lines, until the mages dispersed to points all over Ozran. Occasionally, they reconverged.

"This big spike indicated when the eight mages found Plennafrey's hidey-hole," Carialle said, narrating, "followed by the big one when everyone came to see the fun. Here comes the chase scene. A huge buildup as the others left Chaumel's peak. And—"

Abruptly, the lines thinned, some even disappearing for a moment.

"That has happened before," Plenna repeated. "Not often, but more often now than before."

"Absolute power corrupts, and I'm not just talking about political." Carialle finished the ley geographic review.

"Can you run that image again, Cari?" Keff said, leaning close to study it. "Magic shouldn't cause imbalances in planetary fields."

"But it does, depending on where it comes from," Carialle said. "What's it for? Why is there a worldwide network of force lines? It must have been put here for a reason." She turned to Plenna. "Where does *your* power come from, Magess?"

"Why, from my belt amulet," Plennafrey explained, displaying the heavy buckle. "The sash is an amulet, too, but it was my father's, and I don't like to use it." She undid her waist cincture and held it out to Carialle.

Carialle had her image shake its head. "I'm not solid, sweetie." Instead, she directed the artifact to Keff. Carialle turned on an intense spotlight in the ceiling and aimed it so she and her brawn could have a better look. Keff turned the belt over in his hands. Carialle zoomed in a camera eye to microscopic focus.

The five indentations were there, as Chaumel had said, part of the original design. The buckle had been adapted for wear by some unknown metal smith at least eight hundred years ago, Carialle judged by a quick analysis. Braces and a tongue had been welded to its sides. The whole thing comprised approximately ninety cubic centimeters, and was plated with fine gold, which accounted for its retaining a noncorroded surface over the centuries. Carialle recorded all data in accessible memory.

"Can you teach me how to use it?" Keff asked, smiling hopefully at her. Plennafrey seemed uneasy, but allowed herself to be persuaded by the fatal Von Scoyk-Larsen charm.

"Well, all right," she said. "I'll trust you." Her expression said that she didn't trust often or easily. Such behavior on this world, Carialle noted, would not be a survival trait.

Plenna stood behind Keff and showed him how to place his fingers in the depressions. "Do not push down, not . . . solidly," she said.

"Physically," Keff corrected IT's translation. He cradled the buckle in his other hand, raising it to eye level.

"Correct," Plenna said, unaware of the box's simultaneous transmission as she spoke. "Imagine your fingers pressing deep into the heart, where they will contact the Core of Ozran."

"Is that why you wear the finger extensions?" Keff asked, after trying to fit his hand into the depressions. His thumb and little finger had to curve unnaturally to touch all five spots, while Plenna, with her pinky prosthesis, could cover them without effort, bending only her thumb.

"Yes. Most mages do not have fingers long enough. It is one way in which we are inferior to the great Ancient Ones who left us these tools," Plenna said with a trace of awe. "Now, think hard. Do you feel the fire inside? It should run up inside your arm to your heart."

"I feel something," Keff said after a while. "Now what?"

She looked around and pointed at the pedometer lying on the console. "Make that box fly," she said.

Keff stared fixedly at the pedometer. His face turned red with effort. To Carialle's satisfaction, the device lifted a few centimeters before clattering back to its resting place.

"There, you see?" she said. "Mechanics."

Plennafrey held out her hand for the belt, and Keff gave it back. "Now, here is how I do it." Barely touching the five depressions, the magiwoman glanced at the box. It shot up to dangle in midair. Keff walked over and tried to push down on the hovering device. It didn't budge. He yanked at it with all his strength.

"It's as if you fixed it there," Keff said, sweeping Plenna off her feet and kissing her. "Carialle, we're both right. They do use machines, but it's more than that. I can't duplicate what she just did. I nearly got a hernia raising the pedometer as far as I did. She set it like a point plotted in a three-dimensional grid, and she's not even flushed."

The Lady Fair image didn't show the exasperation that Carialle let creep into her voice.

"All right, so they have natural TK and psi abilities which are amplified by the mechanism. Probably increased by selective breeding over centuries—you see what they've done to the Noble Primitives."

"Sour grapes," Keff said cheerfully. "And this gizmo can work from anywhere on the planet?" he asked Plennafrey.

"Yes," the magiwoman said, "but closer to the Core of Ozran makes it easier."

Keff nodded and sat down next to Plenna so he could examine the buckle once again. "Chaumel mentioned that, but he wouldn't say what it is. Is that the power source? Do you know how it works?"

"I do—or I think I do." Plennafrey's eyes grew dreamy as she raised her hands to sketch in the air. "It is a great, glowing heart of power, somewhere deep beneath the surface of Ozran. It was the Ancient Ones' greatest work." For a moment, the young woman looked sheepish. "My power is weak compared with the others. I have tried to figure out more about the Ancient Ones and the Core to try and increase my power, though not . . . not in the way some did." She glanced uneasily at Carialle.

"I know all about your father, Magess," Carialle said. "Whatever Keff sees and hears, I do, too."

That reminded Plennafrey of what Carialle must have seen and heard that morning, and she blushed from the roots of her hair to her neckline.

"Oh," she said. Carialle kindly tried to take the sting out of the revelation.

"I also agree with everything he said about your situation. You're very brave, Magess."

"Thank you. Hem! As I said, I wished to make my connection to the Core greater with harm to none. I have some ancient documents that I am sure hold the key to the power of the Core, but I cannot read them." She appealed to both brain and brawn. "I dared not ask anyone for help, lest they take away my small advantage. Perhaps you might help me?"

"Documents?" Keff perked up. He rose and paced around the cabin. "Documents possibly written by the Ancients? Will you let me see them? I'm a stranger; I have no reason to rob you. I'm also very good with languages.

Will you trust me?" He stopped at Plennafrey's chair and took her hand.

"All right," Plennafrey said. She looked lovingly up into his eyes. "There is no one else I would rather trust."

"She's completely out of her league in this game," Carialle said in Keff's ear. "What a pity there isn't a place on this nasty planet for nice guys. . . . We have one problem," she said aloud. "I can't lift tail from where I'm sitting, and at present, there's a surveillance team of overgrown marbles flying around my hull."

"Where are Chaumel and the others?" Keff asked.

Carialle consulted her monitors, reanimating the globe. The enormous mass of purple had thinned away, leaving single points scattered along the crisscrossing lines. "Everyone's gone home except a few who are hanging around Chaumel's peak."

"I am sure they will be looking for me in my stronghold," Plenna said resignedly. "All is lost."

"We need a conspirator," Keff said. "And I know just the fellow."

"Who? I told you all the others would steal my documents, and then you will be forced to read for them."

Keff's eyes twinkled. "He's not a mage. Cari, can you get me out of here unobserved through the cargo hatch? I'm going to go enlist Brannel."

"Who is Brannel?" Plenna asked, trailing behind Keff and Carialle as they headed toward the cargo hold.

"He's one of the workers who lives in the cave out there," Keff said, pointing vaguely outward.

"A four-finger? You wish to entrust one of Klemay's farmers with secrets of the Core of Ozran?"

"You don't know what's in your files," Carialle said. "Might be a book of recipes from the Dark Ages. Listen, Magess." Carialle's image stopped in the hold as Keff began to move containers out of the way. Plennafrey trotted to a halt to avoid bumping into her. "We need help. Something very wrong is happening to your world and I think it has been going bad since your ancestors were babies. Your documents are the first piece of real information we've heard about. Brannel can do what none of us can: he can go in and out of your house without being noticed by the other magimen."

"Cari?" Keff gestured at the larger boxes blocking the ladder to the hatch. Service arms detached from the walls and began to stack and move them to other shelves. "I'm also going to have to jump down three meters. You'll have to create a diversion."

"Leave that to me," Carialle said.

She led the magiwoman back toward the main cabin. "Now, we're going to have some fun."

Devoting screens around the main console to three of her external cameras for Plenna's benefit, Carialle tuned into the eye-spheres, the service door, and the main hatchway.

They watched the eyes cluster as Carialle let down her ramp and slid open her airlock to disgorge a servo. The low robot rolled down onto the plateau and trundled off into the bushes with the cluster of spy-eyes in pursuit. The door slid closed.

"Go!" Carialle said, pitching her voice over the speaker in the cargo hold. She slid open the door just a trifle.

Leaving some skin behind, Keff slipped out the narrow opening, and dropped to the ground in a crouch. He ran down the hill and across the field toward where the workers were gathering at the cave mouth for their daily toil.

Trusting Keff to take care of that half of the arrangements on his own, Carialle watched with amusement through one of the servo's guiding cameras as the spies followed. It rumbled downhill into a gully and plunged into a sudden puddle, splashing some of the eyes so they recoiled. Plennafrey laughed.

The servo rumbled forward into the midst of a cluster of globe-frogs, who rolled hastily backward and gesticulated at one another inside their cases, croaking in alarm. They moved into the servo's path, continuing their tirade, as if scolding the machine for scaring them. Cari guided it carefully so it wouldn't bump into any of them and headed it for the deepest part of the swamp.

Low-frequency transmissions buzzed between the spy-eyes. Carialle hooked the IT into the audio monitors. From the look of concentration on her face, Plenna was already listening to them in her own way, and enjoying being in the know for a change.

"Where is it going?" asked Potria's voice. "Do you suppose it's going to where *they* are?"

Plennafrey giggled.

"Is the stranger's house doing this on its own?" Nokias asked. "It is a most powerful artifact."

Carialle huffed. "They still think I'm an object! Oh, well, there's nothing I can do about that yet."

"If they knew you were a living being," Plenna said, "they would not treat you as an object. Oh," she said, reality dawning, "they would, wouldn't they? They did with Keff. Oh, my, what has my world become?"

Carialle felt sorry for Plenna. She might be one of the upper class, but she wasn't happy about the status.

On the screen, the spy-eyes were buzzing busily to one another, circling the area, trying to second-guess the servo's mission. Serenely, the robot rolled into a swampy place where pink-flowering weeds grew. Carialle set its parameters to seek out a marsh weed that had exactly fifteen leaves and twelve petals.

"That should keep it busy for a while," Carialle said.

"What does it want in that terrible wet place?" Asedow's

voice wailed. "I am getting aches in my bones just watching it!"

"Keep your eyes open," Nokias's voice cautioned them. "There might be a clue in what this box seeks that will lead us to the stranger."

Carialle joined Plennafrey's delighted chuckle.

Keff ran to the far side of the cave mouth so the hill would block the view of him from the spy-eyes' position. The Noble Primitives, still wiping traces of breakfast from their faces and chest fur, were listening to their crew chiefs assigning tasks for the day. Brannel, near Alteis's group, seemed bored with the whole thing. Keff now suspected that there was something in the Noble Primitive's metabolism that rejected the amnesia-inducing drug, or he was cleverer than his masters knew. He was banking on the latter possibility.

"Ssst, Brannel!" he whispered. A child turned around at the slight noise and saw him. Sternly, Keff shook his head and twirled his finger to show the child she should turn around again. Terrified, the youngster clamped her hands together and returned to her original posture, spine rigid. Keff fancied he could see her quivering and regretted the necessity of scaring her. It was easier to frighten the child into submission than make friends. He hissed again.

"Ssst, Brannel! Over here!"

This time Brannel heard him. The Noble Primitive's sheeplike face split into a wide grin as he saw Keff beckoning to him. He rose to hands and knees and crawled away from the work party.

Alteis saw him. "Brannel, return!" he commanded.

Wordlessly, Brannel pointed to his belly, indicating the need to go relieve himself. The leader shook his head, then lost all interest in his maverick worker. Keff admired Brannel's quick mind; the fellow had to be unique among the field workers on Ozran.

"I am so glad to see you safe, Magelord," Brannel said, when they had retreated around the curve of the hill. "I was concerned for your safety."

Keff was touched. "Thank you, Brannel. I was worried for a while, too. But as you see, I'm back safe and sound."

Brannel was impressed. Only yesterday Mage Keff could speak but a little of the Ozran tongue. Overnight, he had learned the language as well as if he had been born there.

"How may I serve, Magelord?"

"I wonder if you would be willing to do me a favor. I need someone with your injenooety," Keff said. Brannel shook his head, not comprehending. "Er, your smart brain and wits."

"Ah," Brannel said, docketing "injenooety" as a word of the linga esoterka he had not previously known. "You are too kind, Mage Keff. I'd do anything you wish."

Inwardly, Brannel was jubilant. The mage had sought him out, Brannel, a worker male! He could serve this mage, and in return, who knew? Keff possessed many great talents and wide knowledge which, perhaps, he might share as a reward for good service. One day, Brannel, too, might be able to achieve his dream and take power as a mage.

Keff looked around. "I don't wish to talk here. We might be overheard. Come with me to the silver tower." When Brannel looked askance at him, he asked, "What's wrong?"

"The noise it made, Mage Keff," Brannel said, and put his fingers in his ears. "It drove me outside."

"Oh," Keff said. "That won't happen again. I want you to come in and stay this time. All right?"

Brannel nodded. The magelord rose to a stoop and began to make his way across the field. None of the workers looked his way. Brannel hurried after him, full of hope.

Instead of entering by the ramp through the open door, Keff directed Brannel around the rear of the tower and pointed upward. A slit as wide as his forearm was long had opened in the smooth silver wall.

"But why . . . ?" he asked.

"The front's being watched," Keff said. He joined his hands together and propped them on one knee. "Put your foot here—that's good. Now, reach for it. Up you go."

Brannel grabbed the edge of the opening and heaved himself into it. Once he was up, he helped pull Mage Keff into a room crowded with boxes. They had to climb down from a high shelf with great care. When Brannel and Keff were inside, the opening in the wall closed. The female voice of the tower spoke in its strange tongue.

"Aha," it said. "Come on through."

"Come with me," Keff said, in Ozran.

They walked down a short corridor. Two figures sat together in front of the great pictures of the outside. One of them rose and stared at him in horror and surprise.

The feeling was mutual.

"Magess Plennafrey!" Brannel, with one fearful glance at Keff, dropped to his knees and stared at the floor.

"It's okay, Brannel," Keff said, reassuringly, plucking at the worker male's upper arm. "We're all working together here."

"Hush, everyone," the other magess said in the tower's voice. "Here comes our diversion. I don't want the spies to pick up any sound from in here."

Carialle turned on a magnetic field in the airlock, strong enough to disable the spy-eyes, should any be bold enough to try to pass inside, but not enough to stop the servo. She slid the door upward. The low-slung robot rumbled imperturbably up the ramp and through the arch. In one slim, black, metal hand it held very carefully a single marsh flower.

Immediately, the spy-eyes thought they had their opportunity to storm the tower and zoomed after the servo. One hit the field before the others and clanked noisily to the ground, disabled. The over-the-air chatter became excited, and the other spheres reversed course at once, speeding away.

"That'll make them crazy," Carialle said. The first spy sphere rolled halfway down the ramp before its owner, on the other side of the continent, was able to take charge of it once again. As soon as it was airborne, it flitted off.

"Good riddance," Carialle said, and returned her attention to the situation inside the cabin.

Keff stood between Plennafrey and Brannel with his hands out. Brannel was on his feet, with his mutilated hands balled into fists by his sides. Plenna had both her long-fingered hands planted protectively on her belt buckle. The Ozrans were glaring at each other.

"Now, now," Keff said. "I need you both. Please, let's make peace here."

"You intend to explain to a worker what we are doing?" Plenna asked, appealing to Keff. "This one only has four fingers! You can give them directions, but they cannot understand detailed instructions or complicated situations."

Brannel, following the secondary dialect with evident difficulty, replied haltingly in that language, which surprised the magiwoman as much as his daring to speak out in her presence. "I *can* understand. Mage Keff has agreed to give me a chance to help. I will do whatever Mage Keff wants," he said staunchly.

Carialle made her image step forward. "Lady Plennafrey, you are suffering from a preconceived notion that all the people who have had the finger amputation are stupid.

Brannel is the exception to almost any rule you can think of. He has superior intelligence for someone brought up with the hardships he suffered. I think he's far smarter than the favored few who live in the mountains with you mages. You're not that different. You belong to the same species," she said, reaching for an example, "like . . . like Keff and I do."

"You?" Plennafrey asked.

Almost amazed that such a thought had come from her own speakers, Carialle had to pause to consider the change of attitude she had undergone. Much of it was due to seeing the division of a single people on this world into masters and slaves. She now realized that it was counterproductive to separate herself from her parent community. Yes, she was different, but compared with everything else she and Keff encountered, the similarities were more important. Acknowledging her humanity at last felt right and proper. In spite of the way she always pictured herself, she knew inside the metal shell and the carefully protected nerve center was a human being. She felt warmed by the perception.

"Yes," she said, simply. "Me."

Keff beamed at her pillar. Her Lady Fair image beamed happily back at him. Plennafrey fumed visibly at the interplay. If Carialle was human, then the Ozran had a genuine rival. This, combined with her lover's liberal attitude toward the lower class, obviously dismayed the young woman. As she had proved before, she was resilient and adaptable. Plenna seemed to be considering Keff's point of view, but she thoroughly disapproved of Keff having another woman in his life. To disarm the magiwoman, Carialle made her image step back onto the wall. Plennafrey relaxed visibly.

"So I think you should understand that Brannel deserves an explanation if he is to help us."

"Well . . ." Plennafrey said.

"I heard that some of the mages are descended from Brannel's kind of people," Keff said persuasively. "Isn't Asedow's mother one like that? I heard Potria call her a dray-face."

"That's true," Plenna said, nodding. "And he is intelligent. Not good at thinking things through, but intelligent." She smiled ruefully at Keff. "I don't wish to make things harder for my people or for myself. I will cooperate."

"For what am I risking myself?" Brannel asked hoarsely, looking from one mage to another.

"For a sheaf of papers," Keff said. "I need to see them. Magess Plenna will describe them, and Carialle will create an image for you to see."

Brannel seemed unsatisfied. "And for me? For what am I risking myself?" he repeated.

"Ah," Keff said, enlightened. "Well, what's your price? What do you want?"

Plennafrey, losing her newfound liberalism, drew herself up in outrage. "You dare ask for a reward? Do the mages not give you food and shelter? This is just another task we have given you."

"We have those things, Magess, but we want knowledge, too!" Brannel said. Having begun, he was determined to put his case, even in the face of disapproval from an angry overlord, though somehow he was begging now. "Mage Keff, I . . . I want to be a mage, too. For a tiny, small item of power I will help you. It does not need to be big, or very powerful, but I know I could be a good mage. I will earn my way along. That is all I have ever desired: to learn. Give me that, and I will give you my life." Keff saw the passion in the Noble Primitive's eye and was prepared to agree.

"To give a four-finger power? No!" Plenna protested, cutting him off.

"Not good for you, Brannel," Carialle said, emphatically, siding unexpectedly with Plennafrey. "Look what a mess your mages have made of this place using unlimited power. How about a better home, or an opportunity for a real education, instead?"

"What about redressing the balance of power, Cari?" Keff asked under his breath.

"It doesn't need redressing, it needs de-escalating," Carialle replied through her brawn's mastoid implant. "Could this planet really cope with one more resentful mage wielding a wand? We still don't know what the power was for originally."

Brannel's long face wore a mulish expression. Carialle could picture him with donkey's ears laid back along his skull. He was not happy to be dictated to by the flat magess, nor was he comfortable being enlisted by a genuine magess.

"No one speaks of what went before this," he said. "The promises of mages to other than themselves always prove false. I served Klemay, and now he is dead. Who killed him? I know whoever kills is not always the newest overlord in a place."

Plenna's mouth dropped open. "How do you know that? You're uneducated. You've never been anywhere but here."

"You talk over our heads as if we aren't there," Brannel said flatly. "But I, *I* understand. Who? I wish to know, for if it was you, I cannot help."

Plennafrey looked stricken at the idea that she could willingly commit murder. Keff patted her hand.

"He doesn't know, Plenna," Keff said soothingly. "How could he? It was Ferngal," he told Brannel. "Chaumel said so last night."

"Yes, then," Brannel said eagerly, "I will do what you want. For my price."

"Impossible," Plenna said. "He is ignorant."

"Ignorance is curable," Keff said emphatically. "It wasn't part of his brain that was removed." He made a chopping motion at his hand. "He can learn. He's already proved that."

Brannel looked jealously at Plenna's long fingers. "But I cannot use the power items without help."

Carialle was immediately sorry Keff had mentioned the amputation. "Brannel, there's nothing that can be done about that now. Some of the other magimen use prosthetics—false fingers. You can, too."

"If we were home," Keff said thoughtfully, "surgery could be done to regrow the fingers." He glanced up to find Plenna gazing at him.

"I must see these wonders," Plenna said, moving closer. "Should I not come back with you? After all, you said you are here to learn about my people on behalf of your own. I can teach you all about Ozran and see your world. Someday we can come back here together." She laid one long hand on his arm.

"Uhhh, one thing at a time, Plenna," Keff said, his smile fixed on his face. Her touch sent tingles up his arm. Her scent and her lovely eyes pulled him toward her like a magnet, but the sudden thought of having a permanent relationship with her had never crossed his mind. Evidently, it had hers. He reproached himself that he should have thought of the consequences before he took her to bed. "Carialle, we may have a problem," he subvocalized.

"We *have* a problem," Carialle said aloud. "The eyes are back. They're circling around outside."

"Oh!" Plenna ran to the screen. "Nokias, Chaumel, and the other high mages. They are trying to decide what to do."

"Have they figured out that we're in here?" Keff asked.

"No," Plenna said, after listening for a moment. "All

of their followers are still searching." Carialle confirmed it.

"Then we'd better make our move, pronto, if we want a chance at those papers," Keff said. "All that remains is for our agent here to agree to fetch them for us."

Brannel had been standing beside the console, listening to the three bare-skins talk. He folded his arms over his furry chest.

"I would do anything for you, Mage Keff, but such a chance comes only once to one such as myself. You asked me my price. I told you my heart's desire. Will you pay it?"

Keff appealed to Plennafrey.

"I think he deserves a chance."

Clearly uneasy, Plennafrey eyed the Noble Primitive. "If all goes well, I agree he will be worthy of an opportunity," she said slowly. "I do not know where to find him an object of power yet, but I *will* try."

"All right, Brannel? Magess Plennafrey will teach you how to *use* a power object. She'll be your teacher, so she will control what you do to a certain extent—but you'll have your chance. She'll also teach you other things an educated man needs to know. Agreed?"

"Agreed," Plennafrey said.

Brannel, his eyes shining, fell to his knees before the magiwoman. "Thank you, Magess."

"There may be no power left for anyone," Carialle reminded them. "If those power drops have been increasing in frequency over time, it may mean that whatever's powering the magic here on Ozran is finally running down."

"What do I look for?" Brannel asked meekly.

Following Plenna's instructions, Carialle created the holographic image of a sheaf of dusty documents, yellow with age, and rotated it so the Noble Primitive could see all sides.

"They are very fragile," Plenna said. "They could shiver to dust if you breathe on them."

"I will be careful, Magess, I promise."

"We're left with only one problem," Keff said. "How do we get Brannel to Plennafrey's stronghold?"

Carialle's Lady Fair image drew an impish smile. "It might be worth a try to count on one of those power drops. If we can attract everyone's attention again, I might be able to break loose when the lights go off. After all, I'm not dependent on the Core of Ozran. I only need a moment. I can be set to launch at any second, and you'll have your diversion to teleport there in peace."

"How can we do that?" Keff asked, bemused.

"By letting them know where you are," Cari said. "You zoom outside and start the Wild Hunt all over. That will bring everyone here with a view-halloo, and if I'm right, overload the power lines. As soon as the tractor beam on my tail lets go, I'll take off and distract them away from you. I'll lead them on an orbit of Ozran while Brannel is getting your papers."

"Do you have enough fuel?" Keff asked.

"Enough for one try," Carialle said, showing an indicator of her tank levels, "or we may not have the wherewithal to get home. I burned a lot trying to break loose before. Don't fail me."

"Did I burst my heart in the effort I never would, fair lady," Keff said, kissing his hand to her. "We'll rendezvous here in two hours."

With a final reproachful glance at Carialle's image, Plenna took her place on her chariot. Keff crouched behind her like the musher on a dogsled, and Brannel, hunched on hands and knees, clung to the back, white knuckles showing through the fur on his fingers.

"Ready, steady, go!" Carialle threw up the airlock door, and the chariot shot out the narrow passage.

"Yeeeee-haaaah!" Keff yelled as they zoomed over the Noble Primitives' cave. The spy-eyes froze in place.

Suddenly, the air was full of chariots. The mages in them looked here and there for Plennafrey, who was already kilometers away from Carialle.

"Look!" shouted Asedow, pointing with his whole arm, and the mob turned to follow them.

Chaumel blinked in, with Nokias and Ferngal alongside him. Like well-trained squadrons, the wings of mages fell in behind. Keff turned and thumbed his nose at them.

"Nyaah!" he shouted.

Two hundred bolts of red lightning shot from two hundred amulets and rods toward their backs. Plennafrey threw up a shield behind them, which deflected the force spectacularly off in all directions.

"If it's coming, it's coming now," Carialle said in Keff's ear. "Building . . . building . . . now!"

"Hold tight!" Keff yelled, as the floor dropped out from under them when the power failed. Plennafrey's shoulders tensed under his hands, and Brannel moaned.

Shrieks and shouts echoed off the valley floor as the other mages were deprived of their power and fell helplessly earthward. Some were close enough to the ground to strike it before the blackout ended. One magess ended up sitting dazed, in the midst of broken pieces of chair, staring around in complete bewilderment.

As before, the power-free interval was brief, but it sufficed for Carialle to kick on her engines and break loose from her invisible bonds. With a roar and an elongating mushroom of fire, she was airborne. As one, the hundreds of mages swiveled in midair, ignoring Plennafrey and Keff, to pursue her. Her cameras picked up images of astonished and furious faces. Chaumel was hammering his chair arm.

"Catch me if you can!" she cried, and took off toward planetary north.

◻   ◻   ◻

Another fifty meters, and Plennafrey transported them from Klemay's valley to an isolated peak. Brannel, a huddled bundle of knees and elbows at her feet, was silent. Keff thought the Noble Primitive was terrified until Brannel turned glowing eyes to them.

"Oh, Magess, I want to do *this*!" he exclaimed. "It would be the greatest moment of my life if I could make myself fly. I could never even imagine this out of a dream. I beg you to teach me this *first*."

Keff grinned at the worker male's enthusiasm. "I hope you'll feel as energetic when you find out how much work it is to do magic," he said.

"Oh, it feels so good to be free again!" said the voice in his ear. Carialle, knowing in advance where they were going, reconnected instantly with Keff's implants. "I have to keep slowing down so I don't lose my audience. They're such quitters! I've almost lost Potria twice."

"Any unwanted watchers out there, Cari?" Keff asked, pointing his finger so the ocular implants could see.

"No spy-eyes here yet," Carialle's voice said after a moment.

Plenna shot in over the balcony, which was a twin to the one at Chaumel's stronghold, and hovered a few centimeters above the gray tiles.

"I mustn't land, or the ley lines will indicate it," she said.

Brannel hopped off and dashed inside.

"Good luck!" Keff called after him. Plenna lifted the chair up and looped over the landing pad's edge to wait beneath the overhang.

Brannel felt the floor humming through his feet and forced himself to ignore it. The discomfort was a small price to pay for associating with mages and having them treat him as a friend, if not an equal. Even a true Ozran magess had been kind to him, and the promise Mage Keff had made him—! The knowledge put a spring in his step all along the corridor walled with painted tiles. At the green-edged door, he turned and put his hand on the latch.

"Ho, there!" Brannel turned. A tall fur-face with five fingers strode toward him. He had a strange, flat-nosed face, and his eyes turned up at the corners, but he was handsome, nearly as handsome as a mage. "You're a stranger. What do you think you're doing?"

"I have been sent by the magess," Brannel said, leaning toward the house servant with all the aggression of a fighter who has survived tough living conditions. The servant backed up a pace.

"Who? Which magess?" the servant demanded. He eyed Brannel's prominent jaw with disdain. "You're not one of us."

"Indeed I am not," Brannel said, drawing himself upward. "I am Magess Plennafrey's pupil."

That statement, and the casual use of the magess's name, shocked the house male rigid. His tilted eyes widened into circles.

Brannel, ignoring him, pushed through the door. The room was lined with hanging cloth pictures. He went to the fourth one from the door and felt behind it at knee level. Gently, he extracted from the hidden pocket a thick bundle. He forced himself to walk, not run, out the door, past the startled house male, down the hallway, and out onto the open balcony.

The chariot appeared suddenly at the edge of the low wall overlooking the precipice, startling him. Keff cheered as Brannel held up the packet and waved him onto the chair's end.

"Good man, Brannel! Where are you, Cari?" Mage Keff

asked the air. "We're on our way back to the plain. Yes, I've got them! Cari, I can almost read these!"

The chair swept skyward once more. Now that his task was done and reward at hand, Brannel indulged himself in enjoying the view. One day, he would fly over the mountains like this on his own chariot. Wouldn't Alteis stare?

"Are those what they look like?" Carialle asked, from her position over the south pole.

"Yes! They're technical manuals from a starship," Keff said, gloating. "One of *our* starships. The language is human Standard, but old. Very old. Nine to twelve hundred years is my guess from the syntax. Please run a check through your memory in that time frame for," he held a trembling finger underneath the notation to make sure he was reading it correctly, "the CW-53 TMS *Bigelow*. See when it flew, and when it disappeared, because there certainly was never a record of its landing here."

Keff turned page after page of the fragile, yellowing documents, showing each leaf to the implants for Carialle to scan.

"This is precious and not very sturdy," he said. "If anything happens to it before I get there, at least we'll have a complete recording." The covers and pages had been extruded as a smooth-toothed and flexible but now crackling plastic. In a tribute to technology a thousand years old, the laser print lettering was perfectly black and legible. He wondered, glancing through it, what the original owners would have said if they could see to what purpose their record-keeping was being put.

"Are these documents good?" Plennafrey asked, over the rush of the wind.

"Better than good!" Keff said, leaning over to show her the ship's layout and classification printed on the inside front cover of the first folder. "These prove that you are the descendant of a starship crew from the Central Worlds who landed here a thousand years ago. You're a human, just like me."

"That makes everything wonderful!" Plennafrey said, clasping his wrist. "Then there will be no difficulty with us staying together. We might be able to have children."

Keff goggled. Without being insulting there was nothing he could do at the moment but kiss her shining face, which he did energetically.

"One thing at a time, Plenna," Keff said, going hastily back to his perusal of the folders. "Ah, there's a reference to the Core of Ozran. If I follow this correctly, yes . . . it's a device, passed on to them, not constructed by, the Old Ones, pictured overleaf." Keff turned the page to the solido. "Eyuch! Ug-*ly*!"

The Old Ones were indeed upright creatures of bilateral symmetry who could use the chairs reposing in Chaumel's art collection, but that was where their similarity to humanoids ended. Multi-jointed legs with backward-pointing knees depended from flat, shallow bodies a meter wide. They had five small eyes set in a row across their flat faces, which were dark green. Lank black tendrils on their cylindrical heads were either hair or antennae, Keff wasn't sure which from the description below.

"Erg," Keff said, making a face. "So now we know what the Old Ones looked like."

"Oh, yes," Brannel said, casually standing up on the back to look, as if he flew a hundred kilometers above the ground every day. "My father's father told us about the Old Ones. They lived in the mountains with the overlords many years past."

"How long ago?" Keff asked.

Brannel struggled for specifics, then shrugged. "The wooze-food makes our memories bad," he explained, his tone apologetic but his jaw set with frustration.

"Keff, something has to be done about deliberately retarding half the population," Carialle said seriously. "With the diet they're being forced to subsist on, Brannel's people could actually lose their capacity for rational thought in a few more generations."

"Aha!" Keff crowed triumphantly. "Tapes!" He plucked a sealed spool out of the back cover of one of the folders. "Compressed data, I hope, and maybe footage of our scaly friends. Can you read one of these, Carialle?"

"I can adapt one of my players to fit it, but I have no idea what format it's in," she said. "It could take time."

Keff wasn't listening. He was engrossed in the second folder's contents.

"Fascinating!" he said. "Look at this, Cari. The whole system of remote power manipulation comes from a worldwide weather-control system! So that's what the ley lines are for. They're electromagnetic sensors, reading the temperature and humidity all across Ozran. They were designed to channel energy to help produce rain or mist where it was needed. . . . Ah, but the Old Ones didn't build it. They either found it, or they met the original owners when they came to this planet. Sounds like they were cagey about that. The Old Ones adapted the devices to use the power to make it rain and passed them on to you," he told Plennafrey. "They were made by the Ancient Ones."

"The Ancient Ones," Plenna said, reverently, pulling the folder down so she could see it. "Are there images of them, too? None know what they looked like."

Keff thumbed through the log. "No. Nothing. Drat."

"Rain?" Brannel asked, reverently. "They could make it rain?"

"Weather control," Carialle said. "Now that does smack of an advanced technological civilization. Pity they're not still around. This planet is an incipient dust-bowl. Keff, I'm within fifty klicks of the rendezvous site. Beginning landing procedures . . . Uh-oh, power traces increasing in your general vicinity. Company!"

Keff heard cries of triumph and swiveled his head, looking for their source. A score of magimen, led by Potria and Chaumel, had just jumped in and were homing in on them along a northwest vector.

"They've found us!" Plenna exclaimed, her dark eyes wide. Keff stood upright and grasped the back of her chair.

The magiwoman started to weave her arms in complicated patterns. Brannel, realizing that he was in the firing line of a building spell, dropped flat. Plenna launched her sally and had the satisfaction of seeing three of the magimen clear the way. The rattling hiss of the spell as it missed its mark and vanished jarred Keff's bones.

"Can you teleport?" Keff asked, clinging to the chair's uprights.

"Someone is blocking me," Plenna said, forcing the words through her teeth. "I must fight, instead."

"You'd be a sitting duck in here anyway," Carialle interjected crisply, "because the tractor grabbed me again as soon as I touched down. Keep moving!"

Plenna didn't need Carialle's message relayed to her. She took evasive maneuvers like a veteran fighter, zigzagging over the pursuers' heads and diving between two so their red lightning bolts narrowly missed each other. Keff saw Potria's face as he passed. The golden magiwoman had abandoned her look of elegant boredom for a grim set. If her will or her marksmanship had been up to it, she would have spitted them all.

Contrarily, Chaumel seemed to enjoy toying with them. He shot his bolts, not so much to wound, but more as if he were seeing what Plennafrey would do to avoid them. He seemed to have observed that she wasn't spelling to kill, obviously a novelty among Ozran mages.

Plennafrey dived low into the valleys, defying the magifolk to chase her through the nooks and crannies of her own domain. Keff felt the crackle of dry branches brush his shoulders as she maneuvered her chair through a narrow passage and down into a concealed tunnel. While the others circled overhead squawking like crows, she flew through the mountain. Brannel's keening echoed off the moist stone walls. Just as swiftly, they emerged into day.

Keff thought they might have shaken off their pursuers, but he had reckoned without Chaumel's determination. The moment they cleared the tunnel mouth, the silver magiman was there in midair, winding nothingness around and around his hands. Brannel gasped and threw his hands over his head to protect it.

Plenna flattened her hands on her belt buckle, and a translucent bubble of force appeared around her.

"Oh, child." Chaumel grinned and flicked his fingers. The chair started to sink toward the ground.

"He made the force shield heavy!" Keff said. "We're falling!"

Abandoning her defensive tactic at once, Plennafrey popped the sphere and threw a few of her own bolts at Chaumel. Almost lazily, the other gestured, and the lightning split around him, rocketing toward the horizon. He made up another bundle of power, which Plenna averted. She returned fire, sending a handful of toroid shapes that grew and grew until they could surround Chaumel's limbs and neck. Two made contact, then fell away as open arcs, snaring and taking the other rings with them.

A moment later, Potria and Asedow appeared.

"You found them!" Potria called. The pink-gold magess was jubilant. Plenna turned in her seat and fired a doublebarrel of white spark lightning at her. Potria shrieked when her fine clothes and skin were burned by some of the hot sparks. At once she retaliated, weaving a web with missiles of force around the edge that propelled it toward the younger magess.

Asedow chose that moment to drive in at them from the other side. His methods were not as smooth as his rival's. He produced a steady stream of smoky puffs that hung in the air like mines until Plennafrey, trying to avoid Potria's web, was forced back into them.

Keff was nearly shaken off when the first exploded against his back. Plennafrey turned her chair in midair, seeking to steer her way clear of the obstacles. No matter how she turned, she collided with another, and another. By then, Potria's web had struck.

All around him Keff felt rolls of silk fabric, invisible and magnetic, drawing him in, surrounding him, then smothering his nose and mouth. As the spell established itself, it threatened to draw every erg of energy out of his body through his skin. He gasped, clawing with difficulty at his throat. He was suffocating in the middle of thin air. Plennafrey, her slender form slumped partway over one chair arm, her skin turning blue, still fought to free them, her hands drawing primrose fire out of her belt buckle. Her will proved mightier than the other female's magic. The sunlight flames consumed the air around her, then caught on the veils of web clinging to Keff and Brannel, turning them into insubstantial black ash. She was about to set them all free when they were overcome by dozens and dozens of bolts of scarlet lightning, striking at them from every direction.

As Keff lost consciousness, he heard Potria and Asedow shrilling at each other again over who would take possession of him and his ship. He vowed he would die before he would let anyone take Carialle.

A sharp scent introduced itself under his nose. Unwittingly, he took a deep breath and recoiled, choking. He batted at the bad smell, but nothing solid was there.

"You're awake," a voice said. "Very good."

With difficulty, Keff opened his eyes. Things around him began to take focus. He lay on his back in the main cabin of his ship. Beside him was Plennafrey, also in the throes of regaining consciousness. Brannel lay in a motionless heap under Plenna's feet. And leaning over Keff with a distorted expression of solicitousness was Chaumel.

¤ CHAPTER ELEVEN

Carialle fought against the blackness that abruptly surrounded her, refusing to believe in it. Between one nanopulse and the next, Chaumel had appeared in the main cabin, past the protective magnetic wall she had set up, and stood gloating over the contents of a captive starship. Outraged at the invasion, Carialle set up the same multi-tone shriek she used on Brannel to try and drive him out. Chaumel threw up protective hands, but not over his ears.

Suddenly she could move nothing and all her visual receptors were down. She could still hear, though. The taunting voice boomed hollowly in her aural inputs, continuing his inventory and interjecting an occasional comment of self-congratulation.

She spoke then, pleading with him not to leave her in the dark. The voice paused, surprised, then Carialle felt hands running over her: impossible, insubstantial hands penetrating through her armor, brushing aside her neural connectors and yet not detaching them.

"My, my, what are you?" Chaumel's voice asked.

"Restore my controls!" Carialle insisted. "You don't know what you're doing!"

"How very interesting all of this is," he was saying to someone. "In my wildest dreams I could never have imagined a man who was also a machine. Incredible! But it isn't a man, is it?" The hands drew closer, passed over and *through* her. "Why, no! It is a woman. And what interesting things she has at her command. I must see *that*."

Invisible fingers took her multi-camera controls away from her nerve endings, leaving them teasingly just out of reach. She sensed her life-support system starting and stopping as Chaumel played with it, using his TK. She felt a rush of adrenaline as he upset the balance of her chemical input, and was unable to access the endorphins to counteract them. Then the waste tube began to back up toward the nutrient vat. She felt her delicate nervous system react against pollution by becoming drowsy and logy.

"Stop!" she begged. "You'll kill me!"

"I won't kill you, strange woman in a box," Chaumel said, his voice light and airy, "but I will not risk having you break away from my control again as you did when the magic dropped. What a chase you led us! Right around Ozran and back again. You made a worthy quarry, but one grows tired of games."

"Keff!"

"I'm here, Carialle," the brawn's voice came, weak but furious. Carialle could have sung her relief. She heard the shuffling of feet, and a crash. Keff spoke again through soughing pain. "Chaumel, we'll cooperate, but you have to let her alone. You don't understand what you're doing to her."

"Why? She breathes, she eats—she even hears and speaks. I just control what she sees and does."

For a brief flash, Carialle had a glimpse of the control room. Keff and the silver magiman faced one another, the

Ozran very much in command. Keff was clutching his side as if cradling bruised ribs. Plenna stood behind Keff, erect and very pale. Brannel, disoriented, huddled in a corner beside Keff's weight bench. Then the image was gone, and she was left with the enveloping darkness. She couldn't restrain a wail of despair.

It was as if she were reliving the memory of her accident again for Inspector Maxwell-Corey. All over again! The helplessness she hoped never again to experience: sensory deprivation, her chemicals systems awry, her controls out of reach or disabled. *This time*, the results would be worse, because *this time* when she went mad, her brawn would be within arm's reach, listening.

Swallowing against the pain in his ribs, Keff threw himself at Chaumel again. With a casual flick of his hand, Chaumel once more sent him flying against the bulkhead. Plennafrey ran to his side and hooked her arm in his to help him stand.

"You might as well stop that, stranger," Chaumel advised him. "The result will be the same any time you try to lay hands on me. You will tire before I do."

"You don't know what you're doing to her!" Keff said, dragging himself upright. He dashed a hand against the side of his mouth. It came away streaked with blood from a split lip.

"Ah, yes, but I do. I see pictures," Chaumel said, with a smile playing about his lips as his eyes followed invisible images. "No, not pictures, *sounds* that haunt her mind, distinct, never far from her conscious thoughts—tapping." The speakers hammered out a distant, slow, sinister cadence.

Carialle screamed, deafeningly. Keff knew what Chaumel was doing, exercising the same power of image-making he had used on Keff to intrude on his consciousness. Against this particular illusion Carialle had no mental defenses. To dredge up the long-gone memories of her accident coupled with Chaumel's ability to keep her bound in place and deprive her of normal function might rob her of her sanity.

"Please," Keff begged. "I will cooperate. I'll do anything you want. Don't toy with her like that. You're harming her more than you could understand. Release her."

Chaumel sat down in Keff's crash couch, hands folded lightly together. Swathed in his gleaming robes, he looked like the master of ceremonies at some demonic ritual.

"Before I lift a finger and free my prisoner"—he leveled his very long first digit at Keff—"I want to know who you are and why you are here. You didn't make the entire over-lordship of this planet fly circuits for amusement. Now, what is your purpose?"

Keff, knowing he had to be quick to save Carialle's sanity, abandoned discretion and started talking. Leaving out names and distances, he gave Chaumel a precis of how they had chosen Ozran, and how they traveled there.

" . . . We came here to study you just as I told you before. That's the truth. In the midst of our investigations we've discovered imbalances in the power grid all of you use," Keff said. "Those imbalances are proving dangerous directly to you, and indirectly to your planet."

"You mean the absences that occur in the ley lines?" Chaumel said, raising his arched eyebrows. "Yes, I noticed how you took advantage of that last lapse. Very, very clever."

"Keff! They're crawling over my skin," Carialle moaned. "Tearing away my nerve endings. Stop them!"

"Chaumel . . ."

"All in good time. She is not at risk."

"You're wrong about that," Keff said sincerely, praying

the magiman would listen. "She suffered a long time ago, and you are making her live it over."

"And so loudly, too!" Chaumel flicked his fingers, and Carialle's voice faded. Keff had the urge to run to her pillar, throw himself against it to feel whether she was still alive in there. He wanted to reassure her that he was still out there. She wasn't alone! But he had to fight this battle sitting still, without fists, without epee, hoping his anxiety didn't show on his face, to convince this languid tyrant to free her before she went mad.

"I've discovered something else that I think you should know," Keff said, speaking quickly. "Your people are not native to Ozran."

"Oh, that I knew already," Chaumel said, with his small smile. "I am a historian, the son of historians, as I told you when you . . . visited me. Our legends tell us we came from the stars. As soon as I saw you, I knew that your people are our brothers. What do you call our race?"

"Humans," Keff said quickly, anxious to get the magiman back on track of letting go of Carialle's mind. "The old term for it was 'Homo sapiens' meaning the 'wise man.' Now, about Carialle . . ."

"And you also wish to tell me that our power comes from a mechanical source, not drawn mystically from the air as some superstitious mages may believe. That I also knew already." He looked at Plennafrey. "When I was your age, I followed my power to its source. I know more than the High Mages of the Points about whence our connection comes to the Core, but I kept my knowledge to myself and my eyes low, having no wish to become a target." Modestly, he dropped his gaze to the ground.

If he was looking for applause, he was performing for the wrong audience. Keff lunged toward Chaumel and pinned his shoulders against the chair back.

"While you're sitting here so calmly bragging about

yourself," Keff said in a clear, dangerous voice, "my partner is suffering unnecessary and possibly permanent psychic trauma."

"Oh, very well," Chaumel said, imperturbably, closing his hand around the shaft of his wand as Keff let him go. "What you are saying is more amusing. You will tell me more, of course, or I will pen her up again."

Sight and sensation flooded in all at once. Carialle almost sobbed with relief, but managed to regain her composure within seconds. To Keff, whose sympathetic face was close to her pillar camera, she said, "Thank you, sir knight. I'm all right. I promise," but she sensed that her voice quavered. Keff looked skeptical as he caressed her pillar and then resumed his seat.

"Keff says that our power was supposed to be used to make it rain," Plenna said. "Is this why the crops fail? Because we use it for other things?"

"That's right," Keff said. "If you're using the weather technology as you have been, no wonder the system is overloading. Whenever a new mage rises to power, it puts that much more of a strain on the system."

"You have some proof of this?" Chaumel asked, narrowing his eyes.

"We have evidence from your earliest ancestors," Keff said.

"Ah, yes," Chaumel said, raising the notebooks from his lap. "These. I have been perusing them while waiting for you to wake up. Except for a picture of the inside of an odd stronghold and an image of the Old Ones, I cannot understand it."

"I can only read portions of it without my equipment," Keff said. "The language in it is very old. Things have changed since your ancestors and mine parted company."

"It's a datafile from the original landing party," Carialle said. "That much we can confirm. Humans came to Ozran on a starship called the TMS *Bigelow* over nine hundred years ago."

"And where did you get this . . . datafile?"

"It's mine!" Plenna said stoutly. She started forward to reclaim her property, but Chaumel held a warning hand toward Carialle's pillar. With a glance at Keff's anxious face, Plenna stopped where she stood.

"Yours?" The silver magiman looked her over with new respect. "I didn't think you had it in you to keep a deep secret, least of magesses. Your father, Rardain, certainly never could have."

Plenna reacted with shame to any mention of her late father. "He didn't know about it. I found it in an old place after he . . . died."

"Does that matter?" Keff said, stepping forward and putting a protective arm around Plenna's waist. The tall girl was quaking. "We're trying to head off what could become a worldwide disaster, and you're preventing us from finding out more about the problem."

"And this 'datafile' will tell you what to do?" Chaumel was delicately skeptical.

Carialle manifested her Lady Fair image on the wall. After a momentary double take, Chaumel accepted it and occasionally made eye contact with it.

"Given time, I can try to read the tapes," Carialle said. "In the meantime, Keff can translate the hard copy."

Chaumel settled back. "Good. We have all the time you wish. The curtain you set about this place will prevent the others from finding us. In a little while they will be tired of chasing shadows and go home. That will leave us without disturbance."

"Can I use my display screens?"

The silver magiman was gracious. "Use anything you wish. You can't go anywhere."

Grumbling at Chaumel's make-yourself-at-home attitude,

Carialle spent a few minutes re-establishing the chemical balances in her system. Two full extra cycles of the waste-disposal processor, and her bloodstream was clear of everything but what belonged there. She increased the flow of nutrients and gratefully felt the adrenaline high fade away.

She assessed the size of the tape cassette Keff held up and noted that there was one place for a spindle on the small, airtight capsule. Two of her input bays were made to take tapes as well as datahedrons. Carialle rolled the capstan and spindle forward from the rear wall of the player, narrowed the niche so the tape wouldn't wobble, then opened the door.

"Ready," she said.

"Here goes nothing at all," Keff said, and slid the tape in.

Carialle closed the door. As she engaged the spindle, the cassette popped open, revealing the tape, and letting go a puff of air. Carialle, who had been expecting just that, captured the trace of the thousand-year-old atmosphere in a lab flask and carried it away through the walls to analyze its contents.

Slowly, she rolled the tape against the heads, comparing the scan pattern produced on her wave-form monitor with thousands of similar patterns.

"Can you read it?" Keff asked.

"We'll see," Carialle said. "There are irregularities in the scan, which I attribute to poor maintenance of the recording device that produced it. Of all the lazy skivers, why did one have to be recording this most important piece of history? It would have been no trouble at all to keep their machinery in good repair, damn their eyes."

"Did you want it to be easy, lady fair? Do you know, I just realized I'm hungry," Keff announced, turning to the others. "Plenna, we've had nothing since last night, and damned little then. May I buy you lunch?"

The magiwoman turned her eyes toward him with

relief. Her face was beginning to look almost hollow from strain.

"Oh, that would be very nice," she said thinly. A timid croak from the side of the weight bench reminded him Brannel was still with them. He was hungry, too.

"Right. Three coming up. Chaumel?"

"No, very kindly, no," the silver magiman said, waving a hand, although keeping an eye on him that was anything but casual. Keff gave instructions to the synthesizer, and in moments removed a tray with three steaming dishes.

"Very simple: meat, potatoes, vegetables, bread," Keff said, pointing the food out to his guests.

"Hold it, Keff," Carialle said. "I don't trust our captor." Keff aimed his optical implants at each plate in turn. "Uh-huh. Just checking."

"Thank you, lady dear. I count on your assistance," Keff said subvocally. Placing the first plate on its tray in Plenna's lap, he handed the second filled dish and fork to Brannel before he settled on the weight bench to enjoy his own meal.

Brannel was still staring at the divided plate when Keff turned back.

"What's the matter?" Keff asked. "It's good. A little heavy on the carbohydrates, perhaps, but that won't spoil the taste."

Wordlessly, Brannel turned fearful eyes up to him.

"Ah, I see," Keff said, intuiting the problem. "Should I try some first to show you it's all right? We're all eating the same thing. Would you like my dinner instead?"

"No, Mage Keff," Brannel said after a moment, glancing wild-eyed at Chaumel, "I trust you."

If he had any misgivings, one taste later the worker was hunched over his lunch, shoveling in mouthfuls inexpertly with his fork. He probably would have growled at Keff if he had tried to take it away. In no time the dish was empty.

"You packed that away in a hurry. Would you like another plate? It's no trouble."

Eyes wide with hope, Brannel nodded. He looked guilty at being so greedy, but more fascinated that "another plate" was no trouble. As soon as the second helping was in his hands, he began wolfing it down.

"Huh! Crude," Chaumel said, fastidiously disregarding the male. "Well, if you want to keep pets . . ."

Brannel didn't seem to hear the senior mage. He sucked a stray splash of gravy off his hairy fingers and scraped up the last of the potatoes.

"How's my supply of synth, Cari?" Keff asked, teasingly. The worker stopped in the middle of a mouthful. "I'm teasing you, Brannel," he said. "We're carrying enough food to supply one man for two years—or one of you for six months. Don't worry. We're friends."

Plenna ate more sedately. She smiled brightly once at Keff to show she enjoyed the food. Keff patted her hand.

"Bingo!" Carialle said, triumphantly. "Got you. Gentlemen and madam, our feature presentation."

A wow, followed by the hiss of low-level audio, issued from her main cabin speakers. Carialle diverted her main screen to the video portion of the tape. On it, a distant, spinning globe appeared.

"The scan is almost vertical across the width of the tape," Carialle explained. "Very densely packed. You could measure the speed in millimeters per second, so where glitches appear there's no backup scan. Because this was done on a magnetic medium, some is irrevocably lost, though not much. I have filled in where I could. This is not the full, official log. I think it was a personal record kept by a biologist or an engineer. You'll see what I mean in the content."

The tape showed several views of Ozran from space, including technical scans of the continents and seas. Loud static accompanied the glitches between portions. Carialle found the technology was as primitive as stone knives and bearskins compared to her state-of-the-art equipment, but she was able to read between the lines of scan. She put up her findings on a side screen for the others to read.

"Looks like a damned fine prospect for a colony," Keff said, critically assessing the data as if it were a new planet he was approaching. "Atmosphere very much like that of Old Earth."

"Ureth," Plennafrey breathed, her eyes bright with awe.

Keff smiled. "Uh-huh, I see why they made planetfall. *Their* telemetry was too basic. We wouldn't miss above-ground buildings and the signs of agriculture from space, no matter how slight, but they did. Hence, first contact was made."

The *Bigelow's* complement had been four hundred and fifty-two, all human. Keff fancied he could see a family resemblance to the flamboyant Mage Omri in the dark-skinned captain's face.

Chaumel lost his veneer of sophistication when the first Old One appeared on screen. He stared at it open-mouthed. Keff, too, was amazed by the alien being, but he could appreciate that, to Chaumel, it was analogous to the gods of Mount Olympus visiting Athens.

"I have never seen anything like them. Have you, Carialle?"

"No, and neither has Xeno," Cari said, running a hasty cross-match through her records. "I wonder where they came from? Somewhere else in R sector? Tracing an ion trail at this late date would be impossible."

What could not have been indicated by the still image in the folders which Keff has seen was that each of the alien's five eyes could move independently. The flat bodies were faintly amusing, like the pack of card-men in *Through the Looking-Glass*. The tapes compressed many of the early meetings with the host species, as they showed the crew of the *Bigelow* around their homes, introduced them to their offspring, and demonstrated some of the wonders of their seemingly inexplicable manipulation of power.

The Old Ones had obviously once had a thriving civilization. By the time the crew of the *Bigelow* arrived, they were reduced to two small segments of population: the number who lived singly in the mountains and the communal bands who tilled the valley soil. Being few, they hadn't put much of a strain on the available resources, but it wasn't a viable breeding group, either.

Keff listened to the diarist's narration and repeated what he could understand into IT for the benefit of the Ozrans.

"The narrator described the Old Ones and how happy they were to have the humans come to live with them. He's talking about ugly skills possessed—no, fabulous skills possessed by these ugly aliens, who promised to share what they knew. Whew, that is an old dialect of Standard."

An Old One was persuaded to say a few words for the camera. It pressed its frightful face close to the video pickup and aimed three eyes at it. The other two wandered alarmingly.

"I can understand what it says," Chaumel said, too fascinated to sound boastful. "How it speaks is what we now call the linga esoterka. 'How joy find strangejoy find strange two-eyes folk,' is what this one says."

"He's pleased to meet you," Keff said with a grin. He directed IT to incorporate Chaumel's translation into his running lexicon of the second dialect of Ozran. "It sounds as though a good deal of Old One talk was incorporated into a working language, a gullah, used by the humans and Old Ones to communicate."

The mystical sign language Keff had observed was also in wide usage among the green indigenes, but the narrator of the tape hadn't yet observed its significance. Keff could feel Carialle's video monitors on him, as if to remind him of the times that IT ignored somatic signals. He grinned over his shoulder at her pillar. This time, IT was coming through like the cavalry.

"So that is where the expression 'to look in many directions at once' comes from," Chaumel said excitedly. "We cannot, but the Old Ones could."

In his corner, Brannel was hanging on to every word. Keff realized that his three guests comprehended far more of the alien languages than he could. The two mages chimed in cheerfully when the Old Ones spoke, giving the meaning of gestures and words in the common Ozran tongue, which Keff knew now was nothing more than a dialect of Human Standard blended with the Old Ones' spoken language. Somewhat ruefully, he observed that, with Carialle's enhanced cognitive capacity, he, the xenolinguist, was the one who would retain the least of what was going by on the screen. Carialle signaled for Keff's attention when a handful of schematics flashed by.

"Your engineer identifies those microwave beams that have been puzzling me," she said. "They're the answerback to the command function from the items of power telling the Core of Ozran how much power to send. Each operates on a slightly different frequency, like personal communicators. The Core also feeds the devices themselves. Hmm, slight risk of radioactivity there." One of Carialle's auxiliary screens lit with an exploded view of one of the schematics. "But I haven't seen any signs of cancers. In spite of their faults, Ozrans are a healthy bunch, so it must be low enough to be harmless."

Another compression of time. In the next series of videos, the humans had established homes for themselves and were producing offspring. Some, like the unknown narrator, had entered into apprenticeships to learn the means of using the power items from the Old Ones. The rest lived in underground homes on the plains.

"Hence the division of Ozrans into two peoples," Keff said, nodding. "It's hard to believe this is the same planet."

The video changed to views of burgeoning fields and broad, healthy croplands. Ozran soil evidently suited Terran-based plant life. The narrator aimed his recorder at adapted skips full of grain and vegetables being hauled by domesticated six-packs. The next scene, which made the Ozrans gasp with pleasure, showed the humans and one or two Old Ones hurrying for shelter in a farm cavern as a cloudburst began. Heavy rain pelted down into the fields of young, green crops.

In the next scene, almost an inevitable image, one proud farmer was taped standing next to a prize gourd the size of a small pig. Other humans were congratulating him.

Keff glanced at the Ozrans. All three were spellbound by the images of lush farmland.

"These cannot be pictures of our world," Plenna said, "but those are the Mountains of the South. I've known them since my childhood. I have never seen vegetables that big!"

"It is fiction," Chaumel said, frowning. "Our farms could not possibly produce anything like that giant root."

"They could once," Carialle said, "a thousand years ago. Before you mages started messing up the system you inherited. Please observe."

She showed the full analysis of the puff of air that had been trapped in the tape cassette. Keff read it and nodded. He understood where Carialle was headed.

"This shows that the atmosphere in the early days of human habitation of Ozran had many more nitrogen/oxygen/carbon chains and a far higher moisture content than the current atmosphere does." Another image overlaid the first. "Here is what you're breathing now. You have an unnaturally high ozone level. It increases every time there is a massive call for power from the Core of Ozran. If you want more . . ."

In the middle of the cabin Carialle created a three-dimensional image of Ozran. "This is how your planet was seen from space by your ancestors." The globe browned. Icecaps shrank slightly. The oceans nibbled away at coastline and swamped small islands. The continents appeared to shrink together slightly in pain. "This is how it looks now."

Plenna hugged herself in concern as Ozran changed from a healthy green planet to its present state.

"And what for the future?" she asked, woebegone eyes on Carialle's image.

"All is not lost, Magess. Let me show you a few other planets in the Central Worlds cluster," Carialle said, putting up the image of an ovoid, water-covered globe studded with small, atoll-shaped land masses. "Kojuni was in poor condition from industrial pollution. It took an effort, but its population reclaimed it." The sky of Kojuni lightened from leaden gray to a clear, light silver. "Even planet Earth had to fight to survive." A slightly flattened spheroid of blue, green, and violet spun among them. The green masses on the continents receded and expanded as Carialle compressed centuries into seconds. For additional examples, she showed several Class-M planets in good health, with normal weather patterns of wind, rain, and snow scattering across their faces. The three-dimensional maps faded, leaving the image of present-day Ozran spinning before them.

Chaumel cleared his throat.

"But what do you say is the solution?" he asked.

"You overlords have got to stop using the power," Keff said. "It's as simple as that."

"Give up power? Never!" Chaumel said, outraged, with the same expression he would have worn if Keff had told him to cut off his right leg. "It is the way we are."

"Mage Keff." Brannel, greatly daring, crept up beside them and spoke for the first time, addressing his remarks only to the brawn. "What you showed of the first New Ones and their land—that is what the workers of Klemay have been trying to do for as long as I have lived." He looked at Plenna and Chaumel. "We know plants can grow bigger. Some years they do. Most die or stay small. But I know—"

"Quiet!" Chaumel roared, springing to his feet. Brannel was driven cowering into the corner. "Why are you letting a fur-face talk?" the silver mage demanded of Keff. "You can see by his face he knows nothing."

"Now, look, Chaumel," Keff said, aiming an admonitory finger at him, "Brannel is intelligent. Listen to him. He has something that no other farmer on your whole world does: a working memory—and that's your fault, you and your fellow overlords. You've mutated them, you've mutilated them, but they're still human. Don't you understand what you saw on the tape? Brannel knows when, and probably *why* your crops have failed, so let the man talk."

Brannel was gratified that Mage Keff stuck up for him. So he gathered courage and tried, haltingly, in the face of Chaumel's disapproval, to describe the failed efforts of years. "We seek to feed the earth so it will burgeon like this—I know it could—but every time, the plants either die or the cold and dryness come back when the mages have battles. The farms could feed us so much better, if there was more water, if it was warmer. Of the crops"—he held up all eight of his digits—"this many do not survive." He folded down five fingers.

"You're losing over sixty percent of your yield because you like to live high," Keff said. "Your superfluous uses of power, to show off, to play, to *kill*, is irresponsible. You're killing your world. One day your farms won't be able to sustain themselves. People will die of starvation. No matter what you think of their mental capacity, you couldn't want that because then *you'd* have no food and no one to do the menial labor you require."

Chaumel looked from Keff's grim face to the spinning globe of Ozran, and sat down heavily in the crash couch.

"We *are* doing that," he said, raising his long hands in surrender. "Everything he says, he knows. But if I lay down my items of power to help, my surrender will not stop all the others, nor will appealing to wisdom. We mages distrust each other too much."

"Then we need to negotiate a mass cease-fire," Carialle said.

"Not without a ready alternative," Chaumel returned promptly. "Our system is steeped in treachery and the counting of coup."

"I found references to that, too," Keff said, consulting a page of the first manual. "Somebody made a bad translation for your forefathers of instructions given to officers seeking promotion. It says 'consideration for continued higher promotion will be given to those individuals who complete the most successful projects in the most efficient manner.' It goes on to say that those projects should benefit the whole community, but I guess that part got lost over time. There's a similar clause in our ship's manual, just in updated language."

Chaumel groaned.

"Then all this time we have been making an enormous mistake." He appealed to Keff and the image of Carialle. "I didn't know that we were acting on bad information. All my life I thought I *was* following the strictures of the First Ones. I sought to be worthy of my ancestors. I am ashamed."

Keff realized that Chaumel was genuinely horrified. By his own lights, the silver mage was an honorable man.

"Well," Keff said, slowly, "you can start to put things right by helping us."

Chaumel chopped a hand across.

"Your ship is free. What else do you want me to do?"

"Seek out the Core of Ozran and find out what it was really meant to do, what its real capacity is," Carialle said at once. "It's possible, although I think unlikely, that you can retain some of your current lifestyle, but if you are serious about wanting to rescue your planet and future generations—"

"Oh, I am," Chaumel said. "I will give no more trouble."

"Then it's time to redirect the power to its original purpose, as conceived by the Ancient Ones: weather control."

"But what shall we do about the other mages?" Plennafrey asked.

"If we can't convince 'em," Carialle said, "I think I can figure out how to disable them, based on what our long-gone chronicler said about answerback frequencies. With a little experimentation, I can block specific signals, no matter how tight a wave band they're broadcast on. The others will learn to live on limited power, or none at all. It's their choice."

"We'd employ that option," Keff said quickly when he saw Chaumel's reaction, "only if there is no other way to persuade them to cooperate."

"And that is where I come in," Chaumel said, smiling for the first time. "I am held in some esteem on Ozran. I will use my influence to negotiate, as you say, a widespread mutual surrender. With the help of the magical pictures you will show us"—he bowed to Carialle's image—"we will persuade the others to see the wisdom in returning to the ways of the Ancient Ones. We must not fail. The size of that gourd . . ." he said, shaking his head in gently mocking disbelief.

"I still think you're wrong to leave Brannel behind," Keff argued, as Plenna lofted him over the broad plains toward Chaumel's stronghold.

"It is better that only we three, with the aid of Carialle and her illusion-casting, seek to convince the mages," the silver magiman said imperturbably. He sat upright in his chariot, hands folded over his belly.

"But why not Brannel? I'm not a native. I can't explain things in a way your people will understand."

Chaumel shook his head, and pitched his voice to carry over the wind. "My fellows will have enough difficulty to believe in a woman who lives inside a wall. They will not countenance a smart four-finger. Come, we must discuss strategy! Tell me again what it said about promotion in the documents. I must memorize that."

The chariots flew too far away even to be seen on the magic pictures. Brannel, left alone in the main cabin, felt awkward at being left out but dared not, in the face of Chaumel's opposition, protest. He remained behind, haunting the ship like a lonely spirit.

The flat magiwoman appeared on the wall beside him, and paced beside him as he walked up and back.

"I don't know when they'll be coming back," Carialle said very gently, surprising him out of his thoughts. "You should go now. Keff will come and get you when he returns."

"But, Magess," Brannel began, then halted from voicing the argument that sprang to his tongue. After all, this time she was not driving him away with painful sounds, but he was unhappy at being dismissed whenever the overlords had no need of him. After all the talk of equality and the promise of apprenticeship following his great risk-taking in Magess Plennafrey's stronghold, he, the simple worker, was once more ignored and forgotten. He sighed.

"Now, Brannel." The picture of the woman smiled. "You'll be missed in the cavern if you don't go. True?"

"True."

"Then come back when you've finished your work for the day. You can keep me company while I'm running the rest of the tapes." The voice was coaxing. "You'll see them before Magess Plenna and Chaumel. How about that as an apology for not sending you out with the others?"

Brannel brightened slightly. It would be hard to return to daily life after his brush with greatness. But he nodded, head held high. He had much to think about.

"Oh, and Brannel," Carialle said. The flat magess was kind. She gestured toward the food door which opened. A plate lay there. "The bottom layer is soft bread. You can roll the rest up in it. We call it a 'sandwich.'"

He walked down the ship's ramp with the "sandwich" of magefood cradled protectively between his hands. The savory smell made his mouth water, even though it hadn't been long since he had eaten his most delicious lunch. How he would explain his day's absence to Alteis Brannel didn't yet know, but at least he would do it on a full belly. Associating with mages was most assuredly a mixed blessing.

"Why not relax?" Chaumel said, leaning back at his ease in a deeply carved armchair that bobbed gently up and down in the air. "He will come or he will not. I shall ask the next prospect and we'll collect High Mage Nokias later. Sit down! Relax! I will pour us some wine. I have a very good vintage from the South."

Keff stopped his pacing up and back in the great room of Chaumel's stronghold. Chaumel had decided on the first mage to whom he would appeal, and sent a spy-eye with the discreet invitation. Evening had fallen while the three of them waited to see if Nokias would accept. The holographic projection table from the main cabin was set up in the middle of the room. He went over to touch it, making sure it was all right. Plennafrey watched him. The young magiwoman sat in an upright chair in her favorite place by the curtains, hands folded in her lap.

"It's important to get this right," Keff said.

"I know it," Chaumel said. "I am cognizant of the risks. I may enjoy my life as it is, but I love my world, and I want it to continue after I'm gone. You may find it difficult to convince my fellows of that. I achieve nothing by worrying about what they will say before I have even asked the question. The evidence speaks for itself."

"But what if they don't believe it?"

"You leave the rest to me," Chaumel said. He snapped his fingers and a servitor appeared bearing a tray holding a wine bottle and a glass. He poured out a measure of amber liquid and offered it to Keff. The brawn shook his head and resumed pacing. With a shrug, Chaumel drank the wine himself.

"All clear and ready to go," Carialle said through Keff's implant.

"*Receiving*," Keff said, testing his lingual transmitter, and let it broadcast to the others.

"I have pinpointed the frequencies of all of Chaumel's and Plennafrey's items of power, including their chariots. They're all within a very narrow wave band. Will you ask Plenna to try manipulating something, preferably not dangerous or breakable?"

Plenna, grateful for something to do to interrupt the waiting, was happy to oblige.

"I shall use my belt to make my shoe float," Plenna said, taking off her dainty primrose slipper and holding it aloft. She stepped away, leaving it in place in midair.

"But you're not touching the belt," Keff said. "I've noticed the others do that, too."

Plenna laughed, a little thinly, showing that she, too, was nervous about the coming confrontation. "For such a small thing, concentrating is enough."

"Here goes," Carialle said.

Without fanfare, the shoe dropped to the ground.

"Hurrah!" Keff cheered.

"That is impossible," Plenna said. She picked it up and replaced it, this time with her hand under her long sash.

"Do it again, Cari!"

Carialle needed a slightly more emphatic burst of static along the frequency, but it broke the spell. The shoe tumbled to the floor. Plennafrey put it back on her foot.

"No answerback, no power," Carialle said simply, in Keff's ear. "Now all I have to do is be open to monitor the next magiman's power signals and I can interrupt *his* spells, too. I'm only afraid that with such narrow parameters, there might be spillover to another item I don't want to shut off. I'm tightening up tolerances as much as I can."

"Good job, Cari," Keff said. He smacked his palms together and rubbed them.

"You are very cheerful about the fall of a shoe," Chaumel said.

"It may be the solution to any problems with dissenters," Keff said.

A flash of gold against the dark sky drew their attention to the broad balcony visible through the tall doors. Nokias materialized alone above Chaumel's residence and alighted in the nearest spot to the door. As their message had bidden him, he had arrived discreetly, without an entourage. Chaumel rose from his easy chair and strode out to greet his distinguished guest.

"Great Mage Nokias! You honor my poor home. How kind of you to take the trouble to visit. I regret if my message struck you as anything but a humble request."

Nokias's reply was inaudible. Chaumel continued in the same loud voice, heaping compliments on the Mage of the South. Keff and Plenna hid behind the curtained doors and listened. Plenna suppressed a giggle.

"Laying it on thick, isn't he?" Keff whispered. The girl had to cover her mouth with both hands not to let out a trill of amusement.

Nokias mellowed under Chaumel's rain of praise and entered the great hall in expansive good humor.

"Why the insistence on secrecy, old friend?" the high mage asked, slapping Chaumel on the back with one of his huge hands.

"There was a matter that I could discuss only with you, Nokias," Chaumel said. He beckoned toward the others' place of concealment.

Keff stepped out from the curtains, pulling Plenna with him.

"Good evening, High Mage," he said, bowing low. Nokias's narrow face darkened with anger.

"What are they doing here?" Nokias demanded.

Chaumel lost not a beat in his smooth delivery of compliments.

"Keff has a tale to tell you, high one," Chaumel said. "About our ancestors."

Carialle, alone on the night-draped plain a hundred klicks to the east, monitored the conversation through Keff's aural and visual implants. Chaumel was good. Every move, every gesture, was intended to bring his listeners closer to his point of view. If Chaumel ever chose to leave Ozran, he had a place in the Diplomatic Service any time he cared to apply.

She kept one eye on him while running through her archives. Her job was to produce, on cue, the images Chaumel wanted. Certain parameters needed to be met. The selection of holographic video must make their point to a hostile audience. And hostile Nokias would be when Chaumel got to the bottom line.

"You are no doubt curious why I should ask you here,

when we spent all day yesterday and all morning together, High Mage," Chaumel said, jovially, "but an important matter has come up and you were the very first person I thought of asking to aid me."

"I?" Nokias asked, clearly flattered. "But what is this matter?"

"Ah," Chaumel said, and spoke to the air. "Carialle, if you please?"

"Carialle?" Nokias asked, looking first at Plennafrey, then at Keff. "Has he two names, then?"

"No, high one. But Keff does come from whence our ancestors came, and his silver tower has another person in it. She cannot come out to see you, but she has many talents."

That was the first signal. Using video effects she cadged from a 3-D program she and Keff watched in port, she spun the image up from the holo-table as a complicated spiral, widening it until it resolved itself as the globe of Ozran, present day.

Nokias was impressed by Keff's "magic," according him a respectful glance before studying the picture before him. Chaumel led him through a discussion of current farming techniques.

At the next cue, Carialle introduced the image of Ozran as it had been in their distant past.

" . . . If more attention were paid to farming and conservation," Chaumel's smooth voice continued.

Maybe a little video of a close-up look at the farms run by the four-fingers would be helpful. Pity the images taken through Keff's contact button were 2-D, but she could coax a pseudo-holograph out of the stereoscopic view from his eye implants. She found the image from the dog-people's commune, and cropped out images of the six-packs hauling a clothful of small roots.

" . . . Higher yield . . . water usage . . . native vegetation . . . advantage in trade . . ."

In the seat of honor, Nokias sat up straighter. Chaumel's sally regarding superior trading power among the regions had struck a chord in the southern magiman's mind.

"My people farm the tropical zone," Nokias noted, nodding toward Plennafrey, who was all large eyes watching her senior. "We harvest a good deal of soft fruit." Chaumel reacted with polite interest as if it were the first time he'd heard that fact. "If the climate were warmer and more humid, I could see a greater yield from my orchards. That does interest me, friend Chaumel."

"I am most honored, High Mage," the silver magiman said smoothly, with a half-bow. "As you see, there has been a deterioration. . . ."

Keeping the holo playing, Carialle ran through the datafile, looking for specific images relating to yield. With some amusement, she discovered the video from her servo's search for the marsh flower. Globe-frogs clunked into one another getting out of the low-slung robot's way. They gestured indignantly at the servo for scaring them.

"Help us save Ozran," Chaumel was saying, using both gesture and word to emphasize his concept. "Help us to stay the destruction of our world by our own hand."

"Help," Carialle repeated to herself, translating the sign language Chaumel used.

"It would also be good to cease dosing the workers with forget-drugs so they will be smart enough to aid us in saving our world," Plennafrey spoke up, timidly.

"That I am not sure I would do," Nokias said.

"Oh, but consider it," Plenna begged. "They are part of our people. With less power, you will need more aid from them. All it would take is giving them the ability to take more responsibility for their tasks. Help us," she said, also making the gesture.

Carialle played the video of the first landing, including

the encounters with the Old Ones. Nokias was deeply impressed.

"This proves, as we said, that the workers are of the same stock as we. There is no difference," Chaumel concluded.

"I will think about it," Nokias said at last.

"Help," Carialle said again. "Now, where else have I seen that gesture used?" She ran back through her memory. Well, Potria had used it during the first battle over Keff and the ship, but Carialle was certain she had seen it more recently—wait, the frogs!

She replayed the servo's video, reversing the data string to the moment when the robot surprised the marsh creatures. The frogs weren't reacting out of animal fright.

"They were talking to us!" Carialle said. She put the image through IT. The sign language was an exact match.

Intrigued, Carialle ran an analysis of every image of the amphibioids she had and came out with an amazing conclusion.

"Keff," she sent through Keff's implant. "Keff, the globe-frogs!"

"What about them?" he subvocalized. "I'm trying to concentrate on Nokias."

"To begin with, those globular shells were manufactured."

"Sure, a natural adaptation to survive."

"No, they're artificial. Plastic. Not spit and pond muck. *Plastic*. And they speak the sign language. I think we've found our equal, spacefaring race, Keff. They're the Ancient Ones."

"Oh, come on!" Keff said out loud. Nokias and Chaumel turned to stare at him. He smiled sheepishly. "Come on, High Mage. We want you to be prosperous."

"Thank you, Keff," Nokias said, a little puzzled. Favoring Keff with a disapproving glare, Chaumel reclaimed his guest's attention and went on with his carefully rehearsed speech.

Carialle's voice continued low in his ear. "They're so easy to ignore, we went right past them without thinking. That's why the Old Ones moved up into the mountains— to take the technology they stole out of reach of its rightful owners, who couldn't follow them up there. When the humans came, they didn't know about the frogs, so they inherited the power system, not knowing it belonged to someone else. They thought the globe-frogs were just animals. It would explain why they're so interested in any kind of power emission."

"I think perhaps you're on to something, lady," Keff said. "Let's not mention it now. We're asking for enough concessions, and the going is hazardous. We can test your hypothesis later."

"It's *not* a hypothesis," Carialle said. But she controlled her jubilation and went back to being the audio-video operator for the evening.

"Very well," Nokias said, many hours later. "I see that our world will die unless we conserve power. I will even discuss an exchange of greater self-determination for greater responsibility from my workers. But I will let go of my items only if all the others agree, too. You can scarcely ask me to make myself vulnerable to stray bolts from disaffected . . . ah . . . friends."

"High Mage, I agree with you from my heart," Chaumel said, placing a hand over his. "With your help, we can attain concord among the mages, and Ozran will prosper."

"Yes. I must go now," Nokias said, rising from his chair. "I have much to think about. You will notify me of your progress?"

"Of course, High Mage," Chaumel said. He turned to escort his guest out into the night.

Gasping, Plennafrey pointed toward the curtains. The

others spun to see. A handful of spy-spheres hovering there flitted out into the window and disappeared into the night.

"Whose were they?" Chaumel demanded.

"It was too dark to see," Plenna said.

"I am going," Nokias said, alarmed. "These eavesdroppers may be the enemy of your plans, Chaumel. I have no wish to be the target of an assassination attempt."

Escorted by a wary Chaumel, Keff, and Plennafrey, the golden mage hurried out to his chariot. He took off, and teleported when he was only a few feet above the balcony.

"I do not wish to distress you, but Nokias is correct when he says there will be much opposition to our plans," Chaumel said. "You would be safe here tonight. I am warding every entrance to the stronghold."

"No, thank you," Keff said, holding Plennafrey's hand. "I'd feel safer in my own cabin."

Chaumel bowed. "As you wish. Tomorrow we continue the good work, eh?" In spite of the danger, he showed a guarded cheerfulness. "Nokias is on our side, friends. I sense it. But he is reasonable to be afraid of the others. If any of us show weakness, it is like baring one's breast to the knife. Good night."

✿ CHAPTER TWELVE

Keff mounted the platform behind Plenna's chair, and put his hands on the back as the blue-green conveyance lifted into the sky. He watched her weave a shield and throw it around them. Chaumel, his duties as a host done, went inside. The great doors closed with a final-sounding *boom!* He suspected the silver mage was sealing every nook and cranny against intrusion.

Nothing was visible ahead of them but a faint jagged line on the horizon marking the tops of mountains. Plenna's chair gave off a dim glow that must have been visible for a hundred klicks in every direction. The thought of danger sent frissons up his legs into the root and spine of his body, but he found to his surprise that he wasn't frightened.

His arms were nudged apart and off the chair back, making him jerk forward, afraid of losing his balance. He glanced down. Plennafrey reached for his hands and drew them down toward her breast, turning her face up toward his for a kiss. The light limned her cheekbones and the delicate line of her jaw. Keff thought he had never seen anything so beautiful in his life.

"Am I always to feel this excited way about you when we are in peril?" Plenna asked impishly. Keff ran his hands caressingly down her smooth shoulders and she shivered with pleasure.

"I hope not," he said, chuckling at her abandon. "I'd never know if the thrill was danger or love. And I do care about the difference."

They didn't speak again for the rest of the journey. Keff listened with new appreciation to the night-birds and the quiet sounds of Ozran sighing in its sleep. In the sky around them was an invisible network of power, but it didn't impinge on the beauty or the silence.

The airlock door lifted, allowing Plennafrey to steer her chair smoothly into the main cabin. This time she was able to choose her landing place and parked the conveyance against the far bulkhead beside Keff's exercise equipment. Keff handed Plenna off the chair and swung her roughly into his arms. Their lips met with fiery urgency. Her hands moved up his back and into his hair.

"Keff, can we talk?" Carialle asked in his ear.

"Not now, Cari," Keff muttered. "Is it an emergency?"

"No. I wanted to discuss my findings of this evening with you."

"Not now, please." Keff breathed out loud as Plenna ran her teeth along the tendon at the side of his neck.

Crossly, Carialle gave him a burst of discordant noise in both aural implants. He winced slightly but refused to let her distract him from Plennafrey. His thumbs ran down into the young woman's bodice, brushed over hard nipples and soft, pliant flesh. He bent his head down to them.

Plennafrey moaned softly. "Carialle won't watch us, will she?"

"No," Keff said reassuringly. He bumped the control with his elbow and the cabin hatch slid aside. "Her domain ends at my door. Pray, lady, enter mine!"

In the circle of his arm, Plenna tiptoed into Keff's cabin.

"It is like you," she said. "Spare, neat, and very handsome. Oh, books!" She picked one off the small shelf by his bed and lightly fingered the pages. "Of course, I cannot read it." She glanced up at Keff with a bewitching dimple at the corner of her mouth. Her eye was caught by the works of art hanging on the walls. "Those are very good. Haunting. Who painted them?"

"You're standing in her," Keff said, grinning. "Carialle is an artist."

"She is wonderfully talented," Plenna said, with a decided nod. "But I like you better."

There was only one answer Keff could give. He kissed her.

At the end of their lovemaking, Keff propped himself up on his elbow to admire Plennafrey. Her unbound hair tumbled around her white shoulders and breast like black lace.

"You're so lovely," Keff said, toying with a stray strand. "I will feel half my heart wrenched away when I have to go."

"But why should I not come with you to your world?" Plenna asked, her fingers tracing an intricate design on his forearm.

"Because I'm in space eighty percent of my life," Keff said, "and when I'm planet-side I'm seldom near civilization. My usual job is first contact with alien species. It's very strange and full of so many dangers I couldn't even describe them all to you. You wouldn't be happy with the way I live."

"But I am not happy here now," Plenna said plaintively, clasping her hands together in appeal. "If you take me with you, I would cede my claim of power to Brannel and keep my promise to him. There is nothing here to hold me; no family, no friends. I would be glad to learn about other people and other worlds."

"Yes, but . . ."

She touched his face, and her eyes searched his. "We suit one another, do we not?"

"Yes, but . . ."

She silenced him with a kiss.

"Then please consider it," she said, cuddling into his arms. Keff crushed her close to him, lost in her scent, lost in her.

In the early morning hours, Carialle monitored her exterior movement sensors until she heard sounds of life from the marshy area downhill from her bluff. She let down her ramp and sent her two servo robots forth into the pink light of dawn. The boxy units disappeared through the break in the brush and over the edge of the ridge. Carialle, idly noting a half dozen spy-eyes hovering at a hundred meters distant, heard clunks and high-pitched squawking as they reached their goal. In a little while, the servos returned to view, herding before them a pair of globe-frogs. The amphibioids tried to signal their indignation, but had to keep paddling on the inside of their plastic spheres before the boxes bumped into them from behind. With some effort, the servos got their quarry up the ramp. Carialle shut the airlock door and pulled up her ramp behind them.

As the frogs entered the main cabin, Carialle hooked into the IT, calling up all the examples of sign language that she and Keff had managed to record over the last few days.

"Now, little friends," she said, "we're going to see if that sign you made was a fluke or not." She manifested the picture of another frog on the side screen at their level, like them but with enough differences of color and configuration to make sure they knew it was a stranger. "Let's chat."

A few hours later, Keff's door opened, and the brawn emerged, yawning, wearing only uniform pants. Plenna, wrapped in his bathrobe, followed him, trailing a lazy finger down his neck.

"Good morning, young lovers," Carialle said brightly. "We have guests."

Red lights chased around the walls and formed an arrow pointing down at the two globe-frogs huddled together in the corner nearest the airlock corridor. Keff goggled.

"But how did they get past Plenna's barrier? She told me she warded the area. Any intrusion should have set off an alarm."

"We're protected against magic only," Plenna said, eyeing the marsh creatures with distaste. "Not vermin."

"They aren't vermin and they're aware you don't like them," Carialle said indignantly. "We've been exchanging compliments."

On her main screen she displayed an expanded image of the small creatures staring at a strange-looking frog on the wall.

"That's my computer-generated envoy," Carialle explained. "Now, watch." The image made a gesture, to which the native creatures responded with a similar movement. As the complexity and number of signs increased, the frogs became excited, bumping into one another to respond to their imaginary host.

Keff watched the data string, glancing once in a while at the frogs.

"Monkey see monkey do," Keff said, shaking his head. "They observed the Ozrans making signs and copied them. This little performance is without meaning."

"Beasts Blatisant," Carialle countered. Keff grimaced. "Keff, I didn't make a subjective judgment on the frequency and meaning of these symbols. Check IT's function log. Read the vocabulary list."

When Keff lifted his eyes from the small readout screen, they were shining.

"Who'd have thought it?" he said. "Cari, all praise to your sharp wits and powers of observation."

Plennafrey had been listening carefully to the IT box's translation of Carialle's and Keff's conversation. She pointed to the frogs.

"Do you mean they can talk?" she asked.

"More than that," Keff said. "They may be the founders of your civilization." Plenna's jaw dropped open, and she stared at the two amphibioids. "Your belt buckle—may I borrow it?"

The belt flew out of Keff's room and smacked into Plenna's hands. She started to extend it to him, then withdrew it. "What for?" she asked.

"To see if they know what to do with it. Er, take it off the belt. It's too heavy for them." Obligingly, Plenna detached the buckle and handed it to him.

Very slowly, Keff walked to where the frogs stood. They waited passively within their globes, kicking occasionally at the water to maintain their positions and watching him with their beady black eyes. Keff hunkered down and held out the buckle.

Wearing a startled expression on its peaky face, the larger frog met his eyes. Immediately, the case opened, splitting into two halves, splashing water on the cabin floor, and the frog stretched out for the power item. Its skinny wrist terminated in a long, sensitively fingered hand which outspread was as large as Plennafrey's. The ends of the digits slid into the five apertures. There was a nearly audible *click*.

"It is connected to the Core of Ozran," Plennafrey said softly.

The water that had been inside the plastic ball gathered around the frog's body as if still held in place by the shell. Thus sheltered, the amphibioid rose on surprisingly long, skinny legs and made a tour of the cabin. Its small face was alive with wonder. Keff directed it to the astrogation tank showing the position of Ozran and its sun. The frog looked intelligently into the three-dimensional star map, and studied the surrounding control panels and keyboards. Then it returned to Keff.

"Help us," it signaled.

"You win, lady dear. Here're your Ancient Ones," Keff said, turning to Plennafrey with a flourish. "They were among you all the time." The young magiwoman swallowed.

"I . . ." She seemed to have trouble getting the words out. "I do not think that I can respect _frogs_."

Chaumel was more philosophical when confronted by the facts.

"I refuse to be surprised," he said, shaking his head. "All in the space of a day or so, my whole life is thrown into confusion. The fur-faces turn out to be our long-lost brothers and we have cousins in plenty among the stars ready to search us out. Some of them live inside boxes. Why should we not discover that the Ancient Ones exist under our noses in the swamps?"

"Try talking to one of them," Keff urged him. Doubtfully, Chaumel looked at the three globe-frogs Keff and Plenna had brought to his stronghold. They were rolling around the great room, signing furiously to one another over an artifact or a piece of furniture.

"Well . . ." Chaumel said, uneasily.

"Go on," Keff said. With a few waves of his hands, Keff got their attention and signed to them to return to him. Once or twice the "courtiers" turned all the way over, trying to negotiate over the slick floor, but the biggest maintained admirable control of his sphere.

After the initial attempts at communication, Keff had let Carialle's two subjects go, asking them to send back one of their leaders. Within an hour, a larger frog speckled with yellow to show its great age had come up the ramp, rolling inside a battered case. A pair of smaller, younger frogs, guards or attendants, hurtled up behind it. The first amphibioid rolled directly over to Plenna and demanded her belt buckle. For his imperious manner as well as his great size, Keff and Carialle had dubbed him the Frog Prince. From the two symbols with which he designated his name, Keff decided he was called something like Tall Eyebrow.

"I'm sure it loses something in the translation," he explained.

Chaumel knelt and made a few signs of polite greeting. He was unsure of himself at first, but grew enthusiastic when his courtesies were returned and expanded upon.

"These are not trained creatures," he said with delight. "It really understands me."

"Tall just said the same thing about you," Keff noted, amused.

"It has feet. What are the globes for?"

"Ozran used to have much higher humidity," Keff said. "The frogs' skins are delicate. The shells protect them from the dry air."

"We cannot tell the other mages about them until we have negotiated the 'cease-fire,'" Chaumel told him seriously. "Already Nokias regrets that he said he will cooperate. He suspects Ferngal of sending those spy-eyes the other night and I have no reason to doubt him. If we present them with speaking animals who need bubbles to live, they will think we are mad, and the whole accord will fall apart."

Neither Keff nor Carialle, listening through the implant contacts, argued the point.

"It's too important to get them to stop using power," Keff said. "It goes against my better judgment, but it'll help the frogs' case if we don't try to make the mages believe too many impossible things before breakfast."

During the successive weeks, the brawn and the two magifolk traveled to each mage's stronghold to convince him or her to join with them in the cause of environmental survival.

Keff spent his free time, such as remained of it, divided between Plennafrey in the evenings and the frogs in the early morning. He had to learn another whole new language, but he had never been so happy. His linguistic skills were getting a good, solid workout. Carialle's memory banks began to fill with holos of gestures with different meanings and implications.

Since the mages had always used the signs as sacred or magical communion, Keff had to begin all over again with the frogs on basic language principles. The mages had employed only a small quantity of gestures that had been gleaned from the Old Ones in their everyday lives, giving him a very limited working vocabulary. Chaumel knew only a few hundred signs, Plenna a few dozen. Keff used those to build toward scientific understanding.

Mathematical principles were easy. These frogs were the five-hundredth generation since the life-form came to this world. That verified what Keff had been coming to believe, that none of the three dominant life-forms who occupied Ozran were native to it.

Knowledge of their past had been handed down by rote through the generations. The frogs had manufactured the life-support bubbles with the aid of the one single item of power that remained to them. The other devices had all been borrowed, and then stolen by the Flat Ones, by whom Keff understood them to mean the Old Ones.

For a change, IT was working as well as he had always hoped it would. An optical monitor fed the frogs' gestures into the computer, and the voice of IT repeated the meaning into Keff's implant and on a small speaker for the benefit of the others. Keff worked out a simple code for body language that IT used to transcribe the replies he spoke out loud. Having to act out his sentence after he said it made the going slow, but in no time he picked up more and more of the physical language so he could use it to converse directly.

He was however surprised at how few frogs were willing to come forward to meet with the Ozrans and help bridge the language barrier. The Frog Prince assured him it was nothing personal; a matter of safety. After so many years, they found it difficult to trust any of the Big Folk. Keff understood perfectly what he meant. He was careful never to allude to the frogs when on any of his many visits to the mages' strongholds.

On his knees at the end of another dusty row of roots, Brannel observed Keff and Plennafrey returning to the silver ship. Scraping away at the base of a wilted plant as long as he dared, he waited for Keff to keep Carialle's promise and come get him. It seemed funny they couldn't see him, but perhaps they hadn't looked his way when he was standing up. He knew he could go up to the door and be admitted, but he was reluctant to do so until asked as they seemed disinterested in asking him. Weighing the question of waiting or not waiting, he pushed his gathering basket into the next row and started digging through the clay-thick soil for more of the woody vegetables.

His thoughts were driven away by a stunning blow to the side of the head. Brannel fell to the earth in surprise.

Alteis stood over him, waving a clump of roots from his basket, spraying dirt all over the place. Some of it was on Brannel's head. A female with light brown fur stood beside the old leader, her eyes flashing angrily.

"You're in the wrong row, Brannel!" Alteis exclaimed. "This is Gonna's row. You should go that way." He pointed to the right and waited while Brannel picked up his gear and moved.

"Your mind in the mountains?" Fralim chortled from his position across the field. What traces of long-term memory the others retained came from rote and repetition, and they had been witness to Brannel's peculiarities and ambitions since he was small. Everyone but his mother scorned the young male's hopes. "We saw the Mage Keff and the Magess Plennafrey fly into the tower. You planning to set yourself up with the mages?" He cackled.

Another worker joined in with the same joke he had been using for twenty years. "Gonna shave your face and call yourself Mage, Brannel?"

Brannel was stung. "If I do, I'll show you what power the overlords wield, Mogag," he said in a voice like a growl. Alteis walked up and slapped him in the head again.

"Work!" the leader said. "The roots won't pull themselves."

The others jeered. Brannel worked by himself until the sun was just a fingertip's width above the mountain rim at the edge of the valley. Any time, food would arrive, and he would be able to sneak away. Perhaps, if no one was looking, he might go *now*.

It was his bad luck that Alteis and his strapping son were almost behind him. Fralim yanked him back by the collar and seat of his garment from the edge of the field, and plunked him sprawling into his half-worked row.

"Stay away from that tower," Alteis ordered him. "You have duties to your own folk."

Moments crept by like years. Brannel, fuming, finished his day's chores with the least possible grace. As soon as the magess kept her promise to teach him, he would never return to this place full of stupid people. He would study all day, and work great works of magic, like the ancestors and the Old Ones.

At the end of the day, he hung back from the crowd hurrying toward the newly materialized food. With Alteis busy doing something else, there was no one watching one discontented worker. Brannel sneaked away through the long shadows on the field and hurried up to the ship.

As he reached the tall door, it slid upward to disgorge Magess Plennafrey and Keff on her floating chair.

"Oh, Brannel!" Mage Keff said, surprised. "I'm glad you came up. I am sorry, but we've got to run now. Carialle will look after you, all right?" Before Brannel could tell him that nothing was "all right," the chair was already wafting them away. "See you later!" Keff called.

Brannel watched them ascend into the sky, then made his way toward the heart of the tower.

Inside, Magess Carialle was doing something with a trio of marsh creatures.

"Oh, Brannel," she said, in an unconscious echo of Keff. "Welcome. Have you eaten yet?" A meal was bubbling in the small doorway even before he had stopped shaking his head. "I promised you a peep at the tapes. Will you sit down in the big chair? I've got to keep doing another job at the same time, but I can handle many tasks at once."

Keff's big chair turned toward him and, at that direct invitation, Brannel came forward, only a little uneasy to be alone in the great silver cylinder without any other living beings. Marsh creatures didn't count, he thought, as he ate his dinner, and he wasn't sure what Carialle was.

Though she didn't seem to eat, in deference to his appetite, Magess Carialle had prepared for him a meal twice the size of the one he had eaten last time. Each dish was satisfying and most delicious. With every bite he liked the thought less and less of returning to raw roots and grains. He was nearly finished eating when the big picture before him lit up and he found himself looking into the weird green face of an Old One. He stopped with a half-chewed mouthful.

"Here's the first of the tapes, starting at the point we left off last time," Carialle's voice said.

"Ah," Brannel said, recovering his wits.

He couldn't not watch for he was fascinated and her voice kept supplying translations in his tongue. Brannel asked her the occasional question. She answered, but without offering as much of her attention as she gave one of Keff's inquiries. He glanced back over his shoulder, wondering why she had made a picture of the marsh creatures, and what they found so interesting in it.

"   . . . And that's the last of the tapes," Carialle said, sometime later. "What a fine resource to have turn up."

"What am I to do now?" Brannel asked, looking around him. Carialle's picture appeared on the wall beside him. The lady smiled.

"You've done so much for us—and for Ozran, by telling us about farming," she said. "All we can do now is wait to see what the mages think of our evidence."

"I would tell the mages all I know," Brannel said hopefully. "It would help convince them to farm better." The flat magess shook her head.

"Thank you, Brannel. Not yet. It would be better if you didn't get involved—less dangerous for you," she said. "Now, I don't have any tasks that need doing. Why don't you go home and sleep? I'm sure Keff will find you tomorrow, or the next day. As soon as he has any definite news to tell you."

Brannel went away, but Keff didn't come.

The worker spent the next day, and the next, waiting for Keff to stop off to see him between his hurried journeys to the far reaches of Ozran on the magess's chair. He never glanced at Brannel. In spite of his promise, he had forgotten the worker existed. He had forgotten their growing friendship.

Worse yet, Brannel now had a head full of information about the ancestors and the Old Ones, and what good did it do him? Nothing to do with teaching him to become a mage, or getting him better food to eat. In time his disappointment grew into a towering rage. How *dare* the strangers build up his hopes and leave him to rot like one of the despised roots of the field! How dare they make him a promise, knowing he never forgot anything, and then pretend it had never been spoken? Brannel swore to himself that he would never trust a mage again.

Ferngal's stronghold stood alone on a high, dentate mountain peak, set apart by diverging river branches from the rest of the eastern range. The obsidian-dark stone of its walls offered little of the open hospitality of Chaumel's home. In the dark, relatively low-ceilinged great hall, Keff had the uncomfortable feeling the walls were closing in on him. Brown-robed Lacia and a yellow-coated mage sat with Ferngal as Chaumel gave his by now familiar talk on preserving and restoring the natural balances of Ozran.

Chaumel, in his bright robes, seemed like a living gas-flame as he hovered behind Carialle's illusions. He appealed to each of his listeners in turn, clearly disliking talking to more than one mage at a time. He had voiced a caution to Keff and Plenna before they had arrived.

"In a group, there is more chance of dissension. Careful manipulation will be required and I do not know if I am equal to it."

Keff had felt a chill. "If you can't do it, we're in trouble," he had said. "But we need to speed up the process. The power blackouts are becoming more frequent. I don't know how long you have until there's a complete failure."

"If that happens," Chaumel told his audience, "then mages will be trapped in the mountains with no means of rescue at hand. Food distribution will end, causing starvation in many areas. We have made the fur-faces dependent upon our system. We cannot fail them, or ourselves."

Early in the discussion, Lacia had announced that she viewed the whole concept of the Core of Ozran as science to be sacrilege. She frowned at Chaumel whenever the silver magiman made eye contact with her. The mage in yellow robes, an older man named Whilashen, said little and sat through Chaumel's speech pinching his lower lip between thumb and forefinger.

"I do not like this idea of relying more upon the servant class," Ferngal said. "They are mentally limited."

"With respect, High Mage," Keff said, "how would you know? Chaumel tells me that even your house servants are given a low dose of the docility drug in their food. I have done tests on the workers in the late Mage Klemay's province and can show you the results. They are of the same racial stock as you, and their capabilities are the same. All they need is more nurturing and education, and of course for you to stop the ritual mutilation and cranial mutations. In the next generation all the children will return to normal human appearance, with the possible exception of retaining the hirsutism. That may need to be bred out."

"Tosh!" Ferngal's ruddy face suffused further.

"I can't wait to see what happens when we tell him about the Frog Prince," Carialle said through the implants. "He'll have apoplexy."

Keff leaned forward, his hands outstretched, making an

appeal. "I can explain the scientific process and show you proof you'll understand."

"Proof you manufacture proves nothing," Ferngal said. "Illusions, that's all, like these pictures."

"But Nokias said . . ." Plennafrey began. Chaumel made one attempt to silence her, but it was too late. "Nokias—"

Ferngal cut her off at once. "You've talked to Nokias? You spoke to him before you came to me?" The black magiman's nostrils flared. "Have you no respect for protocol?"

"He is my liege," Plenna said with quiet dignity. "I was required. You would demand the same from any of the mages of the East."

"Well . . . that is true."

"Will you not consider what we have said?" she pleaded.

"No, I won't give up power and you can stuff your arguments about making the peasants smarter in a place where a magic item won't fit. You're out of your mind asking something like that. And if Nokias has softened enough to say yes, he will regret it." Ferngal showed his teeth in a vicious grin. "I'll soon add the South to my domain. Chaumel, you ought to know better."

"High Mage, sometimes truth must overcome even common sense."

Abruptly, Ferngal lost interest in them.

"Go," he said, tossing a deceptively casual gesture toward the door behind him. "Go now before I lose my temper."

"Heretics!" screamed Lacia.

With what dignity he could muster, Chaumel led the small procession around Ferngal toward the doors. Keff gathered up the holo-table and opened his stride to catch up without running.

He heard a voice whisper very close to his ear. Not Carialle's: a man's.

"Some of us have honor," the voice said. "Tell your master to contact me later." Startled, Keff turned around. Whilashen nodded to him, his eyes intent.

In spite of Chaumel's pleas for confidentiality, word began to spread to the other mages before he had a chance to speak with them in person. Rumors began to spread that Chaumel and an unknown army of mages wanted to take over the rest by destroying their connection to the Core of Ozran. Chaumel spent a good deal of time on what Keff called "damage control," scotching the gossip, and reassuring the panic-stricken magifolk that he was not planning an Ozran-wide coup.

"No one will be *compelled* to give up all power," Chaumel said, trying to calm an angry Zolaika. He sat in her study in a hovering chair with his head at the level of her knees to show respect. Keff and Plennafrey stood on the floor meters below them, silent and watching. "Each mage needs to be allowed free will in such an important matter. But I think you see, Zolaika, and everyone will see in the end, that inevitably we must be more judicious in our use of power. You, in your great wisdom, will have seen that the Core of Ozran is not infinite in its gifts."

Zolaika was guarded. "Oh, I see the truth of what you *say*, Chaumel, but so far, you have offered us no proof! Pictures, what are they? I make pretty illusions like those for my grandchildren."

"We are working on gathering solid proof," Chaumel said, "proof that will convince everyone that what we say about the Core of Ozran is the truth. But, in the meantime, it is necessary to soften the coming blow, don't you think?"

"I'm an old woman," Zolaika snapped. "I don't want words to 'soften the coming blow.' I want facts. I'm not blind or senile. I will be convinced by evidence." Her eyes lost their hard edge for a moment, and Keff fancied he saw a twinkle there for a moment. "You have never lied to me, Chaumel. You say a thousand words where one will do, but you are not a liar, nor an imaginative man. If you're convinced, so will I be. But bring proof!"

As they flew off Zolaika's balcony, Chaumel sat bolt upright in his chariot, a smug expression on his face. "That was most satisfactory."

"It was? She didn't say she'd support us," Keff said.

"But she believes us. Everyone respects her, even the ones who are spelling for her position." Chaumel made a cursory pass with one hand in the air to show what he meant. "Her belief in us will carry weight. Whether or not she actually says she supports us, she does by not saying she *doesn't*."

"There speaks a diplomat," Carialle said. "He makes pure black and white print into one of those awful moire paintings. Progress report: out of some two hundred and seventeen mages with multiple power items, I now have one hundred fifty-two frequency signatures. It is now theoretically possible for me to selectively intercept and deaden power emissions in each of those items."

"Good going. We might need it," Keff said, "but I hope not."

With Zolaika four of the high mages had given tentative agreement to stand down power at the risk of losing it, but meetings with some of the lesser magifolk had not gone well. Potria had heard the first few sentences of Chaumel's discourse and driven them out of her home with a miniature dust storm. Harvel, the next most junior mage above Plenna, had accused her of trying to climb the social ladder over his head. When Chaumel explained that their traditional structure for promotion was a perversion of the ancestors' system, the insulted Harvel had done his best to kill all of them with a bombardment of lightning. Carialle turned off his two magic items, a rod and a ring, and left him to stew as the others effected a hurried withdrawal. "I think that among the remaining mages we can concentrate on the potential troublemakers," Chaumel said as they materialized above his balcony. "Most of the others will not become involved. A hundred of them barely use their spells except to fetch and carry household items, or to power their flying chairs."

"They'll miss it the most," Keff said, "but at least they aren't the conspicuous consumers."

"Oh, well put!" Chaumel said, chortling, as he docketed the phrase. "The 'conspicuous consumers' have been making us do most of the work for them. I laughed when Howet said he'd agree if we talked to his farm workers for him—Verni, what are you doing out here?"

Below them, clinging to the parapet of Chaumel's landing pad, was his chief servant. As soon as the magiman angled in to touch down, Verni ran toward him, wringing his hands.

"Master, High Mage Nokias is here," he whispered as Chaumel rose from the chariot. "He is in the hall of antiquities. He has warded the ways in and out. I have been trapped out here for hours."

"Nokias?" Chaumel said, sharing a puzzled glance with Keff and Plennafrey. "What does he want here? And warded?"

"Yes, master," the servant said, winding his hands in his apron. "None of us can pass in or out until he lets down the barriers."

"How strange. What can frighten a high mage?"

Chaumel strode through the great hall. The servant, Keff, and Plennafrey hurried after him, having to scoot to avoid the tall glass doors closing on their heels.

The silver mage stood back a pace from the second set of doors and felt the air cautiously. Then he moved forward and pounded with the end of his wand.

"High Mage!" he shouted. "It is Chaumel. Open the door! I have warded the outside ways."

The door opened slightly, only wide enough for a human body to pass through. Chaumel beckoned to the others and slipped in. Keff let Plenna go first, then followed with the servant. No one was behind the door. It snapped shut as soon as they were all inside.

Nokias waited halfway down the hall, seated on the old hover-chair, his hands positioned and ready to activate his bracelet amulet. Even at a distance, Keff could see the taut skin around the mage's eyes.

"Old friend," Chaumel said, coming forward with his hands open and relaxed. "Why the secrecy?"

"I had to be discreet," Nokias said. "There's been an attempt on me at my citadel already. You've stirred up a fierce gale among the other mages, Chaumel. Many of them want your head. They're upset about your threats of destruction. Most of the others don't believe your data—they do not want to, that is all. I came to tell you that I *cannot* consider giving up my power. Not now."

"Not now?" Keff echoed. "But you see the reasoning behind it. What's changed?"

"I do see the reasoning," the Mage of the South said, "but there's revolt brewing in my farm caverns. I can't let go with violence threatened. People will die. The harvest will be ruined."

"What has happened?" Chaumel asked.

Nokias clenched his big hands. "I have been speaking to village after village of my workers. Oh, many of them were not sure what I meant by my promises of freedom, but I saw sparks of intelligence there. The difficulties began only a day or so ago. My house servants report that, among the peasantry, there is fear and anger. They cry that they will not cooperate. It is stirring up the others. If I lose my ability to govern, there will be riots."

"It's only their fear of the unknown," Chaumel said smoothly. "They should rejoice in what you're offering them, the first high mage in twenty generations to change the way things are to the way things might be."

"They cannot understand abstract thinking," Nokias corrected him sternly.

"I will go and talk to them on your behalf, Nokias," Chaumel said. "I've done so for Zolaika. It's only right I should also do it for you."

"I would be grateful," Nokias said. "But I will not appear in person."

"You don't need to," Chaumel assured him. "I and my friends here will take care of it."

The farm village looked like any of the others Keff had seen, except that it also boasted an elderly but well cared for orchard as well as the usual fields of crops. A few lonely late fruit clung to the uppermost branches of the trees nearest the home cavern. Nokias's farmers were harvesting the next row's yield.

The Noble Primitives glanced warily at the three "magi-folk" when they arrived, then went about their business with their heads averted, carefully keeping from making eye contact with them.

"Surely they are wondering what brings three mages here," Keff said.

"They dare not ask," Plenna said. "It isn't their place."

Chaumel looked at the sun above the horizon. "It's close enough to the end of the working day."

He flung his hands over his head and the air around him filled with lights of blue and red. Like will-o'-the-wisps the sparks scattered, surrounding the farmers, dancing at them to make them climb down from the trees, gathering them toward the three waiting by the cavern entrance. Keff, flanking Chaumel on the left, watched it all with the admiration due a consummate showman. Plennafrey stood demure and proud on Chaumel's right.

"Good friends!" Chaumel called out to them when the whole village was assembled. "I have news for you from your overlord Nokias!"

In slow, majestic phrases, Chaumel outlined the events to come when the workers would have greater capacity to think and to do. "You look forward to something unimaginable by your parents and grandparents. You workers will have greater scope than any since the ancestors came to Ozran."

"Uh-oh," Carialle said to Keff. "Someone out there is not at all happy to see you. I'm noting heightened blood pressure and heartbeat in someone in the crowd. Give me a sweep view and I'll try to spot them."

Not knowing quite what he was looking for, Keff gazed slowly around at the crowd. The children were openmouthed, as usual, to be in the presence of one of the mighty overlords. Most of the older folk still refused to look up at Chaumel. It was the younger ones who were sneaking glances, and in a couple of cases, staring openly at them the way Brannel had.

" . . . Nokias has sent me, Chaumel the Silver, to announce to you that you shall be given greater freedoms than ever in your lifetime!" Chaumel said, sweeping his sleeves up around his head. "We the mages will be more open to you on matters of education and responsibility. On your part, you must continue to do your duty to the magefolk, as your tasks serve all Ozran. These are the last harvests of the season. It is vital to get them in so you will not be hungry in the winter. In the spring, a new world order is coming, and it is for your benefit that changes will be taking place. Embrace them! Rejoice!"

Chaumel waved his arms and the illusion of a flock of small bluebirds fluttered up behind him. The audience gasped.

"No! It's a lie!" A deep male voice echoed over the plainlands. When everyone whirled right and left to see who was talking, a rock came whistling over the heads of the crowd toward Plenna.

With lightning-fast gestures, the magiwoman warded herself. The rock struck an invisible shield and fell to the ground with a heavy *thud*. Keff saw the color drain from her shocked face. She was controlling herself to keep from crying. Keff pushed in front of the two magifolk and glared at the villagers. Some of them had recoiled in terror, wondering what punishment was in store for them, harboring an assailant. The male who had thrown the stone stood at the back, glaring and fists clenched. Keff hurtled through the crowd after him.

The farmer was no match for the honed body of the spacer. Before the panicked worker could do more than turn away and take a couple of steps, Keff cannoned into him. He knocked the male flat with a body blow. The worker struggled, yelling, but Keff shoved a knee into his spine and bent his arms up behind his head.

"What do you want done with him, Chaumel?" Keff called out in the linga esoterka.

"Bring him here."

Using the male's joined wrists as a handle, Keff hauled upward. To avoid having his wrists break, the rest of the worker followed. Keff trotted him along the path that magically opened up among the rest of the workers.

"Who is in charge of this man?" Chaumel asked. A timid graybeard came forward and bowed deeply. "Even if there is to be change, respect toward one another must still be observed. Give him some extra work to do, to soak up this superfluous energy."

"Is this what the new world order will be like? If we allow the workers more freedom of thought, there will be no safe place for me to go," Plenna said to Keff in an undertone with a catch in her voice. He put an arm around her.

"We'd better get out of here," Keff said under his breath to Chaumel.

"It would have been better if you'd pretended nothing had happened," Chaumel said over Keff's shoulder. "We are supposed to be above such petty attacks. But never mind. Follow me." Though he was obviously shaken, too, the magiman negotiated a calm and impressive departure. The three of them flew hastily away from the village.

"I don't understand it," Chaumel said, when they were a hundred meters over the plain. "In every other village, they've been delighted with the idea of learning and being free. Could they enjoy being stupid? No, no," he chided himself.

Keff sighed. "I'm beginning to think I put my hand into a hornet's nest, Cari," he said under his breath. "Have I done wrong trying to set things straight here?"

"Not at all, Sir Galahad," Carialle reassured him. "Think of the frogs and the power blackouts. Not everyone will be delighted with global change, but never lose sight of the facts. The imbalances of power here, both social and physical, could prove fatal to Ozran. You're doing the right thing, whether or not anyone else thinks so."

When they returned to Chaumel's residence, another visitor awaited them. Ferngal, with a mighty entourage of lesser eastern Mages, did not even trouble to wait inside.

The underlings covered the landing pad with wardings and minor spells of protection like a presidential security force. Chaumel picked his way carefully toward his own landing strip, passing a hand before him to make sure it wasn't booby-trapped. He set down lightly and approached the black chariot on foot.

"High Mage Ferngal! How nice to see you so soon," Chaumel said, arms wide with welcome. "Come in. Allow me to offer you my hospitality."

Ferngal was in no mood for chitchat. He cut off Chaumel's compliments with an angry sweep of his hand.

"How dare you go spreading sedition among *my* workers? You dare to preach your nonsense in my farmsteads? You have overreached yourself."

"High Mage, I have not been speaking to your farmers. That is for you to do, or not, as *you* choose," Chaumel said, puzzled. "I would not presume upon your territories."

"Oh, no. It could only be you. You will cease this nonsense about the Core of Ozran at once, or it will be at your peril."

"It is not nonsense, High Mage," Chaumel said mildly but with steel apparent in his tone. "I tell you these things for your sake, not mine."

Ferngal leveled an angry finger at Chaumel's nose.

"If this is a petty attempt to gain power, you will pay heavily for your deceit," he said. "I hold domain over the East, and your stronghold falls within those boundaries. I order you to cease spreading your lies."

"I am not lying," Chaumel said. "And I cannot cease."

"Then so be it," the black-clad mage snarled.

He and his people lifted off from the balcony, and vanished. Chaumel shook his head, and turned toward Keff and Plenna with a "what can you do?" expression.

"Heads up, Keff!" Carialle said. "Power surge building in

your general area—a heavy one. Focusing . . . building . . . Watch out!"

"Carialle says someone is sending a huge burst of power toward us!" Keff shouted.

"An attack," shrieked Plenna. The three of them converged in the center of the balcony. The magiwoman and Chaumel threw their hands up over their heads. A rose-colored shell formed around them like a gigantic soap bubble only a split second before the storm broke.

It was no ordinary storm. Their shield was assailed by forked staves of multicolored lightning and sheets of flaming rain. Hand-sized explosions rocked them, setting off clouds of smoke and shooting jagged debris against the shell. Torrents of clear acid and flame-red lava flowed down the edges and sank into the floor, the ruin separated from their feet only by a fingertip's width.

The deafening noises stopped abruptly. When the smoke cleared, Chaumel waited a moment before dissolving the bubble. He let it pop silently on the air and took a step forward. Part of the floor rocked under his feet. Keff grabbed him. Two paces beyond the place they were standing, the end of the balcony was gone, ripped away by the magical storm as if a giant had taken a bite out of it. The pieces were still crashing with dull echoes into the ravine far below. Plenna mounted her chair to go look. She returned, shaking her head.

"It is . . ." Chaumel began, and had to stop to clear his throat. "It is considered ill-mannered to notice when someone else is building a spell, especially if that person is of higher rank than oneself. I believe it has now become a matter of life and death for us to behave in an ill-mannered fashion."

"Ferngal," Carialle said. "Using two power objects at once. I have both their frequencies logged." Keff passed along the information.

"Sedition, he said." Chaumel was confused. He appealed to Keff. "What sedition was Ferngal talking about? I have talked to no one in his area. I *would* not."

"Then someone else is talking to them," Keff said. "Nokias mentioned something similar. We'd better investigate."

A quick aerial reconnaissance of the two farmsteads from which Nokias and Ferngal's complaints came revealed that they were very close together, suggesting that whatever set off the riots was somewhere in the area, and on foot, not aloft. Chaumel asked help from a few of the mages who had tentatively given their promise to cooperate. They sent out spy-eyes to all the surrounding villages, looking for anything that seemed threatening.

Nothing appeared during the next day or so. On the third day, a light green spy-eye found Chaumel as he was leaving Carialle's ship.

"Here's your trouble," Kiyottal's mental voice announced.

Plennafrey, sensing the arrival of an eye-sphere from inside the ship, interrupted their attempts at conversation with the Frog Prince to run outside. Keff followed her.

"We've located the troublemaker," Chaumel said, after communing silently with the sphere. "It's your four-finger. He's making speeches."

"Brannel?" Keff said. He glanced out at the farm fields. Wielding heavy forks, the workers were turning over empty rows of earth and bedding them down with straw. He searched their ranks and turned back to Chaumel.

"You're right. I forgot all about him. He's gone."

"Follow me," Kiyottal's voice said. "I have also alerted Ferngal. Nokias is coming, too. It's in his territory."

In the center of the clearing in a southern farm village,

Brannel raised his arms for silence. The workers, who had long, pack beast-like faces, were gently worried about this skinny, dirty stranger who had arrived at their farmstead with an exhausted dray beast at his heels.

"I tell you the mages are weakening!" Brannel cried. "They are not all-powerful. If we have an uprising, every worker together, they will come out to punish us, but they will all fall to the ground helpless!"

"You are mad," a female farmer said, curling back her broad lips in a sneer.

"Why would we want to overthrow the mages?" one of the males asked him. "We have enough to eat."

"But you cannot think for yourselves," Brannel said. He was tired. He had given the same speech at another farmstead only days before, and once a few days before that, with the same stupid faces and the same stupid questions. If not for the flame of revenge that burned within him, the thought of journeying all over Ozran would have daunted him into returning to Alteis. "You do the same things every day of your lives, every year of your lives!"

"Yes? So? What else should we do?" Most of the listeners were more inclined to heckle, but Brannel thought he saw the gleam of comprehension on the faces of a few.

"Change is coming, but it won't be for our sakes—only the mages'. If you want things to change for *you*, don't eat the mage food. Don't eat it tonight, not tomorrow, not any day. Keep roots from your harvest, and eat them. You will *remember*," Brannel insisted, pointing to his temples with both hands. "Tomorrow you will see. It will be like nothing you have ever experienced in your life. You *will* remember. You need to trust me only for one night! Then you will see for yourselves. You grow the food! You have a right to it! We can get rid of the magefolk. On the first day of the next planting when the sun is highest, throw down your tools and refuse to work."

The whirring sound in the air distracted most of the workers, who looked up, then threw themselves flat on the ground. Brannel and his few converts remained standing, staring up at the four chariots descending upon them.

The black and gold chairs touched down first.

"Kill him," Ferngal said heatedly, pointing at the sheep-faced male, "or I will do so myself. His people have been without an overlord too long. They are getting above themselves."

"No," Keff said. He leaped off Plenna's chair, putting himself between the high mage and the peasant. "Don't touch him. Brannel, what are you doing?"

At first Brannel remained mulishly silent, then words burst out of him in a torrent of wounded feelings.

"You promised me, and I risked myself, and Chaumel knocked me out, and you threw me out again with nothing. Nothing!" Brannel spat. "I am as I was before, only worse. The others made fun of me. Why didn't you keep your promise?"

Keff held up his hands. "I promised I'd do what I could for you. Amulets aren't easy to find, you know, and the power is going to end soon anyway. Do you want to fill your head with useless knowledge?"

"Yes! To know is to understand one's life."

Ferngal spat. "If you're going to waste my time by talking nonsense with a servant, I'm away. Just make certain he does not come back to my domain. Never!" The black chair disappeared toward the clouds. Nokias, shaking his head, went off in the opposite direction. The workers, freed from their thrall by the departure of the high mages, went on to eat their supper, which had just appeared in the square of stones. Brannel started away from Keff to divert the villagers. The brawn grabbed him by the arm.

"Don't interfere, Brannel. I won't be able to stop

Ferngal next time. Look, man, I guaranteed only that Plenna would teach you."

Brannel was unsatisfied. "Even that did not happen. You sent me away, and I heard nothing for days. When I saw you at last, you were in too much of a hurry to speak to me."

"That was most discourteous of me," Keff agreed. "I'm sorry. But you *know* what we're doing. There's a lot to be done, and mages to convince."

"But we had a bargain," Brannel said stubbornly. "*She* could give me one of her items of power, and I can learn to use it by myself. Then I will have magic as long as anyone."

"Brannel, I want to offer you a different kind of power, the kind that will last. Will you listen to me?"

Reluctantly, but swayed by the sincerity of his first friend ever, the embittered Noble Primitive agreed at last to listen. Keff beckoned him to a broad rock at the end of the field, at a far remove from both the magifolk and the dray-faced farmers.

"If you still want to help," Keff said, "and you're up to continuing your journey, I want you to go on with it. Talk to the workers. Explain what's going to happen."

"But High Mage Ferngal said . . . ?"

"Ferngal doesn't want you to make things more difficult. Help us, don't hinder. Tell them what they stand to gain— in cooperation." Keff saw light dawning in the male's eyes. "Yes, you do see. In return, we'll supply you with food. We might even be able to manage transporting you from region to region by chair. Arriving in a chariot will give you immediate high status with the others. You like to fly, don't you?"

"I love to fly," Brannel said, easily enough converted with such a shining prospect. "I will change my message to cooperation."

"Good! Tell them the truth. The workers will get better

treatment and more input into their own government when the power is diminished. The mages will need you more than ever."

"That I will be happy to tell my fellow workers," Brannel said gravely.

"I have a secret to tell you, but you, and only you," Keff said, leaning toward the worker. "Do you promise? Good. Now listen: the mages are not the true owners of the Core of Ozran. Remember it."

Brannel was goggle-eyed. "I never forget, Mage Keff."

Seven days later, Chaumel returned to his great room dusting his hands together. A quintet of chariots lifted off the balcony and disappeared over the mountaintops. He stood for a moment as if listening, and turned with a smile to Plenna and Keff.

"That is the last of them," he said with satisfaction. "Everyone who has said they will cooperate has also promised to press the ones who haven't agreed. In the meantime, all have said that they will keep voluntarily to the barest minimum of use. On the day you designated, two days hence, at sunrise in the eastern province, the great mutual truce will commence."

"Not without grumbling, I'm sure," Keff said, with a grin. "I'm sure there'll be a lot of attempts before that to renegotiate the accord to everyone else's benefit. Once the power levels lessen, it'll give me the last direction I need to find the Core of Ozran."

"Leave the last-minute doubters to me," Chaumel said. "At the appointed moment, you must be ready. Such a treaty was not easily arranged, and may never again be achieved. Do not fail."

¤ CHAPTER THIRTEEN

The high mountains looked daunting in their deep, pre-dawn shadow as Plenna and Chaumel flew toward them. Keff, on Plenna's chair, had the ancient manuals spread out on his lap. As he smoothed the plastic pages down, they crackled in the cold.

"The sun's about to rise over Ferngal's turf," Carialle informed him. "You should see a drop in power beginning in thirty seconds."

"Terrific, Cari. Chaumel, any of this looking familiar?"

Chaumel, in charge of three globe-frogs he was restraining from falling off his chair with the use of a mini-containment field generated by his wand, nodded.

"I see the way I came last time," he shouted. His voice was caught by the great mountains and bounced back and forth like a toy. "See, above us, the two sharp peaks together like the tines of a fork? I kept those immediately to my left all the way into the heart. They overlook a narrow passage."

"Now," Carialle said.

Chaumel's and Plenna's chariots shot forward slightly

and the "seat belts" around the globe-frogs brightened to a blue glow.

"That's kickback," Keff said. "Every other mage in the world has turned off the lights and the power available to you two is near one hundred percent."

"A heady feeling, to be sure," Chaumel said, jovially. "If it were not that each item of power is not capable of conducting all that there is in the Core. I must tell you how difficult it was to convince all the mages and magesses that they should not each send spy-eyes with us on this journey. Ah, the passageway! Follow me."

He steered to the right and nipped into a fold of stone that seemed to be a dead end. As the two chairs closed the distance, Keff could see that the ledge was composed of gigantic, rough blocks, separated by a good four meters.

The thin air between them was no barrier to communication between Keff and the Frog Prince. Lit weirdly by the chariot light, the amphibioid resembled a grotesque clay gnome. Keff waved to get his attention.

"Do you know where we are going?" he signed.

"Too long for any living to remember," Tall Eyebrow signaled back. "The high fingers—" he pointed up, "mentioned in history."

"What's next?"

"Lip, hole, long cavern."

"Did you get that, Carialle?" Keff asked. Flying into the narrow chasm robbed them of any ambient light to see by. Chaumel increased the silver luminance of his chariot to help him avoid obstructions.

"I did," the crisp voice replied. "My planetary maps show that you're approaching a slightly wider plateau that ends in a high saddle cliff, probably the lip. As for the hole, the low range beyond is full of chimneys."

"That's what the old manuals can tell me," Keff said, reading by the gentle yellow light of Plennafrey's chair.

"According to this, the cavern where the power generator is situated is at ninety-three degrees, six minutes, two seconds east; forty-seven degrees, fifteen minutes, seven seconds north." He held up a navigational compass. "Still farther north."

"The lee lines lead straight ahead," Chaumel informed him. "Without interference from the rest of Ozran, I can follow the lines to their heart. You are to be congratulated, Keff. This was not possible without a truce."

"We can't miss it," Keff said, crowing in triumph. "We have too much information."

The sun touched the snow-covered summits high above them with orange light as the pass opened out into the great central cirque. Though scoured by glaciers in ages past, the mountains were clearly of volcanic origin. Shards of black obsidian glass stuck up unexpectedly from the cloudy whiteness of snowbanks under icefalls. The two chairs ran along the moraine until it dropped abruptly out from underneath. Keff had a momentary surge of vertigo as he glanced back at the cliff.

"How *high* is that thing, Cari?" he asked.

"Eight hundred meters. You wonder how the original humans got here, let alone the globe-frogs who built it."

At his signal, Plenna dropped into the dark, cold valley. Keff shivered in the blackness and hugged himself for warmth. He glanced up at Plenna, who was staring straight ahead in wonder.

"What do you see?" he asked.

"I see a great skein of lines coming together," she said. "I will try to show you." She waved her hands, and the faintest limning of blue fire a fingertip wide started above their heads and ran down before them like a burning fuse. A moment later, a network of similar lines appeared coming over the mountain ridges all around them, converging on a point still ahead. Her glowing gaze met

Keff's eyes. "It is the most amazing thing I have seen in my life."

"Your point of convergence is roughly in the center of your five high mages' regions," Carialle pointed out. "Everyone shares equal access to the Core."

"Has anyone else ever come here?" Keff asked Chaumel.

"It is considered a No-Mages'-Land," the silver magiman said. "Rumors are that things go out of control within these mountains. I could not come this far in my youth. I became confused by the overabundance of power, lost my way, and nearly lost my life trying to fly away. Here is the path, all marked out before us, as if it was meant to be."

"We should never have lost sight of the source of our power," Plenna said. "Nor the aims of our ancestors." Her own tragedy, Keff guessed, was never far from the surface of her thoughts.

The two chariots began to throw tips of shadows as they ran over the broken ground. Soot-rimmed holes ten meters and more across punctuated the snow-field. Keff followed the indicator on his compass as the numbers came closer and closer to the target coordinates.

All at once, Chaumel, Carialle, and the Frog Prince said, "That one."

"And down!" Keff cried.

The tunnel mouth was larger than most of the others in the snow-covered plain. Keff felt a chill creep along his skin as they dropped into the hole, shutting off even the feeble predawn sunlight. Plenna's chariot's soft light kept him from becoming blind as soon as they were underground. Chaumel dropped back to fly alongside them.

They traveled six hundred meters in nearly total darkness. Plenna's hand settled on Keff's shoulder and he squeezed it. Abruptly the way opened out, and they emerged into a huge hemispherical cavern lit by a dull blue luminescence and filled with a soft humming like the purr of a cat.

"You could fit Chaumel's mountain in here," Carialle said, taking a sounding through Keff's implants.

The ceiling of this cavern had been scalloped smooth at some time in the distant past so that it bore only new, tiny stalactites like cilia at the edges of each sound-deadening bubble. Here and there a vast, textured, onyx pillar stretched from floor to roof, glowing with an internal light.

The globe-frogs began to bounce up and down in their cases, pointing excitedly. Keff felt like dancing, too. Ahead, minute in proportion, lay a platform situated on top of a complex array of machinery. It wasn't until he identified it that he realized they had been flying over an expanse of machinery that nearly covered the floor of the entire cavern.

"I have never seen anything like it in my life," Chaumel whispered, the first to break the silence. His voice was captured and tossed about like a ball by the scalloped stone walls.

"Nor has anyone else living," Keff said. "No one has been here in this cavern for at least five hundred years."

"Stepped field generators," Carialle said at once. "Will you look at that beautiful setup? They are huge! This could light a space station for a thousand years."

"It is amazing," Plennafrey breathed.

She and Chaumel leaned forward, urging speed from their chariots, each eager to be the first to land on the platform. Keff clenched his hands on the chair back under his hips until he thought his fingers would indent the wood, but he was laughing. The others were laughing and hooting, and in the frogs' cases, jumping up and down for pure delight.

"The manual says . . ." Keff said, piling off the chair,

pushed by Plenna who wanted to dismount right away and see the wonders up close. "The manual says the system draws from the core below and the surface above to service power demands. It mentions lightning—Cari, this is too cracked to read. I must have lost a piece of it while we were flying."

Carialle found the copy in her memory bank. "It looks like the generators are made to absorb energy from the surface as well to take advantage of natural electrical surges like lightning. Sensible, but I think it got out of hand when the power demands grew beyond its stated capacity. It started drawing from living matter."

Plenna surrendered her belt buckle to the Frog Prince. He left his shell and joined Keff and Chaumel at the low-lying console at the edge of the platform. The brawn, on his knees, displayed the indicator fields to Carialle through the implants while signing with the amphibioids. Stopping frequently to compare notes with his companions, the Frog Prince read the fine scrawl on the face of each, then tried to tell the humans through sign language what they were.

"So that says internal temperature of the Core, eh, Tall?" Keff asked, marking the gauge in Standard with an indelible pen. "And by the way, it's hot in here, did you notice?"

"Residual heat from years of overuse," Carialle said. "I calculate that it would take over two years to heat that cavern to forty degrees centigrade."

"Well, we knew the overuse didn't occur overnight," Keff said. "Ah, he says that one is the power output? Thanks, Chaumel." He made another note on a glass-fronted display as the magiman gesticulated with the amphibioid. "Pity your ancestor didn't have any documentation on the mechanism itself, Plenna."

"Isn't that level rising?" Plennafrey asked, pointing over

Keff's shoulder. Keff looked up from the circuit he was examining.

"You're right, it is," he said. Subtly, under their feet, the hum of the engines changed, speeding up slightly. "What's happening? I didn't touch anything. None of us did."

"I'm getting blips in the power grid outside your location," Carialle replied. "I'd say that some of the mages have gotten tired of the truce and are raising their defenses again."

Keff relayed the suggestion to Chaumel, who nodded sadly. "Distrust is too strong for any respite to hold for long," he said. "I am surprised we had this much time to examine the Core while it was quiescent."

Swiftly, more and more of the power cells kicked on, some of them groaning mightily as their turbines began once again to spin. The gauge crept upward until the indicator was pinned against the right edge, but the generators' roar increased in volume and pitch beyond that until it was painful to hear.

"It's redlining," Keff shouted, tapping the glass with a fingernail. The indicator didn't budge. "Listen to those hesitations! These generators sound like they could go at any moment. We didn't get here any too soon."

"The sound is still rising," Plenna said, her voice constricted to a squeak. She put out her hands and concentrated, then recoiled horrified as the turbines increased their speed slightly in response. "My power comes from here," she said, alarmed. "I'm just making it worse."

The frogs became very excited, bumping their cases against the humans' knees.

"Shut it down," Tall commanded, sweeping his big hands emphatically at Keff. "Shut it down!"

"I would if I could," he said, then repeated it in sign language. "Where is the OFF switch?"

"Is it that?" Chaumel asked, pointing to a large, heavy switch close to the floor.

Keff followed the circuit back to where it joined the rest of the mechanism. "It's a breaker," he said. "If I cut this, it'll stop everything at once. It might destroy the generators altogether. We have to slow it down gradually, not stop it. This is impossible without a technical manual!" he shouted, frustrated, pounding his fist on his knee. "We could be at ground zero for a planet-shattering explosion. And there's nothing we could do about it. Why isn't there a fail-safe? Engineers who were advanced enough to invent something like this must have built one in to keep it from running in the red."

"Perhaps the Old Ones turned it off?" Chaumel suggested. "Or even our poor, deceived ancestors?"

"Off?" Plennafrey tapped him on the shoulder and shouted above the din. "Couldn't Carialle turn off every item of power?"

"Good idea, Plenna! Cari, implement!"

"Yes, sir!" the efficient voice crackled in his ear. "Now, watch the circuits as I lock them out one at a time. The magifolk won't notice—they'll think it's another power failure. You and the globe-frogs should be able to trace down where the transformer steps kick in. See if you can make a permanent lower level adjustment."

The turbines began to slow down gradually as the power demands lessened. The Frog Prince and his assistants were already at the consoles. As the only one with his hands outside a plastic globe, the leader had to monitor the shut-downs and incorporate the readings his assistants took through the controls. His long fingers flicked switches one after another and poked recessed buttons in a sequence that seemed to have meaning to him. The whining of the turbos died down slowly. In a while, the amphibioid raised his big hand over his head with his fingers forming a circle and blinked at Keff in a self-satisfied manner.

"You're in control of it now," Keff signed.

"I am now understanding the lessons handed down," the alien replied, his small face showing pleasure as he signed. "'To the right, on; to the left, off,' it was said. 'The big down is for peril, the small downs like stairs, to your hands comes the power.' Now I control it like this." He held up Plennafrey's belt buckle. His long fingers slid into the depressions. "This one is in much better condition than the single we have, which has done service for our whole population for all these many years."

Tall glanced toward the controls. The switches pressed themselves, dials and levers moved without a hand touching them. The great engines stilled to a barely perceptible hum.

"At last," he gestured, "after five hundred generations we have our property back. We can come forward once again."

He seemed less enthusiastic once the extent of the damage began to emerge. Series of lights showed that several of the turbines were running at half efficiency or less. Some were not functioning at all. At one time, some unknown engineer had tied together a handful of the generators under a single control, but the generators in question were nowhere near one another on the cave floor.

"It'll take a lot of fixing," Keff said, examining the mechanism with the frogs crowded in around him. The indicators in some of the dials hadn't moved in so long they had corroded to their pins. He snapped his fingernail at one of them, trying to jar it loose. "We'll have to figure out if any of the repair parts can be made out of components I have on hand. If they're too esoteric, you might need to send off for them, providing they're still making them on your home planet."

"Home?" one of the globe-frogs signed back, with the fillip that meant an interrogative.

"If you have the coordinates, we have your transportation," Keff offered happily, signing away to the *oops, eeps,* and *ops* of IT's shorthand dictation. "Our job is to make contact with other races, and we're very pleased to meet *you.* My government would be delighted to open communications with yours."

"That is all well, Keff," Chaumel asked, "but do not forget about us. What of the mages? They will be wondering what happened to their items of power. Blackouts normally last only a few moments. There will be pandemonium."

"And what for the future?" Plenna asked.

"Your folk will have to realize that you now coexist with the globe-frogs," Keff said thoughtfully. "And, Tall, she's right. You are going to have to do something about the mages. They're dependent upon the system to a certain extent. Can we negotiate some kind of share agreement?"

"They can have it all," Tall said, with a scornful gesture toward the jury-rigged control board. "All this is ruined. Ruined! You come from the stars. Why do you not take my people back to our homeworld? We are effectively dispossessed. We've been ignored since the day we were robbed by the Flat Ones. No one will notice our absence. Let the thieves who have used our machinery have it and the husk that remains of this planet."

"We'd be happy to do that," Keff said, carefully, "but forgive me, Tall, you won't have much in common with the people of your homeworld anymore, will you? You were born here. Five hundred generations of your people have been native Ozrans. Just when it could start to get better, do you really want to leave?"

"Hear, hear," said Carialle.

One of the amphibioids looked sad and made a

THE SHIP WHO WON 303

gesture that threw the idea away. The Frog Prince looked at him. "I guess we do not. Truth, *I* do not, but what to do?"

"What was your people's mission? Why did you come here?"

"To grow things on this green and fertile planet," Tall signed, almost a dance of graceful gestures, as if repeating a well-learned lesson. He stopped. "But nothing is green and fertile anymore like in the old stories. It is dry, dusty, cold."

"Don't you want to try and bring the planet back to a healthy state?"

"How?"

Keff touched the small amphibioid gently on the back and drew Chaumel closer with the other arm. "The know-how is obviously still in your people's oral tradition. Why not fulfill your ancestors' hopes and dreams? Work together with the humans. Share *with* them. You can fix the machinery. I agree that you should make contact with your homeworld, and we'll help with that, but don't go back to stay. Ask them for technical support and communication. They'll be thrilled to know that any of the colonists are still alive."

The sad frog looked much happier. "Leader, yes!" he signed enthusiastically.

"Help us," Keff urged, raising his hands high. "We'll try to establish mutual respect among the species. If it fails, Carialle and I can always take you back once we've fixed the system here."

Chaumel cleared his throat and spoke, mixing sign language with the spoken linga esoterka. "You have much in common with our lower class," he said. "You'll find much sympathy among the farmers and workers."

"We know them," Tall signed scornfully. "They kick us."

Keff signaled for peace.

"Once they know you're intelligent, that will change. The human civilization on this planet has slid backward to a subsistence farming culture. Only with your help can Ozran join the confederation of intelligent races as a voting member."

"That's a slippery slope you're negotiating there, Keff," Carialle warned, noticing Plenna's shocked expression. Chaumel, on the other hand, was nodding and concealing a grin. He approved of Keff's eliding the truth for the sake of diplomacy.

"For mutual respect and an equal place we might stay," the Frog Prince signed after conferring with his fellows.

"You won't regret it," Keff assured him. "You'll be able to say to your offspring that it was your generation, allied with another great and intelligent race, who completed your ancestors' tasks."

"To go from nothing to everything," the Frog Prince signed, his pop eyes going very wide, which Keff interpreted as a sign of pleasure. "The ages may not have been wasted after all."

"Only if we can keep this planet from blowing up," Carialle reminded them. Keff relayed her statement to the others.

"But what needs to be done to bring the system back to a healthy balance?" Chaumel asked.

"Stop using it," Keff said simply. "Or at least, stop draining the system so profligately as you have been doing. The mages will have to be limited in future to what power remains after the legitimate functions have been supplied: weather control, water conservation, and whatever it takes to stabilize the environment. That's what those devices were originally designed to do. Only the most vital uses should be made of what power's left over. And until the frogs get the system repaired, that's going to be precious little. You saw how much colder and drier Ozran has become over the time human beings have been here. It won't be long until this planet is uninhabitable, and you have nowhere else to go."

"I understand perfectly," Chaumel said. "But the others are not going to like it."

"They must see for themselves." Plenna spoke up unexpectedly. "Let them come here."

"Your girlfriend has a good idea," Carialle told Keff. "Show them this place. The globe-frogs can keep everyone on short power rations. Give them enough to fly their chariots here, but not enough to start a world war."

"*Just* enough," Keff stressed as the Frog Prince went to make the adjustment, "so they don't feel strangled, but let's make it clear that the days of making it snow firecrackers are over."

"Hah!" Chaumel said. "What would impress them most is if you could make it snow *snow*! Everyone will have to see it for themselves, or they will not believe. The meeting must be called at once."

The Frog Prince and his companions paddled back to Keff. "We will stay here to feel out the machinery and learn what is broken."

Keff stood up, stamping to work circulation back into his legs.

"And I'll stay here, too. Since there is no manual or blueprints, Carialle and I will plot schematics of the mechanism, and see what we can help fix. Cari?"

"I'll be there with tools and components before you can say alakazam, Sir Galahad," she replied.

"I had better stay, too, then," Plenna said. "Someone needs to keep others from entering if the silver tower leaves the plain. She attracts too much curiosity."

"Good thinking. Bring Brannel, too," Keff told Carialle. "He deserves to see the end of all his hard work. This will either make or break the accord."

"It will be either the end or the beginning of our world," Chaumel agreed, settling into the silver chair. It lifted off from the platform and skimmed away toward the distant light.

¤ CHAPTER FOURTEEN

The vast cavern swallowed up the few hundred mages like gnats in a garden. Each high mage was surrounded by underlings spread out and upward in a wedge to the rim of an imaginary bowl with Keff, Chaumel, Plenna, Brannel, and the three globe-frogs at its center on the platform. All the newcomers were staring down at the machinery on the cave floor and gazing at the high platform with expressions of awe. The Noble Primitive gawked around him at the gathering of the greatest people in his world. All of them were looking at him. Keff aimed a companionable slap at the worker's shoulders and winked up at him.

"You're perfectly safe," he assured Brannel.

"I do not feel safe," Brannel whispered. "I wish they could not see me."

"Whether or not they realize it, they owe you a debt of gratitude. You've been helping them, and you deserve recognition. In a way, this is your reward."

"I would rather not be recognized," Brannel said definitely. "No one will shoot fire at a target that cannot be seen."

"No one is going to shoot fire," Keff said. "There isn't enough power left out there to light a match."

"What is going on here?" Ilnir roared, projecting his voice over the hubbub of voices and the hum of machinery. "I am not accustomed to being summoned, nor to waiting while peasants confer!"

"Why has the silver tower been moved to this place?" a mage called out. "Doesn't it belong to the East?"

"Why will my items of power not function?" a lesser magess of Zolaika's contingent complained. "Chaumel, are you to blame for all this?"

"High Ones, mages and magesses," the silver magiman said smoothly. "Events over the past weeks have culminated in this meeting today. Ozran is changing. You may perhaps be disappointed in some of the changes, but I assure you they are for the better—in fact, they are inexorable, so your liking them will not much matter in the long run. My friend Keff will explain." He turned a hand toward the Central Worlder.

"We have brought you here today to see this," Keff said, pitching his voice to carry to the outermost ranks of mages. "This"—he patted the nearest upthrust piece of conduit— "is the Core of Ozran."

"Ridiculous!" Lacia shouted down at him from well up in the eastern contingent. "The Core is not this thing. This is a toy that makes noise."

"Do not dismiss this toy too quickly, Magess," Chaumel called. "Without it you'd have had to walk here. None of you have ever seen it before, but it has been here, working beneath the crust of Ozran for thousands of years. It is the source of our power, and it is on the edge of breaking down."

"You've been misusing it," Keff said, then raised his hands to still the outcry. "It was never meant to maintain the needs of a mass social order of wizards. It was intended"—he had to shout to be heard over the rising murmurs—"as a weather control device! It's supposed to control the patterns of wind, rain, and sunshine over your fields. We have asked you here so you will understand why you're being asked to stop using your items of power. If you don't, the Core will drain this planet of life faster and faster, and finally blow up, taking at least a third of the planetary surface with it. You'll all die!"

"We're barely using it now," Omri shouted. "We need more than this trickle." A chorus of voices agreed with him.

"This is the time, when everyone can see the direct results, to give up power and save your world. Chaumel has talked to each one of you, shown you pictures. You've all had time to think about it. Now you know the consequences. It isn't whether or not the Core will explode. It's *when!*"

"But how will we govern?" the piping voice of Zolaika asked. The room quieted immediately when she spoke. "How will we keep the farms going? If the workers don't have us in charge of everything they won't work."

"They don't need you in charge of everything, Magess. Stop using the docility drugs and you'll find that you won't need to herd them like sheep," Keff said. "They'll become innovators, and Ozran will see the birth of a civilization like it has never known. You're dumbing down potential sculptors, architects, scientists, doctors, teachers. The only thing you'll have to concentrate on," Keff said with a smile, "is to teach them to cook for themselves. Maybe you can send out some of your kitchen staff, after you build them stoves—geothermal energy is available under every one of those home caverns. You could have communal kitchens in each one of the farmsteads in a week. After that, you can discontinue all the energy you use in food distribution."

Keff urged Brannel to center stage. "Speak up. Go on. You wanted to, before."

"Magess," Brannel began shyly, then bawled louder when several of the mages complained they couldn't hear him. "Magess, we need more rain! We workers could grow more food, bigger, if we have more rain, and if you do not have battles so often." At the angry murmuring, he was frightened and started to retreat, but Keff eased him back to his place.

"Listen to him!" Nokias roared. Brannel swallowed, but continued bravely.

"I . . . the life goes out of the plants when you use much magic near us. We care for the soil, we till it gently and water with much effort, but when magic happens, the plants die."

"Do you understand?" Keff said, letting Brannel retreat at last. The Noble Primitive huddled nervously against an upright of the control platform, and Plennafrey patted his arm. "Your farmers know what's good for the planet—and you're preventing their best efforts from having any results by continuing your petty battles. Let them have more responsibility and more support, and less interference with the energy flow, and I think you'll be pleasantly surprised by the results."

"You go on and on about the peasants," Asedow shouted. "We've heard all about the peasants. But what are *they* doing here?" The green-clad magiman pointed at the frogs.

Keff smiled.

"This is the most important discovery we've made since we started to investigate the problems with the Core. When Carialle and I arrived on Ozran, we hoped to find a sentient species the equal of our own, with superior technological ability. We were disappointed to find that you mages weren't it." He raised his voice above the expected plaint. "No, not that you're backward! We discovered that you are *human* like us. We're the same species. We've found in you a long-lost branch of our own race."

"You are Ozran?"

"No! *You* are Central Worlders. Your people came to Ozran a thousand years ago aboard a ship called the *Bigelow*. That's the reason why I could translate the tapes and papers they left behind. The language is an ancient version of my own. No, Carialle and I still managed to achieve our goal. We have found our equal race."

"Where?" someone shouted. Keff held up his hands.

"You know all about the Ancient Ones and the Old Ones. You know what the Old Ones looked like. There are images of them in many of your strongholds. Your grandparents told you horror stories, and you've seen the holographs Chaumel had me play for you from the record tapes saved by your ancestors. But you've never seen the Ancient Ones. You know they built the Core of Ozran and founded the system on which your power has been based for ten centuries. These," he said, with a triumphant flourish toward the Frog Prince and his assistants, "are the Ancient Ones."

"Never!" Ferngal cried, his red face drawn into a furious mask.

Over shouts of disbelief, Keff blasted from the bottom of his bull-like chest:

"These people have been right here under your nose for ten centuries. These are the Ancient Ones who invented the Core and all the items of power."

The murmuring died away. For a moment there was complete silence, then hysterical laughter built until it filled the vast cavern. Keff maintained a polite expression, not smiling. He gestured to the Frog Prince.

The amphibioid stepped forward and began to sign the discourse he had prepared with Keff's help. It was eloquent, asking for recognition and promising cooperation. The mages recognized the ancient signs, their eyes widening in disbelief. Gradually, the merriment died down. Every face in the circle showed shock. They stared from Tall Eyebrow to Keff.

"You're not serious, are you?" Nokias asked. Keff nodded. "*These* are the Ancient Ones?"

"I am perfectly serious. Chaumel will tell you. They helped me—*directed* me—on how to make temporary repairs to the Core. It was overheating badly. It'll take a long time to get it so it won't blow up if overused. I couldn't do it by myself. I've never seen some of these components before. Friends, this machine is brilliant. Human technology has yet to find a system that can pull electrical energy out of the solid matter around it without creating nuclear waste. What you see here at my side is the descendant of some of the dandiest scientists and engineers in the galaxy, and they've been living in the marshes like animals since before your people came here."

"But they *are* animals," Potria spat.

"They're not," Keff said patiently. "They've just been forced to live that way. When the Old Ones moved to the mountains you call your strongholds, they robbed the frogfolk of access to their own machinery and reduced them to subsistence living. They *are* advanced beings. They're willing to help you fix the system so it works the way it was intended to work. You've all seen the holo-tapes of the way Ozran was when your ancestors came. Ozran can become a lush, green paradise again, the way it was before the Old Ones appropriated their power devices and made magic items out of them. They passed them on to you, and you expanded the system beyond its capacity to cope and control the weather. It's not your fault. You didn't know, but you have to help make it right now. Your own lives depend upon it."

"Hah! You cannot trick me into believing that these trained marsh-slime are the Ancient Ones!" Potria laughed, a harsh sound edged with hysteria. "It's a poor joke and I have had enough of it." She turned to the others. "Do you believe this tale?"

Most mages were conferring nervously among themselves. Keff was gratified that only a few of them cried out, "No!"

"You say we should share," Asedow said, "but these so-called Ancient Ones might have their own agenda for its use."

"They were here first, and it is their equipment," Keff said. "It is only fair they have access now."

"They could hardly use it worse than we have," Plennafrey shouted daringly.

"What has become of the rest of our power?" Ferngal asked.

"The turbines were overheating. We've turned them down to let them cool off," Keff explained. "There's enough power for normal functions. Nothing fancy. It's either that, or nothing at all, when the system blows up. You'll just have to learn to live with it."

"I won't 'just live with it.' How can you stop me?" Asedow asked obnoxiously.

"Shut up, brat, and listen to your betters," the old woman named Iranika called out.

"Who is with me?" Potria called out, ignoring the crone. "We've been insulted by this stranger. He *claims* he has stopped our power for our benefit, but he is going to give it to *marsh-creatures*. He wants to rule Ozran with that skinny wench at his side and Chaumel as his lackey!"

"Potria!" Nokias thundered, spinning his chariot in midair to face her. "You are out of order. Asedow, back to your place."

"Friends, please," Chaumel began.

"You give more consideration to a fur-face than to one of your own, Nokias," Asedow taunted. "Perhaps you'd rather be one of them—powerless, and fingerless!"

He started to draw up power to form one of his famous smoke clouds. All he could generate was a puff. Keff could see him strain and clench his amulet, trying to find more power. The cloud grew to the size of his head, then dissipated. Asedow panted. Nokias laughed.

"To me, Asedow!" Potria called. "We must work together!" Her chariot flew upward, out of its place in the bowl. Asedow, Lacia, Ferngal, and a handful of others joined her in a ring. At once, a lightning bolt rocketed from their midst. It would have struck the edge of the platform but for the thin shield Chaumel threw up.

"This is thin," he said to Keff. "It will not hold."

Nokias, Zolaika, Ilnir, and Iranika flew down from their places toward the platform.

"This means trouble," Nokias called. "How much power is there left?"

"Not much beyond what it takes to run your chariots," Keff said.

"They can pervert that, too," Zolaika warned. "See!"

Recognizing the beginnings of a battle royal, many of the other mages turned their chairs and headed for the exit. The chariots started to falter, dipping perilously toward the rows of turbines as the combined will of the dissidents drew power away from them. Many turned back and crowded over the platform, fighting for landing space.

"I will stop them," Tall said, his huge hands clenched over the belt-buckle amulet.

"No," Keff said. "If you turn off the power, all these mages will fall."

"I will end this," Zolaika said. "Brothers and sisters, to me." At once, Nokias, Ilnir, and a cluster of other magifolk added their meager strength to that of the senior magess.

Accompanied by straining sounds from the generators, she built a spell and threw it with all the force left in her toward the ring of dissidents.

Cries of fear came from the fleeing mages, whose chairs faltered like fledgling birds. The great chamber rumbled, and infant stalactites cracked from the ceiling. Sharp teeth of rock crashed to the platform. The mages warded themselves with shields that barely repelled the missiles. Keff jumped away as a three-foot section of rock struck the standard next to him. It bounced once and fell over the side, clattering down into the midst of the machinery.

In the circle of dissidents high up in the cavern, Potria and her allies held out their hands to one another. Keff could see bonds of colored light forming between them, one ring for each mage or magess that joined them.

"Problem, Keff," Carialle said. "They've reestablished their connection to the Core's controls."

"They are pulling," Plenna said, grabbing Keff's arm. "They're pulling at the Core, trying to break the barrier holding the power down—they've done it!"

"Tall, stop them!" Keff shouted.

"No can," the amphibioid semaphored hastily. "Old, broken."

"Coming on full now," Carialle's voice informed him.

With a mighty roar, the generators revved up to full force. The mages whose chariots were limping toward the exit hurtled out of the cavern as if sling-shot. Keff groaned as he smelled scorched silicon. He and the frogs hadn't been able to do more than patch the fail-safes. Now they were melted and beyond repair.

"As your liege I command you to cease!" Nokias shouted at the dissidents.

"You do not command *me*, brother," Ferngal jeered. He raised his staff and aimed it at Nokias. A bolt of fire, surprising even its creator in its size and intensity, jetted toward Nokias. The golden mage dodged to one side to avoid it. His chair, also oversupplied by the Core, skittered away on the air as if it were on ice. It was a moment before he could control it. In that short time, Ferngal loosed off several more bolts. They all missed but the last, which took off one of Nokias's armrests. Fortunately, the golden mage's arms were raised. He was readying a barrage of his own.

Lacia had engaged Chaumel. The two of them exchanged explosive balls of flame that grew larger and larger as each realized that the Core had resumed transmission. Dissidents dive-bombed the platform. With admirable calm and dead aim, Chaumel managed to keep them all from getting any closer.

"Stop!" Keff yelled. "The more power you use the closer we come to blowing up!"

With an eldritch howl, Potria swooped down at Keff, taloned fingers stretched out before her. He saw the red lightning forming between them and dove under the low console. Brannel and the frogs were already huddled there. Tall Eyebrow stood with his back to his companions, protecting them. Keff wished for a weapon, any kind of weapon. He saw his faux-hide toolkit, hanging precariously near the edge of the platform, anchored only by the edge of a chair that had landed on it. He rose to his hands and knees, and scrambled out of his hiding place, shielded by the cluster of chariots.

With power restored, Brochindel the Scarlet chose that moment to lift off in an attempt to flee the battle going on over his head. Keff threw himself on his belly with one hand out. He managed to grab one centimeter of strap by one joint of one hooked finger. Potria saw him lying there exposed, and screamed, coming around in the air and diving in anew. Wincing at the weight of the tool bag, Keff hoisted it up and dragged it into the lee of the console. He turned out the contents in search of a weapon. Hammers, no. Spanners, no. Aha, the drill! It had a flexible one-meter bit.

"The knight shall have his sword," Carialle said. "Get 'er, Sir Keff."

His fingers scrabbled on the chuck, trying to get the bit loose. Potria, her power overextended by the immediacy of the Core, threw a ball of fire that left a molten scar in the platform's surface. Keff bounced up as she passed and snapped his erstwhile sword-blade out. He smacked Potria on the back of the hand. She dropped her amulet, but it fell only into her lap.

"You . . . you peasant!" she screamed, for lack of a better epithet. "You struck me!"

Plennafrey hurried to Keff's side. The Frog Prince had her belt buckle, but she still possessed her father's sash. Working the depressions with her long fingers, she formed a thin shell of protection around the two of them and the console. Potria veered upward when her target changed, and retreated, but not until Plennafrey poked a small hole in the shield. She scooped up a chunk of fallen rock and threw it after the pink-gold magess. It struck Potria in the back of the arm, provoking a colorful string of swear words as, this time, the magess lost her grip on her power object. She swooped down to retrieve it before it fell into the machinery.

"Good throw, Plenna!" Keff said, hugging her with one arm.

"Conservation of energy," Plenna said brightly, grinning at Keff.

Asedow zoomed in, his mace at the ready. Keff ducked flat to the floor, avoiding the smoke-bubble bombs, then sprang up. With a flick of his improvised epee, he engaged Asedow and disarmed him, flinging the mace away into the void. Swearing, Asedow reversed. He glanced down at the spinning engines, and felt among the robes at his chest. He uncovered a small amulet and planted his fingers in it.

"Damn!" Carialle said. "I don't have a record for that one."

Fortunately, Asedow didn't use it immediately. Too soon, Potria reappeared over the edge of the platform, her teeth set.

"I just wanted to say farewell," she said, her eyes shining with a mad light. "I'm going on a frog hunt! Are you with me, Asedow!"

"I am, sister!" the green mage chortled. "Our new overlords will be so surprised we came to visit!"

Sounds of alarm erupted from underneath the console. Tall emerged, signaling frantically. Potria, as a parting gesture, threw a handful of scarlet lightning at him. Tall shielded almost automatically, and went on gesturing, panic-stricken.

"My people," he repeated over and over. "My people!"

"We have to stop them!" Keff said. Plennafrey broke the bubble around them, and the three headed for her chair.

"I will guard our friends," Chaumel said, making his way across the platform toward them. Ferngal threw forked lightning, aiming for the silver and golden mages at once. Chaumel ducked, and it sizzled over his head. A second later, he had a thin and shining globe of protection raised around himself and the console, withstanding the attacks of the dissidents.

Plennafrey lifted off the platform. Asedow and Potria were already most of the way to the tunnel. Suddenly, half a dozen chariots loomed over them and dropped into their path, cutting them off. Jaw set grimly, Keff hung on. Tall clutched Plennafrey around the knees as she tried to evade the others, but there were too many of them.

"Traitor!" Lacia screamed, peppering them with thunderbolts.

"Upstart!" Ferngal shouted at Plennafrey. "You don't know your place, but you will learn! Together—*now*!"

The young magiwoman set up a shield, but spells from six or more senior mages tore it apart like tissue paper. Fire of rainbow hues consumed the air around them. An explosion racked the chariot beneath them. Keff, blinded and choking, felt himself falling down and down.

Something springy yet insubstantial caught him just a few meters above the tops of the generators. When his eyes adjusted again, Keff looked around. A net of woven silver and gold bore him and the others upward. Scattered on the surface of the machinery were the pieces of Plennafrey's chariot. It had been blasted to bits. Plenna herself, clutching Tall, was in a similar net controlled by Chaumel and Nokias. Ferngal and the others were halfway down the cavern, turning to come in again for another attack.

"Are you all right?" Chaumel asked them, helping them back onto the platform.

"Yes," Keff said, and saw Plenna's shaky nod. "The generators are running out of control. We have to slow them down."

Tall kicked loose from Plenna's arms and hurried over to the console. Using the amulet, he flicked switches and rolled dials, but Keff could see that his efforts were having little effect. Ferngal and the others were almost upon them. A bolt of blue-white lightning crackled between him and the console, driving him back. Bravely, the little amphibioid threw himself forward. Keff interposed himself between Tall and the dissidents, ready to take the brunt of the next attack.

"That's enough of this!" Carialle declared loudly. Suddenly, the power items stopped working. The dissidents' chariots all slowed down, even dipped. Everyone gasped. Lacia clutched the arms of her chair.

"Stop this attack at once!" Keff roared, flinging his arms

up. "The next thing we turn off will be your chairs! If you don't want to fall into the gear-works, cease and desist! This isn't helping your cause or your planet!"

Furious but helpless, Ferngal and the others drew back from the platform. With as much dignity as he could muster, Ferngal led his ragged band out of the cavern.

"Nice work, Cari," Keff said.

"I wasn't sure I could select frequencies that narrow, but it worked," Carialle said triumphantly. "They won't fall out of the air, but that's it for their troublemaking. I'm *not* turning their power items on again. Tall can do it someday, if he ever feels he can trust them." Keff glanced at the globe-frog, who, in spite of the small burns that peppered his hide, was working feverishly over the console. The turbines slowed down with painful groans and screeches, and resumed a peaceful thrum.

"I doubt it will be soon," Keff said. Plennafrey grabbed his arm.

"We have to stop Potria," Plenna said urgently. "She's going to kill the Ancient Ones and she doesn't need power to do it. She's mad. If she can fly to where they are, that's enough."

Keff smote himself in the forehead. "I've been distracted. We have to stop them right away."

"She's gone mad," Nokias said. "I will go." The golden chair lifted off the platform.

"I will help, Mage Keff," Brannel volunteered, emerging from his hiding place.

"We've got to follow her, Chaumel," Keff said, turning to the silver magiman. "Can you take us, too?"

"Not to worry," Carialle said cosily in Keff's ear. "She's out here. In the snow. Swearing."

"Carialle stopped her," Keff shouted. Nokias turned his head, and Keff nodded vigorously. The others cheered, and Plenna threw herself into his arms. He gave her a huge hug, then dropped to his knees beside Tall. The other two globe-frogs had come out from beneath the console to aid their chief. They all acted alarmed.

"Can I help?" Keff asked.

"Big, *big* power, stored," Tall signed, pointing to the battery indicator. "Made by them," he gestured toward the departed Ferngal and his minions. "Must do something with it, now!"

"A glut in the storage batteries?" Keff said. He could see the dials straining. The others, who knew from long use what the moods of the Core felt like, wore taut expressions. "What can you do? Can you discharge it?"

Tall nodded once, sharply, and bent over the controls with the amulet clutched in his paws.

On the surface, Carialle's fins rested on an exposed outcropping of rock not far from the entrance. She watched with some satisfaction as Potria shook, then pulled, then kicked her useless chariot. Asedow lay unconscious on a snowbank where he'd fallen when his chair stopped. The pink-gold magess hoisted her skirts and tramped through the permafrost to his. It wouldn't function, either. She kicked it, kicked him, and came over to apply the toes of her dainty peach boots to Carialle's fins.

"Hey!" Carialle protested on loudspeaker. "Knock that off."

Potria jumped back. She retreated sulkily to her chair and seated herself in it magnificently, waiting for something to happen.

Something did, but not at all what Potria must have had in mind. Carialle detected a change in the atmosphere. Power crept up from beneath the surface of the planet, almost simmering up through solid matter. Instead of feeling ionized and drained, the air began to feel heavy. Carialle checked her monitors. With interest, she observed that the temperature was rising, and consequently, so was the humidity.

"Keff," she transmitted, "you ought to get everyone out here, pronto."

"What's wrong?" the brawn's voice asked, worriedly.

"Nothing's wrong. Just . . . bring everyone topside. You'll want to see this."

She monitored the puzzled conversation as Keff gathered his small party together for the long flight to the surface. By the time they appeared at the chimney entrance, clouds were already forming in the clear blue sky.

Plennafrey rode pillion on Chaumel's chair with the three globe-frogs clinging to the back while Keff and Brannel shared the gold chair with Nokias. Nokias's remaining followers straggled behind. The group settled down beside Carialle's ramp. Potria, her nose in the air, ignored them pointedly.

"What's so important, Cari?" Keff asked after a glance at Asedow to make sure the man was alive.

"Watch them," Carialle suggested. The Ozrans were all staring straight up at the sky. "It's not important to you, but it is to them. In fact, it's vital."

"What's happening?"

"Just wait! You nonshells are so impatient," Carialle chided him playfully.

"The air feels strange," Brannel said after a while, rubbing a pinch of his fur together speculatively with two fingers. "It is not cold now, but it is *thick*."

The crack of thunder startled all of them. Sheet lightning blasted across the sky, and in a moment, rain was pummeling down.

As soon as the first droplets struck their outstretched palms, Chaumel and the others started shrieking and dancing for joy. A few of the mages gathered in handful after handful of the cold, heavy drops and splashed them on their faces. Plennafrey grabbed Keff and Brannel and whirled them around in a circle.

"Rain!" she cried. "Real rain!"

Under his wet, plastered hair, the Noble Primitive's face was glowing.

"Oh, Mage Keff, this is the best thing that has ever happened to me."

In the center of their little circle, the three globe-frogs had abandoned their cases and stood with their hands out, letting the water sluice down their bodies.

"Thank you, friends," Chaumel said, coming over to throw soaked sleeves over their backs. "Look how far the clouds spread! This will be over the South and East regions in an hour. Rain, on my mountaintop! What a treasure!"

"This is what'll happen if you let the Core of Ozran run the way it was meant to," Keff said. Plenna gave him a rib-cracking hug and beamed at Brannel.

"This welcome storm will convince more doubters than any speeches or caves full of machinery," Nokias said, coming to join them. "More of these, especially around planting season, and we will have record crops. My fruit trees," he said proudly, "will bear as never before."

"Ozran will prosper," Chaumel said assuredly. "I make these promises to you now, and especially to you, my furry friend: no more amputations, no more poison in the food, no more lofty magi sitting in their mountain fastnesses. We will act like administrators instead of spoiled patricians, eating the food and beating the farmers. We will come down from the heights and assume the mantle of our . . . humanity with honor."

Brannel was wide-eyed. "I never thought I would live to be talked to as an equal by one of the most important mages in the world."

"You're important yourself," Keff said. "You're the most intelligent worker in the world, isn't he, Chaumel?"

"Yes!" Chaumel spat water and wiped his face. "My friend Nokias and I have a proposition for you. Will you hear it?"

Nokias looked dubious for a moment, then silent communion seemed to reassure him. "Yes, we do."

"I will listen," Brannel said carefully, glancing at Keff for permission.

"Ozran will need an adviser on conservation. Also, we need one who will liaise between the workers and the administrators. It will be a position almost equal to the mages. There will be much hard work involved, but you'll use your very good mind to the benefit of all your world. Will you take it?"

Brannel looked so pleased he needed two tails to wag. "Oh, yes, Mage Chaumel. I will do it with all my heart."

"Shall I tell him now?" Plenna whispered in Keff's ear. "He can have my sash and my other things when I come away with you. Tall Eyebrow already has my belt."

"Um, don't tell him yet, Plenna. Let it be a surprise. *Uh-oh*, Cari," Keff subvocalized. "We still have a problem."

"I'm ready for it, sir knight. Bring her in here."

"Now, friends," Nokias said, wringing out one sleeve at a time. "I am enjoying this rain very much, but I am getting very wet. Come back to my stronghold, where we may watch this fine storm and enjoy it from under a roof." He beckoned to Brannel. "Come with us, fur-face. You have much to learn. Might as well start now."

Brannel, hardly believing his good fortune, mounted the golden chair's back and prepared to enjoy the ride. Nokias gathered his contingent, including the recalcitrant Potria, and Asedow, who was coming to with all the signs of a near-fatal headache.

"Go on ahead," Keff said. "We've got some things to take care of here."

Carialle's Lady Fair image was on the wall as Keff, Plennafrey, Chaumel, and the trio of globe-frogs came into the cabin. At once, she ordered out her servos, one with a heavy-duty sponge-mop, and the other with a shelf-load of towels.

"There, get warmed up," she said sweetly. "I'm making hot drinks. Whether or not you've forgotten, you were still standing on top of a glacier with wet feet."

Keff stepped out of his wet boots and went into his sleeping compartment. "Come on, Chaumel. I bet you wear the same size shoes I do. Everybody make themselves at home."

Plennafrey kissed her hand lovingly to Keff. He kissed his fingers to her and winked.

"Oh, Plenna," Carialle said with deceptive calm. "I've got some data I wanted to show you." Keff's crash-couch swung out to her hospitably as the magiwoman approached. "Sit down. I think you need to see these."

When Keff and Chaumel appeared a few minutes later, freshly shod, Plennafrey was sitting with her head in her hands. The Lady Fair "sat" sympathetically beside her, murmuring in a soothing voice.

"So you see," Carialle was saying, "with the mutation in your DNA, I couldn't guarantee your safety during prolonged space travel. And Keff couldn't settle here. His job is his whole life."

Plenna raised a tear-streaked face to the others.

"Oh, Keff, look!" The young woman pointed to the wall screen. "My DNA has changed over a thousand years, Carialle says. And my blood is too thin—I cannot go with you."

Keff surveyed the DNA charts, trying to make sense of parallel spirals and the data which scrolled up beside them. "Cari, is it true?" he subvocalized.

"I wouldn't lie to her. *No one* can guarantee anyone's complete safety in space."

"Thank you, lady dear, you're the soul of tact— How terrible," he said out loud, kneeling at Plenna's feet. "I'm so sorry, Plenna, but you wouldn't have been happy in space. It's very boring most of the time—when it isn't dangerous. I couldn't ask you to endure a lifetime of it, and truthfully, I wouldn't be happy anywhere else."

"I am glad this is the case," Chaumel said, examining the charts and microscopic analysis on Carialle's main screen. From the look in the mage's eye, Keff guessed that perhaps he had been eavesdropping on their private channel. "You cannot take such a treasure as Magess Plennafrey off Ozran."

Standing before the magiwoman, he took her hand and bowed over it. Plennafrey looked startled, then starry-eyed. She rose, looking up into his eyes tentatively, like an animal that might bolt at any moment. Chaumel spoke softly and put out a gentle hand to smooth the tears from her cheeks.

"I admire your pluck, my dear. You are brave and resourceful as well as beautiful." He favored her with a most ardent look, and she blushed. "I would be greatly honored if you would agree to be my wife."

"Your . . . your wife?" Plenna asked, her big, dark eyes going wide. "I'm honored, Chaumel. I . . . of *course* I will. Oh!" Chaumel raised the hand he was holding to his lips and kissed it. Keff got up off the floor.

"Listen up, sir knight. This fellow could give you some pointers," Carialle said wickedly. Chaumel aimed a small smile toward Carialle's pillar and returned his entire attention to Plennafrey.

"We will share our power, and together we will teach our fellow Ozrans to adapt to our future. Our society will be reduced in influence, but it will be greater in number and scope. The Ancient Ones can teach us much of what we have forgotten."

"And one day, perhaps, our children can go into space," Plenna said, turning to Keff and smiling, "to meet yours." Leaning over, she gave Keff a sisterly peck on the cheek and moved into the circle of Chaumel's arm.

Over the top of her head, Chaumel winked.

"And now, fair magess," he said, "I will fly you home, since your own conveyance has come to grief." Beaming, Plennafrey accompanied her intended down the ramp. He handed her delicately onto his own chariot, and mounted the edge of the back behind her.

"That man never misses a trick," Carialle said through Keff's implant.

"Thank you, Cari," Keff said. "Privately, in a comparison between Plenna and you as a lifelong companion, I'd choose you, every time."

"Why, sir knight, I'm flattered."

"You should be flattered," Keff said with a smirk. "Plenna is intelligent, adaptable, beautiful, desirable, but she knows nothing about my interests, and in the long transits between missions we would drive one another crazy. This is the best possible solution."

Chaumel's well-known gifts for diplomacy and the unexpected treat of the thunderstorm began to bear fruit within the next few days. Mages and magesses began to approach Keff and the globe-frogs in the cavern to ask if there was anything they could do to help speed the miracle to their parts of Ozran. Spy-eyes were everywhere, as everyone wanted to see how the repairs progressed.

The greatest difficulty the repair crew faced was the

sheer age of the machinery. Keff and Tall rigged what they could to keep it running, but in the end the Frog Prince ordered a halt.

"We must study more," Tall said. "Given time, and the printout you have made of the schematic drawings, we will be able to determine what else needs to be done to make all perfect. The repairs we have made will hold," he added proudly. "There is no need to beg the homeworld for aid. I would sooner approach them as equals."

"Good job!" Keff said. "We'll take our report home to the Central Worlds. As soon as we can, we'll come back to help you to finish the job. I expect that by the time we do, between you and the Noble Primitives, you'll teach the mages all there is to know about weather management and high-yield farming."

"The fur-faces will show them how to till the land and take care of it. We do not retain *that* knowledge," Tall said with creditable humility. "Brannel is our friend. We do need each other. Together, we can fulfill the hopes of all our ancestors. Others will take us up and back to the Core after this," the Frog Prince assured them. "Many are protecting us at all times. You've done much in helping us to achieve the respect of the human beings."

"No," Keff said, "you did it. I couldn't convince them. You had to show them your expertise, and you did."

Tall signaled polite disbelief. "Come back soon."

Carialle and Keff delivered Tall and his companions back to Brannel's plain for the last time. The globe-frogs signed them a quick good-bye before disappearing into the brush. Five spy-eyes trailed behind them at a respectful distance.

Chaumel and Plennafrey arrived at the plain in time to see Keff and Carialle off.

"You've certainly stirred things up, strangers," Chaumel said, shaking hands with Keff. "I agree there's nothing else you could have done. My small friends tell me that shortly Ozran would have suffered a catastrophic explosion, and we would all have died without knowing the cause. For that, we thank you."

"We're happy to help," Keff said. "In return, we take home data on a generation ship that was lost hundreds of years ago, and plenty of information on what's going to be one of the most fascinating blended civilizations in the galaxy. I'm looking forward to seeing how you prosper."

"It will be interesting," Chaumel acknowledged. "I am finding that the certain amount of power the Ancient Ones have agreed to leave in our hands will be used as much to protect us from disgruntled workers as it will be to help lead them into self-determination. Not all will be peaceful in this new world. Many of the farmers are afraid that their new memories are hallucinations. But," he sighed, "we brought this on ourselves. We must solve our own problems. Your Brannel is proving to be a great help."

Plennafrey came forward to give Keff a chaste kiss. "Farewell, Keff," she said. "I'm sorry my dream to come with you couldn't come true, but I am happier it turned out this way." She bent her head slightly to whisper in his ear. "I will always treasure the memory of what we had."

"So will I," Keff said softly. Plenna stepped back to stand beside Chaumel, and he smiled at her.

"Farewell, friends," Chaumel said, assisting the tall girl down the ramp and onto his chariot. "We look forward to your return."

"So do we," Keff said, waving. The chair flew to a safe distance and settled down to observe the ship's takeoff.

"They do make rather a handsome couple," Carialle said. "I'd like to paint them a big double portrait as a wedding present. Confound their combination of primrose and silver—that's going to be tricky to balance. Hmm, an amber background, perhaps cognac amber would do it."

Keff turned and walked inside the main cabin. The airlock slid shut behind him, and he heard the groaning of the motor bringing the outer ramp up flush against the bulkhead. The brawn clapped his hands together in glee.

"Wait until we tell Simeon and the Xeno boffins about the Frog Prince and his tadpole courtiers on the Planet of Wizards," Keff gloated, settling into his crash-couch and putting his feet up on the console. He intertwined his hands behind his head. "Ah! We will be the talk of SSS-900, and every other space station for a hundred trillion klicks!"

"I can't wait to spread the word myself," Carialle said with satisfaction as she engaged engines and they lifted off into atmosphere. "We did it! We may be considered the screwball crew, but we're the ones that get the results in the end. . . . Oh damn!"

"What's wrong?" Keff asked, sitting up, alarmed.

Carialle's Lady Fair image appeared on the screen, her face drawn into woeful lines.

"I forgot about the Inspector General!"